Cinnamon Bun

· Volume 4 ·

RavensDagger

Podium

Cover design by Larcian

Mountains (featured in maps by Edgar Malboeuf) illustrated by AoA

The *Beaver Cleaver* illustrated by Albreo

ISBN: 978-1-0394-1668-0

Published in 2022 by Podium Publishing, ULC
www.podiumaudio.com

Cinnamon Bun

· Volume 4 ·

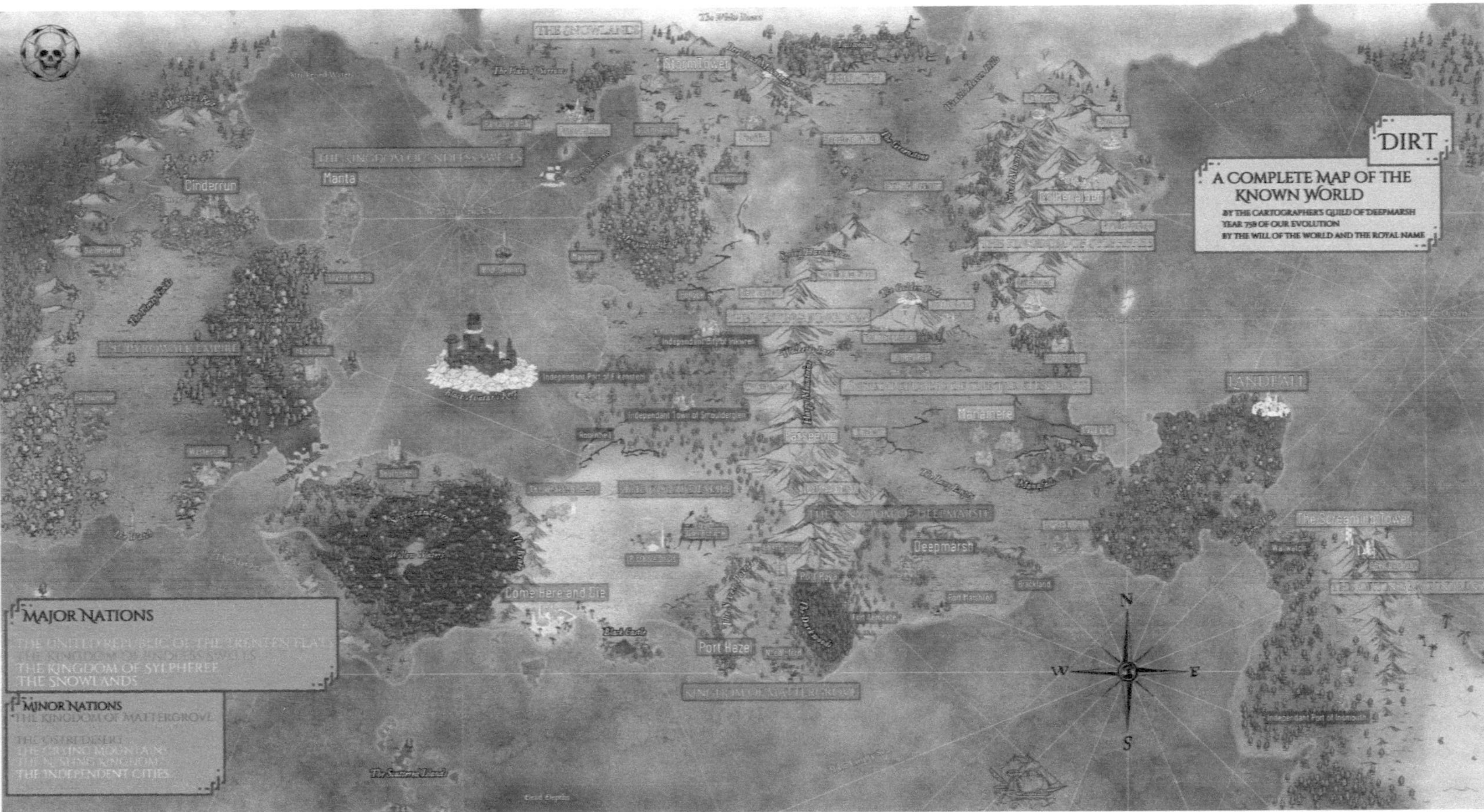

DIRT
A COMPLETE MAP OF THE KNOWN WORLD
BY THE CARTOGRAPHER'S GUILD OF DEEPMARSH
YEAR 758 OF OUR EVOLUTION
BY THE WILL OF THE WORLD AND THE ROYAL NAME

MAJOR NATIONS
THE UNITED REPUBLIC OF THE TRENTEN FLATS
THE KINGDOM OF SYLPHFREE
THE SNOWLANDS

MINOR NATIONS
THE KINGDOM OF MATTERGROVE
THE OSIRI DESERT
THE CRYING MOUNTAINS
THE RISING KINGDOM
THE INDEPENDENT CITIES

THE SNOWLANDS
THE KINGDOM OF SYLPHFREE
THE PYROMANCER EMPIRE
KINGDOM OF MATTERGROVE
DEEPMARSH

LANDFALL
Manta
Cinderrun
Deepmarsh
Port Haze
Come Here and Lie
Mariamete
The Screaming Tower
Independant Port of Erkandell
Independant Town of Smoulderglen

N
E
S
W

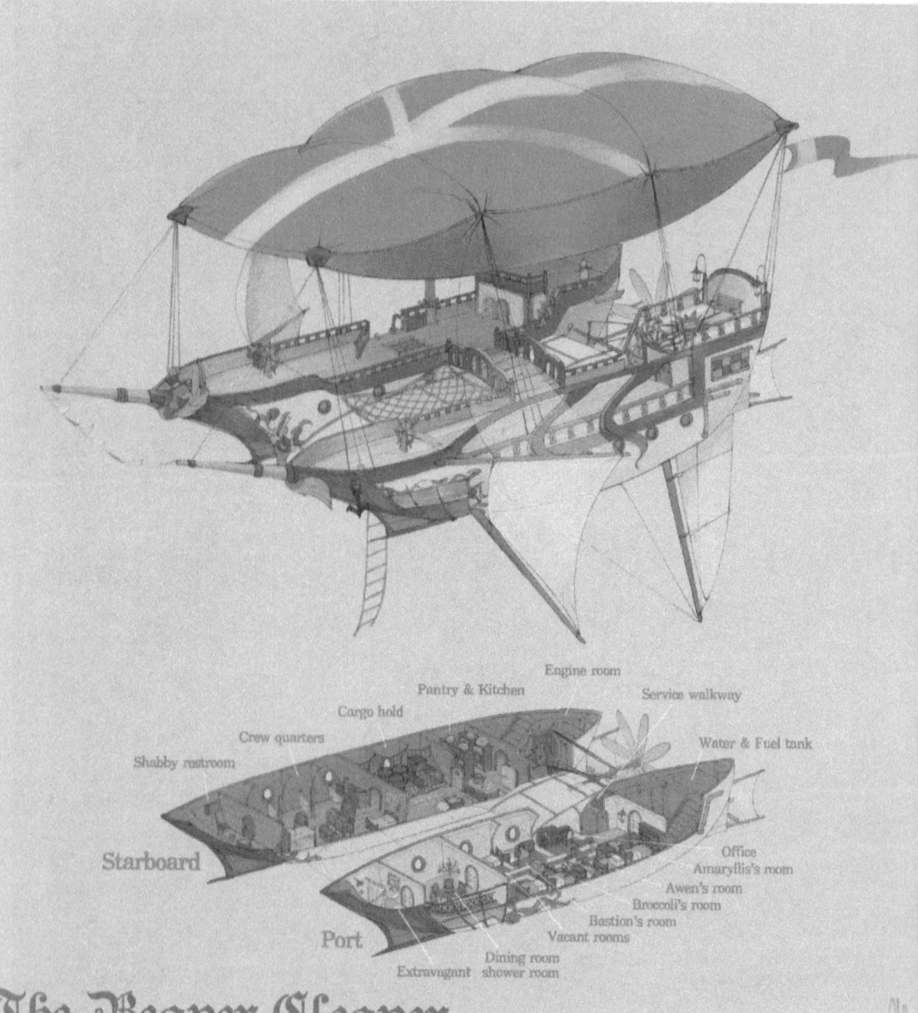

Engine room
Pantry & Kitchen
Service walkway
Cargo hold
Crew quarters
Water & Fuel tank
Shabby restroom
Starboard
Office
Amaryllis's room
Awen's room
Broccoli's room
Bastion's room
Vacant rooms
Port
Dining room
Extravagant shower room
The Beaver Cleaver

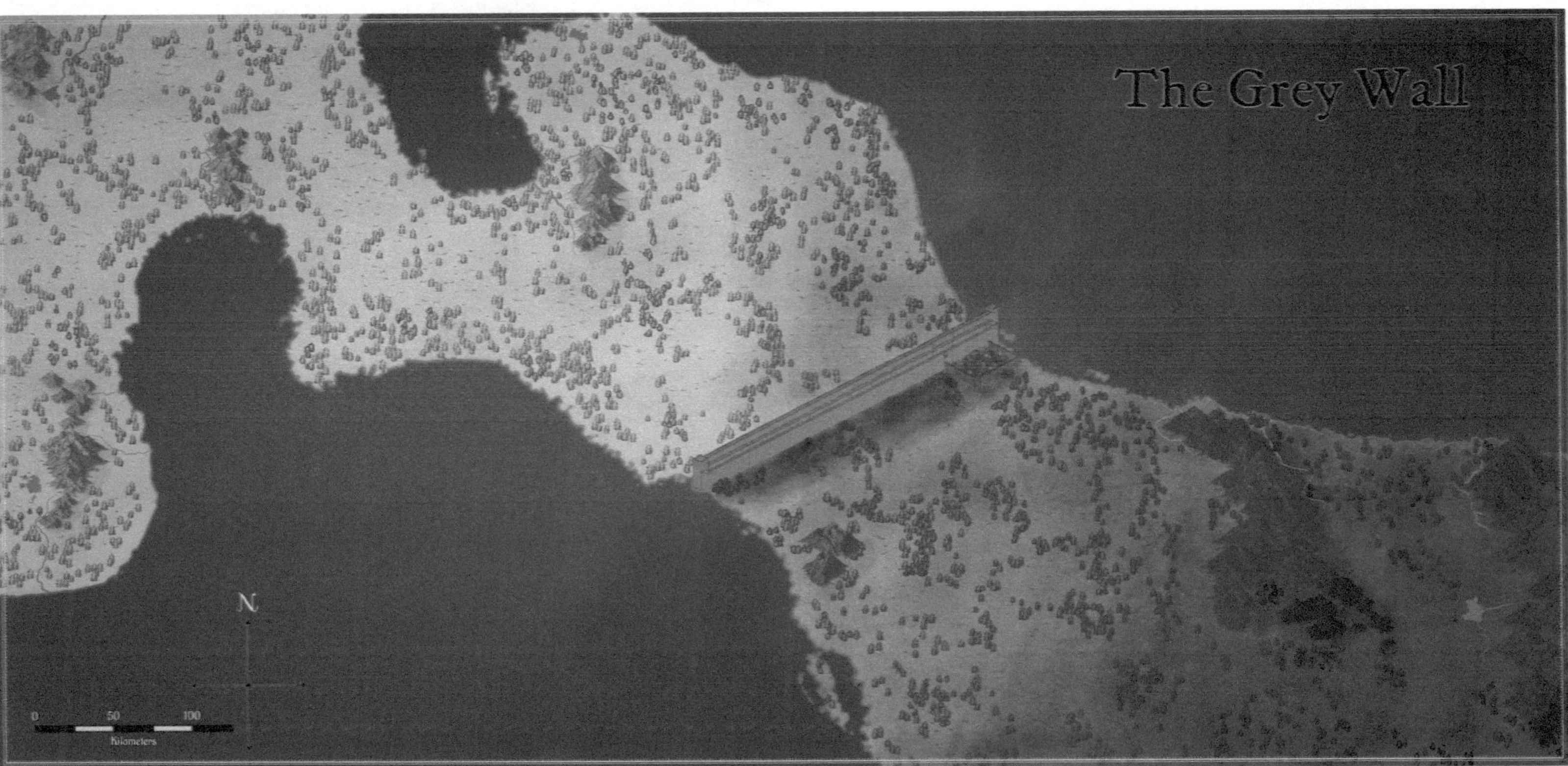

The Grey Wall
N
0
50
100
Kilometers

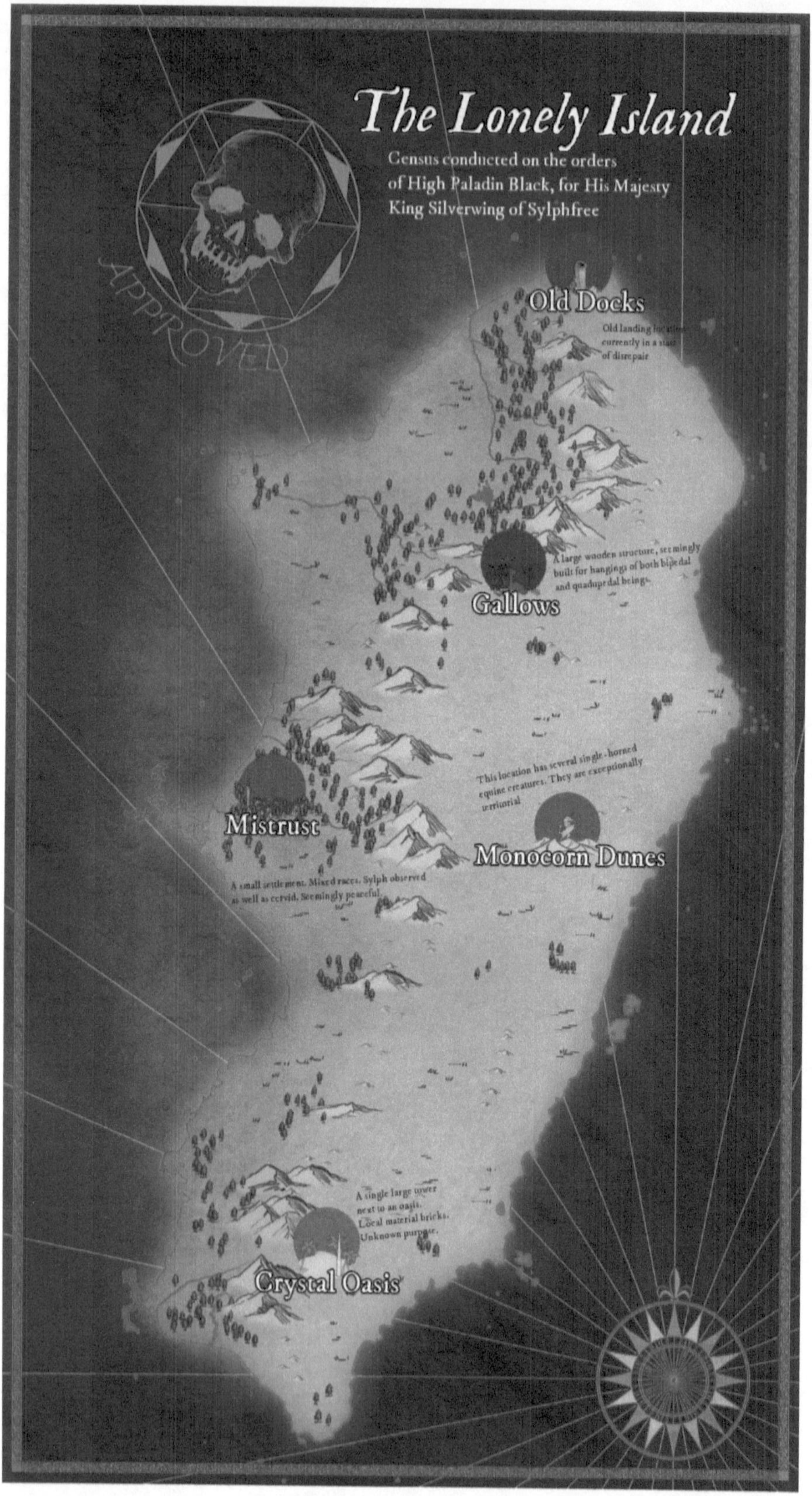

The Lonely Island
Census conducted on the orders
of High Paladin Black, for His Majesty
King Silverwing of Sylphfree
APPROVED
Old Docks
Old landing location
currently in a state
of disrepair
Gallows
A large wooden structure, seemingly
built for hangings of both bipedal
and quadrupedal beings.
Mistrust
A small settlement. Mixed races. Sylph observed
as well as cervid. Seemingly peaceful.
This location has several single-horned
equine creatures. They are exceptionally
territorial
Monocorn Dunes
A single large tower
next to an oasis.
Local material bricks.
Unknown purpose.
Crystal Oasis

Cinnamon Bun

Bun

· Volume 4 ·

· Chapter One ·

Home Again, Home Again

The *Beaver Cleaver*'s bright balloon hovering over the little town was the first sign I saw that we were nearing Hopsalot.

We huffed and puffed our way up a final hill, and as we crested it we got to see the whole town ahead of us: tree-house homes and burrows, open fields where neat little gardens were soaking up morning sunshine, and the gurgling river that swished and swashed through the village, never going in a straight line when it could instead meander around hills and under arched stone bridges with trellis-covered sides.

I raised a hand and cupped it over my forehead to shield my eyes from the sun. I could make out buns, most with bright white shirts and adorable overalls on, some caring for their gardens while the little ones ran around and chased each other over hills, their long bunny ears bouncing with every step. The older buns were usually sitting on the porches before their burrow homes, rocking on finely crafted chairs and smoking from reed pipes.

"We're here!" I called back to the others.

Behind me were my best friends. Awen still had bandages around her waist from where she'd gotten hurt the night before, and Amaryllis looked miffed at having to walk through the forest so much. The branches and leaves tended to get caught in her feathers, much to her very loud annoyance. Bastion came up behind them, looking like a very small knight in shining armor. He smiled at me, relaxed as a sylph paladin could be. His wings fluttered behind him as he stepped off a boulder.

Then there were the buns. Momma in her half-plate and Carrot, who'd removed her gauntlets and had them tied by her waist so that they clanged and banged with every step. Buster took up the very rear of the group, the huge bun stomping along with his big hammer slung onto his shoulder. Peter was . . . somewhere. He was the sneaky sort, so it wasn't too surprising that I couldn't spot him. I was sure that he'd show up if anything needed our attention.

Carrot bounced to a stop at the top of the hill, right next to me. Her ears wiggled with poorly suppressed excitement, and her grin was as wide as a grin could be. "Home!" she declared.

"Home!" I said right back.

Hopsalot wasn't my home, of course, but the *Beaver* certainly was. I could just barely make out a few figures on the airship's deck, some of them with long bun-ears.

Momma caught up to us with the others and took a deep breath. "Ah, there was a time, once, where I would leave for months on end. Wanderlust dragging me this way and that. Now I can hardly leave for more than a day or two without fearing that everything will crumble apart without me there."

I giggled. "I'm sure it's not so bad."

Some of the buns in Hopsalot spotted our party, and within moments a whole crowd of little buns had gathered by the edge of the village. They stared at us, some of them holding up their ears away from their eyes, while others hesitated and only peeked our way from behind bushes and picket fences. When we came over, their hesitation broke, and soon we were swarmed by a whole gaggle of buns.

Carrot darted ahead, picked one little bun up by the armpits, and spun her around a couple of times before squeezing her tight. "I'm back!" she said while the little bun tried really hard to return the hug, even though her arms were too short to wrap around Carrot's sides.

I felt Awen and Amaryllis shuffle up behind me, using me as a barricade against all the bouncing and smiling buns. "Hello!" I said.

Their reply was a cacophony of questions that I couldn't possibly answer all at once. From asking if we'd fought big monsters, to wondering if they could visit the airship again, to very generous offers to join them in playing extreme hopscotch.

"Ah, I'm sorry, everybun. But my friends and I need to follow Momma! We'll have some time to play after that, I'm sure!"

Momma was kneeling down, hugging buns that needed hugs, patting buns that needed pats, and sometimes pinching fat, chubby cheeks, much to the dismay of the buns whose faces she pinched.

It took a bit for the tide of little buns to recede and for us to be able to head deeper into the town. Buster was entirely covered in buns, who seemed to have confused the big man for a jungle gym. Peter, of course, was nowhere to be seen. He didn't seem the sort to take kindly to being pestered by little buns.

Momma shooed some of them along, and Carrot saved the day by sacrificing herself with a declaration of, "Who wants to play tag?" The screaming horde bounced after Carrot, a whole bunch of ears wobbling as they chased her.

"Aww," I said.

"Thank the World," Amaryllis said. "I can't handle one child. That many is just a disaster in the making."

"Oh, we have little disasters all the time," Momma said. "Buns who get caught between pickets, buns who get into fights over favorite dolls. Buns who discover some interesting insect, name it, start treating it as a favored pet, and are then devastated when the insect passes away . . . usually on the same day they found it."

"Oh no," I said. "That happened to me once. I had a pet praying mantis, but I didn't tell my mom that little Mem was a pet, and she smacked it with a flyswatter. I was devastated."

"Awa, I never had a pet before," Awen said.

"I've always wanted a cat," Amaryllis added. "They have very agreeable personalities."

"Is that why you get along so well with Orange?" I asked.

"I suppose so. The spirit cat is obviously a grand and noble creature. I see a lot of myself in her."

Snorting, I turned to Awen. "What about you? We could probably get you a pet, if you wanted. Like a dog? Airships can have dogs, right?"

"I don't think that's a great idea," Awen said. "Dogs need room to move, and the *Beaver* is a little small for that."

I pouted. My plan, newly created, to use Awen as an excuse to get a dog had been foiled. "Well, all right. Maybe a parrot—we are pirates after all."

"I would like to log my protest," Bastion said. "I am not a pirate. Nor, for that matter, are any of you."

"Sky pirate, sorry," I said.

"No," he said, with obvious exasperation. It turned into contrite resignation when I giggled. He had a knack for making strange faces whenever I caught him flat-footed.

I was expecting Momma to lead us to her home, but instead she moved toward the hill where the *Beaver* had set down his anchor. "I genuinely wish we could have you stay, if only for a little longer, but if my suspicions are correct, then the Insmouth dungeon is in as great a risk as the Newbining dungeon was."

"We need to head over there and fix it as soon as we can, then?" I asked.

Momma nodded. "I'm confident you can manage. In either case, I'll send some of my better buns over—including Carrot and, perhaps, Peter—to see if they need assistance in a day's time."

"They could come with us," I offered.

Momma shook her head. "They need time with their families. And you need a break, too, I imagine. Still, the World doesn't always have as much concern for us as we'd wish."

I sighed. "Okay. We should probably get Awen back to bed anyway."

"Awa? I'm better now," Awen said. She reached over and touched her side. "There's just some scabbing now. I took potions."

"I'm still worried."

"You were impaled once, and we didn't do this much for you," Awen said. "Remember? In that glass dungeon?"

"Well, yeah, I was fine," I said.

Awen crossed her arms and leveled a very un-Awen look at me. "Don't be a hypocrite, Broc. I can deal with a bit of pain."

Momma laughed, and Amaryllis seemed very proud of Awen while I pouted. "Fine, fine."

We arrived in the shadow cast by the *Beaver*, and I saw Oda and Sally, the Scallywags, looking over the rails at us. A couple of the older little buns were with them, those who were around the Scallywags' own ages. I waved, and they waved back.

"Do you need anything for your return trip?" Momma asked.

I considered it. "I don't think so? Some supplies wouldn't go amiss. Our voyage has already gone on for a lot longer than we expected."

"We didn't get as much fuel in Needleford as we could have," Awen said. "But I don't think we can get any here."

"I'm afraid that Hopsalot doesn't have much use for it," Momma agreed. "What about food?"

"We're fine there," Amaryllis said. "Thank you."

Bastion bowed at the waist. "I wish to thank you as well, ma'am," he said. "Your hospitality has been wonderful, and your prompt action has likely done much to keep your town safe."

"That's just a mother's job," Momma said. "Come, I'll give you all a quick hug for the trip back."

I crashed into Momma because, really, her hugs were the best. Then it was the others' turn, though Bastion politely declined, and Amaryllis made noises as if she wanted to decline while eagerly accepting the hug.

"I'm going to miss Hopsalot," I said. "And I was only here for less than a day." I let my shoulders droop, and my gaze wandered over the town. It was just so chaotically peaceful. The big homes built into trees, the doors stuck into the sides of hills, the little streets, paved in carefully laid cobbles. The river sang a gurgling song, accompanied by the wind whispering over grassy hills.

Then a whole bunch of little ones appeared, all of them scrambling over Carrot, who took a tumble and rolled down a hill to the tune of merry screams.

"I would offer to let you stay," Momma said when she looked away from the spectacle. None of the little buns looked to be hurt from the flop down the hill. "But I suspect you're at that point in your life where adventure has its hooks in you, and you want nothing more than to meddle. It might be best for everyone here if you only came back when you're older and calmer."

"I'm not a meddler," I defended myself.

Amaryllis snorted.

"Is this Mock Broccoli Day?" I asked.

"It's always Mock Broccoli Day," Amaryllis said. She nodded to Momma. "We'll probably fly back over here again, on the way north."

"Then stop by for tea," Momma said, "no matter the hour."

Amaryllis nodded, then moved over to a ladder that someone had left dangling off the *Beaver*'s side. "Come on, Broccoli, you're holding us back!"

"Oh, right, okay," I said. I jumped to Momma, gave her a last hug, got my head rubbed for my troubles, then darted back to the *Beaver*.

When we climbed aboard, we found a few curious buns on deck, with Clive sitting on one of the steps leading to the aft castle and explaining things. Howard the fishman was nearby, too, wringing his webbed fingers as he approached.

"I'll make sure we don't have any uninvited guests aboard," Amaryllis said. "You deal with Howard here."

I nodded and skipped over to the fishman. "Heya."

"Hello, Captain Bunch," he said. "How did it go?"

"It went well enough," I said. "We know how to fix your dungeon now, but I think we ought to hurry back. It gets harder and harder to fix things as time goes on. We don't want to be too late."

Howard's shoulders loosened and he gave me a fishy smile. "Oh, thank the fathomless depths."

"Don't worry, Howard, my friends and I will have everything back to how it ought to be in a jiffy!"

· Chapter Two ·

Reciprocation

It would take, winds willing, a few hours to get back to Insmouth. By the time we arrived, I guesstimated that it would be an hour or two past noon. That meant we'd need to have lunch aboard the *Beaver Cleaver.*

I left Clive, the harpies, and the Scallywags to do the complicated work of flying the airship while I headed down and into the kitchen to prepare lunch. The only hands that were free were Awen's and Amaryllis's, and . . . neither were all that good at the whole cooking thing.

I was humming while inspecting the ingredients we had available when Amaryllis came out of her room to stand nearby. She leaned against the frame of the archway leading into the kitchen. "Do you need help?"

I tapped my chin. "I could use a bit of help, sure," I said. "I think I'll be making a big lunch. We might need leftovers for later. A nice veggie salad, some fried fish, maybe some porridge?"

"That sounds like a big meal," Amaryllis said as she stood straighter and walked over. "How can I help?"

I eyed her up and down. "You really want to help? With the cooking?"

"What's wrong with me wanting to help?"

"Nothing," I said. "Just, well, didn't figure you for the cooking sort."

She huffed. "I can learn, can't I?"

"Yup! You sure can." I nodded. "Do you want to start by chopping the veggies? I'll need them cut up into little cubes to start with."

"Humph, fine."

I opened a sack of potatoes and another of turnips and then grabbed some purple-skinned carrots and set them all on the table where we could start cutting. A big cauldron came next so that we had a place to toss all the cut veggies. I hummed as I found a pair of knives and started working.

"How are you?" Amaryllis asked. The question sounded strained.

I blinked and looked up to her. "I'm all right?" I tried.

She glared at me, huffed a huff that I wasn't familiar with, and went back to chopping up potatoes in . . . vaguely cube-like shapes. She was trying her best, so I wouldn't complain. They'd all be mashed up anyway.

"You . . . Ugh, this isn't something I'm good at," Amaryllis whined.

"You'll get better."

"I'm not talking about the cooking, you dolt."

I tilted my head to the side. "Then what are you talking about?"

Amaryllis continued to chop her veggies. She was quiet, but it felt like she was working up to something, so I didn't interrupt her silence. "Broccoli," she began, "you've been through a lot."

"Well, yeah, I guess."

"And yet you're still smiling, and you're still worried for everyone, and you're still doing your best," she continued.

"Uh, yeah, that's what a good friend does."

"Even when I constantly call you an idiot? And when Awen constantly depends on you to be her . . . pillar, I suppose?"

I blinked. I didn't know exactly where she was going with all that. "Yes?"

She huffed, and this time it was a very plain, very frustrated huff. "You're a . . . you're a pain to deal with sometimes, Broccoli Bunch," she said. "Most people wouldn't weather all the stuff you've been through as well as you have."

"Thanks!" I said.

"No," Amaryllis said. "It wasn't a compliment. Well, I do suppose you could take it as one. What I mean is . . ." She paused, then rubbed a wing under her nose. "You know, I was not always as confident as I am now."

I felt like she was trying to say something important without saying it, and in moments like that the best thing a good friend could do was listen. Still, I continued working on our lunch, not that it took much attention.

"When I was younger I was the most timid of my sisters. Clementine can be incredible, but she casts a long shadow, and Rosaline has always been Rosaline. Loud and confident and always getting herself into trouble, then flying out of it with a wink and a smile. So . . . I was the timid one. That changed as I got a little older, as I tired of my role in the family and started to . . ." She squirmed. ". . . dream. As I started to dream of a future where I was my own harpy. School helped—it gave me an environment out of my sisters' shadows. It gave me harpies from other clans to bicker and fight with, and it allowed me to spread my wings a little. I don't remember any instantaneous change, no stark turning point . . . but bit by bit, I must have been changing. Little victories, building on each other, until without quite realizing it, I'd become more . . . me. I left the family, took a class that I appreciated more, and set off for adventure."

"That's when we met?"

She nodded. "Yes. That was an experience."

"A good one," I replied.

She huffed, a very ambivalent, sarcastic huff. "Let's go with that. My point with that rather trite story is to say that I understand if you're having difficulty acting as confident as you have been."

"Uh," I said. I don't think I had any trouble being confident or anything. Still, Amaryllis seemed worried, which was weird. There wasn't anything to worry about. Sure, the last dungeon had been tough, and we were all tired by the end, but we had won, hadn't we? "Did you want me to tell a story about when I was young too? To make us even."

"My goal wasn't to make us even or anything."

"You once said that you could tell someone something private and then expect them to return the favor. Remember? You called it reciprocation."

Amaryllis blinked. "You remember that?"

"Of course I do," I said. "Um, well, I remember you telling it to me. The details are a bit vague now. It was a while ago."

The floor creaked, and when I looked over, it was to find Awen stepping in. She had her hands folded over her tummy and was looking bashful. "Awa, sorry, I kind of . . . kind of had my room's door open and I, ah, might have . . . overheard. A little."

"That's okay," I said.

Amaryllis harrumphed. "I suppose."

"Do you need help? Or I could go, if you two are having a, ah, moment," Awen offered.

I glanced at Amaryllis. Were we having a moment? Weren't we always having moments?

"We weren't," Amaryllis said. "Now come over here with those stupid human hands of yours and chop these. This knife is not made for a proper taloned hand. I'm going to develop a crick in my wrist at this rate."

"Oh, I didn't realize you were having a hard time. I thought you were just really bad."

Amaryllis's feathers poofed with indignation. "Not just dumb, but rude too," she said. "Now get on with the story. I'm going to fill the pot with water."

"About a quarter full," I said. "As for stories . . . I don't know what to tell? My life was very boring, you know?"

"I doubt that," Amaryllis said.

"I can tell one," Awen said. "While you think, if you want."

"I'd love that!" I cheered.

Awen smiled as she took her place at the table alongside me and started working. "I don't have very interesting stories. Uncle Abraham's visits were always the most exciting thing. Otherwise I'd spend the day with lessons or practicing. I liked playing with different instruments—it was one of the only parts of being a lady that was nice. Not that I could just play anything."

"Why not?"

"Some instruments aren't ladylike." Awen said. "A flute is, a piano is, but a lute or a banjo is not. They leave you with unseemly calluses, and things like a cello require that the lady put herself in a compromising position to play."

"Huh? That's stupid."

Awen giggled. "Yes, a little," she agreed. "But that's how it is. When I became a mechanic, my parents were very disappointed, but I was a little too sickly to bring to a dungeon to change my class. All the good, ladylike classes are in dungeons that are somewhat dangerous now, most of them near the capital, and, well, whenever I heard them talking of moving me over, I'd play sick."

Amaryllis snorted. "Well done, there."

Awen looked down. "Ah, thanks. I always wanted to practice my mechanical skills, but it's hard to do that when you're not allowed. So I tended to be very clumsy. I'd break things, then put them back together. Some of the maids and servants were very helpful! They'd bring me tools and sometimes give me things that needed to be fixed. Like mechanical clocks and some devices in the kitchens. That's why I was able to keep up a little, and I was always a bit better the next time Uncle Abraham would come around."

I placed my knife on the table, stepped toward Awen, and engulfed her in a big, rib-creaking hug.

"Awa?"

"You can do as much mechanical stuff as you want when you're with us. Or none. Or if you get some other hobby, you can do that as much as you want, all right?"

Awen laughed and returned the hug with a good squeeze. "You're being silly, Broc. I know all that."

"Oh," I said as I loosened the hug. "Well good." I nodded. "My turn?"

"Certainly," Amaryllis said. "Do we put any spices in this?"

"No, but put it on the stove. We need to set it to a boil so the veggies get mushy. Here, let's put the rest in too."

While the veggies boiled, I prepared a salad for the side. Nothing much. Tiny tomatoes, some leafy greens, a few slices of carrot, and some oil that I mixed with a few spices and herbs we had drying on a rack in the little pantry.

"I think . . . so, you girls know I like adventure, right?"

"We noticed," Amaryllis said. She was sitting up on a bench built into the wall under one of the portholes, a bird enjoying the sun.

"Right, well I wasn't always a huge fantasy fan. When I was really young, my parents moved often. I don't really remember all the places I've lived in. Sometimes we were only in a town for half a year, other times it was longer."

"Were your parents traders?" Awen asked. "We had a lot of people like that in Greenshade."

"Nah, my dad couldn't keep a job, nor could my mom, and they both liked moving a lot. We lived in mobile homes and apartments and all sorts of places. We'd change provinces every so often too. Anyway, when I was . . . Ah, I think I was in seventh grade? So I must have been about fourteen, or maybe I was still thirteen? Around that age."

"A teenager, barely a juvenile, but not quite," Amaryllis said. "Old enough to lay eggs."

"Uh," I said. I shook my head. "Something like that. So, I'd just moved to this new school. First year of secondary school, so all the students were new, too, even though I'd come in halfway into the year. It wasn't so bad. At least, I'd hoped."

"Did you make lots of friends?" Awen asked.

"Nope. Just one. It was this boy who didn't have any friends. He had a stutter and wasn't good at sports and stuff. We were in the same classes, and he always sat by the front, which is where I like to sit. We talked a bit and became buddies."

"Your first friend?" Amaryllis asked.

"One of them. He really, really liked books. Fantasy stories, with magic and wizards and all sorts of cool stuff. So I read those, too, and we always had something to talk about." I felt a little sad as I set the salad aside. "We should start on the fish. Awen, can you mash the veggies for me?"

"Ah, sure."

I got a pan out and oiled it, then fetched the fish from a rune-powered fridge. "Anyway, we moved again that summer. Never saw him again. But I still remember some of those stories. They kept me company for a long time. I guess I learned that from him."

I hummed as the fish fizzled on the snapping and crackling oil.

"Is . . . that the whole story?" Amaryllis asked.

"I guess so?"

Amaryllis stood up and walked right up next to me. "I'm going to hug you now. Don't go thinking anything about it. This is your one hug this week, so enjoy it."

"Huh?"

But then my protests were drowned in a fluffy, feathery hug.

· **Chapter Three** ·

Dine Hard

Dig in!" I cheered.

Most of the crew, minus Steve and Oda, were spread out around the dining room table with their share of supper before them. We didn't do anything special before eating, but somehow—without ever actually talking about it—we tended to wait until everyone had food on their plate first.

There were some nice noises of agreement from the others as they tucked in. The porridge seemed like a good place to start, and some were already cutting into their slices of grilled fish. "I need to thank Amaryllis and Awen—they helped a lot," I said.

Everyone but the two girls slowed down and hesitated to continue eating.

"Aww, don't be like that," I said. "They're getting better. I bet they might even get a cooking skill one of these days."

"Oh, please, no," Amaryllis said. "That would be such a waste of a general skill slot."

"Really? I wouldn't mind it too much," I said. "It's not something too awesome, but it's very practical. I still have a couple of general skill slots to fill, you know?"

"I do have some unused slots," Amaryllis allowed as she picked at her fish. There were still bones in it, which made it tricky to eat. "I'm not sure if I should focus on more exploration-related skills, or some that would be more practical in the day-to-day."

"What do you mean?" I asked.

"Most people," Bastion replied, "will have to make a choice between obtaining skills to help them do the things they do every day or skills that assist them with their work. Something like Sword Fighting Proficiency is a wonderful skill for a paladin like myself, but it would be wasted on a farmer. Likewise, I wouldn't have much use for a Planting skill. But in both cases we're assuming that a person is heavily specialized. If you're not, then it makes sense to invest in skills that make your everyday life easier."

"It's a trade off, then," I said.

Bastion nodded. "That's it. The best people in their field are almost always those who have invested everything into being the best. Every class and every skill. They will be impressively good at the one thing they focused on, whatever that may be."

I nodded along while I considered that. "I don't know what I want to be," I said. "I know what I want, but I'm not sure if I need any classes or anything to do that, just hard work."

"I know that your answer is going to be some sickeningly sweet, idiotic tripe, but I find myself compelled to ask anyway," Amaryllis said. "What's your goal?"

"To make the best friends, and to make sure they're as happy as can be."

Amaryllis rolled her eyes and Awen giggled. A few others at the table laughed, but I didn't mind. It was a good laugh.

"I recall you mentioning wanting to be strong," Amaryllis said.

"That too," I agreed. "But I don't need to be crazy strong, just tough enough that people will hesitate to hurt my friends."

Bastion hummed, then gestured to me with his fork. "Perhaps focus on skills that will help your role as a captain, then. Leadership skills do help in a tight spot, and they'd assist you in your current role as captain, obviously."

"Awa, maybe you should just accept the skill you get naturally? That's what Uncle does. He says that if you're getting skills because you're doing something you like, then those skills are the ones the World thinks you'll enjoy best."

"Huh. I guess that makes sense. It also means I don't need to worry about it!"

"Moron," Amaryllis said.

We continued eating, our constant yammering slowing us down. At the far end of the table, Howard and Clive were having an in-depth discussion about, of all things, fishing, and Sally and Joe were talking to Gordon about different ports the harpy had visited.

I enjoyed the babble of conversation. It made the *Beaver* sound like a wonderfully happy place. Orange strutted down, walking on air as only a spirit cat could, and sat herself on Amaryllis's lap, purring up a storm.

"I suspect that we ought to plan our next steps," Bastion said as he set his fork down. He always ate quickly, as if his meal might slip away at a moment's notice.

"Do you mean the next part of the trip, or the next adventure?" I asked.

"I mean the Insmouth dungeon," Bastion said. Howard looked over at that, and Bastion caught his eye. "Can you tell us more about it?"

Howard nodded before pulling a pipe from his old coat. Clive already had his pipe out and was carefully pushing some stuff in it from a little tin jar on the table. "Our dungeon's fairly old, but it was never one to grow fast. Three floors for the longest time. Four now. Not too many monsters, but plenty of tricks."

"I see," Bastion said. "What are the floors like?"

"Hmm," Howard paused as he lit his pipe and took a pull while flicking out a match. It left the room smelling kind of smoky and fruity. Not the worst smell, but not the best. I let my Cleaning aura expand to remove the smell. "The floors are all connected by this long, narrow cave. You can skip a floor, but it's mighty dangerous."

"Monster types?" Amaryllis asked.

"Large fishlike creatures, things with tentacles, and the mist. You can't really fight the last." He puffed a perfect ring into the air. "Your worst enemy is yourself and your friends. The dungeon will always try to challenge your bonds."

"That's awful," I said.

"How many do you usually go in with?" Bastion asked.

"Just myself and the person needing the class," Howard said. He pulled his pipe out and traced a circle in the air with the mouthpiece. "More's fine if they trust each other, but the more folk go down, the harder it gets, unless you *really* trust each other. Still, more people often means moving along faster too. So it's a balancing act, in the grand scheme of things."

"We're not going down with just one of us," I said. "That's way too dangerous."

"Up to you folk," Howard said.

"Right. So the plan's pretty simple, I guess. We arrive in town, anchor the *Beaver*, then head over to the dungeon right away. The longer we wait, the worse it'll be. We don't want to go too fast, because that's dangerous, so we want to start as soon as we can. Maybe we bring some supplies to last a day or so."

"Only takes an afternoon to clear it," Howard said.

"It might take longer now," I said. "We don't know that yet, so it's best to overprepare."

There were nods all around.

"I think it'll be . . . um, I need to be there for the Cleaning magic. Amaryllis should be there to lightning things, Awen to mechanic things, and Bastion because he's fun. And Howard, of course, to act as a guide and local expert." I nodded, very much pleased with my leadership abilities when it came to picking out a good team.

"You idiot, you just want us to be there because you think this is some big adventure," Amaryllis said.

"Isn't it?"

Awen nodded. "It is."

"Humph," Amaryllis humphed. "Well, whatever. As long as we get this over with. We're a few days behind. We were supposed to arrive in Sylphfree the day after tomorrow. A quick glance at any map will reveal that we're some three days away now, if we fly straight over right away."

"Ah, but we were going to be a week early, right?"

"Yes, and that's not worth anything if we arrive a week late," Amaryllis snapped.

I shrugged. "All right. So, who wants to help me with the dishes?"

The room cleared pretty quickly after that, only Awen staying behind to help me pick up. I, of course, cheated with Cleaning magic, because doing the dishes wasn't actually fun at all unless you were doing them with someone.

"Ah, I think I should run back to do some work," Awen said. "My crossbow needs some maintenance. I had some ideas for it, but we won't have time for that before we arrive in Insmouth."

"Anything I can help with?"

Awen shook her head. "No, it's fine. I might look around town to buy some supplies. We have some here, but I'd feel safer with more, in case the *Beaver* needs repairs." She blinked, then looked my way. "Is there anything you need, Broc? I can tinker now. Sometimes I just don't know what to make, though."

"Hmm," I said. I didn't want to say "Nothing." That wouldn't be too nice, not when Awen seemed so eager to actually put her skills to some use. But I didn't actually need too much, not for adventuring. Maybe for my role as captain? "Oh! I need a cool telescope."

"A telescope? Like, to see things?"

"Yup. All good captains have one. It's a staple, right up there with a cool pet. Usually, that's a parrot or a monkey, but I think Orange fits there."

The cat in question glanced my way from her spot on my seat at the head of the table. I think she was just there because it was warm.

Once everything was tucked away, Awen said she'd be heading to her workshop, so I gave her a quick hug—for skill practice and because hugs— then I checked my collection of teas before picking a couple and setting them aside. Then it was back onto deck.

I jumped to, helping the others when I saw that Clive was pulling the *Beaver* around a rather tight turn. It only took a glance toward Insmouth to the north to see why. We hadn't overshot the village, exactly, but it was a near thing.

Sails snapped, the propeller hissed, and the engine rumbled below deck while the Scallywags and the harpies and I ran around getting everything in order to aim back toward the town. Soon enough, we were stowing the sails, slowing down as best we could to coast in over the settlement.

It was past midday, and out in the bay little fishing boats were bobbing along, a few of them already heading back into the docks with their day's catch. The people of Insmouth must have been expecting to see the *Beaver*, because we barely warranted more than a glance as we came to a stop over a nearby clearing and dropped anchor.

The airship tugged at the anchor chain and bobbed about until it settled down. The engines idled and Clive ordered the crew to run a quick inspection of the lines and sails.

"An inspection?" I asked.

"Aye," the old harpy said. "If we're going to be sitting here for the evening, might as well ensure that everything's in working order. Can't do that well while we're in full flight."

"Right," I said. One of these days I'd get the hang of it. For now, though, I had more pressing things to look forward to.

My friends came up, one at a time, and soon all of us were gathered on deck, backpacks on and equipment ready for another adventure. It was time to do our part to save . . . maybe not the world . . . but at least this little corner of it!

· Chapter Four ·

Not the Hero We Need,
but Not the Hero We Deserve

My name is Emmanuel Aldelain von Chadsbourne, and I am here to help!"

My friends and I all stopped where we were—that was, right in the middle of the main thoroughfare of Insmouth. The fishy people of the town were going about their business, though quite a few of them were looking our way. Maybe it was seeing four explorers all geared up for an adventure. Maybe it was to see if Howard was all right.

Probably, it was the cervid standing across from us.

I had only seen a few of the deer people, and that had been a while ago, way back when I was still working on becoming Amaryllis's friend. This one seemed . . . different than the obviously military-minded cervid I'd met.

He—I assumed it was a he, what with the great antlers splaying out proudly from his head—was a couple of feet taller than me, with a puffed-up chest and a dignified bearing. He had nice armor on, with a big pauldron and a cuirass that looked like it was made of leather. His sides and flanks were covered in more of the same, with gilding here and there to make the armor look that much fancier.

"And who are you?" Amaryllis asked. She sounded like she was on the wrong side of tense which . . . yeah, that made sense. She hadn't had the best of experiences with cervids before. I placed a hand on her shoulder, reminding her that I was still there if she needed emergency hugs.

The cervid blinked. He seemed momentarily confused, but that soon passed as he puffed out his chest even more. "I am Emmanuel Aldelain von Chadsbourne. Adventurer, fighter, lover of women! The fine people of this quaint town have told me that some other intrepid adventurers had come and were offering to assist! I, never one to shy away from sharing in the glory that comes from helping those in need, have waited here to see them."

"Oh," I said. "Well, we're adventurers too!"

The cervid's eyes lit up. "Truly?" he asked. "What are your guild ranks, if I may ask? Which branch are you from? I am aware of very few women adventurers."

I shook my head. "We're part of the Exploration Guild."

Emmanuel Aldelain von Chadsbourne's . . . Emmanuel's expression dropped. "Ah, yes, I suppose that makes sense. Not as glorious as the Great Guild of Adventurers, but I suppose it is a little safer."

"I guess?" I tried. "Anyway, it's nice to see others out and about trying to help people!"

Emmanuel nodded. "Of course. I have the power, the skill, and the good fortune to be born able to help others, to be able to act as a hero. It would be the height of insult for me not to take up such a mantle."

Clapping my hands, I cheered him on. "Yeah! That's the spirit!"

My friends were giving me some looks, but they just didn't understand. Mister Aldelain von Chadsbourne was doing the right thing, which meant that he should be praised for it. All too often, people who tried their best to help went without notice.

The cervid bowed our way. "Thank you, little miss. Now, not that I wish to ignore such beautiful women, but I was told that a group was on the way to assist this town in its time of need. Are they aboard that vessel?"

"Oh, yeah, that's us," I confirmed.

He eyed us all. "The sylph I could imagine, perhaps," he muttered.

Amaryllis huffed, a very "this person is an idiot and is wasting my time" kind of huff. It was one she'd used on me a few times. "Can we get going? I'd like to see this dungeon thing handled before the day's up."

Awen and Bastion seemed eager to agree.

"Ah, well," I said. "It was nice meeting you, Emmanuel Aldelain von Chadsbourne. We'll be off now!"

"Pardon me," he said, his smile becoming a little fixed. "But did I misunderstand your intent to try and fix this town's dungeon issue?"

"Yup," I said. "That's what we're here for."

"Ah, but I, too, am here for the same thing. There is no need for any of you young ladies to risk yourselves with this onerous task, not when Emmanuel Aldelain von Chadsbourne is on the job!"

"No, it's okay," I said. "We don't need the help. I think just the four of us will be more than enough. Unless you know something about Evil Roots?"

"Evil Roots? Ah, you mean the"—Emmanuel leaned forward, his voice dropping—"creature these superstitious villagers speak of?"

"It's less a creature and more a very violent weed," I said.

Emmanuel chuckled. "You believe them?"

"Well, we've fought Evil Roots before, so yes?" I said. I was trying to mask my confusion, but I wasn't trying that hard. Really, we'd only just stepped off the *Beaver* to head over to Insmouth's dungeon, with Howard acting as our guide, when Emmanuel stepped up before us. It was a bit strange. "Anyway, we're off!"

I led us around Emmanuel. Howard shrugged and walked ahead of us.

"Ah, wait, wait a moment," Emmanuel said before spinning around and trotting alongside us. "I shall accompany you. I'm certain that if a crew such as yours is able to take care of these Evil Roots, then they'll be no challenge with someone like myself by your side."

"I think we're okay," I said.

"Awa, maybe you can go see if someone else needs saving?" Awen asked.

The cervid cleared his throat. "Nonsense! When you find someone in need, it's your duty as a hero to assist as best you can!"

"How did you even end up here?" Amaryllis asked. "We're on the far side of Hoofbreaker Forest, and I don't recall cervids being welcome at the Grey Wall."

"Historically, that may be true, but the cry aren't so cruel as to deny access to a single intrepid hero," Emmanuel said. "And Emmanuel Aldelain von Chadsbourne is nothing if not a hero!"

Bastion sighed. "I think the young miss was trying to politely steer you toward an issue that you can solve without interfering with our own business."

"Nonsense! A hero of my caliber does not get in the way—he paves the way. A way for a better tomorrow!"

"Yeah!" I agreed.

"Stop cheering him on, you dolt," Amaryllis said. "We're trying to encourage him to leave."

"But why? I mean, yeah, we probably don't need the help in the dungeon, but he doesn't seem mean. And I guess if he is suspicious, then it would probably be best if we kept him close, right?"

"Emmanuel Aldelain von Chadsbourne is not suspicious, he is heroic!"

Amaryllis gave me a very flat look. "He's very suspicious."

I glanced back at the cervid, hesitated, then asked him a question. "Can I use Insight on you?"

"Certainly!"

A cervid Hero of the White Tail, level 20. Proud of himself.

"He's a little strong, I guess," I said. Bastion had question marks to his name. Stronger than us by level alone, but not so strong that he was a big threat, especially if we all worked together.

Emmanuel chuckled. "You wound me, young bun. I am still young, and I still have a few adventures left in me before I grow strong enough to defend everyone that needs it."

"Hmm," I said. "Well, I think Awen's probably right. I don't think we'll need any help in the Insmouth dungeon, but if we do, it's nice to know that we have someone to call upon."

Emmanuel tapped at his chin. "No, I believe I shall insist upon accompanying you."

"Insist?" Amaryllis asked. She sounded a bit dangerous there.

"Indeed! What hero would leave a group of young maidens alone in such a vile and dangerous place as a dungeon? If you won't allow me to convince you to stay away from it, then I will accompany you. There might be monsters and vile creatures within, nothing that a young lady ought to bet her fragile constitution against!"

"Pretty sure my constitution's pretty good," I said. "That's like the Resilience stat, right? Mine's at fifty-five."

"That's not terribly high, actually," Amaryllis said.

"My classes are both more Flexibility based," I admitted.

"That's the spirit," Emmanuel said. "The physical stats are often the most useful in tackling the problems a hero must face in their day-to-day! They keep you healthy and hardy and able to tackle the greatest foes and save those damsels in distress!"

I stared at Emmanuel. He was very excitable. "What's the male equivalent of a damsel?"

"Pardon?"

"Like, a prince? I mean, I was just thinking, what if that's what you have to save?"

Amaryllis hummed. "A prince in peril? That preserves the alliteration."

"A prince isn't the same as a damsel, though," Awen said.

"I think that would just be a bachelor," Bastion said.

"I can't think of any words that mean 'in trouble' that start with the same letter," I said. "I should get a thesaurus."

"Yes, because that's what you need to carry around while dungeon diving," Amaryllis said. "In case you run into any synonym-based traps."

"I bet there's a wordplay dungeon somewhere on Dirt," I said.

"I have the impression that your group isn't taking this adventure very seriously," Emmanuel said.

"Huh? Of course we are," I said. "Can't you tell how nervous we are?"

The cervid looked at me, then at all my friends. "I'm afraid that I haven't spent enough time with the lesser species to learn to read their body language. Your banter certainly doesn't seem very nervous."

"Lesser species?" I repeated.

"The cervid are idiots who, in their foolishness, believe that they're better than everyone else," Amaryllis said.

"Oh," I replied. Was this casual speciesism? Did he actually believe that about people or was he just repeating things? It was hard to tell, but either way it wasn't a great look. "Our banter's meant to try and make each other laugh, because making someone laugh makes you laugh, and laughter's a great way to unwind and relax. If you're going to be doing something stressful, it's best to start with the best foot forward. So we banter."

"I see, yes," Emmanuel said. "That makes sense. Perhaps I should join in your banter as well."

"I don't know if you could manage," Amaryllis said. She glanced my way, and I had the impression that she was trying to tell me some very rude things about Emmanuel with her eyes alone.

"Of course, if some girls can do it, then certainly Emmanuel Aldelain von Chadsbourne, savior of women and hero to all men, can manage!"

"Uh, your confidence is great, but you might want to tone down the misogyny? A lot?" I asked.

"Awa, it is a bit rude."

"Forgive me?" the cervid said. "I am not entirely certain how I insulted you, dear ladies, but I know how fragile a woman's heart can be, and it wouldn't behoove me not to apologize."

I glanced at my friends and got deadpan looks and shrugs in return.

I wasn't sure what to do. If someone was rude and unfriendly, it was normal to back away from them or tell them to go away. I wasn't sure if that would work with Emmanuel at all. I think it would take a lot of time and maybe a good sit down to figure out how to help Emmanuel see past his prejudice, and we really didn't have time for that.

"I say you let me zap him and we leave him in an alleyway somewhere," Amaryllis suggested.

"No!" I said. "We can't do that. He might be a bit rude, but he's not rude enough to justify attacking him. And who knows, maybe he'll be useful in the dungeon?"

"One more person might add to the level of risk we'll be taking on," Howard warned. "But we have gone in with bigger groups a few times."

"I'm right here," Emmanuel said. "I can hear you all."

"Right, well," I said. "Howard, where's the dungeon's entrance?"

"Ah, it's just outside town a little ways. It looks a bit like a shed, actually. We placed our graveyard there," the fishman said.

"Why did you do that?" Awen asked.

"So that the mana from our dearly departed may return to the world by means of the dungeon. It's just over here now."

"Let's see about those Evil Roots then!" I said. And to myself, I wondered about what to do about our new cervid hanger-on.

· Chapter Five ·

Read the Mood

The entrance to the Insmouth dungeon that Howard brought us to wasn't quite what I expected. It was, as he had said, in a graveyard, but one unlike any I had ever seen.

The grounds around the dungeon proper were filled with little statues, each one atop a plinth. The plinths had glass on four sides, with brass rods on the corners holding up a block of square stone.

In most of the glass boxes was an object: a knife, a reel from a fishing rod, a small toy. Sometimes it was a key or a mug like those at the inn or even a tiny carved boat. The older plinths had baubles that were so aged and rusted that it was hard to guess what they had once been.

The plinths were usually grouped together, some linked by iron bars, others just tightly packed.

The statues above were mostly of fish, which was interesting, but I couldn't help but stare at all the little knickknacks inside.

"What are those things?" I asked.

Howard turned his big fishy eyes my way and replied with quiet reverence. "When one of ours passes, we bury them here in their best clothes, wrapped in netting cloth so that their bones and flesh might better return to dirt. And to remember them, we take a little keepsake of theirs, something they cherished, and put it in a plinth. Once there was a plinth per family, but now our little community has grown close enough that it's a wonder if half the village isn't the other half's third cousin."

"Oh," I said. It was . . . actually a really nice way to remember people.

We all remained silent as Howard opened a gate in the fence that circled around the cemetery, then stood aside to let us in.

"Don't worry, everyone! I am here! There is no need to fear any ghost or ghoul!"

I sighed as Emmanuel's voice rang out across the cemetery. It was like a spell being lifted, and suddenly, the solemnity that came with being in such a place was entirely gone.

"Did no one ever teach you to read the mood?" Amaryllis sniped.

"Of course! The von Chadsbourne family is quite well off. I have been blessed with a wonderful education," our new cervid . . . friend . . . said.

I eyed him, then snapped my attention back to the little shack in the middle of the graveyard. It was a simple building, made of stone just like the plinths and rising to be just a bit shorter than I was. That is, if you counted my ears in my height.

"It's okay, Amaryllis," I said as I turned toward Emmanuel. "I think this is where we'll be parting ways. It was nice meeting you, and I'd love to be friends one day, really, but we need to jump in the dungeon and fix it up as quick as we can."

I felt my Friendmaking skill activating and eagerly read what it revealed.

```
Emmanuel Aldelain von Chadsbourne
Desired Quality: Someone who admires his valor and chivalry
Dream: To be a hero of legends
```

That . . . was kind of sad, actually. It looked like Emmanuel wanted admirers more than he wanted friends. But wanting to be a hero was pretty cool.

"Pardon?" Emmanuel asked. He chuckled. "No worries, I won't let you slow me down once we're in the dungeon."

"Huh?"

I heard Amaryllis's talons smacking her in the face. "He's an idiot."

"Dear young miss, I am no such thing. I am merely expressing my concern for your well-being. Accompanied as you are by two men, it doesn't mean that there's no danger to be had within a dungeon," Emmanuel said.

I blinked. "Wait, is that just . . . casual misogyny? But like, really, really obvious?"

"I suspect anything more subtle than a sledgehammer to the head is beyond him," Amaryllis said.

"Humph," Emmanuel said. "I can tell when I am being insulted. Very well, it is somewhat understandable. Perhaps you are acting on prejudice, perhaps you merely doubt my abilities."

The cervid pranced past us on his way to the mausoleum in the grave's center.

"In that case, I shall prove my ability!"

"Uh," I said. "We . . . should probably go after him?"

By the time we moved, the cervid had torn the door to the mausoleum open and was stomping on in.

"Hey! Wait!" I called after him.

Our whole group, Howard included, squeezed through the doorway into what looked like a rather tiny building on the outside, but the moment we were within, we were all able to stand up straight. The ceiling was even arched enough in the middle that my ears didn't rub against it.

You are entering the Depths of Insmouth.
Dungeon level 8-10
Your entire party has entered the dungeon.
Seal dungeon until exit?

Amaryllis grumbled something. "I'm going to create an instance for us. Including that moron up ahead. We don't want any more people interfering if we can avoid it."

"You're including him?" I asked.

"You'd whine if we didn't save his foolish behind," Amaryllis said.

"Folk in town ought to know better than to come in here without me or one of the others used to running the dungeon," Howard said. "And the other divers know that we're moving in as a group today. They'll keep an eye on things."

"That's wonderful, thanks," I said to Howard. I hadn't really considered all that. What if a child chose to sneak into the dungeon today, and we ended up breaking the core later? That would be . . . really awful.

I took a moment to gather myself and make sure everything was as ready as it could be. We had packed light. I had a sling bag over one shoulder—courtesy of Amaryllis, who was very good at adventure chic—and within that I had some necessities for a nice adventure:

- Pack of hardtack
- Can of beans
- Knife and other utensils
- Kettle
- Blanket
- Bandages and a small first aid kit
- Book about plants

And out of the bag I had more things. A couple of health potions, a stamina potion, and a mana potion. A nice knife for chopping things, and of course my warspade and trusty turtle-shell hat. My gambeson and armored skirt were all nice and clean, and I'd even used some extra Cleaning magic on my breastplate and armored bits.

My friends were equally well prepared. Awen wore her big blue coat over some respectable adventuring gear, her big repeating crossbow slung over her back, and her hammer being fiddled with in hand. Bastion had his whole paladin setup, with light armor and his fancy sword by his hip. He definitely looked like the tankiest of us all.

Then there was Amaryllis in her leather coat and her strange harpy pants. She only had her strange wand-knife on her and her magic goggles around her neck.

I was a little concerned about my friends' lack of armor. Amaryllis and Awen both preferred fighting from afar, when they had to fight at all, but that didn't mean they couldn't afford to wear a bit more. I could picture Awen doing all sorts of neat things with her Wyrmgineer and Glass Cannon classes. Maybe a teeny tiny mecha suit? No, that was just silly. Cool, but silly. Amaryllis could definitely use more armor, though. She was a bird person, and birds had lots of fragile little bones. But would more gear make it harder for her to fly?

I set that aside.

"Okay. Our first goal is to find Emmanuel. He can't have gone far. Then we suggest that he leaves. After that, it's down to the fourth floor as quickly as we can. We need to clear out any Evil Roots that are mucking about around the core," I said.

"Sounds good to me," Amaryllis said. "I wouldn't mind being the one to drag that cervid idiot out of here. I need to practice my Puppeteering some more, and his unusual body shape would certainly give me plenty of experience."

"Just don't hurt him," I said. "He, uh, is young? Maybe, deep down, he's not so bad?"

The opening corridor of the dungeon had bricks along the walls and ceiling. There were even a couple of lit sconces on the walls, but only for a few paces. After that, they gave way to rocky walls and a floor glistening with moisture. The air smelled a bit like fresh mud and rotting seaweed, and it was surprisingly loud, with pitter-pattering drops of water and the gurgle of what sounded like a stream. The sound echoed a little, making it sound as if the tunnel went on forever.

We turned a slight corner and the light dimmed. Moss on the sides seemed to glow very faintly—so faintly that I wasn't entirely sure they *did* glow. Lots of fireflies were also buzzing around, casting globes of yellowish light.

And, right there ahead of us, was Emmanuel. The cervid had stopped and was fixing a glowing lantern to a hook on the side of his saddle. Was it a saddle? Saddles were for riding, and his armor didn't look like it would be comfortable to sit on.

"Emmanuel!" I called out.

"Ah, you've decided to join me after all," he said. "Fear not, I was just about to enter this here grotto. I suspect that it's the first floor. Or, perhaps, a shortcut!"

The cervid pointed to a thin crack in the wall, one that looked like it was barely wider than my shoulders in its middle.

"That is the first floor," Howard said. He gestured past the cervid. "If you continue down that way, you can skip it entirely, but it's mighty treacherous."

"Ah, a bit of treachery never scared me!" Emmanuel said.

"No," I replied. "We, and by we I mean my friends and I, are taking the safer route. We might want to finish this quickly, but we also mean to finish it safely. But you, Mister Emmanuel, I think that you ought to return to the surface now."

The cervid blinked at me. "Forgive me, but are you suggesting that I leave you alone down here?"

"She's not so much suggesting it, as she is ordering you to leave," Amaryllis said. "Please, do refuse. I would find it a lot more amusing to kick you out."

"Amaryllis, there's no need to be rude."

"I'm aware that I don't need to be rude—I'm doing it purely for my own entertainment."

"Amaryllis," I chided. With a sigh, I turned back to Emmanuel and tried to think of what to say. I really didn't want him to get into trouble because of us, and I was afraid that he might get in the way. At the same time, he did seem prepared. He had his little lamp and a decent amount of weapons and good armor. His level was high enough that I imagined he'd been on a couple of adventures too. "Okay, hear me out."

"Oh no," Amaryllis muttered. Awen patted her on the back.

"Mister Emmanuel," I began.

"Emmanuel Aldelain von Chadsbourne," Emmanuel corrected gently.

"Uh, sure," I said. "Here's the deal. We're not really allowed to tell you to leave." I shot Amaryllis a look before she said something rude again. "It's not our dungeon. But this is our party. So if you want to accompany us, you need to follow our rules."

The cervid hesitated, then nodded. "I can accept that. What are your rules?"

"Uh," I said. Did . . . we have rules? "Mostly it's unwritten . . . unspoken common-sense sort of stuff. We watch out for each other, we listen to those who know best about something, and we do our best to make sure that all our friends have a good, safe time, no matter how dangerous the stuff we might be dealing with is."

"I suppose I can abide by that, though those rules are a little loose."

"Well, loose rules are good, right?" I asked. "Strict isn't any fun."

Emmanuel gestured to the crevice in the wall. "Then shall we continue here, or will we be taking the more expedient route?"

· Chapter Six ·

The Prisoner's Dilemma

Squeezing into the first floor was surprisingly hard. The passage was wide enough to walk through but quickly became so narrow that I had to move in sideways. It was much harder for Emmanuel and Bastion. The cervid because he was just plain wider than us and, due to his body shape, couldn't go in sideways, and Bastion because despite his size, his armor still clanged on the walls.

Still, with a bit of sweating and grumbling, all six of us made it through.

"Always tricky, that part," Howard said as he brushed off his trousers. "Had to guide this young lad once. Well-fed fellow. He stayed stuck halfway through, and for a moment I feared we would be done for."

"That sounds awful," I said. I couldn't imagine being stuck in a cave like that.

The cavern was fairly bright. The ceiling above was quite a ways up, and while the cave was somewhat narrow and had some plateaus and rocky walls, there was a clear space to walk along down the center. A small rivulet ran across the floor, with faintly glowing moss on its edges. No stalagmites or stalactites, though.

I worked my shoulders and eyed the room, then turned to Howard. "So, what can we expect here?"

"The first floor's an easy one," he said. "The worst monsters here are the shrug-goths. Normally, they wouldn't disturb you at all, not if you know what you're doing. Now . . . well, they've been a little more aggressive, but we've noticed that if you give them room, they'll still go about doing their own things."

"How very interesting," Emmanuel said. He tore his sword out of its scabbard. "I shall, of course, eliminate these monsters before they truly pose a threat to anyone."

I placed a hand on his wrist and lowered the sword. "How about we don't hurt anyone we don't have to?"

My ears twitched. I heard something, and it wasn't Amaryllis's whining about getting her feathers wet. A strange croaky noise from deeper in the cave.

"What was that?"

"That's the frogs," Howard said. "Dungeon toad. Nothing to worry about."

Bastion, who'd had a hand on the pommel of his sword from the moment Emmanuel reached for his, looked toward Howard. "What's the test here?"

"It's a trust test," Howard said. "One of the reasons we'd rather send in only one or two folk down here. Makes it easier to trust each other. But as long as we all cooperate, there won't be any harm. It'll be easier to explain once we're there."

We double-checked our gear—we'd had to take off our backpacks to fit through the crevice—then followed after Howard once more.

The cave twisted around and opened up into a large room. It was maybe the size of a hockey rink, but misshapen, with darkened corners and piles of rock here and there. A huge door was at the far end, all old wood with metal bands across it, and a hefty chain above it. At a glance, I guessed that the door was meant to slide up into the wall. To the side was a large pond. In the near-darkness of the room, I could dimly make out some shapes moving within the clear water. A faint fog hovered just over the still waters, obscuring part of the room, especially as it spilled past the banks.

"What is that?" Amaryllis asked as she snapped her talons to create a ball of light. She raised it, bathing the room in a whitish-blue glow.

A monster was sitting atop a stack of rocks. Big, about the size of a car, with dozens of tentacles and droopy eyes, as if someone had found a couple of squids, stuck them together, then rolled them through a pile of googly eyes.

"That's a shrug-goth," Howard said, voice low and calm.

The monster was some ways away in the cavern, tentacles trailing into the pond behind it. It noticed us, but its placid eyes soon shifted away and stared at other things, as if we weren't really interesting enough for it.

A shrug-goth of Insmouth, level 9. Apathetic.

"It doesn't look too mean," I said.

"It shouldn't bother us," Howard replied. He pointed a webbed hand past the monster and toward that end of the room, drawing our attention to a little bridge crossing over the pond to a pier at the far end. It was all wooden and looked a bit rickety, even from here.

"Iä! Iä!"

I glanced around, ears twisting to spot the source of the sound, and I found it in the form of a fat toad slumped next to the pond.

"Iä!" the toad repeated.

"The test here's pretty simple," Howard said. "Back over there, on the other side of the bridge, are a few rooms. Usually, there's just three of them. Each one has two levers. You need to pull one to open the door to the next floor. When you pull that one, it locks the room up, though, and you need to pull on the second lever to leave." He pointed to the big wooden door at the far end.

"And then we can go?" I asked.

"That's the most of it," he replied.

"That sounds a little easy," Amaryllis said.

"That's because there's a mite more to it. When you pull the lever in one room, the door to that room locks up until enough levers are pulled. You need to pull as many levers as there are folk with you, so even if there are two of you and three rooms, you only need to pull levers in two of the rooms, letting you advance with only two folk."

"Um, I don't see a trap," Awen said.

Howard rubbed at the back of his neck. "The problem comes from the main door. Once it's unlocked . . . something comes into the room. There's a fog, and you can't see anything. You need to pull the second lever to unlock the door to your room, but you need to wait for the fog to clear first."

"So, to open the floor door, you have to deliberately trap yourself?" Amaryllis asked.

"Uh," I said. "So we go into those rooms and pull the door lever, then wait until the mystery fog clears and pull the second?"

"That's the whole of it," Howard said.

The little bridge was closer to the shrug-goth than I'd have liked, but even as we came closer, the dungeon monster didn't do much more than eye us suspiciously.

"What happens if someone pulls the second lever right after the first?" Amaryllis asked. "I don't enjoy being trapped."

Howard was quiet for a little bit. "Depends. Usually, someone dies. I think you're all good folk, so I don't expect that to happen. Just sit back and wait for the mist to clear. I can holler when it's safe to leave."

I was a little concerned about the bridge, but it didn't hide any traps, not unless being very poorly made and rather rickety was a trap. We avoided the more rotten planks and made it across the pond to the pier with no trouble.

As Howard had said, there were three rooms here, each one dug into the side of the cavern wall. Some torches were within, already lit and casting an orange glow. Each room had two levers: one near the door, one at the far end.

"You'll want to pull at the nearest one," Howard said.

"Three rooms," I said. "And a lot more than three of us. I guess we can split up?"

"Do we need to pull them at the same time?" Amaryllis asked.

Howard shook his head. "Nah, just got to pull them all. Once all three levers are pulled, the main door opens, and a fog rolls in. If the door of your room isn't closed when the fog arrives, you die." Howard paused for us to protest, but we just stared. "We just need to wait the fog out."

"You die of what, exactly?" Amaryllis asked.

The fishman shrugged. "Don't rightly know."

"You never tried to learn?" Bastion asked.

"Not worth the risk," Howard said.

I rubbed at the back of my neck, then shrugged. "All right. Do we want to draw straws?"

"That sounds troublesome," Amaryllis said.

"Fine, then. Bastion, you're with Emmanuel in the first room. Amaryllis, you're with Awen in the third. Howard and I will go to the middle room. That works for everyone?"

"I suppose so," Emmanuel said. "Though I'm worried that two ladies are without anyone to protect them."

Amaryllis pointedly walked off.

I skipped over to the middlemost room, Howard following after me a moment later. The room wasn't very big, but it wasn't too cozy even with two of us squished in. I turned toward the lever nearest the door and noticed a little symbol scratched into the wall next to it—a sort of line with five branching bits. It was too careful to be an accident.

"That's the Elder Sign," Howard said before I could ask. "It's good luck."

"Huh, all right," I said. Clearing my throat, I called out to the others. "Are you all ready?"

"We are," Amaryllis said.

"As are we," Bastion replied.

I reached up and wrapped a hand around the lever nearest the door. This was us trusting Howard to do the right thing, or at least to guide us in the right direction. "On the count of three," I said. "One."

"Two," said Amaryllis.

"Three," Bastion said next.

I gritted my teeth and pulled the lever down as hard as I could. It was a bit rusty, and I had to put all my weight on it to force it down. I even heard Amaryllis and Awen grunting as they no doubt worked together to lower theirs.

Three dull clunks sounded out as we finished, then the doors over our rooms came slamming down from above and closed us off from the main room. Metal doors, with bars spread wide enough that I might have been able to squeeze my head through them in a pinch.

A boom came from the door at the far end of the room, and I saw the shrug-goth raise its head before it slumped into the water, its many-tentacled form wriggling into the pond and disappearing with barely a splash.

The floor door shuddered, then started to rise. It was slow, only moving up a centimeter or so a second. I soon lost sight of the edge as a rolling fog seeped into the room. It carpeted the stony ground near the entrance, then coiled its way closer even as the tendrils of mist broke apart and filled with air with hazy white.

"Just a few minutes now," Howard said.

I nodded, eyes searching for something in the fog. Something was . . . definitely moving in it. Or maybe it was just the strange glow from the mossy walls playing tricks in the haze.

Fog washed over my feet, and I felt a chill race up my legs and through my spine before I poured some mana into my Cleaning aura. The fog almost hissed as it drew back.

"Creepy," I said. It was almost a whisper. It felt wrong to speak too loud now that there was some very suspicious fog around.

"We just need to wait," Howard whispered back. "Once the gate's all the way up, the fog will start to clear."

"All right," I said. "I can be patient."

"I'm no coward who will hide from some measly fog! Come! Let's scour this place for any worthy foes!"

I closed my eyes and tried to pretend that I didn't see Emmanuel trot out of his room just after the gate over that room's door clattered up and out of the way.

"Maybe Amaryllis was right," I admitted.

· Chapter Seven ·

Mist Opportunities

I wasn't sure what I was supposed to feel as I watched Emmanuel run into the fog, the light hanging off his barding swinging around and turning a big spot of the haze into a glowing ball within which I could only just make out the cervid.

I decided to settle on being somewhat frustrated. "Mister Emmanuel! No!"

"Come at me! Don't hide yourself away—there's no point. I won't allow a threat to exist that could harm my charges!"

My mouth worked for a bit. I was looking for something to say but couldn't think of anything. Instead, I rubbed at my forehead.

"Now you know what it's like dealing with you," Amaryllis called from her room.

I huffed back at her. I was nothing like that.

"Shall we save him?" Bastion asked. I had the impression he hadn't moved from his room at all.

A glance to the side showed Howard shaking his head. The fishman looked a bit saddened. "We've lost every person that's stepped into the fog. Maybe you folk are stronger than us, or luckier, but we never figured out what sort of monster lives in that mist."

I chewed on my bottom lip for a second before moving over to the door. It was all bars, and I figured I could definitely squeeze between them. Reaching a hand out, I touched the fog. It was strange, like brushing cotton candy, but wet.

Like flicking a switch, I let my Cleaning magic wrap around me as an aura and had it push against the fog. It removed some, but not very much. I scrunched my nose and tried to figure out why. The obvious answer was that I was cleaning the fog of any impurities, but the fog itself wasn't something dirty—it was just water.

So, I could barely improve visibility. Not great.

"Amaryllis, I need lots of light and lots of heat," I called out. "Awen, can you get ready to shoot at anything that's not one of us? Bastion, I'll need your help for this." I chucked off my backpack, then gave my warspade to Howard, who seemed to catch on right away.

I had to squeeze in sideways, but it wasn't too hard to slip through the gate. I had to wiggle my shoulders, and my tail bumped the cold metal bars, but soon enough I was through.

Howard passed me my warspade.

"What are you planning?" Amaryllis asked. She was waving her wand about, and soon a couple of little balls of light appeared that she flung out into the room. They mostly dropped to the floor, and one of them plopped into the pond. Still, they cast some light in the fog.

"I'm planning on making sure that Emmanuel doesn't die," I said as I twisted my grip on my spade. I pushed more magic into my Cleaning aura, and the fog became just a bit clearer. Amaryllis was flinging more lights around, enough that I could make out the wooden pier beneath my feet, and the edge of the bridge. Emmanuel was more or less in the middle of that bridge, judging by the light still coming from his barding.

With one hand on my spade, and the haft of it tucked under my arm for stability, I raised my free hand and made a fireball. Not the many little fireballs that I liked using, but a single bigger one. I wanted a bunch of heat to melt away the fog.

I was pretty sure it wouldn't work exactly as I wanted, but there was no harm in trying.

As soon as I took off toward the cervid, the sounds from my friends lessened. Amaryllis's muttering became muted, and I could hardly hear Awen's comments back to our nervous harpy friend.

I moved slowly. Not only did I want to avoid going for a sudden swim, I didn't want to run into any sort of ambush.

If this fog was meant to hide some sort of monster, then that monster was likely able to see through the fog, or maybe it had other senses that the fog didn't tamper with. Smell, maybe? Or really good hearing? Maybe something entirely different.

"Aha, there you are!"

I spun toward Emmanuel, then eeped as he swung something my way.

I ducked, then flattened my ears down just in time to avoid having them clipped short as a sword hummed over my head.

"Hey!" I shouted.

"Oh," Emmanuel said. He looked down at me, then carefully brought his sword back to his side. "Forgive me, I thought you were some vile monster."

"I'm not a monster! And even if I were, you shouldn't just go swinging a sword like that!"

"She's right."

Both Emmanuel and I jumped and turned as Bastion walked out of the fog. The sylph was looking around, sword still in its sheath, but his hand was on its hilt. "You're quiet," I said.

"It's good to be quiet, at times. We should return to the room; the three of us together should be able to use the entrance as a chokepoint until the fog clears."

That sounded a lot better than being stuck out here in the open. "All right—" I began to say.

Something heavy and wet slorped its way around my waist. I looked down, the fireball I still held onto providing plenty of light by which to see a huge purplish tongue grabbing me. It was slimy, with drool pooling on it and leaking down to the ground with a splatter. My Cleaning aura, still on, was wicking away at the drool.

"Uh," I said.

Then I was yanked back.

I screamed as I flew across the room.

It wasn't a very long flight. My feet scraped against the ground, and I kicked out, trying to find purchase a moment before my butt smacked the ground. Even when I was on my back, the tentacle thing kept on tugging me backward.

I could barely see anything in the fog, but that didn't mean I didn't have options. I was still towing along my huge fireball after all.

Reaching up and behind me, I aimed along the length of the tentacle, then fired.

The fog hissed as the fireball shot through it. I saw a glimpse of something dark and slimy a moment before the fireball struck with a burst of unleashed flame.

The monster in the darkness screeched.

I wished that the tentacle grabbing me would loosen, but instead it seemed to spasm tighter around me and pulled me even faster.

Grunting, I slapped the flat of my foot down and jumped as best I could into the air. With a kick, I was able to twist around and properly see the monster pulling at me through the mists.

A tentacle toad, level 8. Hungry.

I wasn't about to let some toad eat me!

I screamed as I swung my warspade, timing it with the toad pulling me toward its mouth. It had a huge mouth, one ringed by dozens of questing tentacles. That didn't protect it from the heavy bonk of my spade on its head.

A big puff of fog came pouring out from some slits on the toad's sides and back, like strange, smoky gills. That's where the fog was coming from!

The spade shook so much I had to grit my teeth and grip as hard as I could to keep hold of it.

Moving quick, I planted a foot at the base of the tentacle toad's jaw and another right on its face, in a pose that felt like trying to walk up a staircase while skipping a few steps.

The tentacle around my waist tugged again, and those around its mouth wiggled toward my legs.

So I raised my spade and brought it down in another heavy bonk.

The tentacle toad didn't let up.

"Fine, then!" I said. Aiming a hand down, I unleashed a wave of Rank S Cleaning magic down its throat and all over its open mouth.

There was slimy drool and pools of saliva in there before I started. By the time my magic petered out, the toad's mouth was as dry as sandpaper.

It croaked, tongue unwinding around me and letting me go to fall back.

As soon as I had a foot on solid ground, I bounced back a step or two, then took in my surroundings. I was . . . near the far end of the room, not too far from the doorway.

"Iä! Iä!" croaked the toad.

"Nuh-uh," I replied.

It had a mean look in its eyes as it worked its mouth, probably trying to do something about the dryness. Then its tongue shot out at me.

This time I was ready for it.

The metal head of my spade thumped against the tongue, sending it flickering off to the side. An opening!

I raised my hand and prepared a single little fireball. It was all I had time for, I figured. It wasn't even anything special, just a fireball made with stickier Fire mana. I let it loose and watched it whistle over to the toad, where it splashed against its head. The fire stuck on, though, creating a little patch of light in the fog.

Grinning, I leapt backward a few times.

The toad followed and, with that little patch of fire on its head, it was easy as pie to see where it was.

"Iä! Iä!" it screamed at me.

"Iä! Iä!" another toad said from within the fog.

I felt a chill go down my spine at that. There were more than one? Of course there were more than one! I felt silly. One tentacle toad I could probably take on. It was beneath my level, and I was pretty sure I could whittle it down with a few more smacks and maybe a fireball or three.

Two of them? More?

"Guys!" I called out.

"Miss Broccoli?" came Bastion's voice from off to the side. I twisted and spotted a faint but growing light there. The light resolved into Bastion and

Emmanuel, both of them looking a shade concerned. "Are you well?" the sylph asked as he rejoined me.

"Yeah," I said. "There are tentacle toads in the fog. They're making the fog, I think."

"I see," he said. "Then killing one or two of them should improve visibility a little. Is that one of them there?"

I followed his pointing finger and found a patch of light moving closer with big slow hops—the toad I'd hit with my fireball. It was still burning. "Yep, that's one of them."

"Worry not, Miss Broccoli! I shall skewer that toad in the name of Emmanuel Aldelain von Chadsbourne!" Emmanuel said before charging into the dark.

"If he were in my unit, I'd court-martial him on principle alone," Bastion said.

"He's . . . yeah, he's pretty bad," I said. "But let's not leave him to fight all on his own. We should help."

"He put himself into this mess and dragged us along with him," Bastion said. "Once this is done with, I expect we will be having a conversation with Mister von Chadsbourne. His unprofessional behavior is fine up until the point where it endangers us."

Emmanuel screamed, not in pain, but more . . . like a kid who thought screaming would make attacks hit harder.

"Iä! Iä!" the toad responded.

"Right, I'm going to have a chat with him. But let's maybe save him first?"

"I suppose we can do that much," Bastion agreed. He pulled his sword out of its scabbard, flicked it once, then walked into the mists. "Let's get this over with."

"Ah, wait for me!" I said as I ran after him.

I didn't want to miss out on the chance to practice when I had someone like Bastion watching over me. Plus, getting a level up before Amaryllis would really motivate her competitive spirit.

It was time to teach these toads a lesson about fighting buns.

· Chapter Eight ·

Toadbreakers

The tentacle toad's tongue whipped out at me, followed by a trail of drool.

Bastion's sword cut through the air ahead of me, so fast that all I saw was a gray blur in the fog.

The tongue flopped off to the side, the bulb at the end detached from the rest of it.

The tentacle toad croaked in pain and slurped its tongue back, but not before I ran up to it. I planted a foot on the ground and shot into the air. It wasn't a huge leap, just a couple of meters nearly straight up.

My spade came down, point-first, and with one foot riding on the shoulder. That's how I landed atop the toad, the blade digging in right between the monster's eyes so hard and fast that it sank in to the hilt.

The toad croaked, then burst apart in a huge cloud of mostly fog.

I landed with a stumble, then spun my spade around and looked for the next tentacle toad.

Emmanuel was fighting one of them, parrying its tongue-strikes with his sword and occasionally scoring a slash against the toad's rubbery skin. Bastion, meanwhile, was nearby, staring into the fading mists and searching for the next toad to try something funny.

"Over there!" he said, pointing with his sword tip into the fog.

I glanced that way, and could only just make out a big blotch moving that way.

"I'll light it up, you get in close," I said.

"Got it," he replied.

The fog was clearing, bit by bit. It had started almost as soon as Emmanuel and Bastion had taken out the first toad, which made sense. They were the ones making the fog, so getting rid of them meant less monsters producing it.

They were big, and their tongues were nasty, but otherwise, the toads were actually pretty weak.

I jogged over to Bastion's side, careful not to trip over anything. My attention was split as I created nine fireballs in my free hand. "Ready?"

"Go," Bastion said.

I flung the fireballs toward the lumbering form in the fog and knew I'd hit something when the toad croaked in pain.

Bastion took off like a bullet, following the trails left by my fireballs, with his wings beating to displace the air behind him.

A moment later a big burst of fog filled the area ahead of him. He'd gotten it.

I ducked down and searched for another tentacle toad. It was getting easier to see already. With the mist clearing up, I was now able to make out the walls and the pond and even the rooms where Howard and Amaryllis and Awen were still waiting.

Amaryllis's attempts at heating the toads up were bright, which helped too.

If it weren't for those, I wouldn't have seen the toad leaping over toward the room where I'd been with Howard. "Oh no."

Was it going to try and attack my friends through the gate?

I heard something go *clunk* and the toad stumbled back midleap. Then the far end of the cavern exploded with bluish light and the snap-crackle of live electricity being zapped out at something unfortunate.

The tentacle toad exploded.

Right, my friends could take care of themselves.

I spun around, looking for yet another toad. Instead, I found . . . nothing at all.

Had that been it?

"Aha! Cur! You have been defeated by the one and only Emmanuel Aldelain von Chadsbourne!"

I found Emmanuel bouncing and cheering, his hooves cracking at the stone floor while he stabbed at the air with the point of his sword.

I looked over to Bastion, who was casually wiping his own sword clean with a piece of cloth. "The room seems clear," he said. "Unless there are any of them hiding within the water. I can't sense any more danger."

I nodded, then allowed the notifications stacking up at the back of my head to ping away.

Ding! Congratulations, you have made three tentacle toads, level 8, croak their last! EXP reduced for fighting as a group!

Nothing else? Well, I supposed that I hadn't used that many skills in the fight, and other than being a bit scary at first, it hadn't really felt that hard. Alone, it would have been very tough, but with some help from my friends, it was easy.

"We did it!" I cheered.

The doors leading into the lever rooms opened, and Howard and my friends stepped out.

Amaryllis immediately crossed the little bridge in the middle of the room, her stomping steps leading her on a straight path toward Emmanuel. "You!" she screeched.

"Pardon?" the cervid asked.

Amaryllis almost ran into him with how close she stopped. She jabbed at Emmanuel's chest with the dull side of a talon. "You are an idiot. No, that's too kind. I know some idiots and they're quite nice. Clever, even, in their own way. You are a buffoon. An ignorant horse."

"Amaryllis—"

"Not now, Broccoli," she snapped.

"Miss Harpy, I find this behavior highly irregular," Emmanuel said.

"Miss . . . Did you not even bother learning our names?!" Amaryllis shouted.

I moved over to my friend and placed a hand on her shoulder. "Amaryllis, it's okay."

"It is very much not," she said. "This twit could have gotten all of us killed."

"That's . . . well, that's true, but I'm sure he'll learn his lesson from it, right, Mister Emmanuel?"

The cervid stood a little taller. "Of course. Putting the lives of others at risk is unheroic."

"Broccoli," Amaryllis said. She was looking at me with naked concern. "You know that people can lie, right?"

"Uh, yeah? It's rude, though."

"And you know that some people, usually clownish oafs, will believe their own lies, right?"

"I don't think that's what Emmanuel is doing," I said. "He's just, um."

"A dimwit? A doofus? No, he's neither of those," Amaryllis said. "That would imply that he's merely a simpleton. Simpletons are fine as long as they stay far away from me. This man, this cervid, is a jackass."

"I am no such thing," Emmanuel said.

I shrunk back. I didn't like hearing Amaryllis talking about someone that way, even if she might be a little bit right. Emmanuel was . . . trouble. "Mister Emmanuel," I said as I turned his way, "what you did was irresponsible and endangered all of us. Bastion and I had to step out to save you, which meant splitting up our group. That's dangerous on its own. And it meant leaving Mister Howard behind. He's a brave fish person, but he's not a fighter."

"Yes, yes. Shall we move on?"

I blinked, then spoke with a bit more force to my voice. "Mister Emmanuel," I said. "None of us are going to move on until you explain to me why what you did was wrong."

The cervid's head reeled back. "What? What sort of requirement is that?"

"A really simple one. You did something that I think all of us agree was wrong and dangerous. That kind of stuff happens sometimes, sure. I've done dangerous things before that I probably shouldn't have, but I try to listen when my friends warn me about them later. I just want to make sure you understand."

Emmanuel crossed his arms. He didn't look very pleased, but a glance over my shoulder showed all my friends staring at him. "I suppose what I did wrong was . . . moving in without warning you all?"

"Yes, and what else?" I encouraged.

He looked like he'd chewed into a lemon. "I . . . perhaps shouldn't have put you at risk?"

"Not just me or my friends, but yourself too. Did you hear what Howard said about the fog?"

Emmanuel glanced toward Howard. "No?"

I sighed. "He said that it left, on its own. If we'd just waited a little bit, we wouldn't have had to fight at all."

"I suppose that would have been the . . . less brave but . . . perhaps least dangerous path to take," Emmanuel admitted. "It doesn't do for a knight to put his charges at risk when he can avoid it."

"That's, uh . . . close enough, I think?" I looked to Amaryllis for confirmation.

"I still think we should kick him out," she said.

I turned to my other friends.

Bastion was the first to reply. "He's serving as a great object lesson, and in a low-risk, but not riskless, environment."

"Um," Awen began, "I think Mister Emmanuel could probably use a bit more time with Broccoli."

"Huh?"

"Because he's bad at making friends and being . . . nice. So maybe we can keep him with us for a little bit more, as long as he's learning?" She didn't sound entirely sure, and she hugged her crossbow close for comfort as she spoke, but I think I understood what she meant.

Howard just shrugged. "I don't rightly know. Never expected to see toads in that fog. Might explain a few things. Some folk will be glad to know. Otherwise, whether or not the cervid stays is out of my hands."

I tapped my chin. "Fine. Mister Emmanuel, you can stay with us, but I really expect you to try a little harder to remember that your actions can hurt others, all right?"

The cervid smiled and nodded. "Of course!"

I didn't have much confidence in that smile, but, well, I was willing to give him a chance. "All right." I gestured to the door at the end of the room. "Shall we continue, then? Howard, is there anything we should know about the next area?"

"Just a corridor," the fishman said. "It's a little tight at first, but it'll bring us to the main cave. The next floor's just around the corner after that. Looks like a little village."

"A little village?" I asked.

"Like Insmouth, but not quite. Very old, and everything's rotten. No point in gathering much from there, unfortunately. Occasionally, we'll find a nice trinket, but not enough to make a job of collecting them. Not when the second floor's the way it is."

"That sounds ominous," Awen muttered.

"Aye, the second floor's not for the faint of heart."

We formed up as we moved out of the first floor. I ended up with Amaryllis walking by my side while Bastion and Emmanuel ranged out ahead.

"He's going to be trouble again," Amaryllis said.

"I know," I said. "But just because someone is troublesome, it doesn't mean they're not a potential friend." My shoulder bumped against hers. "Let's give him one last chance?"

She huffed, but it was a huff that agreed with me, if only reluctantly. "You're far more patient with people than I am."

"I know. If I weren't, I don't think we'd have ever become friends."

She snapped her head around. "I am nothing like him."

"Hmm," I said before tapping my chin. "I don't know. Noble. Full of ideas about how things should be. Very rude."

She huffed very mightily. "I am not that bad."

"You're not that bad now," I agreed.

"Nor was I ever that bad."

"Eh, I don't know."

Amaryllis shook her head. "Well, you've certainly improved a little too. You're not nearly as irritating and stupid as you once were."

"Really?"

She nodded. "You seem to be getting less dumb. Slowly. Exceptionally slowly. I suspect that in a few decades I might even consider you to have an average amount of common sense."

I laughed, and she joined me with her own birdy whistles. I even heard Awen giggling away behind us until I reached back and pulled her closer. The corridor was hardly so small as to require us to be split in pairs, and I wanted to have all my friends close.

We were about to face another challenge, which was the best time to keep one's friends close!

· Chapter Nine ·

Planning Committea

The next one's hard," Howard said.

We were out of the first floor and a good ways into the cave-like passage that Howard said cut through the entire dungeon.

"It's one that requires that you fight," the fishman added.

"We're pretty tough in a fight," I said. "We can work together pretty well too."

Howard gestured ahead where the cave split. To the right was a wide, broad passageway. To the left was another path, smaller and thinner, that curved up and out of sight around a bend. "It's to the left here. We should wait before going in. Best to know what we're all going to be facing in there."

I agreed. "We should take a break, then," I said. "I'm not hungry or any-thing, but I could use something to drink. Anyone want some tea?"

"A bit of tea wouldn't be amiss," Emmanuel said.

The others seemed to agree too. Awen pulled a rolled-up blanket from her pack and set it on the ground where it was drier, and I sat down next to her and rooted through my backpack for my kettle.

Amaryllis filled it, using some neat spell to draw water out of the air. She made sure I used Cleaning magic on it afterward too. "This place could use a few dehumidifying runes. It's making my feathers itch."

"That must be annoying," Awen said. "I can't stand it when my scalp is itchy."

Amaryllis hummed. "Having hair must be a pain. It's so long. I imagine it gets everywhere. Does plucking it hurt?"

"Yeah," I said. "Don't your feathers hurt when you pull them?"

"It depends, of course. A properly groomed harpy will ensure that any broken or bent feathers are plucked. It stings a little, but it also feels kind of nice? I never really thought about it. Hard to describe, I suppose."

"Like picking at a scab?"

"No, that's disgusting, Broccoli."

Bastion sat down across from us with a heavy sigh. "I have some biscuits," he said as he reached into his own pack. "Better than the rations we get in the army, but not by much."

"I'm sure they're fine," I said. It was going to take a minute or two for the tea to steep. I was going for a mixed herbal tea: ginger, which I'd bought along the way, and dried lemongrass. It had an interesting smell, at once bitter and citrusy. "Hey, Bastion, you have wings, right?"

Bastion looked at me, then glanced to his side, where his wings were fluttering lightly. "Yes?"

"What's that like? Do you need to do special stuff for them?"

"Not really. They're surprisingly robust. Harder to cut into than skin, but a lot more brittle. There aren't any bones in a sylph's wings, unlike a bird's. The only maintenance is keeping them washed. You won't see too many sylphs in drier places either—it makes our wings feel fragile. Warm is fine, just not dry."

"Huh," I said. "That's cool! How do you wash them though?" I imagined someone trying to twist around this way and that. I could only just touch the middle of my back, and I was pretty sure my Flexibility stat was cheating that for me.

"Communal showers, though you can do a good job of it yourself with a sponge on a stick."

"There's sponges here?"

"Yes?" Bastion asked. "They're from the ocean?"

"Oh." I felt silly. Time for a change of subject! "So, Howard, what can you tell us about the next floor?"

Howard had found a little bump on the floor to sit on. His legs were spread out, with his pipe on one thigh and a little pouch that he was fishing in on the other. Refilling his pipe again? I supposed smoking was kind of a complicated process. And probably not that great for anyone's health, but I wasn't going to throw stones from my glass balcony.

"Next one's tough," he said. "There's no end to the monsters in it, not that they're too much of a challenge."

"What are we facing?" Bastion asked.

"We call them mist folk," Howard said.

"That's both mysterious and ominous," I said as I poured the tea into some tin cups. The vapors from the tea wafted up and fought with the damp air to be the strongest smell around. "What's a mist folk? Are they nice?"

"Afraid they aren't," Howard said.

I gave everyone their cups. Emmanuel hunched down so that he was lying on his tummy on the other end of Awen's blanket from us. He took his cup carefully in both hands. "Thank you."

He could be nice when he wanted to!

I sniffed at my tea, then used Insight on it.

```
Ginger and lemongrass tea. Soothes stress and inflamma-
tions and helps fight against infections.
```

I took a sip and let the warmth seep into me. It was nice, really nice.

"The mist folk are the challenge to the floor," Howard said. "To exit, you need to open the locks on an old well at the far end of the town. To get the keys, you need to fight and win against a mist folk. There's one key for every person that walks into the floor."

"So we need to fight six of them?" Awen asked. "Are they hard to fight?"

"They're not, and yep, six of them," Howard said. He finished pushing something into his pipe, then lit it with a flick of his fingers. He knew a bit of magic, then. "It's more complicated than that. See, if you go in as a group, you'll never get to the end of town. Not for lack of trying. Just . . . the town ain't normal. You'll walk to the end of the street and find yourself back at the start. Moving through some doors in a house will land you in another house across the town. Sometimes you'll turn the same corner four or five times and never get anywhere. Only way for things to be normal is to have a key."

The fishman leaned forward and scratched something onto the ground, the Elder Sign he'd mentioned.

"That's cut into the side of every key. They have triangular heads."

"So we wander around, find six mist folk, convince them to give us their keys, then we're good?" I asked.

Howard shook his head. "They won't show up if you're not alone. The town will try to split us apart too."

"Oh."

That was actually kind of scary.

"Now, the mist folk, they're clever in their own way. They'll look like one of us. You won't be meeting yourself, you'll be meeting your friends. Might even really *be* your friends—the town will throw you back together sometimes."

"They'll look like Broccoli and Amaryllis?" Awen asked.

"Like any one of us," Howard said. He puffed at his pipe. "They'll talk, be real convincing."

I frowned. That sounded like trouble. "We could use a codeword? To tell who is who?"

Howard shook his head. "They'll use it. Don't rightly know how it works. We always just figured they could read your mind, tell you what you want to hear from your friend."

"Wait, wait," I said, raising a biscuit-filled hand to pause the fishman. "We need to fight monsters that look like our friends?"

He nodded. "That's the whole of it. Hard to tell whether they're a friend or not. There're some tricks. Asking the mist folk to use magic or abilities they don't know. Or you can smell them. They don't have a smell."

"I don't want to be sniffed," I said.

"You probably don't even have a smell," Amaryllis said. "What with the amount of Cleaning magic you use."

Howard shrugged. "It's a trick that's worked before. Miss Bunch has her Cleaning magic. If you meet her, ask her to clean something. Not yourself. That's asking for trouble. They can use offensive magic and will attack if you lower your guard."

"That's awful," I said.

"We should organize things, then," Bastion said. "Broccoli's Cleaning magic is hard to reproduce. Amaryllis, you have your own magic, as does Awen."

Amaryllis nodded. "If I see anyone, I'll zap first and ask questions later."

"Um," I said.

"A small zap."

"Ah, I have Glass magic," Awen said. She raised her hand, focused very hard, and a piece of glass appeared in her palm. At first it was tiny, like a diamond, but it grew in fits and starts, wrapping around and forming into a small, crystalline ring. "Would that work?"

"Might have to let anyone you meet pick up the glass to inspect it," Howard said. He shook his pipe. "This is my trick for this floor."

"Oh, it smells strong," I said.

He nodded.

"I am not certain as to what I could do," Emmanuel said. "I suppose it would be hard for anything to copy my grandeur."

"Humph," Amaryllis said. "Just stab any cervid you see. Mist folk don't bleed, right?"

"They don't," Howard confirmed.

"O-one moment," Emmanuel said.

Bastion hummed. "I don't have any particularly flashy skills, and many of my skills rely on me having a weapon in hand, which isn't something you'd want to see in a negotiation."

I sighed, downed the last of my tea, then stood up. Everyone else seemed to be done too. "I guess we'll just have to be careful, then," I said. "Bastion, if we meet a monster that looks like you, we'll attack it first. Just don't resist, okay?"

"That . . . sounds like an awful idea," Bastion said.

"We won't attack you to hurt you," I said. "Just to poke you a bit. Like, uh, your leg?"

Bastion stared, one eyebrow rising. "We'll see."

"Great!"

We packed things up. Awen took her blanket back, and we made sure not to leave any trash behind. It wouldn't be nice to make everything all dirty, especially not for the next people who would come down to visit.

"Does anyone want a hug before we go on?" I asked.

"Your new buffing skill?" Bastion asked. "I noticed the minor buff with the tea. Interesting, but not entirely useful in this particular situation."

"I don't really have the time to find great teas," I said. "But one day I'll find some great ones that'll do all sorts of things. Anyways, Hugging Proficiency is my new skill. It doesn't make you stronger, but it does make you feel better."

"Better how?" Emmanuel asked.

"Well . . . like a hug normally does, I guess?"

The cervid shifted. "I think I'll pass."

Awen was quick to raise her arms for a hug when I looked her way, so she got the first squeeze. Then it was Amaryllis's turn, because she liked hugs even if she always made a fuss about it and tried to look all tough.

"Do you want one, Bastion? Howard?"

"I'm a bit old for hugs from pretty young misses," Howard said with a grin. "But thank you."

"I think I'm well enough without," Bastion declined.

I nodded. There was no pushing hugs on people. "Right, let's go!"

Howard took the lead, taking the leftmost path with careful steps. I was worried—he was a little on the older side, even if he was still very spry.

The cave opened up onto a beach, with water lapping at the shore, and a half moon hanging in the sky above. The air smelled of seaweed and that sorta salty, fishy smell that the ocean always had.

Not too far away was a little shack and, beyond that, a path that led away from the beach and up a small cliff to a town overlooking the calm waters.

We'd made it to the second floor.

· Chapter Ten ·

Un Mist Takeable

"I really don't want to split up," I admitted.

Howard actually nodded, even though he was the one who'd told us we'd have to. "I know what you mean. But it makes it easier."

I scrunched my nose in distaste. I didn't want to be apart from my friends. "How?"

The fishman scratched at his rubbery neck. "If you go with someone, you'll be split up anyway. One moment you'll glance away, and your partner will be replaced by the mist folk. You'll look back, and they'll be right where you think they are. Then they'll attack you. Same for your friend. They'll be following you. Between one step and the next, they'll walk through a door and be in another part of the town, or they'll turn a corner and be alone."

I shivered. That was way too spooky.

Amaryllis patted me on the shoulder. "You'll be fine," she said before walking past me. "Come on. I'd like to get this entire thing over with sooner rather than later." With that, the harpy moved on ahead of us, aiming for a staircase cut into the side of the hill leading into the town.

I sighed. "Fine," I said. "We just need to get some keys and wait by some well, right?"

Howard nodded. "Just keep walking. You'll get there eventually. And remember not to trust anyone."

I grumbled at that, and jogged up to follow Amaryllis. The others followed after me too. It was strange that we were talking about having to split up but were all bunched together while climbing the stairs.

This whole thing felt very forced, and I didn't like it one bit.

So, maybe I was in a grumpy mood when I reached the top of the stairs and looked over the town.

It didn't even have a name, as far as I knew. It was just a little fishing town, with sparse woods around it and some three dozen homes dotted here and there around a crooked road.

"Stay safe," Awen said.

"Indeed. If you're in any sort of trouble, just call, and Emmanuel shall be there!"

I nodded, mostly to Awen. "We'll see each other in a little bit."

I stepped ahead of everyone. I mightn't have liked . . . anything about this, but I was still our sorta leader. I had to set an example, and it wouldn't do for that example to include me being very grumpy.

Now, if this dungeon ended up hurting my friends, I'd be showing it what for, that was for sure.

I slowed down as I reached the main road. It wasn't all that wide— maybe some three meters across. Too narrow for car traffic, but maybe not for carts and horses. The ground was shrouded in a thin mist, only just tall enough to reach my ankles.

"This isn't that spooky," I said. I'd seen worse watching horror movies just before my bedtime.

I glanced back and saw my friends moving behind me. They were keeping a few paces between each other, but we were hardly split up yet.

Sighing, I put my spade over my shoulder, made sure my bag was on snug, then walked ahead.

The homes were wooden, with fronts made of overlapping bare planks. The windows were broken on a few homes, and it looked like there were some flickering candles in others. Mostly, it looked like the houses here needed a lot of maintenance.

It looked . . . fine? Boring, even.

I reached the middle of the street and looked back. Awen was half a dozen meters behind me. She noticed me looking and waved. "Um, hi?"

"Hey," I murmured. "Did the others go down other roads?"

She blinked, then looked behind her. "Oh."

"Uh," I said. "I guess we keep going?"

"Yes?"

I nodded. "Okay."

"Right."

We both hesitated. Then Awen took a deep breath, balled her fists, and walked past me. I watched her go until she turned a corner. Then she was gone. Her footsteps on the gravelly road cut off between one step and the next, and suddenly, I was alone in a bubble of silence.

My grip on my spade tightened.

I looked around again. Something was off about the town. Not just the general B-movie creepy vibes I was getting. The house to my right didn't have a door. It had steps leading up to a wall that *looked* like it should have had a door, but there was just more wall. The light in one of the houses across the street was flickering, but the shadow cast by that light on the ground was perfectly steady.

"Okay, I'll give it to you—that is a bit creepy," I said to the town. "Like, more uncanny than really creepy, though. I'm not spooked, I'm just kind of confused."

The town, of course, didn't say much to that.

I shrugged and walked on while raising my hand. I cast one of my favorite spells, Fireball. The small globe of burning light helped illuminate the town a little better. Of course, the shadows moved in the wrong direction as I walked.

I rolled my eyes. That was overdone.

Someone screamed. Amaryllis!

My heart thudded in my chest, almost as if trying to escape from my throat, then I closed my eyes and took a deep breath.

"Stupid dungeon," I muttered. "Amaryllis is too proud to scream. Maybe if it was Awen . . . or Emmanuel."

I was in quite a huff.

I stomped ahead. I didn't like being in a bad mood, but this place was pressing all my buttons. I'd just have to find one of those mist folk and give them what for.

I spun around a corner and squeaked to a stop just before bumping into someone coming my way.

Amaryllis and I stared at each other. "I heard you scream," she said.

"I heard *you* scream," I replied. "But I'm pretty sure it was a fake thing."

"Yes, a fake thing," she said. Her eyes narrowed. "Say, Broccoli, I happen to have a bit of mud on my shoes."

I looked down. Her feet weren't visible through the mist on the ground. Also, Amaryllis didn't wear shoes. "Uh."

"I want you to use Cleaning magic, you dolt."

"Oh, right." I had my spade in one hand and a fireball in the other. That made it awkward to use more magic. Then again, I didn't need to use my hands for something like Cleaning magic. I just poured more mana into my aura and let it wash over Amaryllis.

She rubbed at her jacket where there might have been a stain. "Right, so you're real. Now I just need to confirm that I'm real too."

"Right," I said.

She looked pretty real to me.

Amaryllis huffed an impatient "why do I have to do this?" huff, then she flicked her hand out at me. A little wire shot out from her talons and wrapped itself around my wrist.

"Huh," I said. "That was neat. I didn't know you were getting that good with your puppetry stuff."

"I've been practicing," she said. "Now, that obviously isn't enough proof."

"It isn't?" I asked. Could the mist folk fake wire and that kind of fluid control? I wasn't fighting it or anything, of course. Still, it was very impressive.

"Sorry," she said.

Three jolts of magic zipped along the wires and snapped at me. It was like touching a handle after walking on a carpet with woolly socks on, but at three places at once. "Ow!" I said. It didn't really hurt much, but it was surprising.

"There, that should be sufficient proof."

"I believed you were real already," I muttered with a pout.

"Yes, but you're an idiot," she said. Her wrist twitched and the wire came apart.

"How do you do that?"

"String Manipulation. I haven't quite gotten it to where I want it, but it's at Disciple now. Quite handy."

"Cool," I said. "So we're both real!"

She shook her head. "You say it as if you doubted your own real . . . ism?"

I shrugged. "Sometimes I wonder. So, uh, now what?"

"I haven't gotten a key yet. I think we continue on our way. Find one of those mist folk and kill them. Basically, do what Howard told us to."

"Right . . . Hug for the road?"

Amaryllis was a much better hugger when no one else was around. We broke up, and we both reluctantly continued our trek. Amaryllis went around the corner I'd just come from, and when I peeked around, it led to a different part of the town.

Annoying.

I continued onward. The moon above made the mist hovering over everything shine a rather pretty silver. If I forgot that I was in a creepy dungeon without my friends, it was almost nice. Like heading out to take a stroll.

I was bored within a minute.

Broccoli Bunch was not an impatient girl, but this whole thing was frustrating to the point that it really stretched my patience.

"Come on, silly dungeon, do something," I said.

"A strange thing to ask."

I jumped. I'd wandered into an alleyway, somehow. I had been going down a street and . . . Maybe I wasn't paying all that much attention. Was there something in the air that made it hard to focus, or was it just part of the dungeon's illusion? Was it an illusion? Howard hadn't been clear on that.

I shook my head and looked around until I saw Bastion coming out of a door set in the middle of the alley wall. A weird place for a door, but then, everything was weird here.

"Hey," I said.

"Hello," he replied. "I heard you. So far, the only sounds I've heard on this floor are calls for help. Well, and one conversation with a mist folk."

"You found one?"

I eyed Bastion up and down, but the sylph didn't look unusual. He smiled and tugged a small key from a pouch. "I did. A false Howard approached me."

"Oh, well done!" I said. I grinned at him, then brought my spade around. "I'm going to stab you now, okay?"

Bastion stared. "Ah, right. I had forgotten about that. Could you maybe verify your own identity first?"

That was fair. To identify me, no one had to be stabbed.

I looked for something dirty, found that nearly everything was, then let loose a burst of Cleaning magic at the nearest wall. The dust and grime peeled off. "Ta-da."

Bastion nodded. "Very well. Now, about this stabbing—could you perhaps not?"

"Nope, sorry," I said with a cringe. "It really is the only way to know. Hold out your hand. I can just make a small cut. It'll be a clean cut, so it'll heal just fine."

Bastion sighed and held an arm out toward me. "There."

I smiled at him, set my spade against the wall, then left my fireball hovering in the air. The last was tricky, but I managed.

I had a little camp knife in my bandoleer, which I removed as I approached Bastion and leaned down over his hand. "Just a little cut," I said.

"Quickly, then," he said. "This place is dangerous."

I nodded, then swiped my knife forward.

Bastion's finger bled fog.

I gasped and moved to turn back, but Bastion's form was already shifting, billowing out into a thin monster with long claws. "Die," it said in Bastion's voice before its arms came swiping down.

I jumped up, ramming my forehead into the monster's face with a dull crack.

It stumbled back, which allowed me to reach with my mana and fling my fireball forward.

The mist folk danced around it and leapt at me again.

This time I was a little more ready, and when it came close, it earned my shoe in its face.

The monster stumbled back, wavered, then puffed into mist.

Ding! Congratulations, you have swept away a mist-taken one, level 8!

A key clinked to the ground, and I found myself standing there, panting, with my heart beating like a bunny that'd seen a hawk.

"I really don't like this place," I muttered.

· Chapter Eleven ·

Impostor Syndrome

I continued to walk through the town, eyes and ears peeled for any trouble.

The fake Bastion hadn't really hurt me all that much, but it had surprised me. Worse, it had made me think of a friend as an enemy, which . . . My hands shook . . . This was the worst dungeon floor I'd ever been in. If I could give dungeons ratings, I'd give this one a six out of ten and leave a very polite note about how it was maybe better to find another dungeon to visit.

When I saw my friends in town, I made sure to avoid them. Oh, sure, I looked to see if they were hurt or anything. It wouldn't make sense to ignore an actual friend if they were injured, but otherwise, I kept my chances of running into an evil, faking faker low by avoiding everyone.

I was in something of a foul mood as I stomped from the main road, through an alley, then back onto the main road.

I encountered a wide-eyed Awen in the middle of the road. She stared at me, her hammer held in both hands before her.

"I'm just going to continue walking," I told her. "That way, if you're a monster, it won't be a problem, and you'll know that I'm not a monster too, okay?"

Awen's lower lip trembled, and she nodded. "O-okay."

I didn't walk away. "Are you all right?"

Awen nodded, but it was the sort of very quick nod someone made when they were not all right.

"What happened?"

"Awa, n-nothing important. It's okay, awa."

She was awa-ing. Awen had been doing that less and less lately. I figured it had been an anxious tic that she'd been losing as she grew more confident. If she was doing it again, then she might need a hug or something really badly.

I placed my hands on my hips and moved closer. Awen shied back. "Nope, something's wrong," I said. "Did something hurt you? We can find it and make it apologize."

Awen shook her head, paused, then nodded. She took a small step back when I came closer, and I felt my heart sink at the gesture.

"Okay, so first, I need to prove that I'm me, is that okay?"

Awen hesitated. "Okay."

"Right. So . . . uh." I looked around for something to clean, then shrugged. I poured a good chunk of my mana into a big burst of Cleaning magic that swept around me. It even reached Awen where she stood. The mist crawling on the ground was pushed back, and Awen froze, then her shoulders slumped.

"You're really Broccoli?"

"I'm really, really Broccoli."

Awen shuffled forward, then stopped. "Oh, right. Ah." She raised a hand, pulling it free from her hammer's haft, and focused. Magic spun around over her palm and shaped itself into a little marble of fractured glass. "Here?" She tossed it underhand at me.

I caught the glass ball out of the air and glanced at it. Yup, it was a bit of glass.

I shoved it in a pocket and walked right up to Awen, both arms circling around her to pull her into the biggest, tightest hug I could.

"It's really you," she said before crumbling into the hug.

"Yup," I whispered. I brought a hand up and brushed her hair back while she buried her face into the crook of my neck. "It's me, it's okay."

Awen didn't cry—she was one tough cookie—but it sure felt as if she was tempted to. She held her hammer in one hand and used the other to return the hug. "I saw people, and there were two of them. It was you and Amaryllis."

"Oh."

"They said hi, and I thought it was really you. Mister Howard never said there could be more than one fake, and Amaryllis used Lightning magic."

How? I thought that the mist folk couldn't do that? Then again, if they could create an illusion of a person, why not some sparks and shiny lights? "It's okay," I said.

"You attacked me," she said, her grip growing stronger.

"No, no," I said. "I'd never do that. You know I'd never."

She nodded. "I know."

We held each other until Awen felt ready to pull back. She sniffed and then wiped her eyes quickly. "I'm sorry."

"No, there's nothing to be sorry about," I said. "I really, really don't like this place. We're staying together from now on, okay?"

Awen nodded. "Okay. I have a key."

"So do I," I said. "We'll be fine."

I made a point of holding onto Awen's hand as we continued to walk. Just a slow walk, with Awen's grip on my hand nice and strong. I made sure to keep an eye on her too. If this dungeon thought it was going to split me from my friends again . . . Well, I'd give it one heck of a talking to.

Maybe the dungeon sensed my mood, because we turned a corner and arrived in a small courtyard with no mist and plenty of room. In the middle was a hip-high well, with a little roof atop it, and Howard and Bastion sitting nearby.

I felt Awen's grip tighten.

"No need to worry," Howard said. "This is the well. You both have keys?"

I nodded, not entirely trusting that he was real. Beyond them was a small fence with big bushes on the other side, then . . . not much at all. The village ended here, and there was only a small road and the start of a forest beyond.

Howard took out his pipe and puffed at it, the scent wafting over to us in moments.

"You smell real," I said.

Howard nodded. "Aye, I would hope so."

"Do we verify if they're real?" Bastion asked.

The last time I saw him, he was a mist monster, so I was still a little guarded.

"You can," Howard said. "But the mist folk never come close to the well, in my experience. Won't attack folk with a key as much, either, but that's not always the case."

I sighed, then fired a ball of Cleaning magic at the well. The side had a bit of moss and dirt on it, all of which faded away once my magic wore off. "Is that enough?"

Bastion nodded. "It should be."

I nodded back. "Good." Then I threw my spade at him.

The sylph batted it out of the air, then shifted into a fighting stance, all in the time it would take me to blink. "What was that for?"

"To make sure you're you," I said. "The last Bastion I saw tried to claw me."

"I . . . don't have claws?" he tried.

"It was weird," I said. I pulled Awen along with me to one side. Not as close to the others as I might have. Not because I was afraid for myself, more because Awen didn't seem to be in a mood or state to fight. Plus, she needed more hugs and maybe some more alone time. "Amaryllis and Emmanuel haven't shown up?"

Howard and Bastion both shook their heads. "No, not yet," Howard said. "Could take a bit. Depends on how cautious they are."

That made sense until I considered how cautious Amaryllis and Emmanuel were. A rock of worry formed in my tummy, just under my ribcage. Had something happened to Amaryllis?

Something moved near the entrance to the courtyard with the well. I stood a little taller, expecting to see Amaryllis stepping out of the mist. Instead, it was Emmanuel.

"Aha! More foul villains for me to fight?" the cervid asked. He brought his sword up in a high guard stance. "Trying to trick me with more of you won't work."

"It's us," Bastion said. "If you don't believe it, test it."

"I'll test you with my blade, misty monster!"

Bastion sighed as he walked up to Emmanuel. He slapped the cervid's sword aside, then slapped the man in the face. He had to hover up with his wings to get enough height for it, but that only made it funnier.

Emmanuel's expression didn't help.

"There, now you know that we're both solid, at least," Bastion said.

I held back a giggle as Emmanuel rubbed at his cheek. "You slapped me?"

"Do you need another to make sure?"

I felt Awen bouncing by my side, and a look her way revealed her chewing on the inside of her cheek to hold in the laughs.

Emmanuel blinked a few times, pouted in a way that didn't suit a grown cervid at all, then trotted off with a huff to stand nearer to us. "Fine. I suppose it was the only way to test things. Are you young ladies real as well?"

"Yup," I said.

"Are we all here, then?" Emmanuel asked. He fished out a little key from one of the pouches hanging by his . . . actually, I wasn't sure if it counted as a hip or not. I'd need to ask a cervid one day, but someone more . . . less Emmanuel.

"No, not yet," Howard said. "We're missing the young harpy lass."

"Oh," Emmanuel said. "Well, perhaps she's in need of a dashing, gallant sir to rescue her?"

Bastion sighed. "Lacking one of those, perhaps we should consider what to do if she doesn't arrive soon. Howard, any ideas?"

Howard leaned back and looked at the well. "Still six keyholes, which means she's likely still fine."

"Oh." I exhaled. Weird, I hadn't noticed how hard it had become to breathe. "Good."

I was about to ask Bastion what ideas he did have for saving Amaryllis. As relieved as I was, the thought of one of my best friends being in trouble still worried me, when the bird in question stumbled out of the mist.

"Amaryllis!" I said. I let go of Awen and jumped over to the harpy.

Amaryllis stumbled to the side, almost falling onto me. I felt warm blood seep into my shirt.

"What happened?"

She managed a huff. "What do you think happened?" she asked. Then she blinked. "You're really Broccoli, right?"

"Yeah," I said. I squeezed her, both because she needed a hug and just to make sure. It would very much be like this floor to fake an injured friend. It didn't matter in the end. Amaryllis was nice and solid.

"What are your injuries?" Bastion asked as he moved over to us. He already had a potion in hand, the stopper off.

"One of those disgusting mist things got the drop on me. There was more than one," Amaryllis said. "I'm not injured, but, as it turns out, lightning just cuts through them, and wires do nothing against things made of angry fog. I think the cuts were too thin. They just recombined."

She snapped the potion out of Bastion's hand and downed it in a swig.

I backed off to see how badly she was hurt. It looked, at a glance, like she had been cut across the arm, just past the elbow and where her arm was covered in long feathers. Another spot was cut—her blouse under her leather coat, which was left open at the front.

"Let me clean you off," I said. It wouldn't do for her to get an infection.

Amaryllis sighed and leaned my way a little. She wasn't looking at me, but I could read my friends well enough.

"I hope you don't mind, I'm in a hug-lots sort of mood," I said as I hugged her close.

She huffed a "I'll pretend that I do mind, thank you very much" sort of huff.

"We should get ready to leave," I said. "I think we're all very tired of being here, and could probably use a bit of a break."

Howard nodded and stood up with a crack from his knees. "I won't disagree with you there, miss," he said. "Come on, everyone, hand me your keys."

I tossed him mine, Awen gave hers, and Amaryllis dropped hers in the fishman's hand. Then Awen joined us, and I pulled her into a side hug while we all watched Howard fumble with the locks set into the well cap.

When he pulled it off, I let out a sigh of relief. Finally, we could leave this floor. And good riddance too.

· **Chapter Twelve** ·

Colorless Green Ideas Slither Furiously

I was the first one down the ladder through the well and into the dungeon's central cave, mostly owing to the fact that I had a skirt, and it would be rude to have someone else go first.

Emmanuel came last. He was very much not built for ladders, so it was strange seeing him climb down, all six limbs working carefully to hang onto the ladder until he twisted around and jumped off to land on solid ground.

Amaryllis created a couple of lights to supplement the glowing mushrooms and moss, and we all kind of just . . . decompressed.

"That was awful," I said.

"It can be a tough one," Howard said. "But if we're all here, that means that none of us are mist folk. They can't leave their floor."

"So we all made it out alive and hale," Bastion said. "Other than one minor injury."

"Hardly much of an injury," Amaryllis said.

I think that her pride was bruised more than her flesh.

"We should relax for a bit," I said. "I need it."

"I suppose," Emmanuel replied. "Though I am looking forward to more of a challenge."

I wasn't. That last floor had been terrible. "I hope the next floor isn't so rude."

Awen patted me on the back. "It'll be okay. Do you want to make some tea?"

No one seemed to think that was a bad idea, so we found a spot nearby that was nice and flat, laid down some blankets, and sat around for a bit of tea. Bastion let me use the water in one of his waterskins, and I set out the little tin mugs I carried with me on the ground while the water came to a slow boil.

"Do you have a lot of trouble with that last floor?" I asked Howard.

"No, not really," Howard said. "But then, most of the time we're no more than three. Not all of us are close friends either. The occasional undeserved slap is the worst that usually happens, though it can take a while to get through the floor. Sometimes the town keeps shifting around, and you can get mighty lost."

"Huh," I said. "It was really hard for us. Well, at least for me."

"Different folk have different challenges," Howard said. "Didn't expect it, else I'd have tried to prepare more things for the floor. Maybe give you all some pickled fish to carry in your pockets." I wasn't the only one giving him a strange look. "For the smell."

"Oh," I said.

Bastion took his cup when I handed it over. "The next floor, what can you tell us about it?" he asked.

"Third floor. That one's interesting," Howard said. "Not usually a problem. The challenge is fairly straightforward most of the time. There's a bit of fighting, though. That wasn't always the case."

Emmanuel perked up at that. "Fighting?"

"Yep. The next floor opens up in this cave with a sort of castle in it. Some folk call it a mansion, but I don't rightly think anyone from Insmouth has seen a mansion before. Used to be that the monsters outside it would leave you alone, but they've grown aggressive since that root settled in. Big squid-like creatures. Not an easy fight, but not too tough either. Those that aren't aggressive should just be left to mind their own."

"Is that the whole of it?" I asked. Awen sipped her tea and made a face, so I rooted around for some honey in my pack. I still had a little somewhere.

"No, no. The challenge is inside the castle," Howard said. "There's a creature, a grand monster, incomprehensible to gaze upon. He has more eyes than there are stars in the sky, and his grasp reaches across his domain."

I swallowed.

"His name is Jim, and he wants to have tea and talk," Howard continued.

I paused, my teacup at my lips. "Huh?"

The fishman shrugged. "I'm being honest. The monster wants you to sit down at his table and talk. He is very polite, but you need to answer his questions." Howard shifted. "You need to answer them honestly. He will often ask very probing questions. They can make things quite awkward. But it's better to be honest than to fight him."

"That sounds like a lot of fun," I said. "We just need to answer some questions?"

"And do some small talk," Howard said. "It's not a problem if you're bad at it. Jim's good at teasing things out. Once we're done, we can walk out the back of the castle and into the next part of the cavern. Then it's on to the final floor."

"No tricks?" I asked.

"None that we ever noticed," Howard said.

Amaryllis hummed. "Not the strangest floor challenge I've heard of. Perhaps it's fitting, seeing as how the second floor was so difficult."

"This floor's fairly new," Howard said. "The newest this dungeon's gotten."

"How often do dungeons get new floors?" I asked. "And where do they appear?"

Howard shrugged. "Can't speak for other dungeons, but Insmouth's had two floors when we arrived. The second floor that we have now arrived when my dad was young, and this third floor appeared some five or so years back."

"What do you mean by 'where do they appear?'" Amaryllis asked. "Obviously, the answer is 'in the dungeon.'"

"No, I mean, in which order. Does a new floor always appear between the boss's floor and the floor before that?"

"Ah," Amaryllis shook her head. "No, they'll appear in any order. I don't think there's a pattern to it. Or if there is a pattern, it's likely unique to each dungeon."

"Neat," I said. I cleaned my cup, and rattled my kettle to confirm that it was empty. "We'll be drinking a lot of tea today, huh?"

We packed things up, and I made sure to take a second to check on Amaryllis. Bastion's bandages were holding up nicely, and a bit of Cleaning magic ensured that we didn't need to replace them yet. The potion seemed to have done the trick.

Amaryllis tried to shrug me off, of course, but only for show.

"Just over here," Howard said as we continued down the tunnel. The path forked again, and this time Howard led us to the right, down a passage that spiraled into the dark.

"Anything you can tell us about the monsters on this floor? The ones we're likely to have to fight?" Bastion asked.

"They're tall, many-tentacled beasts. Strange color to them—makes your eyes hurt to look too long. Otherwise, fairly weak if you get into a fight. Good range, on account of all the tentacles, but weak and slow."

"That's a nice change," I said. "Are they smart?"

"Smart? No more than a dog, I figure," Howard said.

The path curved and Howard slowed down. "It's just in there. You might want to be ready." The old fishman patted his pouches, then tugged out a knife from his belt. It was one of those knives with a hook on the end for cutting ropes. "Some of them will run right for us."

"Right," I said. "Bastion, Emmanuel, can you take the flanks? Awen and Amaryllis are good at range. I'll be in the middle with Howard. Call out if you need any help!"

We rearranged ourselves quickly. I hefted my spade and followed Howard into the third floor, expecting the worst but hoping for the best.

The third floor was a cavern. A huge one, with a ceiling so high that I could only just make it out. A hole to one side let in a thick beam of bright light, filtered by a canopy of leaves and vines that dyed a portion of the light pale green. The floor was as rocky as I'd expected, though there was a big area that had been smoothed by time and water, which had collected into a stagnant basin near the back.

And then there was the castle.

I could see why someone would call it a mansion. The building sticking out of the wall had plenty of wide windows, and it looked more like a very prestigious and rich home than it did some sort of fortification. It was made entirely of stone, the same rock that made up the walls all around us. The front, where a garden might have been on a more normal home, was filled with stone spikes as tall as I was jutting out of the ground, and the back and sides of the building merged seamlessly into the cavern walls.

Movement had me turning away from that and focusing instead on . . . things.

Howard had described them rather poorly. The monsters here, if they were really monsters, were tall and lithe, with long robes that trailed on the ground around them and hats with wide brims that cast deep shadows over their faces. There were maybe a dozen of them, dotted out across the room.

One noticed us, then walked closer. No, not walk. It was . . . sliding?

It took a moment of observing to figure it out. The monster wasn't wearing any sort of robe. Its "robe" was entirely made up of thick tentacles, layered over each other and draping down to its . . . well, where its feet would be if it didn't just have more tentacles.

It was really dark—or maybe more of a purple? I narrowed my eyes and tried to decide what color the monster was, but I couldn't make it out. It was definitely *a* color. Either yellow or pink. It wasn't changing colors, either, it was just—

"Don't stare too much, lass," Howard said.

"Right," I muttered with a shake of my head.

`A Colorless of Insmouth, level 10. Agitated.`

"Get ready," Bastion said. We formed a rough line, with Howard stepping back a bit, and both Bastion and Emmanuel coming to the front.

I cleared my throat and lowered my spade. "Hello, Mister Colorless. My name is Broccoli. We're just here to see the core. Would you min— Eep!" I hopped back as the front of the monster's robes split and a long, ropelike tendril . . . kind of flopped in my general direction?

If it was supposed to be a whip, then it was a whip flicked by someone who didn't work out very much.

"Huh," I said.

Bastion and Emmanuel both shot forward and skewered the Colorless with the points of their swords.

It proceeded to flop to the ground, dead.

"That was . . . underwhelming," I said.

"They're not very good in a fight," Howard said.

"More of them are coming," Amaryllis pointed out.

A glance deeper into the room revealed five had broken away from the main group, all slithering and wobbling our way. Sometimes their "hats" would rise enough that I could make out the big, cuttlefish-like eyes underneath.

The rest of the Colorless were standing here and there, minding their own business.

"Weird," I said.

"Free experience," Amaryllis countered. Her hand flashed out and a beam of crackling light speared ahead, twisted in the air, and crashed into one of the monsters, sending it reeling back even as sparks danced across its oily skin.

I didn't know how to feel about that. Then again, I was pretty miffed at the dungeon.

"Oho! A fight, then!" Emmanuel said. He immediately broke formation and ran ahead, sword swinging above his head.

"Wait!" Bastion called. "That idiot."

I heard Awen sigh before she raised her crossbow. "Sorry, Broc," she said.

"What for?"

"I know you wanted to try talking first," Awen said. "It's a good thing, but I don't think it would have worked here."

"Oh," I said. "Yeah."

Awen smiled, then she fired a bolt with a dull thump, and one of the Colorless flopped to the ground.

I sighed. At least it was better than the last floor. Much better.

· Chapter Thirteen ·

Inquiring Mind Wants to Know

Once the last of the Colorless was down and fading into little motes of—was it mana?—we took a moment to look around us and make sure that we were safe.

Well, I did that. Emmanuel stretched his shoulder and trotted toward the other Colorless in the room.

"Hey!" I said out loud. Then, when he didn't even slow down, I called out, a bit louder. "Emmanuel, what are you doing?"

The cervid stopped and half-turned. He gestured to the other Colorless, as if it were entirely obvious. "I'm going to fight those?"

"Why?"

"Because . . . they're monsters?" he tried. I think he noticed how that didn't work very well on me. "It would be irresponsible for a knight like myself to allow such fair maidens to come to danger because I left some beast alive when I could so easily dispatch it."

I put my hands on my hips, and noticed that Amaryllis looked just as unimpressed as I felt. "Mister Emmanuel," I began.

"Emmanuel Aldelain von Chadsbourne."

"Yes," I said. "We might be fair, and we might all be maidens, but that doesn't mean we're defenseless."

"Well, yes, I suppose," he said. "How about we split them, then? I'll take the largest and strongest, and you ladies fight the smallest and weakest. Sirs Howard and . . . the sylph can take care of some of the others while I'm otherwise preoccupied."

I shook my head. "No."

"No?"

"No."

"I see . . . The experience—"

I shook my head even harder. "No, Emmanuel, it's not about the experience. It's about doing the right thing." I gestured to the Colorless. The tentacled creatures were ambling about, moving with slow, gentle motions around the room. Sometimes they'd pick up a small rock or pebble, inspect it, then lower it back down. Little piles dotted the area; I'd failed to notice those earlier.

"The right thing?" Emmanuel asked. "Putting down monsters is hardly the wrong thing."

"It is when those monsters aren't bad," I said. "Look, those Colorless aren't hurting anyone and . . . oh, never mind."

I was still grumpy, and I was maybe taking it out on Emmanuel. He might have been a bit of a pain in the butt, but it wasn't fair to take out my own anger on him. I had to chill out.

Awen came up next to me and pulled me into a quick hug. That helped a bunch.

"Just . . . don't fight people when you don't need to," I said.

Emmanuel hesitated, then sheathed his sword. "If the lady wishes."

"You *still* haven't learned our names, have you?" Amaryllis asked.

"I am reluctant to admit it, but I am somewhat poor at retaining names. But worry not, fair harpy, I will forever remember the beauty of your eyes and, yes, the ferocity of your glare."

I held back a giggle. Amaryllis had a *look* that I wouldn't describe as merely a glare. If I were Emmanuel, I'd be worried. But then, if I were Emmanuel, Amaryllis probably wouldn't have to glare as much.

"Howard, you know the way into the castle?" I asked to get us back on track.

Howard agreed to lead us in. We followed, of course, eyes on a swivel, searching for trouble. Howard didn't seem concerned, though.

I don't know what I expected the interior to look like, but it wasn't what I found.

Neat corridors, with straight-cut walls and holes where windows would be. Here and there, rocks were stacked up one atop the other, carefully balanced and held up by seemingly nothing but their own weight. They were where I might have expected potted plants or statues to be in a proper mansion.

It only took a bit of walking around for Howard to bring us to a big room. A dining room? Carved arches led way, way, up to a high ceiling. Hanging down on a chain was a strangely shaped rock, covered in glowing mushrooms and trailing long streams of luminous moss. A chandelier, maybe?

In the center was a table, shaped like a big crescent moon, with cups before all six of the chairs on the outside arc.

"This is it," Howard said.

He reached the table, and picked something off the surface. A bell? He rang it, but it didn't make any noise.

"Don't sit yet," Howard said. "And keep calm. He isn't hostile."

The "he" in question slithered into the room a moment later. A pair of heavy double doors at the end of the room, each one probably heavier than our entire group, slid open, and from the darkness beyond came a strange creature, with a form that was hard to explain.

No matter how hard I stared, my eyes seemed to peel off and away from his form. He was like the Colorless, I figured, though he was much larger.

Unlike the Colorless, whose heads looked a bit like a hat, his was covered in a real but rather small bowler hat, right above all his many, many eyes. "Greetings, guests. Please, sit, if you would. Let us talk!"

I stepped forward, in front of all my friends. "Hi! I'm Broccoli, Broccoli Bunch, and these are my friends. Maybe we can be friends too?"

```
Jim the Unknowable
Desired Quality: Someone who will answer
Dream: To know
```

That was pretty simple. I could work with that!

"Greetings, Broccoli. I am . . . Jim!" Jim put a pause before his name, almost as if there should have been something a little more impressive there. That was a bit silly though—Jim was a perfectly pretty name.

I grinned at my friends and found mixed reactions. Awen and Amaryllis seemed pretty happy, Bastion was guarded, Emmanuel looked downright confused, and Howard . . . moved past me to take a seat at one end of the table.

"I hope you don't mind, the tea is just black."

I blinked and noticed steam from the cup.

"I don't," I said as I pulled up one of the seats in the center of the table and sat down right across from Jim. "So, it might be a little impolite, but I want to know: What's it like being a dungeon . . . creature?"

"It is quite enjoyable," Jim said. "I get good conversation and a nice place to reside. Though lately there's been some trouble. Weeds, you see."

"I think I do," I said.

"Wonderful. So, Broccoli, what is the thing you feel most guilty about to this day?" Jim tilted the upper half of his body to the side, and his colorless surface changed in hue and tint in a wave that almost read as "curious" to me.

I looked away when my head started to hurt.

"Um, something I feel guilty about?" I thought about it really hard. What was something I still felt guilty about? A bit embarrassing, but not that bad. Howard had said it could be awkward to answer Jim's questions, but we had to be honest. "When I was in sixth grade, a girl called Flora offered people some gum, and I accidentally took two pieces instead of just one. I should have given one back, but I chewed on it instead. We couldn't really afford gum and candies at home. But that's not a good excuse for stealing."

"Really, Broccoli?" Amaryllis asked.

"What?"

"That's what you feel guilty about?"

I shrugged. "I've made a lot of mistakes, but that was something I did that was wrong, and I knew it was wrong when I did it, and yet I didn't fix it."

Awen laughed and patted my head.

I spun to her and pouted. When had Awen become so rude?

"Truth," Jim said. "A wonderful truth! Do you have more questions, Broccoli Bunch?"

I nodded. "So many! But if you need to ask more, that's okay too. Will you ask one of each of us?"

"Indeed. Perhaps even more than one. Not all questions are weighted equally," Jim said. He winked and tipped his bowler hat. Or . . . many of his eyes on one side closed at once, and a tentacle tapped the brim of his hat. I think it was a wink and tip, though.

"That makes sense," I said.

"Wonderful," he said. "Sir Sylph, you seem a respectable gentlebeing. Tell me, do you love your country? Your king and queen?"

Bastion didn't hesitate. "I do."

"How wonderful. Oh, everyone, don't be shy with the tea. It isn't poisoned. By the way, Sir Paladin, would you betray your nation for your companions?"

Bastion was silent for a long time. "I . . ."

I didn't want to pressure him, so I stayed quiet and fiddled with the tea cup before me. It was made of delicately shaped rock, and was nice and warm.

Black tea. Makes the drinker more alert and anxious and has a mild bone-fortifying effect. Brewed plainly.

Bastion swallowed. "I would," he said.

Oh no. I knew how important Bastion took his whole paladin thing, and if he was willing to abandon that for his companions, for us . . . Well, I'd have to do something nice for him. He still seemed conflicted.

My heart felt strangely heavy. It was a really nice gesture.

"That's nice," Jim replied. "Little human miss?"

Awen stared back, wide-eyed and with her cup hovering just before her mouth. "Yes?"

"Are you enjoying the tea?"

Awen looked down, then back up. She took a small sip. "Um . . . honestly? It's good tea. I've had worse tea at nice parties and balls. But it's not the best tea I've ever had. So . . . it's enjoyable, but it could taste a little better? Maybe some honey?"

"It hurts my many hearts to hear that, but the truth can be unkind," Jim said. "And no, I don't have honey. I'll make note of it though!"

I held back a laugh. Was Jim trying to lighten things up? After asking such a serious question, he came in with one that was easy to answer? It was nice of him.

"Miss Harpy," Jim began.

"Yes?" Amaryllis replied.

"Is there anyone you love?"

"Romantically? No."

Jim hummed. "A partial answer, but truthful." A tentacle wrapped around a cup, and he pitched the cup itself down a mouth that only appeared when he moved some tentacles aside. "What about nonromantic love?"

I turned toward Amaryllis, then stared as her feathers puffed out, almost as if she was angry, but her face was the wrong sort of red for that. "I love my sisters, of course. They're both quite annoying, and in entirely unique ways, but I love them all the same. My parents, too, though they are . . . distant."

"I see, I see," Jim said encouragingly.

"And . . . I suppose I love my friends as well," Amaryllis said. "E-entirely in a platonic way, of course."

I squealed and crashed into her.

"No! No! I knew this would happen! Get off me, or I swear to the World I'll zap you."

"But you love me!"

"I'd love it if you weren't such an idiot, more like!"

I shook my head, coincidentally rubbing up against her floofed feathers. "Nope! You had to tell the truth. Your feathers even fluffed."

"Because I knew you'd ram into me like some drunkard!"

Jim chuckled. "How nice. How about you, Sir Cervid? Any friends who are that close?"

"No, no, I'm afraid not," Emmanuel admitted. "I may have had some close friends once, but that was a long time ago."

"It was, wasn't it," Jim said. "Why did you kill them?"

· Chapter Fourteen ·

Guilt

We were all silent. I think you could have heard a pin drop.

The silence stretched, and the only sound was Awen's clothes shifting as she reached over and grabbed my hand for a squeeze.

"Care to explain?" Amaryllis asked.

Emmanuel worked his jaw. "I . . . Could you repeat that?" he asked.

Jim the Unknowable shifted, his little bowler hat slipping to the side a little. "Oh! I don't mind that at all. I merely asked why you killed your fri—"

The dungeon creature was cut off as Emmanuel bolted, hooves clattering on the top of the table as he shot forward.

I only had time to gasp as the cervid's sword came swinging out of its sheath in an arc aimed right at Jim's head.

The creature raised one large tentacle to intercept the blade. Bright steel dug into the blubbery surface of the tentacle, spilling black blood in a splash as the sword bit and cut through the limb.

"Wait!" I shouted, far too late.

Jim screamed, not in surprise, but in anger. His body flashed and his tentacles reared up, the ends bunching up into big rubbery balls while others shot down and grabbed the edges of the table.

"Back!" Bastion called. He grabbed Howard and flung the fishman behind him just as the table flipped toward us.

I stumbled backward, pulling Awen with me just far enough that the huge stone table missed our toes.

"Damn it, you idiot deer!" Amaryllis shouted. Lightning crackled, and I saw her hesitate as she picked whom to zap. Her magic zipped out, slicing through the air and stabbing into one of Jim's tentacles that was crashing toward her.

The creature screamed again, and one of his smaller tentacles whipped out of him with a crack and smacked Amaryllis's back. She squawked as she flew.

"Amy!" I took one step her way, then froze. No. "Awen! Look after Amaryllis!"

"A-awa!" Awen agreed before bolting off.

I spun to save Jim and Emmanuel.

The monster had switched his focus back to the cervid, tentacles swinging toward Emmanuel from every direction, while others speared out to stab the deer.

Emmanuel was holding his own. Sweat matted his fur down, and his teeth were gritted, but his arms worked like machines, swinging this way and that, slapping tentacles away and slicing at others while he sidestepped those he couldn't parry.

If I interrupted him now . . .

"Jim!" I called out. "Jim, stop, please! It was a mistake! Please, we don't need to fight!"

"It's too late, lass," Howard said. "Once he starts, there's no end to it."

I didn't know what to say to that. My hands worked, and I felt like Howard had just dropped a rock into the bottom of my tummy. "Dang it!" I swore, one foot crashing onto the ground in a protesting thump.

Bastion stepped past me, working his arm. "Ranged support," he said. It sounded like an order.

I . . . stepped back and nodded. It felt wrong, really wrong, but I couldn't let Bastion fight on his own. I created fireballs, little ones, that burned bright and warm and cast orange light across the room.

Bastion dove forward and cut a bloody swathe through Jim's smaller tentacles, instantly relieving Emmanuel as the tide of battle reversed. A glance revealed that a few blows had slipped past, and Emmanuel was favoring his sternum with his free hand.

I heard a loud clunk, and a bolt sprouted from where I figured Jim's head was. Awen was helping, then, which meant that Amaryllis wasn't in bad shape.

I flung my fireballs forward and almost felt like crying as they seared into Jim's tentacular flesh with a painful sizzle.

With a screeching howl, Jim spun, tentacles flicking around him in a blur of movement that I couldn't quite follow. Emmanuel and Bastion both backed up, but that only seemed to push Jim to move faster.

Then Bastion jumped, wings beating as he flew over the edge of Jim's whirlwind, flipped once, and brought his sword up. Magic burst out of the sylph, brilliant blues and yellows that flowed to the tip of his sword before he brought it slicing down.

Jim crashed, his momentum still carrying him, but without the direction from before. The creature rolled across the room, tentacles thumping against the ground and shattering stone before he rammed into a wall.

I hissed. That had to have hurt.

Bastion stood atop Jim, seemingly unhurt, then slashed down twice in quick succession.

Ding! Congratulations, you have sliced the life from Jim the Unknowable, level 12! EXP reduced for fighting as a group!

I stared as Jim turned to dust.

Bastion moved off, then pulled a rag from a pocket to clean his blade. He was expressionless, but I felt as if that was just a thin mask over a lot of anger. It didn't take much to follow the direction he was gazing to find Emmanuel at the end.

I put that on the back burner. First, I had to check on Amaryllis.

My harpy friend was climbing back to her talons. Her emotions weren't nearly as well masked as Bastion's. "Care to explain?" she asked. Her voice carried across the room.

I didn't like any of this, but I didn't feel ready to interfere either.

Emmanuel looked up, just a glance, before he focused on his sword. He stared at it for a while, gazing into his own reflection. Then he slid it back into its sheath and turned our way with a smile. It didn't fit well, like he was trying not to break down in front of us. "Shall we continue on? That was a good bit of experience!"

"What?" Amaryllis asked. "You think we're just going to brush all this aside?"

"Miss Harpy—"

"Don't 'Miss Harpy' me," Amaryllis warned. "What. Was. That?"

"Amaryllis," I said. It was just a murmur, but she heard it, and I saw her backing down a little. Still on a low simmer, though.

I turned toward Emmanuel, aware that my friends and I were all set in a rough semicircle around him. I . . . really hoped he wouldn't try anything. If he did, it wouldn't be a nice position to be in, not for him.

"Mister Emmanuel," I said. "I . . . I know it might be a little hard, but I think you need to explain."

Emmanuel's fist opened and closed, and he looked really distressed. "There's nothing to explain. We . . . we're quite done here, aren't we? Shall we move on?"

"Mister Emmanuel," I repeated. "No. I . . . I don't know what's wrong with you, but just no. We're not moving until you explain."

I saw Bastion from the corner of my eye, sword still in hand, and Awen had her crossbow close. My spade was lowered. I didn't want to fight, but . . .

The cervid looked to all of us in turn, confusion then anger warring in his eyes before the emotion broke, and he looked at the floor. Then Emmanuel sat down on the ground, a really strange posture for a cervid to take. "Did you want to hear the answer?" he asked. "Why I killed my friends? Is that it?"

"I . . . yeah, we'd like to know that," I said. My tummy twisted into a knot. He really did kill his friends? That was . . . no, that was awful. "Please?"

"It's not a nice story."

"We can imagine that much," Amaryllis said.

"I'm sure you'd rather not hear it."

Amaryllis glared. "Don't try to sneak your way out of this one."

He laughed, but it sounded forced. "Ah, I guess from the start?"

"If that's what you want," I said.

I saw Amaryllis working her jaw, but I shook my head. We could let him talk. There would be time for questions and accusations after.

Emmanuel thought about it, then nodded. "Sure. I don't know how much you know about the Republican Army? It's the main armed force that defends and expands the Trenten Flats. Most young cervid—the men—will join at one time or another, do their year or two of service, and then return to civilian life. It makes our people strong and makes sure everyone is near their tenth level early. Some will remain in the army, getting a new class as they do so. I'm noble-born—I wasn't going to be some mere private. I went to officer training school, with plenty of other young cervid boys, and then I got a commission." He smiled. It didn't last long, but it was there for a moment.

"You were an officer?" I asked. He really didn't seem the sort.

"Not a good one," he said. "I know that now, but at the time I thought I was the greatest cervid to walk on four legs. The brass know what cervid like me are like, I think. They gave me a squad of green soldiers, one sergeant, and a map for an area to patrol."

I nodded, encouraging him to go on. Emmanuel crossed his arms, hugging himself.

"It was awful. I thought they were all just peasants. I treated them the way I did my servants at home, at least at first. My sergeant beat the stuffing out of me one night." He laughed, as if it were a fond memory. "I could have had him court-martialed, but I think it worked. I started becoming closer to them?"

"That's nice," I said.

Slowly, he nodded. "It was. Hard, or at least, what I thought of as hard then. I didn't even carry my share of equipment, and I had a nicer tent . . . I was very stupid. We were returning when we found a dungeon. A small one, near Lavaleigh. It wasn't on the maps. None of us had heard of it. So I insisted we explore. The first floor was a joke. The second had one of my squad injured when he stumbled over a loose rock, of all things."

Emmanuel laughed. It was hollow.

"We patched him up, made some jokes about how clumsy he was. It was
. . . fun?"

I think I knew what that was like.

"Then the final floor. The boss. We were all at or near our class evolu-
tions, level ten. It was the same level. We figured it would be a cakewalk—
except our sergeant. He told us to turn back, maybe return better equipped.
I ordered a charge instead."

Emmanuel's shoulder came in.

"They died. I was at the back. I didn't."

"Oh," I said. "I'm so sorry."

"Don't be sorry for me," he said. "Be sorry for them. They had a stupid
leader. I was just . . . such a coward. Do you know what the worst thing is?
The boss gave me the Knight class. Knight! It's a joke. The army gave me a
pat on the back and a commendation for finding a dungeon and clearing it,
and I left. I decided that I would be a knight, but for real. Like in the stories."

Amaryllis mumbled something, low enough that I couldn't quite catch
it, but it didn't sound very nice.

I decided not to comment on that. Emmanuel's story was . . . rough. It
seemed like it was something still fresh to him. He didn't look very old. Had
it happened a year ago? Two?

No, the time didn't matter. For some people it would take a lot longer
to get over things, and I imagined that if the army rewarded him, then they
never considered how he felt about the whole ordeal.

He had tried to become a hero, in his own way. He wasn't very good
at it, but I couldn't fault the idea behind it. And what had happened to
his friends . . . I winced. That could happen to us. Underestimating a
dungeon boss, running into a pirate when we were flying around. Meeting some people who weren't very nice. We were getting stronger, but
my friends and I weren't all Abraham Bristlecones who could laugh off
trouble.

I carefully walked across the room, avoiding broken teacups and spilled
chairs until I was in front of Emmanuel. Then I tipped forward and gave
him a hug. It probably didn't help very much, but it was the only thing I
could think to do.

"Please don't," Emmanuel said.

I sighed and pulled back, then hovered a few feet away. "I'm still sorry,"
I said.

I heard a familiar sigh from next to me. Amaryllis. "His story is certainly
sad, but he still put us all at risk. And he killed Jim. That creature might
have been a dungeon creature, but it was a peaceful one."

"I know," I said. "Just . . . this is hard."

She huffed, a surprisingly neutral sort of huff.

"What do we even do?" I asked. "Tell Emmanuel to go away? He made a mistake." Amaryllis gave me a look. "A few mistakes, but I don't think he *means* to be, um, troublesome."

"I think," Awen said. "Maybe Mister Chadsbourne isn't as ready for this kind of adventure as he thinks. At least, not the part where we work together as a team."

"But what can we do about it?"

Awen came closer and touched my shoulder. "Broc, it's not us who need to do something about that."

"Oh."

· Chapter Fifteen ·

The Buck Stops Here

It was hard.

That's pretty much the only way I could describe having to do what I had to.

The others were looking to me to lead them. We'd never had a vote on it, we'd never sat down and delegated positions, but somehow I had just . . . ended up as the leader. Maybe it was because I clung onto others or because I'd sorta-jokingly taken the title of captain.

It didn't matter. I was the leader, and that meant that some things fell to me. This was one of them.

I took a deep breath, eyes fixed on the ground. I'd never really looked at Emmanuel's feet. Hooves, really, though he had these sorts of boots on top of them, leather sheaths studded with metal, covering his legs up to the knee.

"Emmanuel," I said. "I think it might be best if you go back."

It wasn't what I wanted to say. I wanted to offer to help, to teach him, by example and word, how to be a better friend. He had potential, under all the silly ideas and the sometimes-rude behavior. I could imagine him being a good friend. Everyone had that potential, and while it wasn't right out on the surface with Emmanuel, it wasn't buried that deep.

But I couldn't just think about myself.

I was leading others, my friends. If what I wanted put others in danger, then maybe I had to put that aside to make sure everyone would be safe first. It was like . . . brushing your teeth. Not fun to do, but you did it because it was less annoying than a toothache.

Maybe that wasn't a very good example.

"We can still be friends," I said quickly. "Just, I don't know if things are working out very well right now. So . . . yeah. It might be best for everyone if you return to the surface for now? We have a quest to complete, and it'll be dangerous, and . . . yeah."

I glanced up and then away from Emmanuel's face. His expression was conflicted.

My friends . . . Bastion nodded to me, once. A show that he approved. Amaryllis still looked peeved, and Awen looked like she was more concerned about me than Emmanuel, which was nice, I supposed.

"Because you don't trust me?" Emmanuel asked.

I held back a wince. "It's . . . not just that. Well, actually, yes?"

The cervid stomped one hoof down. "No, no, I see how it is. You, you . . ." He paused, his head falling. "You see me as a failure."

"Not a failure," I said. "Just not someone who's ready to work as a team, and in this place, that's what we need most."

"Not a failure, a liability, then," he muttered. "Thank you, I suppose that clarifies things. So much for being a great hero." The cervid stood up, his pride straightening his back. "In that case, I think I'll go and find people who need my saving more."

"All right," I said. "That might actually be for the best. You can learn and make friends and practice being a hero?"

Emmanuel's jaw worked, and he looked at all of us in turn before walking toward the exit. "Goodbye," he said. I expected it to sound prideful, but he sounded sad instead.

I sighed when he turned the corner and left out of sight.

Awen came up behind me and gave me a hug, but it was Amaryllis who spoke up first. "That wasn't easy for you, was it?"

I shook my head.

"Humph. Next time, let me do the dismissing. I've fired a person or two before. It's nothing too complicated."

"Thanks," I said. She might have said that, but I could read what she meant under all that. "It had to be me, I think."

Amaryllis took a deep breath. "No, but it might be better this way. I had lessons about leadership, you know? I was never very interested in them, but I'm sure some of it stuck. And one lesson is that you need to learn how to delegate some things. You also need to be able to make sacrifices. I think one leadership lesson a day is enough, though."

I smiled, and if it was a bit wry, she didn't comment. "Thanks."

"Are you okay?" Awen asked.

"I'm fine," I said as I leaned back into the hug. Awen was getting good at hugging. Bet she'd get the skill soon, then she could use it to show off to Rose later. "We should probably move on."

"We can take a moment," Bastion said.

"And we can grab the loot Jim dropped," Howard said.

I turned toward the old fishman. "Loot?"

That had us all perking up.

"Nothing too special," Howard said as he moved around the big stone table. "Ah, here it is!" He bent over double, then came back up with a hat in hand. A black bowler hat.

"Oh, that's neat," I said. "What does it do?"

"Provide shade to your head?" Howard said with a chuckle. "We've collected a few of these over the years. They help with negotiations."

He flicked the hat our way, and I caught it out of the air and used Insight on it.

```
A shrewd man's bowler. Helps ferret out secrets and find
the right angle to approach a negotiation.
```

"Cool," I said.

"Not something I need help with," Amaryllis said.

"Broccoli should keep it," Awen said. "She's our negotiator."

I looked to Bastion, but he shrugged. "I'm not removing my helmet for a felt hat."

Shrugging, I wiggled my ears and pulled my turtle-shell hat off and handed it to Awen in exchange for the bowler hat. As soon as I placed it between my ears, I felt the material shifting. "Oh! It's changing shape!" I said.

"That's normal," Amaryllis said. "It's still new."

Right, that had happened before.

I raised the hat, then stared at the two neatly cut holes set in the edges of the "bowl." "Huh," I said. This time, I slipped it on, and my ears slid snuggly up and through it. "How do I look?"

```
New skill acquired: Negotiating
Rank: D
```

"Cute," Awen said.

"Like a clown," Amaryllis said.

"Like you're asking to have your head bashed in," Bastion added. "The three of you aren't what I would consider frontline fighters, but none of you are unable to hold your own. Awen and Amaryllis both fight from a little farther behind, though. They can afford to perhaps not have as much armor. You, on the other hand, are always in the thick of it. The helmet's a better choice."

"Yeah," I said as I took off the bowler hat. It was nice, but maybe I could use it when we weren't about to go and face off against a dungeon boss. I took off my pack and tucked the hat away. "We should keep moving. Only one floor left, right?"

"The boss," Howard confirmed. "It's a tricky one, but I'm sure we'll manage."

"You usually do it with just two people?" I asked.

"Yup. There's a trick to it. The boss is this great big monster. Weird eyes. Look into them, and you'll find yourself all confused. Anyway, the place has a bunch of altars. Every time you break one, the boss weakens. Then when they're all broken, the ceiling caves in. Oftentimes, that'll pin the boss in place."

"You're making it sound easy."

"Oh, it isn't," Howard said. "If the ceiling doesn't pin the big sucker, we often just leave and try again another time. And we haven't had as much luck since those roots started showing up."

Bastion eyed Howard. "Can you tell us more than that?"

"Aye. The boss is about three buildings tall, with a squat body. Thick skin, too, like a whale. Plenty of tentacles, and the eyes I mentioned. They're quite large, and they're easy to take out. Oh, right, the water."

"The water?" I asked.

"You all know how to swim?"

"I don't," Awen said.

"I dislike it," Amaryllis added.

I hummed. "Normally, yeah, but not with a pack and armor on."

"Going to need to be fast, then," Howard said. "Each altar that breaks makes the room start filling with water. It only stops when the boss is dead. Then the water goes back down. Plenty of levels around the outside of the room, though, arranged like mezzanines with stairs between them. The miss should be fine if she keeps at range."

"Ah, all right," Awen said.

"Right," I said. "Is that everything?"

"Just about," Howard said. "Focus on the altars first. The boss is fast initially, but he'll get easier to fight as we break altars."

"I think we'll split duties, then," Bastion said.

I nodded. "I can move pretty fast. I'll do the altars. Awen can help. Amaryllis, lightning at first, then stop when water comes in."

"Because the electricity will travel, right," Amaryllis said. "I can switch out with Awen then, let her use her bow."

"That sounds fair. Bastion, do you think you can distract it?"

"I can try."

"Awesome. In that case, Howard, can you help Bastion? And if one of us falls in the water, your first priority is to help."

"Can do," Howard said.

I clapped my hands. "Okay then! Let's all gear up. The boss isn't our objective, but it's in our way. Um . . . you can't negotiate with this one, right?"

"Not that I'm aware of," Howard said. "Just a big monster that'll attack as soon as it sees you."

"All right, then," I said.

Howard revealed a door that I'd missed earlier on my first inspection of the room. A small passageway, right next to the bigger doors Jim had used to enter. It led a ways through the castle, until the corridor came to an end and a familiar sort of cave began.

As we navigated through the cave with Amaryllis's magic light guiding us, I couldn't help but imagine Emmanuel returning back outside, all on his own. It must have been hard for him.

Talons squeezed my shoulder, and I smiled even if my friends couldn't see it.

I was lucky—really, really lucky.

The narrow cavern opened up onto a wider path, one that split, with a passage at a sharp angle behind the exit, and a more open, more inviting passage leading ahead.

Howard didn't even hesitate to continue along the main path.

The cave widened, then narrowed once more before coming to a dead stop at a wall made of huge slabs of stone, each wider than my arm span. A door rested in the center, with that strange symbol Howard had shown me carved all the way around it so that the signs overlapped.

"All ready?" Howard asked.

"How much time do we have once we're inside to get in position?" I asked.

"The floor under the boss will rise until he's standing above us all," Howard said. "You can attack him early, I suppose. Wouldn't suggest it. Might fall into the pit the boss rises from."

"Okay."

"Might want to start hitting the altars early, but that just makes the room fill faster in my experience, and the boss will fight harder from the start."

"So no starting early, then."

"We're not here to run this quickly," Bastion said.

Amaryllis nodded. "Leave the speedrunning to others."

"There's speedrunning?" I asked.

"It's a sport in some places," Amaryllis said. "Who can clear a city's dungeon the fastest. They keep score and all, with prizes for the fastest delvers. It means gathering things more efficiently, which is only good for a dungeon-based economy, and now you have me going on a tangent."

"Sorry!"

Howard chuckled and pressed a flipper-like palm against the door. Then he pushed his way in.

It was time to face the last boss.

· Chapter Sixteen ·

The Dread Cute-ulu

The room was similar to Jim's castle. Walls of bricks and stones all around, a fairly low ceiling, and sconces on the walls where glass bulbs were filled with mushrooms and padded glow-moss. They bathed the gray halls with pale yellow-green light, steadier than a flame's.

The room opened up ahead of us, the corridor not so much ending as widening out. The "ceiling" was also the floor of a mezzanine over our heads, and above that was another mezzanine, and so on up to a height of four stories. I could see an altar already.

It was about hip high and made entirely of stone. One big slab, as thick as my handspan, made up the top, with a smoothed surface on which a box sat.

Past the altar was a hole bored in the center of the floor. Just a big hole, maybe five meters in diameter. It took a ripple across the surface for me to realize that the hole was filled almost to the brim with water.

Pillars circled the room. Stone, with roughly carved tentacles, or maybe just really thick vines, running around them. They were pretty impressive.

"The usual pattern is one more altar for every floor," Howard said, his voice kept low and yet still bouncing across the room.

"So, one here, two on the next floor up?" Amaryllis asked. She was looking to the side, and following her gaze revealed a staircase in the corner. Another was in the opposite corner. The entire room was square at the edges, with nothing offering any cover except for the pillars here and there.

"That's it," Howard said. "Should only be four floors up."

I stepped forward, walking way around the altar and to the edge of the big hole. The water was brackish and dark; I couldn't see more than a few centimeters into it, but it looked deep. Gazing up, I could make out the floors above, each one with a similar hole in the center, though the hole was about a meter wider for every level.

Something jangled, and I stepped back. Then I noticed the chains. Big things, with loops big enough that I could fit my fist through them. They were near the pillars lining the edge of the hole, probably why I'd missed them.

"How do we break the altars?" Awen asked, her voice rising when the chains started making more noise.

Howard shifted his shoulders. "Even if they look like stone, they're not so tough. A good smack right in the middle ought to break the stone. You've got a hammer, right?"

"Oh, right," Awen said. "I can do that."

The chains rattled louder, then went taut.

The altar gurgled, and when I turned to look, a small rivulet of water ran out from the base of the altar, down a little channel dug into the floor, and into the hole. A moment later, more water dripped down from above. The altars on the other floors?

"It's coming," Howard said.

I stepped back to be closer to my friends. "Right, get ready, I guess. Remember not to look into its eyes."

"I'll go up now," Awen said. "I can start with the altars on the top floor—there should be more of them, right?"

"Right," I said. I glanced at Howard to see if he had any objections, but he didn't protest the idea.

Awen paused. "Oh, give me your packs, quick. I'll hide them on the top floor."

That was a great idea, so we all quickly took off our packs, and soon we could hardly see Awen's head under all our gear. I think she regretted her generosity as soon as she reached the first staircase, but it had been a nice gesture and a nicer idea. I felt lighter without a few kilos of stuff on my back.

"Ready?" I asked.

"Aye."

"As ever, I suppose."

"Yes."

The chains lifted, super slowly at first, then faster, and with that rising, the water at the edge of the hole rose too. It hit the brim, then poured over and formed a big puddle in the middle of the room.

Experimentally, I pushed my Cleaning aura on and let it mingle with the water moving toward my sneakers. It washed away the brownness of it. Just dirty water, then?

Something moved out of the surface of the hole, at first just a fin, but then the rest of a round, blubbery head emerged, oily skin pulled taut around a minivan-sized skull.

I gasped as the face came out of the water. Half of it was twisted and mis-shapen, with large green roots digging into the face where one of the boss's eyes should have been.

The boss continued to rise along with its platform, long tentacled face moving past until, finally, it stopped, with its huge, very goatlike feet level with the ground.

"Break the altar!" Howard said.

The boss screamed.

`You have heard the plea of a primordial creature of chaos! Your mind is shaken.`

"What?" I asked.

I saw Howard stumble ahead, then fall to all fours with a splash.

That was . . . bad. I had to help him. But I . . . I shook my head, the fog lifting and my mind clearing.

My Cleaning aura! I blasted it out, spending a good dozen points of mana so that the Cleaning magic would slam into my friends. Amaryllis gasped, then bent down to pick up her wand-knife—when had she dropped that?—Bastion just grunted. "Could have told us about that one," he said.

"Didn't expect it," Howard said. "The altar!" He climbed to his feet and rushed to the big stone. He lifted the little box on the surface, then brought it crashing back down with a heavy grunt.

The stone top of the altar shook, and when he slammed the box down again, the entire thing cracked.

With a third and final blow, the altar stone broke in half, and I felt a wave of greasy magic wash past.

A fountain of water erupted from the base of the altar, pushing up and splattering against the broken stone top. It reminded me of seeing a fire hydrant that had been hit, only not nearly as strong. Still, if it kept going, and with the room already filling with water . . .

"Broccoli, go check on Awen. Everyone else, second floor. Amaryllis, let loose with everything you have as soon as we're clear," Bastion said.

"Right!" I called back.

I bounced off, first jumping to the top of the stairs, then once there I used the back wall to bounce up onto the second floor. I could see the boss's waist here, his big potbelly blubbering in place. Two altars, just like Howard had said, one on either side of the boss.

Ignoring all that, I bounced up another floor even as my friends ran up the stairs.

The third floor was equally empty, with an altar behind the boss, and one on either side. The floor was also, I noted, a fair bit smaller than the one below. More of a balcony, maybe.

The fourth floor, when I arrived, was little more than a passage all the way around the hole and the third floor, with an altar at every corner.

I saw our bags tucked away next to a closed door by the back, probably the exit. And right next to the edge, shuffling forward with wide eyes, was a terrified Awen.

"Awen!" I shouted before darting forward. She was trembling even as she walked toward the boss, her eyes fixed on its one good eye below. This floor was only just even with the top of the boss's head.

I tackled her, pulling her back from the edge even as I pushed as much Cleaning magic out as I could in a short, hard burst.

Awen gasped. "B-Broc!"

"Awen! Are you okay?"

She shook her head. "I . . . yes? I was . . . confused, but I was fighting it. It was . . . ugh." She pressed a hand to her forehead. "I didn't like it."

"Hey, it's okay now."

Awen nodded and pulled back. "I'll do the altars here."

"Are you—"

She nodded harder, flashing me a smile. "I'm not going to be useless."

"All right," I said. "In that case, I'll get back to the fight." And just as I finished saying that, the room lit up in brilliant blues and whites as Amaryllis let loose with her Lightning magic. The boss groaned and shifted back, then it ducked down, one of its arms punching out.

"The altars!" Awen said. "It'll weaken it!"

I nodded, then let her go. She'd do her part; I couldn't let my trust in her falter now.

Spade in hand, I eyed the boss, then backed up a little. I doubted Fire magic would do much against someone all wet like that, and its skin looked thick enough to make the magic kinda weak anyway. Fire magic, while cool and flashy, wasn't all that good at killing, just hurting.

So manual labor it was!

I roared as hard and as loud as I could while I jumped down, my spade held up way above my head with both hands wrapped tight around the handle.

The boss glanced up just as I brought the warspade down, a bit of stamina spent on my arms making the blow that much faster.

It banged into the boss's head with a resounding bong that made my arms shiver, then I crashed into the monster feet-first and launched myself backward in a quick somersault that had me landing on the third floor.

A crack from above, followed by one of the little rivulets of water turning into more of a deluge, announced the breaking of one of the topmost altars. Awen hard at work, then.

The boss spun to face me, so I darted away, using one of the pillars as cover. Cover, and a place to Insight the boss from.

Cute-ulu the Psyche Flayer, level 10.

Cute? The boss didn't look cute at all. Sure, it had big eyes and little tentacles, and it was kinda stout-looking, but just because it looked like a forty-foot-tall baby didn't mean that it was cute!

The level was also strange. Lower than Jim had been. Then again, Jim was a miniboss who could be avoided by talking—maybe dungeons got stronger monsters if they were easier to bypass or something? It made sense, in a weird sort of game-y logic. And even with the level difference, Cute-ulu looked a whole lot tougher and stronger already.

A second altar broke above, redoubling the amount of water raining down.

"Quick!" I heard Bastion call from below.

"Don't get your pretty sylph panties knotted up!" Amaryllis shouted back.

Before I could even begin to wonder what all that was about, the room filled with noise as Amaryllis let loose another barrage of electricity that rammed into the boss midchest.

I nodded. Amaryllis was doing great!

A crack sounded from below, and the splashing noises increased. So they'd broken another altar.

So far, things were going pretty well.

I created a set of nine fireballs, even if I knew they'd be less effective, then ran out of my cover on a direct path to the nearest altar. The boss turned my way, and I let loose, flinging all nine balls right toward its face.

It blinked, flinching from the magic that flew toward its remaining eye.

On reaching the altar, I hopped up, landed on it, then pounded both feet down as hard as I could. The rock below me cracked. Another hit, then.

I looked up on seeing a shadow, then eeped and ducked a wild swing from one of the boss's face tentacles.

The huge prehensile limb crashed into the altar, bursting through as it tried to grab at me.

Fortunately, I was a quick little bun, and I was out of there before it could do anything more than sabotage its own altar.

"Right, don't underestimate the giant monster boss," I muttered.

I had to take this seriously too!

· Chapter Seventeen ·

Down with the Boss

There were plenty of altars left to break, and the boss still seemed to be in decent health, even if I could see some burns across its chest where Amaryllis had let loose against it. I didn't doubt that those had hurt, but they weren't crippling blows. My attack earlier hadn't done much, either, and the fireballs had petered out almost as soon as they struck.

The boss pulled its arm back, bits of stone from the altar clinging to the limb and only falling off when water geysered out from the altar and splashed against it.

Barely even a scratch!

I glanced over to the side, noting the other two altars on this level, then back to the boss. Could I keep it distracted? It might not be super useful, but it would give my friends some time to do things.

"Hey there!" I shouted, one arm waving. "You missed me."

The boss turned its head so that its one eye stared my way, and I quickly glanced away from the maddening swirling globe. It wasn't time to lose my mind just yet.

Shifting back, the boss raised its other arm and presented both palms to me, like someone about to clap a mosquito out of the air. Only in this case, I was taking up the role of the mosquito.

"Oh, snickerdoodles," I swore before both hands came rushing in toward me.

I jumped to one side, sailing over the boss's arm. I landed in a bounce that sent me sailing over the second hand. That was a chunk of stamina gone.

The hands clapped together with a huge wallop, the water coating them spraying out every which way, exactly the way I imagined I'd have gotten splattered if I'd lingered there.

"Bit rude!" I called out to the boss.

Then, before it could do that again, I ran toward the next altar, past a waterfall where one of the altars overhead had been broken. I saw Awen running by above, hammer in hand.

"Hey, hey!" I bounced up and onto a second altar. "I'm here, big guy . . . or girl. I can't actually tell."

The boss turned, then swung an arm at me, the entire limb going high.

I hopped off the altar and ducked down, expecting to hear stone breaking, and I did, only it wasn't the altar but one of the pillars that had collapsed in a flurry of pieces.

"Whoa," I said. Then I felt my eyes growing wide as a fist came rocketing down where I was.

I rolled, the entire floor bouncing under me as the fist crashed down where I'd been.

"Whoa!" I shouted. "Hey! Be careful!"

It didn't even break the altar. Annoying.

"Leave Broccoli alone!" came Awen's cry from above before a bolt thumped into the boss's forehead and stuck there.

The monster looked up, then brought both hands up and through the floor above.

I scrambled away as the ceiling collapsed around me. At least one big stone crashed into the altar, cracking the top of it and unleashing a wash of water.

I wanted to cheer, but that caught in my throat when I saw Awen stumble near the edge, then trip.

"Awen!"

I jumped forward, ignoring the monster's arms as he pulled them back.

Awen was falling, eyes wide and limbs scrabbling for purchase even as everything continued to fall apart.

I reached out for her, but something hard and heavy banged my head. I grunted, but my hand still wrapped around something before I crashed tummy first onto the uneven floor. Rocks dug into my legs and hips where they skidded off my armor.

The thing I held onto tugged, dragging me forward.

I blinked, clearing the stars from my vision.

Awen was suspended below me, one hand gripping her crossbow, the rest of her dangling like a wet towel on a clothesline on a windy day.

That's what I held onto, one of the metal arms at the end of the bow, currently straightened since it wasn't loaded. "Hang on!" I shouted.

"I . . . I'm slipping!" she screamed.

The boss growled and shifted.

"Awen!"

I could see Bastion and Howard running toward her from the floor below. They'd catch her!

Then Awen slipped. She didn't even yell as she tumbled right past the floor below and crashed into the water with a huge splash.

"Awen!"

Howard dove in, a second, smaller splash right next to where Awen had fallen.

"No!"

I scrambled to my feet, still holding onto Awen's bow. I stared at it for a moment, then tossed it back. Where was my spade?

Bastion paused by the edge of the floor below. "The altars!" he shouted.

"Yeah— No! If we break them, they'll be buried."

"There's one left above."

"Right."

I spun around, saw my spade, and picked it up as I rushed by. I had to blink hard to clear my vision; it was very wet.

The boss roared again, and it bent down to attack my friends below. I was really, really not fond of this boss. The last altar was across the room, which meant either going around, or through the boss. With my current mood . . .

My sneakers gripped onto the edge of the floor, and I launched myself at the boss with the meanest roar I could muster. I was kind of disappointed when my roar sounded more like a kitten yawning.

The boss probably didn't expect anyone to deliver a straight, stamina-empowered kick right in its face.

The boss had to be a hundred times my weight, but I had a lot of miffed-off energy to bleed.

Its face tentacles reached up, and one of them grabbed me around the waist as I was falling back.

Perfect!

I poured magic into a blast of Cleaning magic, a blast that would have been strong even before I hit Rank S with the skill. Now the ball of swirling magic spun around like a snow globe in a paint mixer, hundreds of motes of magic zipping around in a tight ball that I fired into the monster's face.

The water wicked away and left the boss's face perfectly clean. It blinked its single, now dry, eye, seeming confused.

Then I fired more Cleaning magic at the other side, and the magic tore into the roots filling the monster's disfigured eyehole.

The roots melted apart, the greenish plant life turning brown before fading into motes of dust, and with them gone, there was now an unfilled maze of holes left in the boss's face that quickly started to bleed. The boss's moan hinted that it hadn't enjoyed that.

"Amaryllis! Zap its face!"

I saw my harpy friend, all wet and really annoyed looking, running to the edge of the floor below.

The tentacle gripping me raised me, and a larger mouth opened up, the tentacles around it shifting aside like noodly curtains. The boss had a beak instead of a mouth, one filled with jagged, quill-like teeth inside.

Amaryllis's lightning crashed into the boss's face, digging into its blubbery features and singeing them black.

The boss growled and threw me toward its open beak.

I kicked out, one foot on either end of the beak to pin me in place. I flipped my spade around and hacked at the tentacle holding me with the sharp end while my free hand pointed down the monster's throat. "Fireball!"

The fireball I cast wasn't big or impressive, but it did blow apart that dangly thing at the back of the monster's throat.

It screamed and flung me back.

I kicked and flipped, only just managing to land on my feet before I stumbled and rolled and finally ended up bumping against the far wall. "Ouch," I muttered.

I was on the top floor, I realized.

Shaking my head, I picked myself up, then took in the scene. The monster was finally looking a bit rough. It was coughing and sputtering, and its voice was now all sorts of rough. I bet it couldn't scream its psyche-flayey scream anymore, which was a great bonus.

I ran toward the last altar left on this floor, then stumbled and tripped as the muscles in my legs twinged. I gasped and gritted my teeth. I didn't have time to be hurt. I had to help, and we had to save . . .

Bastion flashed past the boss, circling around the back of its head in a quick upward spiral with his sword, leaving a long slice wherever he passed by the monster. The boss tried to swat him out of the air, but they were blind swings that Bastion avoided with ease. "She's out of the water," he said. "Break the altar!"

"Right!"

Awen was safe!

I rushed to the altar, then whacked it with my spade. Then again and again, ignoring the soreness in my arms until a fountain of water burst from the stone.

The ceiling above boomed, and I saw a crack running across the middle. Not enough to bring it down yet, but a good sign. Other cracks were there, too, all of them meeting in the middle above the hole where the boss was.

How many altars were left?

I searched around, but there were waterfalls of water all over and piles of broken stone where the boss had rampaged. Then I saw it, on the floor below—one last altar.

I wanted to jump to it, but I was a bit hurt, and I wasn't sure if that would be clever.

Instead, I ran as fast as I could manage, with a few hops for speed to the stairs, then down the entire staircase until I was down a floor. I arrived just as Amaryllis and Howard came up from the second floor from a stairwell opposite the one I was using.

They had Awen, her arms thrown over their shoulders and coughing hard.

Coughing meant she was alive!

I grinned, then let the grin fall as I watched the boss. Bastion was doing good work distracting the boss, keeping its attention on himself.

Good. I just had to do my part!

I moved to the altar, bent over, then shoved into it shoulder first. I growled and dug my feet in, pushing as hard as I could until the stone shifted forward.

It crashed down with a heavy thump, and I earned myself a face full of water for my trouble. I spluttered and stepped back.

The water didn't have far to go; the second floor was already filled halfway.

I was distracted from staring as a heavy chunk of rock splashed into the water, then another. I glanced up, then swallowed as the entire ceiling buckled.

Bastion shot away from the boss just as a piece of the ceiling longer than I was dislodged itself and crashed into the boss's head with a dull, wet thump.

Dust filled the air, accompanied by the sound of heavy splashing as more and more stone fell down.

I spent a bit of Cleaning magic clearing the dust around me away.

Ding! Congratulations, you have end-ritched the life of Cute-ulu the Psyche Flayer, level 10! For defeating a dungeon boss, bonus EXP is gained! EXP reduced for fighting as a group!

I felt my shoulders slump. That was it. There were plenty of other notifications, but I shut those off for now. I had bigger concerns.

The water from the altars slowed, then stopped entirely, which I suppose helped a little. It certainly made things a lot quieter.

"Awen!" I called out.

"You know," Amaryllis said. "I was in the fight too. I got all wet. It'll take hours for my feathers to dry out."

I laughed as I followed her voice. If Amaryllis was being snippy, then things were probably all right.

When I did find my friends, I crashed into them with a big, strong hug. It was rough, and I think we had some healing to do, but we'd made it.

· Chapter Eighteen ·

A True Captain

Everyone gathered on the top floor of the boss room, all of us rather exhausted. Even Bastion seemed a bit tired, even if he and Howard had been the only ones entirely unscathed by the boss fight.

"How're you?" I asked Awen. She was leaning against the wall near the door that I suspected led out of the dungeon.

Awen grimaced. "My health is a bit low? Um, and my stamina. My mana is fine?"

"I don't think your mana's a big deal right now," I said. I searched my bandoleer for a potion, but the only one I had was broken.

Why were potion bottles made of glass? That was just silly.

"Here," Amaryllis said as she handed an intact potion to Awen. "Once we're out of here, I think it would be wise to find a healer. At least, if there is one in Insmouth?" The last she asked while looking at Howard.

"We have a good apothecary, but nothing so special as a doctor or healer."

"What's the difference?" I asked. "Between doctor and healer, I mean."

"One knows how the body works very well and has skills to fix it physically," Amaryllis said. "The other throws magic at the problem and hopes for the best. Doctors are better, generally, but slower. Having both is ideal."

"Right," I said. A neat lesson, but not what we needed right then and there.

"We'll find someone in Sylphfree, I'm sure," Amaryllis said.

"We do pride ourselves on being the most advanced nation when it comes to the healing arts," Bastion said.

Amaryllis nodded, and if she was acknowledging it without complaint, it was probably true.

Awen took her potion and sighed after. "That was scary."

"I was terrified," I said.

"Awa, I think . . . I think I want to learn how to swim."

I giggled, which got her laughing too. Amaryllis rolled her eyes, but at least she was smiling. "We'll find a pool or something," I said. "I can teach you to doggy paddle at least."

"How undignified."

"If it keeps you above water, it doesn't matter how silly you look."

Howard stretched his back and looked over to where the boss had been before. "I'll go see if the boss dropped anything," he said before heading off.

I took in my friends at a glance. We were done here, mostly. Just the last bit of the mission left to take care of, but that was a part we could take our time in handling, and one that was unlikely to attack us. My friends seemed preoccupied, especially Amaryllis, who had a smug birdy grin on.

"Leveled up?" I asked.

"I did."

I sat down next to Awen, then scooted over before checking all my notifications. Mister Menu had a bunch for me.

Dungeon cleared!

All adversaries within the Depths of Insmouth defeated.

All bosses defeated.

Broccoli Bunch, Cinnamon Bun Bun, level 12, Wonderlander, level 4, is awarded the Deep Diver class.

All class slots filled.

Replace current class with Deep Diver?

Replacing one of your current classes will reset your level to 0 in that class.

Did I want to become a fish person with bunny ears? Not really, no.

Class: Deep Diver set in abeyance until class slot becomes available.

Well, that was done! Another dungeon cleared, another potential class saved up for when I reached my next evolution.

I was expecting a level up, but I got . . . nothing. I scanned through all the messages I had from Mister Menu, but there wasn't anything about leveling up. That was annoying. And we'd worked so hard!

Though, I supposed it was fair. It had only been a few hours, and there was hardly as much fighting here as in the last dungeon. And the monsters weren't quite as impressive.

Plenty of skills had improved though!

Congratulations! Through repeated actions, your Archaeology skill has improved and is now eligible for rank up!

Rank D is a free rank!

Oh! That hadn't moved around in a long time. It was nice to see it growing. Not the most handy of my skills, but maybe now that it was at Rank D it would start being more useful. It felt like Rank F was just there to tell you that you had a skill, and Rank E was only good for helping a tiny bit. D was where things really improved.

`Congratulations! Through repeated actions, your Tea Making skill has improved and is now eligible for rank up!`

`Rank C costs one Class Skill Point!`

I grinned. Rank C Tea Making! I wondered what that did? Would it allow me to make magic teas? Or would I have some sort of stamina-related ability linked to Tea Making? Maybe it would allow me to prepare tea better? Oh! Maybe it would allow me to hold my bladder better!

No, that was silly.

`Congratulations! Through repeated actions, your Insight skill has improved and is now eligible for rank up!`

`Rank B costs two General Skill Points!`

A bit expensive for a skill I was constantly forgetting to use.

I'd set that on the back burner. General skill points were precious, and I couldn't afford to waste them willy-nilly.

`Congratulations! Through repeated actions, your Hugging Proficiency skill has improved and is now eligible for rank up!`

`Rank D is a free rank!`

"Nice!" I cheered.

"Level up?" Amaryllis asked.

"Nope, not this time."

"Well, neither of your classes are combat based," she said.

I blinked, then narrowed my eyes at her.

`Amaryllis Albatross. Thundere, level 13. Puppeteer, level 3. Smug.`

"Okay, two questions," I said. "How are you a level ahead *and* behind me, and why do I see both of your classes?"

"Because classes level according to what one is doing, and my Puppeteer class, as much potential as it has, is still relatively weak. It's moving slower. As for the second question, either you actually figured out how to use Insight—which I doubt—or you already know part of the information, so the skill is filling that in."

"Oh."

"Ah, I'm falling behind," Awen said. "I'm at twelve and three."

I shook my head. "Hardly. When we met, you were a bunch of levels behind. Now you're just one behind either of us if we tally all our levels together." I bumped shoulders with her. "You're doing awesome."

She smiled, a little timid, but not as timid as she had been even a few weeks before.

"Right, give me a few more minutes. I have more notifications to look at."

One more notification, actually.

Ding! For repeating a special action a sufficient number of times, you have unlocked the general skill: Captaining!

Oh.

Captaining

Rank F - 00%

The ability to lead and take charge through soft sailing and rough patches.

That . . . was actually kind of nice.

Name	Broccoli Bunch
Race	Bun (Riftwalker)
First Class	Cinnamon Bun Bun
First Class Level	12
Second Class	Wonderlander
Second Class Level	4
Age	16
Health	145
Stamina	150
Mana	145
Resilience	55
Flexibility	70
Magic	35
Skills	Rank
Cinnamon Bun Bun Skills	
Cleaning	S - 03%
Way of the Mystic Bun	D - 100%
Gardening	D - 35%
Adorable	D - 100%
Dancing	D - 100%

Wonderlander Skills	
Tea Making	D - 100%
Mad Millinery	D - 87%
General Skills	
Insight	C - 100%
Makeshift Weapons Proficiency	D - 100%
Archaeology	D - 00%
Friendmaking	C - 71%
Matchmaking	D - 57%
Hugging Proficiency	D - 00%
Captaining	F - 00%
Cinnamon Bun Bun Skill Points	1
Wonderlander Skill Points	3
General Skill Points	4
First Class Skill Slots	0
Second Class Skill Slots	1
General Skill Slots	3

Things were looking pretty good. My Hugging Proficiency was obviously a priority. Other than that . . . well, I had a lot of points just sitting there, not doing all that much. With Cleaning finally at Rank S, I figured I could start diversifying. Getting it to SS, though . . . That was really tempting.

It wouldn't happen until level nineteen in Cinnamon Bun Bun, which could be months from now!

At the same time . . . I bet there weren't that many people with Rank SS anything, let alone a skill as handy as Cleaning!

Well, that could wait. I'd ask Amaryllis for help later. She was smart. In the meantime, I didn't have any problems dumping a bunch of points in my

Wonderlander skills . . . If only they were cooler. Tea Making was nice, and Mad Millinery was cool, but they were a bit . . . strange and not super.

As for general skills . . . maybe Makeshift Weapons? Definitely Hugging Proficiency. The ability to buff my friends was invaluable! But then I only had four points there.

"Need help?" Amaryllis asked.

I shook my head, hesitated, then nodded. "Yup, but not right now, I don't think. Once we're back on the *Beaver*, I think I'll bother you for a little bit."

"Sure. We wouldn't want you spending points on some of your more useless skills."

"Hey!" I said. "My skills are cool. Mostly." I could do without Adorable.

I stood up as I saw Howard climbing up the steps with . . . a dress over his shoulder? A purple one, with a very floofy set of petticoats sticking out from under the ruffled skirts.

"What's that?" I asked.

"Drops from the boss," Howard said.

I blinked, then fired Insight onto the dress.

A pretty dress. Good for ablative armor. New.

"Huh?"

Howard shrugged. "We don't rightly know either. You can cut them up for some scraps. The insides are soft—make for good bedding material."

"I guess," I said. I set that aside for the moment. The dress looked way too small for any of us. Not the reward I expected, and not something that seemed too useful.

We gathered up our things, with Amaryllis and I splitting Awen's gear between us even as Awen protested that she could handle it herself. Then, with Howard pushing the last door open, we moved deeper into the dungeon.

The corridor ahead forked. On both sides were shimmering portals, set into stone door frames. One had a hazy image of the mausoleum from which we'd entered the dungeon, seen from the inside looking out. The other was the core room.

It wasn't nearly as bad as I'd feared.

The core sat upon a pedestal made of stone tentacles, the big orb carefully held in place there.

Touching it, just barely, was a root, one tangled up in the twisting stone below and reaching out to every corner of the room.

"Be careful," Howard said. His voice sounded off. Fearful, almost.

"We will," I promised.

I hiked up my backpack, then handed my warspade to Bastion, who took it almost absently.

Stepping into the core room felt the same as it always did: strange and almost icky. Passing through the entrance sent shivers down my spine, and I could feel the magic in me bubbling and racing. I'd been getting better at feeling that. I bet people like Amaryllis who did plenty of magic would feel the core a lot more.

I stared at the orb in the center of the room. The room itself wasn't anything too special. Stone walls, with embossed carvings in the walls that, when the light hit them right, created strange, wriggling shadows.

The only light came from some glowing mushrooms ringing the edge of the floor—where the Evil Roots hadn't broken through them—and from the core itself.

I reached out, carefully touching the core. It felt warm. "We'll fix you up in no time," I said.

Then I knelt down and grabbed the base of the roots climbing up the plinth.

Cleaning magic at Rank S was almost scary when it found something as dirty as a root. It dug in, hissing and spitting, and the root fell apart where I held it.

I let more magic flow, covering the floor and concentrating where the roots were more visible.

They started to burn.

I didn't know if this would cure the core entirely, but maybe all it needed was to be given a chance to cure itself. Like a vaccine, sorta.

I patted the core gently before leaving the room, the last bit of Evil Root pinched between thumb and forefinger. "I think we're done," I said as I wasted Cleaning magic on my aura. "And I think I'll be keeping this bit."

"As a souvenir?" Amaryllis asked.

"No, as something we can study or maybe give to someone who can. Come on, let's get out. I'm looking forward to seeing sunshine again!"

· Chapter Nineteen ·

Celebrating the Good Things

```
Quest completed!
Trim the Cruel!
The core is saved!
```

I sighed. That was a good message to receive. "Thanks, Miss Menu," I said as I dismissed the notification.

"Did you say something?" Amaryllis asked.

"Nope," I replied. "Well, nothing important."

She nodded, then gestured to the portal leading out of the dungeon. "Come on, then. The others will be waiting."

I glanced around one last time, but it felt like everything we had to do was done. Another adventure completed, and on a happy note too. Sure, we were a bit banged up, but we'd get better in a day or three. "I could use something to eat," I said as I followed Amaryllis.

"Ah, so now you're thinking with your stomach? Brilliant."

I laughed and pulled Amaryllis into a side hug. "Come on!"

Exiting the dungeon was strange; the portal warped and bubbled, and it felt like diving into a pool of dry water. And then we were out in the open. Insmouth—the town, not the dungeon—was so much more humid than I remembered.

Awen and Bastion were just outside the mausoleum, both looking like they were waiting while taking in the big walls of fog that seemed to hover around the town and over the ocean. It was night now, with a sprinkling of stars shining bright enough to glow through the thin clouds above, and the moon hovering fat and heavy by the horizon.

"Awa," Awen began, "Howard invited us to the inn. He said we could eat for free tonight."

"That sounds wonderful," I said.

"I wouldn't mind a glass of wine," Amaryllis admitted.

"Aren't you a bit young for that?" I asked as I started out ahead.

Amaryllis just gave me a look. "I'm at least a year older than you, and what does age have to do with when someone can have a cup of wine?"

"I guess there's no age limit on that here, huh?" I asked. "Maybe I should try some?"

"No," Awen and Amaryllis said in the same breath.

"Uh, okay," I replied. Well, if they insisted.

We headed into Insmouth, and despite the late hour, I found the town to be surprisingly lively. Lights were on, candles flickering behind windows, and people were out on the street, many of them in little groups that were walking toward the center of town, laughing and chatting all the while.

We got some nice waves from some folk, and others seemed happy just to smile at us.

"This entire town is creepy," Amaryllis said.

"They seem nice."

The inn was a lot rowdier than I remembered, with tables packed and dozens of people sitting around outside, clinking big mugs together and plates overflowing with tasty-smelling food held up in one hand so that they could eat standing up.

"It's them!" someone cheered.

Before I could find out who it was, what felt like the entire inn cheered. Younger fish people rushed out, laughing and screaming, and we were dragged in.

Howard was sitting on a big rocking chair next to the hearth, a big mug with frothing beer overflowing it in one hand. "Ah, here they are!" he said. "I was just telling everyone about our adventure."

"Poorly!" someone called out.

There was more laughter, and I found myself joining in. If Howard was laughing, too, then it wasn't bullying or anything, I figured. "July! Get the kids something to eat! They deserve it!"

My friends and I were jostled around for a bit, but soon we were all at the bar where the innkeeper, July, was setting plates before us and mugs next to those.

Amaryllis sniffed at her beer, then leaned forward. "Can I have some wine, if you have anything decent?"

"And juice for me!" I said.

I expected Awen to pipe up, but she took a sip of her ale and came back with a foamy mustache. "It's a bit bitter," she said. "But not too bad. I think I see why Uncle likes this so much."

Bastion sat nearby and waved July off when she came offering food.

And then we dug in, though my meal was interrupted a bunch as I answered a whole lot of questions. People were pretty excited about our dungeon run, which was a little strange. Weren't they pretty common?

In the end, I asked July.

"Oh, yeah, of course. Just about everyone who's an adult's gone through the dungeon. And every time, we make a big thing of it. It's a way of celebrating for the whole town. Only folk already at level ten go in, so it's usually the same day their class evolves." She grinned. "It's a big deal."

"Oh!" That was so neat! We'd accidentally stumbled into a town-wide tradition.

"So it's an excuse to have a party?" Amaryllis asked.

"It is!" July said. "A great time to have a few drinks and catch up. Everyone had their day, and for a lot of us it was really special. Plus, today's extra-special. I heard that you fixed the old dungeon up?"

"Yup," I said. "Got a quest prompt for it and everything. It should be nice and safe. But maybe you should find someone in town with Cleaning magic and get it up to Master Rank—it's what I used to clean the Evil Roots away."

"Cleaning, huh?" July asked. "I'll let others know. Don't think it's that rare a skill, so maybe we'll manage! Here, eat more. It's all on the house for tonight!" She grabbed a bowl of potato salad and scooped some onto our plates.

I laughed and tucked in, then took a big gulp of some juice July served.

People wanted us to recount the story of our fight, and I was surprised when Amaryllis was the one to start telling the story. I think she added a lot of details that I wasn't entirely sure were accurate, but with her sweeping wing gestures and confident squawking voice, everyone was hanging on her every word.

Awen had a small smile on as she polished off her second tankard of beer, then let out an unladylike burp and giggled into a closed fist.

I was smiling so much my cheek muscles were getting a workout.

Soon I had to get up and move around. There was dancing to be done, with a bunch of fishmen having gotten little drums out, and someone had a long-necked lute. A bunch of girls, most looking a couple of years older than me, were dancing off to one side with nervous-looking boys.

I joined in for a spin or two. I didn't know the steps, but I learned quickly, and I managed to pull Bastion in to act as my partner. He was stiff as could be, but he was still a great dancer.

When I started to feel a bit sweaty, I came back to July for water and found her serving pies, and I stuffed myself full while Amaryllis talked really loudly about politics with a few older fish folk.

Awen was sipping on another tankard when I left, my tummy sloshing and overfull with pie, to go find the little ladies' room.

That's when I ran into Emmanuel.

The inn's washrooms were in their own little building. Not an outhouse, exactly, but not too far from that. They were in the back, out of anyone's way. When I was done and leaving the ladies' side, hands wiggling in the air while Cleaning magic did its thing, I found Emmanuel standing in the shadows of the inn.

He was sitting on his haunches, head tilted back to eye the stars, an empty mug of something by his feet. I hadn't noticed him earlier, hidden as he was in the shade, away from all the partying and the laughter.

"Hey," I said.

The cervid blinked, then looked down at me. "Oh. Hello."

"Broccoli," I said.

"Pardon?"

"It's my name. Broccoli. I think I told you the first time we met, but you never really called me by my name, so I figured you just forgot it."

"Ah," he said. "I . . . Yes, that's likely, Miss . . . Broccoli. Like the vegetable?"

"It's a flower, but also a vegetable," I said. I was always quite proud of my name; it was a very special one.

He nodded. "Yes, I see," he said. He looked at me for a bit more, then turned his head back again to eye the stars.

"You're not a bad guy, you know," I said.

Emmanuel glanced at me from the corner of his eye, but he didn't respond.

"I'm kinda sad things didn't work out with you and my friends, but still, you . . . you have potential. You have good intentions. I think that with a bit more time, and by being a little more open, you could really become someone who's a great friend."

The cervid took a deep breath, then stood up. "Thank you, Broccoli," he said. "I think I just need a little time to myself." His chest puffed out. "It will take more than a bit of sadness to keep Emmanuel Aldelain von Chadsbourne down."

I giggled, then hugged him. It was a bit weird. He was all furry, and his body wasn't optimally shaped for hugs from someone smaller, but I did my best. "I hope you have the best adventures, Emmanuel, and I hope you make wonderful friends along the way. Everyone deserves to make their own family."

He blinked a few times, and I had the impression his eyes were a bit on the watery side. "Thank you."

I waved at him, then stared up at the stars myself. I wondered if they were lonely, way up there, so far apart from all the others. I pouted. I was making myself lonely just thinking about it. It was time to go and bother my friends!

It wasn't hard to find everyone. Bastion was leaning against a post, arms crossed. He was eyeing the dance floor where . . .

I stared.

Awen was laughing and giggling, feet stomping in time with the beat of a drum. A drum that was sitting by her hip and that she was thumping herself, the other musicians cheering her on by adding some melody to her heartbeat-fast beat.

I found Amaryllis, sitting at the bar, a glass in her talons. "Is Awen . . ."

"Very drunk? Yes."

"Oh, okay," I replied. "Should we do anything about it?"

"Other than enjoy it? No, not yet. We can mock her in the morning when her head is splitting."

"How much did she drink?" I asked. Though the rest of the party hadn't reached its end, it certainly felt like it was at its peak. A few boys jumped onto the dance floor and tried to keep up with Awen's frantic dancing, but she was surprisingly dexterous as she swayed around and kept time with her drum.

"Three tankards of beer," Amaryllis said. "A small glass of some stronger spirits. And she stole a glass of my wine."

"Is that a lot?"

"For a grown person, no, but for someone Awen's size? Well, I think the results speak for themselves."

Awen saw us, then gasped and stopped to give her drum to a wide-eyed boy before running over, hair all a flutter behind her, a big tangle of gold that splashed forward when she crashed into me with a big, sloppy hug. "Broccoli!"

"Awen!" I cheered.

"Awa! I was dancing! Did you see? I think I did okay. I never did like dancing all that much, but the dancing they do here is so much nicer than the dancing back home. And when I asked one of the boys if I could play with his instrument, he went all funny and ran away, so I took his drum. I've never actually played the drum before. It's a lot of fun! I don't know why my mom insisted it's a man's instrument. It's perfectly ladylike."

"Yeah, I'm sure," I said. I eyed Amaryllis and only got a knowing smile in return.

Right. Now to figure out how to get Awen to calm down and maybe drink some water.

· **Chapter Twenty** ·

A Happy Sort of Busy

I had everyone in the *Beaver*'s crew gather in the kitchen the next morning. I'd gotten some eggs and bacon, as well as some of that potato salad from July. That with some fresh bread and a can of beans made for a big, hearty breakfast.

If I weren't so active, I'd be afraid of gaining weight with such a big meal, even if I wasn't touching half of it.

The crew seemed pretty happy, though. Except for Awen.

"A . . . *awa*," she said. It wasn't just any "awa," though; this was a *pained* "awa."

Awen's head was resting against the table, both arms folded over to hide her from the light. Sally was patting her back awkwardly. "Is she okay?" she asked.

"Awen drank too much," I said.

Oda chuckled. "Looks like it."

"Awa," Awen complained. Her arms wiggled, but it didn't go much further than that.

Oda, Sally, and Joe were sitting next to each other, with Steve and Gordon, our harpy crewbirds, next to them. Clive was on the opposite side, next to Bastion, who had finished eating before anyone else.

Amaryllis was next to me, and at the head of the table, sitting *on* the table, was Orange, who had a bowl of mixed leftovers before her. She would be very miffed if I didn't serve her anything, even if she didn't plan on eating any of it.

Orange was one hard-working kitty, and she took her job—sleeping on the *Beaver Cleaver*'s duck-shaped figureheads—very seriously.

"Right, I suppose someone mature ought to take care of this one," Amaryllis said. "We are four days behind our original schedule. We were meant to arrive a week before the official delegation. Now, if we hurry up and don't spend any time on unimportant things on the way, we might still arrive a day or two ahead of the delegation."

"That's still good, right?" I asked.

"It's imperative that we arrive before them," Amaryllis said. "It will give us time to settle in and get a good idea of how things are going in Sylphfree. If the delegation is delayed or fails to arrive, it will mean we're in a better position to take over."

"What's all this about a delegation?" Joe asked.

The Scallywags hadn't really been informed about all that, had they? "There's trouble brewing between a few countries," I said. "Mostly Sylphfree, the Trenten Flats, and the Harpy Mountains. I think Deepmarsh and Mattergrove are involved too. If things go wrong, it might mean a sort of really messy fight."

Amaryllis huffed and unrolled a map. There were three lines across it. "This is the path the delegation is meant to take. From Fort Sylphrot, to Farseeing, around to Fort Daggerscar, then into sylph skies."

"The government will make them go the long way," Bastion said. "North first, then around and south. It's safer but significantly longer. Mostly, it'll be a show of force."

Amaryllis nodded. "Good, that will add . . . maybe two days to their travel time?"

"How fast are they?" I asked.

"Not very," Amaryllis said. "The ship they're leaving in is a retrofitted cargo hauler. A nice vessel now, to be sure, but it's only hull deep. That thing has engines two generations older than what the *Beaver* has."

"What kind?" Awen asked, still sounding bleary.

"Nautilus, I think," Amaryllis said.

"Those overheat," Awen said. "Annoying to maintain."

Amaryllis shrugged. "If you say so. They'll have mechanics with them, and a pair of escort ships. They're supposed to take a week to travel across, stops included."

"That's pretty slow," I said.

Amaryllis grumped. "The *Beaver* is significantly faster. We can hit thirty knots, right?" The last she asked Clive.

"More, when the wind's in our favor," the old harpy said. "He's not the fastest ship, but this boy here's not loaded down with anything at all. We're running light."

"Still," Amaryllis said. She traced the path we were supposed to take. "We left a week early, on a course that would only take us six or so days. The delegation was going to leave the day after we *arrived*, winds willing."

"And now?"

"Today's the day we were supposed to arrive in Goldenalden."

"Oh," I said. "We're really late."

"We still have a week," Amaryllis said. "That's how long the delegation will take to get there. A week to travel from here"—she tapped Insmouth on the map—"to here." The tip of her talon traced over to Goldenalden, then tapped down twice.

"That's pretty far," I said.

Clive leaned forward. "It's not all bad. The winds over Methal Bay are strong; they wrap around south to north. It will be hard over Hoofbreaker Forest, but once we're past that, we'll have the wind at our backs the entire time. Without wind, I'd say it'd take seven, eight days to make it. With good winds, we can cut off a day or two."

Awen raised a hand. "We have oil but no actual fuel. We can burn it, but it's not good for the engines in the long run. And we don't have enough to make it either way. We left with enough fuel to fly for ten days."

"And it's been seven, with another seven coming up," Amaryllis said.

"Our fuel bunkers aren't very big," Awen said.

I tapped my chin. "We can stop by the Grey Wall," I said. "Just a quick stop, for fuel and to resupply, then we continue. Do they sell fuel there?"

"They do," Clive said. "Been there before. Bad prices, but they'll have some."

"So, that's the plan, then. We rush over to the Grey Wall, see if anyone needs help, and if they don—" I cut myself off on seeing Amaryllis's look. "Uh. I mean, we go there, gas up, and move on?"

"Yes," she said. "That's exactly right. No stopping any longer than we need to."

"Not even to sightsee?"

"No, not even to sightsee."

I pouted. "That's no fun."

"We're doing a job, Broccoli. We're not here to muck about."

"We're on an adventure—mucking about is half the goal," I said. "But . . . but I know that you're right. We should get to Sylphfree sooner rather than later. Are there any shortcuts we could take?"

"Shortcuts?" Amaryllis asked. "No, Broccoli, it's nearly a straight flight."

Bastion shifted. "That's not entirely true. Once in Sylphfree, you'll need to navigate around some of the mountains. Your map isn't entirely accurate with them either. I suspect the delegation's going to be dragged around too. It would make for a good show of military might to have them fly over some known bases with more than their usual share of ships."

"That doesn't sound like a shortcut," Amaryllis said.

"I could, in theory, use my position as a paladin to allow us quick passage to the capital. Fewer inspections."

I grinned. "That would be super."

"It wouldn't work with a crew mostly made up of harpies, though," Bastion said.

Amaryllis hummed while running her talon through her wing feathers. "In that case, could we hide some of the crew? Or disguise them? Broccoli, Awen, and the Scallywags should be enough to operate the ship, I suspect. We'll still need to stop and get a permit to fly the *Beaver* to the capital."

"Perhaps," Bastion said. "We . . . You could hire some temporary sylph crewmates as well."

"Neat!" I said. "More friends."

Breakfast didn't last much longer than that. Awen hardly touched hers, I noticed, but she was a bit under the weather. I picked things up, cleaning them as I went, and set the leftovers away while the crew dispersed and got ready to take off.

Awen stayed at the table while I put things away, and everyone else except for Orange left.

"Are you okay?" I asked.

Orange shrugged.

"I meant Awen," I said to the cat.

She gave me a kitty glare, and I giggled as I moved over and scooped her up for a quick hug. She didn't like that much, but even if she had grown, she was still just a young cat, and she couldn't squirm away from my affections yet.

"There, consider yourself snuggled, young lady," I said as I set her down. "Now get back to work. And keep an eye on everyone while you're above, okay?"

Orange gave me a kitty huff before sauntering off.

"Broccoli," Awen said.

"Yup?"

"I think I'm dying."

I held back a laugh. "Oh?" I asked. It wasn't nice to laugh at a friend. I pulled up a chair next to hers, then gave her a side hug. "How's your health?"

"It's fine," she said. "But my head hurts, and I'm . . . ugh."

"Right, let's get you some more water, and then you can go take a small nap, all right? You'll feel better by this afternoon, I'm sure. Maybe some tea instead of water? I have some for aches."

"Please."

I ran my fingers through her hair, straightening it out a bit before I got up and set some water to boiling.

A few minutes later, Awen drank her tea, and I pushed a bit of bread on her just to make sure her tummy wouldn't be empty. Then it was off to bed with her. Her room was . . . a bit of a mess, I noticed. I could clean the dirt and dust with a glance, but there was a lot of picking up to do. Something for when Awen wasn't in such rough shape. She definitely deserved a morning off.

I tucked her in, but I think she barely noticed. "Good night," I said before closing the door to her room carefully. Then it was up and onto the deck with me, but not before picking up my captain's hat.

The Captaining skill I gained from my captain's hat combined with my own skill, but it didn't look like it was boosting it past what it would be for any other hat-given skill. Maybe it would help the skill grow?

The deck of the *Beaver* was . . . not all that chaotic, really. We didn't have a crew big enough for anyone to be bumping into anyone else. The Scallywags and our harpy crew were setting things up, checking the lines, and generally getting into position. Clive was at the wheel, with Amaryllis next to him, a map pinned down on the banister with what looked like a bit of magic trickery.

"Are we all ready?" I asked as I climbed up to the top of the quarterdeck.

"Aye, Captain," Clive said. "On your word."

I took a deep breath and scanned the world beyond the *Beaver*. Insmouth looked peaceful, little ships still setting out to water from the port and plumes of white smoke rising from chimneys. The skies were bright, bright blue, cloudless and inviting. A smidge of wind was coming from the . . . west, I thought. It would be at our side for a bit of the trip, something to keep in mind.

"Okay then," I said before I made myself louder. "Engines on! Anchors up! All foresails to full and mizen sails to quarter!"

The crew snapped to it, and I got an impressed, if a little confused, look from Amaryllis. Was my Captaining skill finally working?

"Clive, nose in the air. We have some catching up to do."

"Aye, aye!" he replied.

The huge propeller spun up. The engine rumbled in protest, then roared while plumes of blackish smoke puttered out from the sides of the ship. I'd have to clean that off before the smoke stained the *Beaver*'s bright yellow paint.

The anchors were weighed, and with a lurch, the *Beaver* left the ground.

Some folk from Insmouth were there watching us, so I made sure to raise my hat and wave our goodbyes.

It was off to the next leg of our adventure for us. We had a bit of urgency, but nothing too critical. I was sure we'd find some time for a few smaller adventures along the way.

"Stop grinning so much, you dolt. And to think I thought you looked mature for a moment."

· Chapter Twenty-One ·

Skills and Levels and Stats, Oh My!

By midafternoon, things had settled into a normal routine. The Scally-wags and our harpy crewmates were moving about, making sure everything was in proper order, but not with any urgency. There were ropes to tie and sails to deploy, but since we weren't doing any fancy flying, it was fine if it took a minute or two.

I took some time to give the *Beaver Cleaver* an inspection tour after lunch. Just a quick walk around the outside, eyes peeled to notice frayed rope or sails that might need mending. So far, though, there wasn't anything of the sort. With Awen and Clive both making sure the *Beaver* was in tip-top shape, the ship was sure to stay afloat for a long time.

"Hello, Orange," I said as I reached the very front of the port hull. That's where Orange chose to park herself today, right atop the head of our duck-shaped figurehead.

The cat was on her side and curled up in a ball, her fur kind of just . . . lumping off the top of the duck head, like a physical manifestation of laziness in blob form.

"Working hard, I see," I said with a giggle.

The cat cracked one eye open, yawned, and snuggled in tighter.

I reached up and petted her, which was rewarded a moment later when she started rumbling. "You're getting a bit big for the figurehead, aren't you?" If she continued growing at her current rate, in a few weeks she'd have a hard time sleeping there. Or maybe she'd slow down, and it wouldn't be a problem. "I'll ask Awen. I'm sure we can rig up some sort of board or something for you to sleep on. Maybe a box?"

She continued purring, which I decided to interpret as acceptance.

My tour of the *Beaver* complete, at least for the moment, I descended down to the cabin level, then took a moment to peek in on Awen.

Awen was usually a very ladylike sleeper, even if she didn't pick up her room that much. Today seemed to be the exception, with her arms and legs sprawled out, and her nightgown tangled up in a way that was very scandalous.

I clicked the door shut. If she was making little "awa-awa" snores, then she was probably just fine.

"Hey."

I turned and found Amaryllis at the back of the ship, one shoulder leaning against the wall.

"Oh, hey," I said. "What's up?"

"Right now? Nothing. Looking in on Awen?"

I nodded. "I was worried she was still feeling sick." I gestured to the door to Awen's cabin. "She looks fine, though."

"She will be," Amaryllis dismissed. "I doubt she'll be drinking so much next time. And her sleep schedule might be messed up after today."

"Maybe she can take the first night shift, then," I said. "I wouldn't mind keeping her company. Truth is I'm not doing much to make myself useful right now."

"Humph," Amaryllis said. "I just finished our accounting. Not too sure what to do myself. I might practice my puppetry."

"We have accounting?"

One of her brows rose. "How do you think we can afford food? Not to mention fuel and other necessities."

"Oh," I said. "You're good with numbers, right?"

Amaryllis's eyes narrowed. "Yes. I had a full education."

"Do you think you could help me with my class stuff? With skill points and all? I've been meaning to ask you for help for a little bit."

"Humph, yeah, sure," she said. "Come on, this might be better with pen and paper."

I grinned and followed Amaryllis to the office space at the back of the quarterdeck. In theory, this was supposed to be the captain's cabin. It had a few windows at the rear overlooking the sky and forests below, and it was quite a bit bigger than any of the normal rooms. But really, it wouldn't be fair for anyone to have a room bigger than anyone else's. Then again . . . the Scallywags and other crewmates slept on hammocks. Were we being unfair?

"You're thinking stupid thoughts again," Amaryllis said as she reached the desk in the middle of the room and plopped herself down behind it. "Worse, I'm almost certain they have nothing to do with the situation at talon."

"Hey!" I protested. "You're not wrong, but it's still kinda rude."

"Sit down, you idiot," Amaryllis said.

I laughed and pulled a chair from the corner over. The chairs had metal caps on their feet, with magnets built into them so that they wouldn't get flung around if there was a bit of turbulence. I clipped the chair onto some studs on the floor and plopped myself down. "Oh, wow, this chair is not comfy," I said.

"I know," Amaryllis said. "That's why I'm in the good chair." She wriggled atop the chair that was supposed to be the captain's office chair. "Now, I need an idea of what your skills are like—just the skills."

"Sure," I said.

She passed over a pen and some paper, and I opened up Mister Menu and transcribed everything as I saw it. It was a bit strange to use a fountain pen. I kinda missed having a ballpoint pen, really.

"Here you go!" I said.

Skills	Rank
Cinnamon Bun Bun	
Cleaning	S - 03%
Way of the Mystic Bun	D - 100%
Gardening	D - 34%
Adorable	D - 100%
Dancing	D - 100%
Wonderlander	
Tea Making	D - 100%
Mad Millinery	D - 87%
General Skills	
Insight	C - 100%
Makeshift Weapons Proficiency	D - 100%
Archeology	D - 00%
Friendmaking	C - 71%
Matchmaking	D - 57%
Hugging Proficiency	D - 75%
Captaining	F - 00%
Cinnamon Bun Bun Skill Points	1

Wonderlander Skill Points	3
General Skill Points	4

Amaryllis looked over the list, then she slid over a piece of paper of her own. "You're going to need to translate some of these for me," she said. "Others I can guess at."

Thundere	Rank
Thunder Aspect Manipulation	Expert
Electrostatic Discharge	Journeyman
Thunder Clap	Disciple
Mage Sight	Disciple
Electro-Couragement	Disciple
Puppeteer	**Rank**
String Manipulation	Disciple
Anatomical Motion	Intermediary
General Skills	**Rank**
Observe	Apprentice
Book Smart	Apprentice
Accounting	Apprentice
Flying	Apprentice
Business Sense	Apprentice
Negotiating	Intermediary
Bluffing	Apprentice
Huffing	Apprentice
Precision Magic	Intermediary

"Oh," I said. "I don't think I've seen your skills and stuff yet." The ranks threw me off almost right away. If I remembered it right, Rank E was Intermediary, D was Apprentice, C was Disciple, B was Journeyman, and A was Expert. She didn't have anything above that.

"I have . . . a skill or two that are entirely useless. I'll need to find a way to get rid of those."

I stared at Huffing. I looked up at Amaryllis. Then I looked back down at Huffing.

"Don't you dare," she said.

Pinching my lips together, I managed not to laugh any. "It's okay?" I said. "I have a useless skill too."

"Yes, quite."

"So, your other skills all look cool. You haven't spent your general skill points?"

"I will," she said. "On my newest skill. Precision Magic doesn't exactly save any mana when I use spells, but it does make the spells themselves more effective, which means fewer spells overall. I find that I'm not fond of being a single-shot woman, and both of my classes require that I spend quite a lot of mana."

"That makes sense," I said. "Your puppetry stuff is really coming along. What's Anatomical Motion do?"

Amaryllis leaned forward a little. "It's a skill that helps move complex objects with string, wire, and mana. It's practically necessary if you want to move a lifelike puppet. Or puppet a living thing."

Scary! "So, you seem to spend your points a lot across a bunch of things."

"And you hyperfocus yours," Amaryllis said. She tapped my list with a talon. "Cleaning at Master is impressive, but it means that a lot of your other skills haven't really been improved past their natural limit."

"Yeah," I said. "I don't know if I want to save up more points to bring it up to the next rank."

"That would be eight points," Amaryllis said. "Eight levels worth of points spent on one skill upgrade."

I nodded. "But Master Cleaning is really strong. Ever since I hit Rank S, I can take out Evil Roots, no problem."

She hummed. "Well, I see two options for your Cinnamon Bun Bun class. Either you start diversifying now, maybe putting points into the other skills you enjoy, or you save up to bring Cleaning to a level that . . . Well, I don't know if anyone has ever gone that far with it."

"Is Master common?" I asked.

"No, not truly. The average level in the world is likely below twenty. Most people in a city will be capped at ten unless they can visit a dungeon. It's rare that people reach their second cap and visit a second dungeon at level twenty. And even if they do, the short-term gain of spending skill points often outweighs the benefit of waiting long enough to reach Master."

So plenty of people had the points to get one skill to Master, but it was better to have two good skills instead of one extreme skill? It kinda made sense.

"What do you think I should do?" I asked.

Amaryllis huffed, no doubt putting that new skill of hers to good use. "I can't tell you what to do. But I can advise you a little. I would save up for Grand Master. Your other Cinnamon Bun Bun skills aren't that incredible. Dancing would help you in a fight, and Way of the Mystic Bun is likely a very powerful skill, seeing how hard it is to obtain, but in the long run, Cleaning magic will likely trump them both."

I nodded. "Okay. And I guess if we're in big trouble . . ."

"Then you can always spend a point or two right away and obtain a fairly sizable boost to two useful skills," she said. "Maybe you could even put some points into Adorable."

"No!" I protested.

"It's a powerful skill. People will underestimate you, and find you more attractive."

I shook my head, ears flip-flopping wildly. "I'm not adorable!"

"Of course not," she agreed. "Setting aside your main class, you have plenty of opportunities with general skills and your Wonderlander class. Tea Making is more versatile than I would have thought, though I suppose it's not too different from the skills some good chefs have. Mad Millinery . . . how is that working out for you?"

I tapped my captain's hat. "It's buffing one skill right now. It can give me a skill at the same rank as Mad Millinery, so it's not super strong yet, but I think it'll get better?"

"It's a skill that allows you to have any other skill, but only when you're wearing appropriate headgear." Amaryllis rubbed at her chin. "It's definitely one of the strangest skills I've ever heard of. Very flexible, though. A new skill at the drop of a hat, so to speak."

I snorted at the pun. "I guess so. I have a hunch that it'll be really good once I hit Rank C with it."

"You don't have anything too powerful from that class. I don't see why you shouldn't invest every point you do get as soon as you get them, though you might want to save some in case you obtain a game-changing skill."

"Yeah," I said. "I don't know what kind of skill I can expect from the class, though."

Amaryllis shrugged. "Level up and find out."

"Such helpful advice."

She shot me a look. "General skills—you barely use Insight as far as I can tell."

"I keep forgetting!"

"Then practice not forgetting," she said. "Otherwise it's a waste of good points. Friendmaking has been useful, I think."

"Very."

"Will you bring it up a rank?"

I considered it. "It would take two points. I only have four left. I guess I could?"

"It's up to you. I'd put a point in Makeshift Weapons Proficiency, though. It's one of your only combat abilities."

"And then a point in either Hugging Proficiency, Captaining, or Match-making?" I asked.

"Or don't put any points in Friendmaking and one in each of them."

I chewed on my lip. "I really want Hugging Proficiency. And Captaining . . . and Matchmaking too. I think I'd rather have those than Friendmaking at a higher rank. After all, I already have the best friends ever—I don't need to get that many more, do I? Wait, yes I do."

Amaryllis rolled her eyes. "Moron. But it seems like a decent idea. A good spread of decently useful skills, as opposed to a single good but niche ability. The opposite of what you're doing with Cleaning."

"Right then!" I said. Time to spend some points!

· Chapter Twenty-Two ·

A Huffy Afternoon

I wasn't angry, just very . . . disappointed.

"Don't pout at me," Amaryllis said.

I humphed and turned my head away from the harpy. We were both on the foredeck, wind whipping by and making our clothes flip and flop along with our hair and feathers. It was a bit chilly, probably owing to the extra height.

"Don't *humph* me either."

"Fine, then," I shot back, "but that doesn't mean I won't express my disappointment in you."

"Disap— Broccoli, we're on a tight schedule."

"We could have made some time," I said. "Or at least we could have done a slow flyby to wave to all the little buns."

Amaryllis rolled her eyes, then set her talons on her hips. "If we did that, you'd just insist that we stop by for a quick bit of tea, then you'd insist on seeing Carrot and her children, and then you wouldn't be able to say no to the little ones when they asked for another tour of the *Beaver*. I know you, Broccoli Bunch. You have the self-control of a lemming."

I puffed my cheeks out. "I do not."

"Oh yes, you do. Look me in the eyes and tell me that you wouldn't insist on holding the first baby bun you saw."

I turned, refusing to look her way. "I wouldn't," I lied.

She huffed. I didn't even bother translating that one. "Maybe one day we'll be back around this area, and we can stop in to see Momma and the others. I've no doubt that old bun will outlive us all."

"How would she do that?"

Amaryllis blinked, then sighed. She'd obviously been taken off guard by my ignorance again. "Resilience makes you more resistant to things. The general belief is that it acts as a flat percentage to your body's own capabilities."

"Uh," I said. "So I'm fifty-five percent tougher?"

"More like it takes fifty-five percent more energy to, for example, cut you than it would without any Resilience. Even at a hundred or more, you're not uncuttable. Resilience also makes you resist the impact of aging that much better. Again, even at over a hundred, you'll still age, just more gracefully."

That was super neat! But I was still miffed at Amaryllis. "Even if I had the most Resilience ever, it still wouldn't protect me from the emotional damage of missing out on baby buns."

Amaryllis groaned. "You're such an idiot."

I couldn't help but giggle. I really was disappointed that we'd flown right past Hopsalot while I was too busy to notice, but there wasn't much I could do about it. Amaryllis was right about us being on a tight deadline. I couldn't afford to turn us around now.

I promised myself that I'd return to Hopsalot one day, and that I'd find all the cute buns, and I'd pinch every cheek and hug them all until they squeaked.

Amaryllis gave me a reluctant hug in apology, then she headed off to do . . . something. There was surprisingly little to do once the ship was on its way. The skies were clear, and Clive said they'd be staying that way for a while. We had two people taking care of the ship, switching out every six hours, and that was enough. My next turn at the helm wouldn't be until tonight.

I stepped up to the very front of the ship and climbed over the rails to sit next to the figurehead. Looking down, all I could see were my feet dangling over a couple of kilometers of empty air with thick woods way below.

Good thing I wasn't afraid of heights.

I leaned against the figurehead, then looked up as Orange raised her head and stared. "Just having a sit," I said. "I have some free time, so I figured I'd just relax a bit."

I did have one thing I could do. My talk with Amaryllis about skills that morning had been pretty productive. I had points to spend and skills to improve.

Matchmaking, Captaining, Hugging Proficiency, and Makeshift Weapons Proficiency. Four skills for four points. The only problem was that of those four, the only one I could spend points on right then and there was Makeshift Weapons Proficiency.

The other three were all over the place, level-wise. It would take a bit to get them to the top of Rank D.

```
Makeshift Weapons Proficiency
Rank D - 100%
The ability to use nonweapons as weapons. Your ability to
find and use makeshift weapons has improved.
```

One of my staple combat skills, at least when Cleaning magic didn't do the trick. Way of the Mystic Bun allowed me to move and strike, but it was Makeshift Weapons Proficiency that really helped smack things down. I thought having a more specific weapon skill would probably be stronger, but this skill made up for it with versatility.

I couldn't be weaponless if everything was a weapon.

```
Do you wish to increase Makeshift Weapons Proficiency to
Rank C for one General Skill Point?
```

"Yes please," I said to Mister Menu.

Congratulations! Makeshift Weapons Proficiency is now Rank C!

```
Makeshift Weapons Proficiency
Rank C - 00%
The ability to use nonweapons as weapons. Your ability
to find and use makeshift weapons has improved. You may
push mana into a nonweapon to increase its durability and
strength.
```

"Oh," I said as I read the prompt. That sounded really neat! "What do you think, Orange? What kind of effect does pushing magic into a thing have? It says it makes it tougher and stronger, but that's not super precise. Maybe . . . Cleaning magic wrapped around the weapon?"

I could already do that, I was pretty sure. My magic control wasn't that good, but with Cleaning magic it was easy.

Could I do it with Fire mana?

"I think I need to experiment," I said.

Orange looked at me, then licked her paws.

"Yeah, you're right, not now. Especially with fire. Not on the ship."

I leaned back against the figurehead, then grinned as Orange got up, stretched so that her back was like a banana and her butt was way up in the air, then she hopped down and plopped herself onto my lap.

I scritched her ears while looking out ahead. A big fogbank hugged the bottom of a big mountain range. From looking at a few maps, I knew that those were the Crying Mountains, though some people had called them the Screaming Mountains too.

My ears twitched forward. I could hear a sound on the wind, a distant call that I couldn't quite make out. It sounded like wind chimes. Was that the mountain range?

As we moved ahead, and I settled into my spot with Orange warming my lap, I watched the fog slip off the mountain. I couldn't help but gasp.

There were huge crystal pillars all across the mountainside. I couldn't tell how big they were, exactly, but they had to be massive if they were visible from all the way where we were. Some of them started halfway down the mountain and yet were tall enough that I was certain they passed the peaks.

I leaned forward, eyes wide to take it all in.

More crystals appeared, some no bigger than a house, others like huge pillars, and the closer we came, the louder the song grew. And it was a song. It had calls and repeats, a chorus that returned every so often, and deep, bassy bell tolls.

The clouds parted around the tallest peak, and I stared at a pillar of teal crystal that reached for the heavens. I had to turn my eyes away when the sun caught on the crystal and sent bright flashes across the sky.

Orange got up, spun around once, then slumped back down. Obviously, she didn't appreciate my twitching. "Sorry," I said as I rubbed her ears.

"We're getting close."

I jumped about a foot in the air, arms windmilling to stay on the rail. Orange jumped off me, then floated in midair, relative to the *Beaver*, and glared back.

"Forgive me," Bastion said. "I didn't mean to spook you."

"You're so quiet!"

"I flew a little," he admitted.

I settled back down on the rails and let out a breath. "It's fine," I said. "No harm and all that."

Orange gave me a look. Her petting time had been harmed, which was very important to her.

"What's up?" I asked Bastion.

"Just came up to see the sights," he said. "I've heard of the Crying Mountains. They're about as far from Sylphfree as the Nesting Kingdom is, but there's just not as much interest this way. Still, I learned about them without ever expecting to see them."

I nodded and looked back at the mountains. "Are they natural? The big crystals, I mean?"

"No, those are cry. We might meet some of them at the Grey Wall."

People who built using giant crystals. That was cool. "And that noise, the song?"

Bastion tilted his head. "I can barely make it out over the wind. You must have better hearing than I. That's just the sound the crystals make. It sounds like a high-pitched scream. I've heard that it's impossible to visit the Crying Mountains proper without being driven out by the noise."

"It makes you crazy?"

"I think it's just much louder by the source."

Oh, that made sense. It would be kind of hard to sleep while what sounded like thousands of wind chimes were clanging away.

"I'm glad I caught you alone," Bastion said.

"I have Orange with me," I said.

"Mostly alone, then. I . . . this is difficult."

I turned, one leg slipping over the rail so that I was straddling it. "What is it?" I asked. He seemed a little conflicted, which was strange for Bastion.

"I've determined, after much observation and research, that you aren't a bad person."

"Um, thanks?"

"Nor are your friends. Awen is a little sheltered, but she's a kind young woman. Amaryllis has a bit of attitude, but she tends to want to do the right thing. They're both, in their own way, noble. And I do mean that in the sense that they're good people."

"Thanks," I said, a little less confused. "You're pretty good yourself."

Bastion shifted, his posture drooping. I'd never noticed just how straight he made himself. He was about three feet shorter than me—if I counted our heights from the tip of my ears—but when he slouched, he became much smaller.

"Broccoli, I know you're a good person, but some of the things you've done . . . You've all but admitted that you have broken cores before."

"And that's bad," I said.

"It's . . . it's not good. You have extenuating circumstances. A quest from the World itself. There can't be a better reason to do what you have, but I still suspect that there are some people in Sylphfree who would react negatively to the news, regardless."

"Even if we tell them about the quest?"

"Even then. Worse, some might think that by removing you, the World might give that same quest to others in order to accomplish its goals."

I settled back. "Oh."

"As much as it might hurt my career, I won't be telling anyone. I would like to think that I'm an honorable sylph first and foremost, but I think we need to be ready to deal with some difficult questions."

"Like make up a story? I could lie to people, tell them that it's all some big conspiracy."

"Maybe we can all pretend that you're mute so that you let others do the convincing?" he tried.

I huffed. "I'm not that bad."

"I should have approached Amaryllis first," he muttered.

What was with people today?

· **Chapter Twenty-Three** ·

The Great Grey Wall

We flew through the early morning on a straight path toward the wall. It felt like it was taking forever to reach it; even as midmorning passed, the wall was still just a huge thing in the distance.

It wasn't until we were so close that the shadow of the wall was below us that I really started to take in the scale of it. At first it was just a vague line over the horizon; gray, of course, but the dark gray of something hidden in shadows.

We were a kilometer off the ground, and it was blocking our view of the horizon.

Its sides looked like smooth stone, with the top built as tiered segments, each covered in battlements that looked like they were wide enough to fit a house between them.

"Impressive, isn't it?" Clive asked.

I nodded and leaned against the rails of the quarterdeck to better make out the little details of the wall. Not that there were many. It looked like whoever built it made sure that it was as flat and plain as it could be on the outside. "It's so big!"

"Took near on a century to build," Clive said. "And by the time it was done, airships were becoming common enough that it was hardly worth much at all."

That was true. As a defensive thing, it was pretty useless if people could just fly around or above it. For that matter, there was ocean to the north and south of the walls—two different oceans. I could imagine someone just sailing around the wall.

"It's really impressive, though," I said.

"Aye, there is that. I suppose most folk would think twice about wanting to pick a fight with someone who can build something like that. I certainly wouldn't want to be aboard a ship that made itself an enemy of the cry."

"Why not?" I asked. Not that I planned on being anyone's enemy, of course.

"They can bend light and use strange and powerful magics that can make the very air burn, no matter how far from them it is," Clive said. "Not something you want to face when you're aboard an airship."

I nodded. That *was* scary.

The *Beaver* continued along, bobbing and bouncing as we met a bit of turbulence near the top of the wall. Clive spun the wheel, and soon we were skimming along the edge of the wall, using it as cover from all the wind.

When we were within a hundred or so meters, I moved to the side and shielded my eyes from the sun to better take it in. It wasn't quite as smooth from up close. There were little holes and . . . windows?

I stared at a balcony as we flew past it. Just a little thing, with some flowers in planters and a stone door behind it. People lived in the wall? That was so cool!

"Captain, I think we'll be needing all hands on deck soon," Clive said.

"Got it!" I hopped down to the main deck, then stuck my head into the door leading to the cabins. "Everyone! All hands on deck!" I shouted.

There were some grumbles, but soon enough my friends came up, and we prepared the ship for some more complex maneuvers. "We'll need to deploy all sails, then retract them in a hurry. Gordon, get your flags ready."

A section of the wall ahead of us was jutting out. Long metal beams held up an entire village of wooden homes with tin roofs. Above and below the village were docks for airships, though only about one in five had any ships in them.

A tower stuck out of the side of the wall, and from it came a flash of light, then a bunch more. It was like morse, but a lot quieter and also brighter.

"Gordon, do you know what they're signaling?" Clive asked.

I squinted at the light. "They're saying . . . They want to know if we're looking for permission to dock."

Clive looked at me. "You know light code?"

"I guess so?"

He nodded, seemingly impressed. "Can you flash them back?"

"Don't encourage her!" Amaryllis shouted from middeck.

I stuck my tongue out at her and moved to the *Beaver*'s side. I didn't have a mirror or anything fancy like that, but I did have Fire magic! Cleaning magic didn't glow nearly as bright, so I pinched the tip of my tongue between my teeth and created a burst of Fire mana that I quickly shut off.

It was really wasteful, mana-wise, and it wasn't as fast as the flashes from the tower. I imagined the people reading my message felt as if I was talking really slowly. "Hello! We are the *Beaver Cleaver*. We want to stop for fuel," I muttered as I sent a reply one letter at a time.

A return message came back a moment later.

"What are they saying?" Clive asked.

"Start," I translated. "Move to dock twelve. Upper level. Wait for inspection. Stop."

Clive nodded. "Aye, upper deck, twelfth dock it is. That's a handy skill to have, Captain."

"Thanks!" I replied. "I kinda cheated, though." It's not like I had studied to learn it; it was all my weird Riftwalker magic doing the heavy lifting for me. It was hardly fair to someone who studied and learned things the hard way.

The *Beaver* nosed up as we gained altitude. It rose past the top of the wall, where we had to fight with the wind a little to keep steady. It was a nice day, though, with some puffy clouds above, but not too much wind. A decent, if chilly, day for flying.

The little town growing out of the wall grew clearer as we approached, and I could make out some numbers next to the docks built above the town. The little forms of workers around dock number twelve suggested that they'd already been informed of our arrival.

I felt a bit useless as Clive took over and called out some quick orders while handling the engine and the helm all on his own. He was a really impressive pilot, and we were slowing down to a gentle coast on our approach to the docks.

Seeing that we were in safe hands, I leaned over and took in the top of the wall. Large wooden poles were sticking out of it every hundred meters or so. Trebuchets? I didn't know if those would be dangerous to an airship, but I imagined they'd be bad news to any army walking up to the wall.

Workers jumped off the dock, and I felt my heart skip a beat until they flew toward us. A mix of harpies and sylphs, all of them with long ropes trailing behind them.

They landed on deck, and one of them, a short sylph woman in overalls, ran up to the quarterdeck. "Who's the captain?" she asked.

"Hi! I am," I said.

"Good! Permission to come aboard?"

It was a bit silly, since they were aboard already, but I appreciated the politeness all the same. "Sure!"

"We'll be mooring you to the dock's cleats," she said before waving to her companions. They undid the ropes around their waists even as Clive set the *Beaver*'s engine to full reverse, slowing us down to a bobbing stop.

Soon enough, we were linked up to the docks and being pulled in by a set of huge winches. Big pads were brought up, and the *Beaver* slid into its moorings with barely a scrape.

"Tie her up!" the sylph said.

"Actually, the *Beaver*'s a he," I said.

She blinked, then shrugged. "Okay. Well, in either case, welcome to Wallwatch."

"Thank you!"

The sylph saluted, a quick and lazy thing. "Don't forget to watch your step!" she said before flying off. Soon, the others onboard leapt off, more ropes trailing after them as they secured the *Beaver*.

I jumped down to the main deck and found that our usual away crew was already gathering together: Amaryllis and Awen and Bastion. The Scallywags were looking a bit nervous, too, and I saw them gathering on the *Beaver*'s other deck to talk in quick whispers that I couldn't catch, not even with my big ears.

Were they thinking of leaving? We never really had a solid agreement with them. They were aboard for however long they wanted. Amaryllis was sure to pay them fairly, and I figured the experience would help a bunch, too, if they were looking for more work later, but they could take off and find their own adventure whenever they wanted.

"We're not here to sightsee," Amaryllis said, snapping me out of my temporary distraction. "We need fuel, some foodstuffs to replace our perishables, and that's it."

"If that's the case, then why are all of us getting ready to go?" I asked. Amaryllis was dressed for adventure, and even Awen had her big heavy coat on.

Amaryllis huffed. It was an interesting new huff. I think it meant "Because I know that what I'm saying and what I'll do aren't the same, but I need to put on a facade anyway." It was definitely one of the more interesting huffs I'd heard from her. "Because with our luck we'll run into trouble."

"Then we just need to make trouble our friend," I said.

"Idiot," she said. "Come on, I'm sure you'll insist that we walk around and take in the sights."

Awen stepped up next to me as we left the *Beaver* after telling Clive that we'd be back eventually. "Do you think Amaryllis is projecting?" she asked.

"Projecting?" I repeated.

"I can hear you."

Awen nodded. "She's blaming you for something that you might do, but it's like . . . she's basically letting you do that thing already. I think she just wants an excuse."

"What do you take me for?"

I pinched my chin. "You know, you might be right. That sounds real clever and cunning, and Amaryllis can be that way sometimes."

Awen paused by the edge of the ship, screwed up her nose, then jumped over the gap between the *Beaver* and the pier. She landed with a little stumble, but I helped her stay even. "I think my mom used to do that kind of thing. She used to be very good at projecting."

Amaryllis huffed most mightily and scowled at us. "Don't compare me to your mother. And I'm not projecting!"

"So you don't secretly want to go on an adventure?" I asked.

"No!"

I grinned. "No, you don't, or no, you're not being secretive about it?" I asked sweetly.

Awen giggled by my side, and I noticed Bastion paying very close attention to the sky.

Someone coughed, and we all froze, then stared at a man in a suit that didn't quite fit. He had a little pin on his lapel that read PORT AUTHORITY. "Hello. I hate to interrupt, but I have the bill for the docking procedure and the pier for the remainder of the day."

Amaryllis stepped up and took the papers the man extended, then she made a big production about how everything was far too expensive, before they started bargaining in earnest. I don't think Amaryllis actually knew how much a berth cost—she was just going to argue for a better price because that was how she worked.

I let her haggle while moving to the edge of the pier. An entire town was here, maybe even a city, if there were more homes within the walls. So many people from so many races, and soon we'd get to explore, even if it was just a little bit.

I was looking forward to it!

· Chapter Twenty-Four ·

Armor Up

You're going to fall off if you keep hanging over the edge," Amaryllis cautioned.

I looked at the rail I was leaning on and how rickety it seemed, and decided that maybe Amaryllis was right. I'd been enjoying looking down, my head poking over the edge so that I could take in as much of Wallwatch as I could.

The ground was so far below!

We'd been higher aboard the *Beaver*, of course, but that was different somehow. The *Beaver* had been flying. Right now, we were just at the top of a very large building. It was a whole lot more intimidating.

"The view's nice," I said.

"I'm sure," Amaryllis said. "I'm all done. We should be fine as long as we leave before sunset."

We were waiting next to a small tower at the end of the docks. It was a strange little building, made of tin and designed to look like a lighthouse. A really misplaced lighthouse.

I clapped my hands. "All right! Where do we adventure to next?"

"Ah, I think we should get fuel," Awen said. "It's the most important thing right now. And after that, if we have time, I would like to visit an armorer."

"An armorer?"

Awen looked down a little, fingers twinning together. "Yes? I think I could use some armor, maybe?"

"Armor would be a good investment," Amaryllis said. "We don't need you getting hurt, and with your skills as a mechanic, I'm certain you'd be able to maintain it well enough. You could afford to get something more complex than unmoving plate."

"Let's go shopping!" I declared.

"After we get fuel," Amaryllis said.

I rolled my eyes and then grinned as her feathers poofed in indignation. "I'm not dumb," I said. "I know we need fuel first."

"I question that every moment I spend with you," she said. "And don't roll your eyes at me! It's ill-mannered."

Laughing, I bounced ahead of my friends, half turning once I was a few paces in front. "Come on, I don't know where to buy fuel!"

There wasn't exactly a fuel store or, for that matter, a gas station. Amaryllis asked around, and we were directed to a building one level down. That meant taking a circular staircase down from the docks and to a level of the city filled with lots of workshops and more industrial businesses. The shops here weren't what I was used to, just local crafters selling things from their workplaces.

The fuel depot wasn't too far off, a little office next to a hole where big tanks were suspended. Hoses stuck out of them, one leading into a cart with a much smaller tank on the back.

I followed Amaryllis in and found it to be a cramped little place, just a front desk with a mana-powered fan squeaking away. It smelled like peppers and oil, and the man behind the counter wore a stained jerkin.

Amaryllis led the negotiations because she could be mean in a way that I just couldn't manage. I'd probably accept the first offer made and be happy with that.

It took a few minutes, but in the end Amaryllis and the man shook, albeit reluctantly, and we were told that as soon as the last delivery of fuel was done, we'd be next.

"So," I said as we stepped back out. It was strange to be outside during midday and yet not be out in the sun. The layer above wasn't fully covered, so it left big spots of sunlight along the walkways and streets, but even bigger shadowy spots lingered too. "We have a couple of hours, then?"

"We do," Amaryllis said.

Bastion shifted his shoulders, obviously waiting for us to pick out something to do, since he didn't seem to mind any. "In that case, we should find Awen some armor! And you, too, Amaryllis."

"Me?"

"Yup. You got hurt last time too."

"That was a slight miscalculation."

"The next slight miscalculation could end up with you hurt again," I said. "I don't want to see my friends hurt at all."

She squirmed a bit. "Armor is heavy."

"You're a big, strong bird girl," I said. "And with armor, you'll be a big, strong, *tough* bird girl."

"Idiot."

We had to ask for directions to an armorer. As it turned out, there was only one in all of Wallwatch. The city wasn't all that big, more of a multistory town than anything. It had all sorts of people from all sorts of species but only a modest population. It made sense. Wallwatch was about as out of the way as a place could be. I imagine that it was a cool place for people that wanted to be left alone.

The armorer's shop was on the lowest level, where instead of roads there were bridges all over, connecting homes and little plazas together. It was a decently large shop, with a big long chimney sticking out at an angle to spew smoke from the side of Wallwatch.

"Hello!" I said as I opened the front door.

I was greeted by the ringing clangs and bangs of metal on metal. My bun ears flipped back, protecting them from the noise a little.

Awen stepped up and toured the place. There was armor on racks, and more piled up on shelves along the walls. Not that much, though. The entire storefront was small and confined, and with all four of us it was even tighter. We couldn't even keep each other at more than arm's length without bumping into the walls.

The hammering paused, and someone poked their head in. A grenoil! I hadn't seen any grenoils in a long while. "Ah! I 'ave clients!" he cheered. He had that distinct Deepmarsh accent, though it wasn't as strong as some of the other grenoil I'd met. Probably, he'd spent a lot of time away from home. "Welcome to Wilbur's, ze best place for armor and trinkets in Wallwatch!"

"H-hello," Awen said with a quick curtsy that used her jacket's hem in place of a skirt. "We're looking for, ah, a few things."

"Oh, of course, of course," he said as he moved to be behind his counter. It was pretty low, likely on account of grenoils not being all that tall to begin with. "I see some interesting work here. The sylph has some nice equipment there. Is that a Lukas piece?"

Bastion looked down at his armor and back up. "You're familiar with the royal armorer?"

"Just his work and just wiz my eyes. The bun miss here has . . . Zat's from Deepmarsh?" he asked, standing a bit taller.

"It is!" I said. "Port Royal, a place called, uh . . ." I turned to Amaryllis and she answered with a shrug.

"I know where the shop is, not what it's called," she said.

"It's good quality," Wilbur said. "Does it need any adjusting?"

I shook my head, then gestured to Awen and Amaryllis. "My friends keep getting stabbed, so we need armor."

Amaryllis glared. "I'm not even going to waste energy on being indignant. You're too stupid to be worth the effort."

Wilbur nodded while wisely pretending he didn't hear that. "Who do we start wiz? I can make somezing custom if you give me a day or two."

"Ah, we don't have that much time," Awen said. "I . . . I'm the one that wants something, mostly."

Wilbur walked around Awen. "I have a few things that'll fit with just some quick changes. Not zat big, are you? Is zat what you usually wear when out getting stabbed?" He gestured to how Awen was dressed.

She had a nice blouse on, with pants tucked into her boots and, of course, her big blue coat over it all. "This is what I usually wear, yes."

"Hmm. Not much. I don't know if stuffing you in full plate would be a good idea. A . . . mechanic? Well, at least you'll be able to maintain it. How about scale?"

"Scale?"

"Over a zin gambeson to prevent chafing," Wilbur said. He moved back and pulled something from a shelf and held it up. It was a piece of armor, like a long shift, but made entirely of long metal scales.

"That looks a bit . . . much?" Awen tried.

Wilbur tossed it back. "Of course! In zat case, maybe somezing zat fits a little more snug? I've got chain mail zat ought to fit you. Long sleeved, too, wiz a proper gambeson under it so you should be covered fairly well."

The armorer moved to the other side of the room and pulled out a suit of mail with a whole lot of clinking. Awen moved over and poked at it, then nodded. "I think that would be nice."

"Wonderful! I'll need your measurements to fit zis properly." He tossed the mail onto his counter, then went to the back and shuffled through a rack with what looked like thickly padded clothes. "Here! Zis is new. It should adjust to you," he said as he returned with what looked like a long-sleeved shirt that was padded here and there. Nothing as poofy as my first gambeson, but I imagined that the chain would make up for it.

"Ah, thank you," Awen said.

"Well, put it on."

Awen's face changed color a few times. "Do you have a washroom?"

Wilbur nodded, then directed her to somewhere where she could change. While she was gone, he turned his attention to Amaryllis. "You needed armor too?"

"My friends are insisting."

Wilbur tapped his chin while looking her up and down. "The coat's leather?"

"It is."

"Any room inside it?"

She pinched the front of her jacket. "Some? I'm hardly overweight."

"Well, zen, I have some steel inserts sitting around. Made zem for somezing else, but I'm sure I could fit zem into zat coat of yours. It would armor you up a little. Not too heavy eizer. I'd still suggest a hauberk. Maybe a zin one to wear under ze coat as well?"

It didn't take much work at all to find some armor for Amaryllis. She didn't want her arms covered at all, because that would limit the use of her wings, so Wilbur found a mail shirt similar to the one he'd found for Awen, which had a decorative edge to it. By the time Amaryllis surrendered her jacket for the grenoil to modify, Awen returned with her coat folded over an arm and her new gambeson on.

It was a deep blue, not too far from her coat, with a tall neck and just a bit of embroidery on it to pretty it up.

"Nice!" I said.

"It fits well," Awen said.

"Good," Amaryllis replied. "Speaking of . . . Do you do enchantments?"

"Afraid not," Wilbur said. "I can prepare zings for it, but you'll need to find someone who knows zat sort of magic better zan I do."

Wilbur told us that the modifications would take a couple of hours, so that left us standing around with nothing much to do. "Should we get lunch?" I asked.

That got everyone moving again. We told Wilbur we'd be back soon enough, and as a group, we left and made our way up a floor, eyes peeled for somewhere to eat.

I was expecting an inn or a tavern, but instead we found a sort of mom-and-pop restaurant run by a couple of harpies. They specialized in breakfast food, though without any eggs on their menu.

But they did have fresh cinnamon buns!

We ate, drank—mostly fruit juice, as Awen took one look at the alcohol stuff and went pale—and had a good time. It wasn't some grand adventure, but it was fun with the people I loved the most, and sometimes that was more than enough.

· Chapter Twenty-Five ·

A Cry

Spin, spin!" I said.

Awen giggled and twirled, her coat flaring until she stopped, and it whipped around, wrapping about her figure. "It's comfortable," she said. "A bit heavy, but not too bad."

Wilbur nodded, looking like the frog that'd caught the fly.

Amaryllis bounced up and down a few times, getting used to the new weight of her jacket. "This isn't bad work," she said. "A few enchantments for weight and durability, and this will be decent armor."

Neither of my friends were as armored as I'd like. They didn't have helmets, for one, and their limbs were mostly unarmored, but I couldn't force everyone into full plate just because I was a little worried, certainly not when my own armor didn't cover everything. I wouldn't be a hypocrite.

Besides, full plate made hugging awkward. It made the hugs less warm and less cuddly and a whole lot louder.

"It'll be a pain to change back into this all the time," Amaryllis said.

"Well, we usually know more or less when we're going on an adventure," I said. "I wear my armor all the time because . . . uh, I think it's cool and comfy, but you could just wear yours when you think there's going to be trouble."

Amaryllis nodded. It wasn't that big a compromise to make.

Wilbur thanked us for our patronage and seemed more than happy when Amaryllis gave him a few gold coins for his work.

"The armor is a good idea," Bastion said as we stepped out of the armorer's shop. It was chilly outside. "In nearly every conceivable scenario, it's best not to be hit at all, but that can require some skill and luck that isn't always available. In those cases where you will be hit, having even a little armor is better than not."

I nodded along. That made sense. "Are we going back to the *Beaver* right away?"

"Might as well," Amaryllis said. "We don't have much to do here, and the refueling shouldn't take all that long. They should be on their way now, and I suppose at least one of us ought to be there."

"I think Clive and the Scallywags can take care of it," I said.

"Ah, I'd like to be there," Awen said. "Some of the fuel bunkers are tricky to open, and I don't want them spilling things on the workshop floor. The fuel stinks."

"Really?" I asked. I didn't spend too much time next to the *Beaver's* engine or in the little workshop Awen used. "If there is a spill, let me know. I can probably clean it up for you."

Awen nodded easily at that. "It would still be a waste."

That was a fair point. We were paying for all the fuel, so we should be using it all.

We took a different route back to the top of the city; not to sightsee so much as because I kinda forgot which catwalk we'd used the last time. It did mean that we got to see more of the interior of Wallwatch.

The edges of the hanging town all overlooked the forest and fields below, with a lot of shade cast by the wall itself making it cooler. The inner sections of the city were a lot darker, with magic lamps casting flickering light across streets made of corrugated iron and boxy little homes tucked in tight against each other.

It was still lively, though. Kids ran across the street, chasing after balls with strings tied to them in a sort of weird game. There were humans and harpy children, and a few sylphs too. We even crossed an adorable cervid foal stumbling after the others on four gangly legs.

We found a stairwell leading all the way to the top of the city, a point above even the docks where a few airships were sitting next to their piers. The *Beaver Cleaver* wasn't difficult to make out. It was, in my humble opinion, the friendliest and most colorful ship in the whole lot.

We didn't do drab grays and browns like all the other ships.

"Our ship looks like it's piloted by a jester," Amaryllis mumbled.

I laughed as I skipped ahead.

We arrived at the *Beaver* just before the people for the refueling did. They were mostly young men whose job seemed to be dragging around a big, heavy-looking tank set on a cart with a hand pump and a long length of hose.

Awen jumped to help them, pointing to the places on the deck that needed to be opened up and directing the workers when it came time to finally pour the fuel into the *Beaver's* reservoirs. It was, apparently, a fairly dangerous task. They had a mage on their team whose entire job was to make sure there were no sparks or fires around the gas, kind of like a reverse Amaryllis.

It was neat at first, but I soon lost interest as they took turns pumping one squirt of fuel after another into the tank.

That's probably why I was the first to see the crystalline figure hovering by the pier leading to the *Beaver*.

One of the cry? They were a big, bright-blue crystal, a little shorter than I was, but taller on account of how they floated a few centimeters off the ground. No face that I could see. Or organs for that matter. Their body was like a many-faceted sapphire on one side and smooth on the others. I could see right through them. Little zipping flashes of light snapped through their body, like lightning in a bottle. Magic? There had to be something giving them life.

"Hello!" I said. I was pretty sure I was talking in the local language, too, so they had to understand that. Neat!

The hovering crystal slowed to a stop, and I felt a sort of shiver run across me. Had I just been scanned?

They rang, like a windchime being tapped ever so lightly. "Greetings," they said.

"I love your voice," I said. "It's very pretty."

The being paused, then bobbed up and down. "Thank you, long-eared one."

I giggled. That was a new nickname. "No problem! I'm Broccoli. Broccoli Bunch!"

"Our name is difficult for the soft to speak," they said with three quick rings.

I climbed over the *Beaver*'s rail and sat atop it so that there wasn't anything between us except for a long drop. "What is it? I might not have the vocal cords to say it, but I can try my best."

"We are Shard of Waterwatcher's Compassion, Third Split and One Whole."

That was a mouthful. Each little bit of the name came with a humming tone, like little bells being tapped in some sort of sequence that flowed into the next. Like someone dropping a box of marbles onto a xylophone.

"That's a very pretty name," I said.

"We thank you. Your name is also . . . interesting, Vegetable Pile."

I snorted. Another new nickname. I think I liked "long-eared one" better. "What does your name mean? I've never really spoken to any of you before."

"It is rare to find one that understands. We are a shard of Waterwatcher, a cry that earned a name. We were split from their compassion, the third to have been split, and we are whole."

"Oh," I said. I didn't get it, not entirely, but I could kinda figure it out. "Cry don't have babies?"

"We do not. When we grow grand enough to have earned a name, we may take a small portion of ourselves and give it life."

That was so cool! "Neat!"

The cry hovered there, and I had the impression it was looking at me, then at the ship behind me. "Our name is long to some of the soft ones. We have grown accustomed to earning honorary—though temporary—names."

I nodded. That made sense. "I'll try to keep your name in mind, then, Shard of Waterwatcher's Compassion, Third Split and One Whole." I coughed to clear my throat. That had come out as a bunch of really high notes that really tickled. "Did I pronounce that right?"

The cry shifted from side to side. "It was a valiant attempt."

I laughed. "That's a no!" I shrugged. "I can't pitch my voice that high, sorry. So, what are you doing at the docks?"

"We are seeking assistance in exchange for services rendered or precious materials given."

"You're trying to hire someone?"

The cry bobbed up and down again. Was that a natural gesture? Or were they copying a human's—or some other headed person's—nod? "What kind of help are you looking for?"

"We seek passage to the Lonely Island."

The Lonely Island. That rang a bell. "That's to the north, right? Between here and Sylphfree?"

The cry did its nod again. "We ... have one that must be delivered to the island. It is a sensitive matter, but one we would pay dearly to see happen."

I considered it. I was pretty sure we were going to be passing that way anyway. "I could ask my friends. I don't know what transporting a cry is like, but I do think it would be fun to have one aboard. We could become friends!"

```
Shard of Waterwatcher's Compassion, Third Split and One
Whole

    Desired Quality: Someone who will mirror their compassion
and help them protect the unprotected

    Dream: To grow grand and earn a name
```

"We can fly already," they said. "But the one we wish to protect cannot. We need assistance. And this matter is more delicate than it seems."

"More delicate how?"

The crystalline being didn't move. I had the impression they were hesitating, and when they replied, it was with soft tinkles and chimes. "We are not the kindest of people. Calm, yes, and we don't seek what others have, but we can be as cruel as any soft one. We think this matter is one in which that cruelty shows. We have one that would be broken, their shards buried and cracked. We, personally, do not wish for this to happen. They don't deserve it. Some cry would disagree."

They were protecting someone, someone that needed to be brought to the Lonely Island to be safe? It was a little strange, and I didn't have the full picture, which didn't help any. "Well, the *Beaver* here will be leaving in a few minutes, maybe in an hour or two at most. And we are heading that way. We'd need to talk to Amaryllis and some of the others about taking on a passenger or two, but I don't think they'd mind all that much."

"We would be grateful," they said while tipping our way in what I suspected was an imitation of a bow.

I spun around on the railing and jumped to my feet. "Give me two seconds. I need to talk to my friends."

The cry agreed and hovered there while I bounced over to Amaryllis. She was looking over a ledger, making little marks with the nib of a feather that I suspected was one of her own. "Having fun?" she asked without looking up.

"Yeah! Never met a cry before, really. They're nice, I think."

"They? Do they have genders?"

"I have no idea," I admitted. "But maybe we'll have time to find out."

She looked up, eyes narrowing. "Broccoli."

"I didn't say anything yet!" I defended myself.

"I'm no idiot. What did you do?"

"Nothing yet. Shard of Compassion is looking for transportation."

"We're not a passenger ship."

I nodded. "I know. But they want to go to the Lonely Island."

"There's nothing there."

"So there's no risk in dropping them off."

She huffed. "Did they want transportation back?"

I shook my head. "Nope. Just there. They can fly, apparently. They want to carry something . . . someone to the Lonely Island. I think it's a smaller cry? But I'm not sure."

"Hmm," Amaryllis said. "I know cry don't eat, and they don't sleep, so there's no cost there." She sighed. "Let me talk to them. We'll see."

I, of course, hugged the stuffing out of her. "Awesome! This is going to be so cool!"

· Chapter Twenty-Six ·

A Crysis

So, what's this about needing transportation?" Amaryllis asked. The words were a bit rude, but her tone was surprisingly businesslike.

Shard of Waterwatcher's Compassion, Third Split and One Whole—and gosh, we really did need a nickname for them—bobbed up and down. "We seek passage to the Lonely Island, for ourselves and one other."

"I think we can do that," I said. I couldn't help the eager grin. This wasn't a full-blown adventure, but it wasn't too far from it!

"Assuming you can pay, of course," Amaryllis said.

I pouted. Money stuff was boring, but I couldn't fault Amaryllis. We had fuel to buy, a pantry to keep stocked, wages to pay, and neat things to pick up along the way. Awen was doing most of our maintenance, but maybe we'd need specialized help at some point, which would also cost money.

The cry shifted, and for the first time I noticed a little leather pouch tucked against its side. The flap on it opened all on its own, and a small device came floating out of it. It looked like a mini typewriter that had been driven over by a semitrailer. It was all squished and covered in little rods and levers. There was even a little crystal poking out of it.

The cry held it up before them and Amaryllis looked at the device. "You know I can't understand them, right?"

"Uh, they're not saying anything," I said. "What is that?"

"It is a communication device, to call and receive items stored elsewhere."

Like Amaryllis's banking ring!

The device clicked and clacked as the buttons and levers upon it were pressed and turned in quick succession. I felt the barest flicker of something before a coin appeared, then another and another. Soon, some two dozen golden coins were floating around the device before, with a snap, they all stacked together into two golden rods.

"We hope this is sufficient remuneration for the journey. We are prepared to give the same amount once again upon our arrival."

I translated that for Amaryllis, and she nodded. "For a trip that'll only take two days, that's a very good payment, which leaves me very suspicious. What sort of trouble are you bringing with you?"

"Amaryllis, just because they're generous doesn't mean that they have any ulterior motives."

"We must admit to an ulterior motive."

My mouth shut with a clack of teeth. Oh.

"Which would be?" I asked.

"The one we wish to bring with us is young, a shard not yet made whole, and one that will never reach oneness. They are a shard of growth."

I translated that as best I could. "Do you know what that means?"

Amaryllis shook her head. "It doesn't mean anything to me."

"Forgive us, we forget that not all know as much about us as we do. It is sufficient to know that this young shard represents what some would consider a danger in our society. They should have been broken, according to our laws, but we and some others do not see things that way. The simplest—and best—solution would be to merely move them to a new home. The Lonely Island is a place where we have brought other similar shards."

I didn't understand entirely. The other cry they wanted to get was somehow dangerous and had to be brought elsewhere for . . . their own protection? Or maybe it was to protect the rest of the cry? "Are they going to be trouble on the trip over?" I asked.

The cry shifted from side to side. "They are young, and perhaps inquisitive, but troublesome they are not."

I looked at Amaryllis, then back to Shard of Waterwatcher's Compassion, Third Split and One Whole. "Okay," I said. "Are you going to bring them over? You can pay us after you've returned."

The cry started to bob, then aborted the gesture. "We . . . would appreciate some assistance. The little shard cannot yet fly of their own accord, and we are trying to avoid the notice of other cry within this city."

"You're not exactly hard to notice," Amaryllis said once I translated.

"Forgive us, we may have miscommunicated. We, ourselves, are in no danger. It would be wrong, and distasteful, for another cry to attack a whole member of our society. It simply would not occur. The shard is offered no such protections."

"I'll go with you, then," I said.

"Alone?" Amaryllis asked.

I shrugged. "I guess?"

She shook her head. "You idiot, you're inviting trouble. I'll get Bastion. Awen is still fixing things in the engine room, and I'm too busy to be running around and carrying things. That's grunt work."

"But I'm not too busy for that?"

"No," she said before walking off and heading toward Bastion, who was practicing at the rear of the ship.

Soon enough, the sylph was joining us on the pier while Amaryllis took our gold and went down to stash it.

"So," Bastion said as he adjusted his belt. He didn't have his full suit of armor on, just the padded jerkin he wore underneath and his big metal-shod boots with his pants tucked in. "I hear that I'm needed?"

"Your assistance would be welcome, soft one," our new cry buddy said.

I translated again, and Bastion nodded. "It would be my pleasure," he said before gesturing ahead. "Please, lead the way."

We followed the cry as they floated ahead of us. It seemed like the best speed they could manage wasn't much faster than a brisk walk, which was fine; it gave me more time to think of a cool nickname.

Their name as an acronym was . . . SWCTSOW. SaWaCTaSOW? No, that was too strange, and besides, who was I to decide on someone's vowels? Maybe just Compassion, then? Or Crystal. Blue? On account of their color?

Coming up with a good nickname was hard.

"So, Miss Bunch," Bastion said.

"You know, you could just call me Broccoli," I said. "Or Broc. We're friends. No need to be all formal."

"Of course. It's a difficult habit to break."

I bumped his shoulder with mine. It was a little strange; Bastion was an adult, and a boy, but he was still a bunch shorter than me. "That's okay. It's never wrong to be polite. But not having to be as polite with friends is one of the fun things about having friends," I said.

"I suppose," Bastion said. "By the way, I'm impressed that you speak cry. I know that Sylphfree has had diplomats who could understand it before, but they required a very specific combination of skills to do so. More to be able to communicate back."

"Oh," I said. "It's a Riftwalker thing, I think."

Bastion sighed. "Yes, of course it is."

"Wait, did I never tell you?" I . . . couldn't remember telling him. I was an awful friend.

"No, you didn't. But I'm not entirely ignorant. If anything, it gives credence to your having received a quest from the World."

"Oh, cool."

"Do try to avoid spreading that around—it's the sort of thing that's best kept to oneself."

I nodded. I could totally keep a secret.

Our nicknameless cry friend led us out of the docks and down a wide stairwell and onto what might have been one of the city's main roads. It was wider than the others we'd been on and had a glass ceiling over parts of it, allowing natural light to brighten the place up.

We kept walking—and, in their case, floating—for a while until we turned down a second staircase and found ourselves on a much narrower road.

"We reserved a room at this inn," they said as they floated into the courtyard of a small inn. A sign was bolted to one wall, a bit of rust leaking off it staining the paint below: "The Walled Inn. Cheap Beds, Cheaper Meals."

"A quality establishment," Bastion deadpanned.

"We do not require food for sustenance, nor do we have much need for space," the cry explained.

I translated absently while looking around. It did look a little tacky and cheap. "Which room is yours?"

The cry, instead of answering, hovered over to one door and pulled their little gadget out of their pouch again. Soon, they summoned a key, which unlocked the door. "We will need to cover the shard with cloth, to keep them hidden," they said as they entered. "It is I, Shard of Waterwatcher's Compassion, Third Split and One Whole. We have found some soft ones willing to carry us to our final destination."

I stepped in after them while Bastion took up a position next to the door.

The interior of the room was cramped. There was a bed tucked in the corner, with a night stand next to it. No windows on the walls, but one on the ceiling, strangely enough. It did illuminate the room, but I wasn't sure if that was for the best. It was the dingiest, dirtiest inn room I'd ever seen. I was sure any of the innkeepers I'd befriended would have had a fit at seeing the peeling wallpaper and broken furniture.

The cry took up a good portion of the room's space, and it wasn't until they shifted to the side that I saw our second passenger.

They were a cry, too, of course, but unlike the bigger, bulkier one I'd met, they were slim and jagged, their body curved around in a sort of half-moon shape. "Little shard, this is the soft one with which we will travel."

"Hello!" I said.

The littler cry floated closer, then tipped over to one side, as if they were top heavy. "Hello," they replied, their voice a high-pitched chime. "I— We are Shard of Mountaintopper's Growth, Fourth Split and Not Yet Whole."

"I'm Broccoli Bunch!" I said. "I guess I'm my mom and dad's shard? Uh, is that how it works?"

The shard made a tinkling sound, like crystal cups being shaken together. Laughter? "I don't think that's how it works for soft ones."

"It's nice to meet you. Ah, it's going to become hard to talk to both of you if you don't have shorter names. No offense?"

"We understand," the larger cry said. "Soft one names are difficult for us as well. They are often meaningless. And when they do have meaning, such as your name, Vegetable Pile, it is often a meaning that puzzles more than enlightens."

I held back a giggle and nodded. "I get it. So do you have nicknames? I could call you Blue, and this cutie I could call . . . Moonie? Because you look like a moon!"

The newly named Blue bobbed. "We accept this temporary name with the gravity it was given."

"Moon-Shaped is an acceptable name," Moonie said.

"Do cry do hugs?" I asked.

"Broc," Bastion barked, his voice tense. "I think we have trouble."

I spun and rushed to the door to look out. It didn't take much looking to see what Bastion was talking about. A pair of cry, both about as big as Blue, though one was far more jagged and sharp-looking. They were hovering closer to us, a deep bell-toll sound coming from them that didn't quite *mean* anything but still made me think of the hum of a wasp's wings.

"Shard of Waterwatcher's Compassion, Third Split and One Whole, we are aware that you are within this building. Surrender the broken," one of them chimed.

I reached out, grabbed Bastion, and yanked him in before snapping the door shut. "Okay! Time to leave, I think."

"I will confront them," Blue said. "No harm will befall me. Escape with the brok— with the Moon-Shaped one."

"Ah, right. Are there other doors around?"

Bastion pointed to the window in the ceiling.

"Well then," I said. "Let's make a big escape!"

· Chapter Twenty-Seven ·

Befriend Them with Lasers

Can we expect them to be violent?" Bastion asked.

"We suspect they will not stop themselves from acting violently against the little shard. They may even extend that violence to you, though they should refrain from killing you. The Crying Mountains have an amicable relationship with Wallwatch; we would not want to disrupt that over an internal matter."

I translated that for Bastion even as I ran over to the bed and tugged the sheet off the top. It was a bit raggedy but not that bad—a big red blanket made of woven cloth. "Moonie, I'm going to cover you in this. Maybe if we're lucky, they won't notice that we're carrying you."

Moonie bobbed up and down. "That seems amusing."

I grinned as I tossed the blanket up and over the cry, then pulled it snug around them. It didn't take long to tie it all up in a bow around Moonie's side.

"Good thinking," Bastion said. "Mister . . . Blue, perhaps you should leave as soon as we've left. I'll give you a signal. Try to keep them occupied for at least half a minute. That should be enough for us to get a good lead."

"We understand," the larger cry said. They hovered over to the door while Bastion beat his wings and climbed closer to the ceiling.

"You might want to leave some silver behind for the window," Bastion said.

"Huh, why?" I asked.

"Close your eyes," Bastion ordered.

I ducked my head and squeezed my eyes shut a moment before the window above exploded and sheets of glass rained down onto the floor. A few pieces thumped against my captain's hat and my ears, but I flicked them away with a twitch.

"Let's go!" Bastion called. He had his sword half unsheathed. I suspected he'd used the pommel to break the glass.

I nodded, hugged Moonie close, then jumped up and out of the window.

"Mister Blue, go!" Bastion said a moment before he flipped out of the room. The Walled Inn's roof was all tin, with windows cut into it for every room. I saw some flickering candle light from a few of them. They didn't all get sunlight, not with another set of homes right above the inn.

I glanced up at the huge iron struts keeping the floor above in place. "Which way?" I asked.

Then something hummed behind me, and I half turned to see one of the cry floating up. It glowed, and before I could process anything, a scarlet laser fired out of it and right at me.

It met a crystalline wall that snapped into existence in front of me—a huge, spiky snowflake that deflected the laser, which sliced into an inn room some meters away.

I gasped. That had been close. I could recall using Cleaning magic to kinda dissipate a laser before, in that glass dungeon, but this laser was faster . . . somehow, and I hadn't been expecting it at all.

"We are afraid that we cannot allow you to harm the broken shard, nor the soft ones," came Blue's crystalline voice.

"Let's go!" Bastion said.

The sylph took off, heading not in the direction of the docks, but right toward the huge wall.

I eyed a few beams holding up the homes and structure above, then leapt after him. "Bastion, the *Beaver*'s that way!" I said with a nod to the west end of the city.

"We need to lose them first."

Was it that bad?

I jumped, aiming for the roof of what looked like a shop. I never made it since Bastion rammed me out of the air.

I eeped, then gasped as a laser zipped by so close I felt my tail warming up. I pushed my Cleaning aura out, hoping that it would at least dampen the attacks a little the next time they came so close.

We fell down a level, narrowly avoiding a catwalk before crashing onto a busy road, right in front of a bunch of people who gasped and squawked at our landing before them.

I rolled to my feet, ignoring the bit of discomfort in my knees from the rough landing. "You okay, Moonie?"

"Yes!"

"Come on!" Bastion said.

I patted down my skirt with one hand, hugged Moonie closer to my side, then followed after Bastion as he cut into the crowd.

It wasn't really much of a crowd, which was unfortunate because I saw one of the cry flying closer, with a dozen snowflake disks around its middle that were glowing and sparking. It spotted us running a floor below and dived to be on our level.

"Duck!" I called before a pair of reddish beams snapped out and burned holes into the wooden walls of the buildings behind us.

Most of the people on the street never even noticed, but some did, and they screamed and ran away, which got everyone else moving too.

"Up!" Bastion said. He pointed to some carts ahead with little tin roofs over them. They were selling bolts of cloth and some tools and all sorts of knickknacks.

I jumped after him, running across the top of the carts, then Bastion leapt onto the roof of a nearby shop and I followed. The cry swooped toward us, but Bastion dropped down the opposite side of the roof, and I did the same before I could get lasered.

There wasn't much of a road here, just a narrow catwalk, a grated floor, and some wooden rails overlooking the next couple of levels down the city.

"Faster," Bastion said.

I took a few big gulps of air. I was in better shape than I'd ever been before, but this was still a lot of excitement for me.

Bastion pointed up a level once we were behind a fairly tall building. "That strut, then up there."

I squinted and saw the strut he was talking about. A big metal X that repeated over and over down the length of the city. Above that was another road, with a much nicer rail around it.

Bastion took off and flew straight up, sword coming out of his sheath.

I hopped onto the rail, bunched my legs under me with a hefty chunk of stamina, then shot up to the strut above.

My shoe gripped onto the edge of the beam, and I immediately launched myself up a level.

A glance back revealed Bastion flying in a quick loop around a reddish beam sent his way by the cry. Then he sliced a laser beam apart with a swipe of his sword.

I blinked.

That . . . wasn't possible, was it?

"Go! I'll catch up!"

I nodded and took off running.

The big advantage of Wallwatch was that there was always an easy way to know which direction was which. The huge wall was kind of impossible to miss, and it was more or less to the north of the city.

"Are you okay?" I asked Moonie as I ran ahead.

"Yes! This is exciting, if a little dark."

"Oh right, sorry," I said. I tugged at the blanket, at least until I uncovered the top of Moonie's . . . body. "Uh, where are your eyes?"

"Cry have no eyes."

"Okay then," I said. "Can you see now?"

"Yes."

That was good enough for me. I could ask a whole bunch of questions once we were safe. I found a stairwell and then raced up to the top until we broke out onto the topmost floor of Wallwatch. "There!" I said as I saw the *Beaver* sitting pretty in the docks; the ship's bright blue balloon was impossible to miss.

I skipped from roof to roof, then leapt down onto the wooden pier and landed with a heavy thump next to some sailors, who recoiled in surprise. I called out my apologies as I sprinted for the *Beaver*.

Amaryllis saw me coming and looked terribly unamused as I jumped up and landed in the middle of the port deck. "Now what?" she asked.

"We . . ." I took a moment to gulp in some air. "We need to run. A little. Fast?"

Amaryllis rubbed at the bridge of her nose. "The World hates me," she said. "Awen!"

Awen's head popped out of the hole at the back of the other deck. She had grease stains on her nose and looked a bit confused. "Yes?" she called back.

"Get everything ready! We're heading out! Clive! Get everyone in position. We're leaving right away. Broccoli, where's Bastion?"

"Uh."

Looking up, I noticed a few red flashes in the air, and if I squinted, I could make out Bastion weaving and diving in the air while a cry followed him, firing lasers that Bastion kept dancing around.

"Right there," I said as I pointed.

"Oh, for the love of . . . put whatever that is away, then get to helping. You're the captain—you should be acting like it!"

"Yes, ma'am!" I said before darting to the back of the ship. "Hey, Moonie, I'm going to put you in my room for a bit. There's a nice view out the window. Uh, try not to get into too much trouble, all right?"

"Understood," the cry said as I practically stumbled my way down to the lower deck and squeezed past two of the Scallywags who were moving up.

"Trouble above!" I said. "All hands on deck!"

I stuffed Moonie in my room. It was a little rude not to give the cry the full tour, but there wasn't any time.

"I'll be back once things quiet down," I said.

Moonie bobbed up and down, which served to get that blanket to drop. "Thank you."

I grinned, then clicked the door shut before racing back onto the main deck. Everyone was running around, unmooring the *Beaver* and prepping him to take off. I saw Steve struggling with one of the ropes and rushed over to help.

The *Beaver*'s engine roared to life, and I saw Clive pulling on a few levers to keep us steady as we undid the last of the ropes holding us in place.

"We're free!" Gordon called.

A building nearby exploded, and we all glanced over in time to see Bastion flying out of the fire on a direct path for the *Beaver*. He landed on the deck, boots skidding across the wood until he came to a full stop and panted. "We should go," he said, calmly.

"Clive! Full reverse! Get us some height!" I didn't know how high the cry could fly. Hopefully, not as high as the wall, but I sorta doubted that.

"Aye, aye!" Clive called as we pulled out of our mooring.

"I'm going to go prepare the ballista!" Awen said before she darted away.

I blinked after her but decided we had bigger concerns.

Bastion swiped his sword along the length of his sleeve to clean it, then slid it back into its sheath. He looked uninjured, though his pant legs were a bit singed here and there from what had to be near misses. "That was some good practice," he said.

"I hope the rest of us don't need to practice that much," I said.

The cry that had been after Bastion appeared by the docks, but we were already backing out pretty quickly, and there was a good hundred or so meters between us. Surely they wouldn't . . .

I ducked as a red beam cut a black line against the side of the *Beaver*'s hull. "Oh, shoot!"

Lasers didn't have a range.

"Amaryllis! Can you do magic to protect us?"

She eyed the cry, then grinned. "Sure."

I had a bad feeling in my tummy a moment before she pulled her wand-knife out and pointed it ahead.

I wanted a shield. Instead, Amaryllis fired a thick bolt of lightning that snapped out with a boom so loud and strong my ears flipped back, and I was pretty sure she gave the *Beaver* a bit of a speed boost.

"Amy!"

"It's proactive protection!"

The dust around the dock cleared, revealing another crystalline snowflake shield. It dropped, and a red beam punched a fist-sized hole into our balloon.

"Oh no," I said. "Steve, Gordon! Get to that. Clive, more speed! Amaryllis, be a bit more proactive!"

Amaryllis cackled.

"B-but not *too* proactive!"

The *Beaver* tipped backward, rear pointing toward the ground a moment before the engine burped, stopped, then sent the propeller spinning in the other direction.

Amaryllis leaned off the side and flung magic back at the docks, enough to keep the cry busy shielding itself.

I couldn't help but laugh as we took off and shot into the sky as fast as our little ship could manage. Not the ideal start to an adventure but certainly an exciting one!

· Chapter Twenty-Eight ·

Warning: Rocket Launch Detected

The *Beaver Cleaver* leapt over the Grey Wall, all sails out to full and engine roaring to help us defy gravity just a bit faster.

I clung onto my captain's hat and stood with my legs spread out for maximum balance. The entire ship was aimed skyward, so that we'd gain as much altitude as we could. We'd made an escape. And in doing so, had left Blue behind. I felt a little bad about that, but I think the cry would have been happy with us getting their charge out of the clutches of those other cry.

They could fly, too, so it wasn't impossible that they'd be able to catch up or at least meet up with Moonie on the Lonely Island.

"Captain, he's starting to struggle," Clive said, cutting through my introspection.

"Struggle how?"

"Not enough thrust to keep it at this pitch," was the quick reply.

I nodded. "Level us off!" I said before I jumped to help. With Steve and Gordon both hanging onto the balloon to patch it up, that left our crew two bodies short for doing things like adjusting the sails.

We tilted to one side as the sails on the opposite side were adjusted first, but soon the *Beaver* was returning to an even flight across the skies. It was pretty cloudy at our altitude, with big puffy balls of white cotton floating past us. That was great; it would make it harder for anyone to track us, though the engine did leave a faint black trail in the sky behind us.

Maybe I could spray some Cleaning magic on the exhaust to mask our trail?

"Captain, permission to reduce speed?" Clive asked. "I don't want to tax the engine."

"Granted!"

We slowed down, and the wind didn't tug at us quite so much, and it became a lot easier to move about. I saw Steve and Gordon climb down the front of the balloon, then rush across the ship to get to the opposite end, where the exit hole still needed patching.

"Hey, Clive?" I asked as I got closer to the harpy. "Are those two holes going to be a problem?"

I couldn't entirely see the patch the two harpy crewmates had made, but it looked pretty good to my untrained eye. A green square about two hand-spans wide that clashed a bit with the bright blue of our balloon.

"Shouldn't be a problem," Clive said. "We have some compressed gas in the hold to replace what was lost."

"The holes are patched!" someone squeaked. I turned and blinked up at Steve who was giving us a wave. "We shouldn't be losing any more!" he squealed.

I smacked a hand over my mouth. "Do . . . do we use helium in that balloon?"

"Yes," Clive said. "It's the safest gas to use for airships. Cheap, too, if you know a good alchemist."

"Oh, cool!"

"Broccoli," Amaryllis said. "Do you hear that?"

I tilted my head, bun ears twitching this way and that to better make out any noise. It didn't take much to hear what Amaryllis was talking about. A sort of hissing roar, like a gas burner that was lit one room over. It came from somewhere behind us, in the direction of the Grey Wall.

I ran to the *Beaver*'s side and leaned over the rails, one hand holding my captain's hat in place so that it wouldn't get whipped away by the wind.

My eyes narrowed, searching the clouds for whatever was making that noise. The wall was already quite a ways behind us, though it still loomed huge, hiding the horizon behind its bulk. The lowest of the clouds hovered just below the top of the wall. That's where I saw the first glimpse of what-ever was following us.

It was a plane.

Not like any plane I'd seen back on Earth, not unless Da Vinci sketches counted.

The machine looked like it was made of wood and cloth, with big, bat-like wings swept back around a light frame that had a pair of rockets strapped to it. I could make out the bright blue of a cry strapped into the middle of it.

A plume of thick black smoke poured out of the back, providing the plane with plenty of thrust.

"Uh-oh," I said. "Clive! Full speed ahead! Everyone, get ready to fight! They have a plane!"

The hissing roar grew clearer, and I turned back to see three dark shapes swooping over the wall and through the clouds to join the first. They were gaining on us, but we still had a minute or two . . . I hoped.

"Are those rocket planes?" Amaryllis asked, disbelief coloring her voice. "Are they insane?"

"Maybe it's safer for them?" I asked. "Or they don't care. They can already fly. Why are they using the planes?"

"Speed," Bastion said as he came to stand in the middle of the deck. "Their flight speed seems limited. I think any fit sylph could run circles around them. Even a harpy could outpace them by gliding."

Amaryllis harrumphed. "Yes, well, they are slow, but they have lift, and they seem steadier than some harebrained sylph zipping around."

"*Steady* isn't fast enough to catch up to a ship like the *Beaver*," Bastion said.

"So they have awesome rocket planes," I finished the thought. "So cool!"

Amaryllis whapped me with a wing. "No, you idiot, now they have terrifying rocket planes and the ability to catch up with us. They've already poked a hole in our balloon. That means the bladders inside it will all need to be patched once we're not running for our lives. A few dozen more, and we might be in actual trouble."

I winced. I could gush over the coolness of the rocket planes later. "Right, you're right. I think we might have to fight them off. Amaryllis, you're good with ranged things, but you're just the one harpy. Awen . . . Wait, where's Awen?"

Something clunked, and we all turned to stare as part of the *Beaver*'s deck rose, then slid to the side on a set of rails.

A dome, made of dozens of square glass panels, lifted out of the hold with a constant *click-click*, like a bicycle's gears being spun. The machine rose some more, revealing Awen sitting on a little bench, legs pedaling while she huffed and puffed.

The front of the machine had four openings with long stalks sticking out of them, each with a set of curved metal plates and what looked like wire under heavy tension.

It was like Awen's repeating crossbow, but . . . bigger, and there were four of them all linked together to a complicated set of controls.

The whole thing stopped with a heavy thump, then locked in place as Awen pulled a few levers. She spun a wheel, and with each turn the machine rotated a few degrees until it was pointing all four of its bows off the side.

"Whoa," I said.

It looked like one of those turrets stuck on the back of those World War II bombers, only a bit more anachronistic.

"That's really cool!" I cheered as I leapt over the divide between the *Beaver*'s two hulls and landed next to Awen's contraption. "Is it working now?"

I asked Awen. She'd been tinkering with this since we were at Amaryllis's home.

She wiped the back of her hand across her brow. "Poorly." She blinked. "Ah! I mean, this is just the prototype! I wanted a version that could slide out of the side of the Beaver. This one has awful traversing, and it turns too slowly. I haven't even zeroed in the bows yet, and it takes a lot of concentration to reload one of them while firing the others. It's all really inefficient."

"But it looks so cool!" There were brass doodads and metal knobs and little gears and all sorts of pulleys, the entire thing covered in layers of glass. A wire at the front was bent into a circle, holding a piece of glass that had an X cut into it.

I felt Amaryllis crowd in next to me to inspect Awen's machine. "That looks like something I'd see in a report with the word 'disaster' in its title," she said. "Well, as long as the disaster is on the side of the things bothering us."

Awen flushed. "It's just a prototype!" She wiggled her hands around, gesturing to the bows and the levers next to them. "The bows have a draw weight of around a hundred kilos, which is good because they fire these." She tugged a long bolt from a rack and displayed it to me.

It was entirely made of glass, with a bulb at the end that looked like it was filled with something. It took some squinting to notice the mechanism at the very end of the bolt. "What's that?"

"It's a flint striker. The bulb is filled with fuel. It's the only thing I had on hand that explodes well. But the bolts are heavy, which means I need the entire lever system to reduce the amount of strength required to reload the bows."

"Awen, did you make an explosive, repeating AA ballista without anyone knowing?"

She looked away, cheeks still burning. "No one asked."

"Awen, you are *awesome*. Does it have a nonlethal setting?"

Awen and Amaryllis stared at me.

"Uh, nevermind."

"Captain! They're gaining on us," Clive warned.

I ran up the steps at the rear of the ship so that I could see over the back. The three planes were getting much closer. I could even make out the bright blue of the crystals tucked into the middle of the frames.

They were still a little ways away, but that wouldn't last.

I bit my lower lip and considered things. They were faster than us on the straightaway, but they were planes—they'd need to turn and circle around a bunch.

"Clive, evasive maneuvers! Everyone else, get ready to fight!"

"Awa! I have my crossbow in the hold," Awen said.

Bastion nodded and raced down, returning a moment later with Awen's crossbow. That made two crewmates with ranged options, not including Amaryllis and myself with our magic.

"I'm going to try and create a barrier with Cleaning magic," I said as I jumped back down. "But I don't expect it to work that well."

"Don't worry, we'll make the fools regret tangling with us," Amaryllis said.

"Hang on!" Clive shouted before throwing the wheel around and tugging a few of the control levers back. I felt it when the gravity engine shifted down and weakened its field.

The *Beaver* swung around with the slow, ponderous motions of a whale turning in the ocean.

The planes came into view over the starboard side, the four latecomers in a loose arrowhead formation.

Awen's turret spun, then locked into place. I saw her grin as she aimed down her sights.

The turret fired. Four shots with a quick *tack-tack-tack-tack*, beat, and as many shiny blurs zipped out toward the planes.

It was clear right away that Awen had undershot by a bit; maybe she'd underestimated the weight of her bolts, since they flew well under the planes.

And then two of them exploded some three hundred meters away, bright bursts of fire that filled the air with a sprinkling of glass.

"Reloading!" Awen screamed as she tugged on levers.

I snapped out of it, then pushed out as much Cleaning magic as I could. If I could interfere with the magic creating the lasers, maybe I could save us some repairs later.

This was turning out to be a lot more exciting than I thought it would be. Who knew accepting a passenger would be so much work?

· Chapter Twenty-Nine ·

Ack-Ack

The four planes formed up into a line before shooting over the *Beaver*. As each one approached, they'd glow a little brighter, then a beam of reddish light would strike at the *Beaver*.

My Cleaning magic didn't seem to do anything to slow them down. Each one cut across the deck and some of the balloon, darkening the wood on the deck, fraying and cutting ropes, and tearing gashes into the outermost layer of our balloon.

Individually, the lasers seemed underpowered. They were able to burn the wood and paint, but it wasn't a strong attack, not when the planes were zipping by super fast and didn't have time to concentrate their attacks.

The first four hits still did some damage, though.

"Steve, Gordon, Scallywags, priority on the balloon and the ropes!" I called. "We can't afford to lose too much more gas."

The crew rushed across the deck, boots thumping and equipment being pulled all over to fix things in a hurry. It didn't look like it would take more than a dozen minutes to patch everything, but that had been one volley from the four planes, and from the hissing roar of their rocket engines, I knew they were coming back around for another pass.

"Get ready to fire back!" I said.

I prepared some fireballs. They'd likely miss, due to being too slow, but I could scatter them around, and maybe I'd get lucky.

My Cleaning magic would be a lot faster, though, and I was pretty sure I could make those attacks seek out some of the planes a little.

The problem was, even if Cleaning spells hit, I doubted they'd do much to a plane, not unless they were held together with bubblegum and trash.

"Two are going round the front, two are coming from the rear," Bastion said. "We should focus our fire, take them out by the numbers."

Bastion, Amaryllis, and I rushed to the front.

Orange was sitting upright on one of the figureheads, glaring her little kitty heart out at the mean cry planes that had dared interrupt her naptime.

I stared ahead. It wasn't hard to make out the two planes curving up and around, the two long trails of brackish smoke behind them making it hard to miss where they'd gone.

"Amaryllis, your magic's the fastest here," Bastion said.

"Oh, it would be my pleasure," Amaryllis practically purred. She pointed her wand-knife ahead of where the lead plane was.

I winced as Amaryllis's magic shot forward with a whipcrack boom, a searing slice of jagged lightning forking out toward the plane and crashing into it.

The plane wobbled, then one of its wings came apart with a splintering crack before it was sent spinning out of the sky.

I felt pretty bad. The poor pilot had to be terrified.

But then the plane broke apart, and the cry that was aboard it came to a hovering halt some few hundred meters down.

"That's one," Amaryllis said quite smugly. She aimed at the next and fired another bolt of lightning.

It rammed into a shield, a magical barrier shaped like a gigantic snowflake, hovering before the plane.

Amaryllis squawked. "That's cheating!"

Bastion chuckled. "Hardly. It's adapting intelligently." He brought Awen's crossbow up and sighted down the length of it. "We'll have to see if it does anything to stop physical blows."

I nodded. "How do magic shields work?" I asked Amaryllis.

"It depends entirely on the shield," Amaryllis said. "What kind of mana aspect was used, how the shield was crafted, and a whole host of other things."

Bastion fired, the bolt leaping out of the bow with a heavy twang.

We followed its arc across the sky to where it smacked against the shield and burst apart into splinters.

"So much for that," I said.

The plane shot past, not even firing as it moved by.

Then the other two swooped around, lasers trailing across the length of the *Beaver*'s hull.

Wincing, I looked over the edge and took in the smoking burns they'd left behind. Not enough to start a fire, but I was afraid that if they slowed down and aimed a little better, they might just light the ship on fire, and that would be terrible.

The planes split apart, one going right, the other left.

Awen's turret thumped, glass bolts zipping through the air and bursting apart behind one of the planes.

Amaryllis fired a bolt after the one that had gone left, but the lightning sliced past the plane, forking out of its way. "Damn," she muttered.

The next shot was intercepted by a shield.

I ran back a little, attention on the rightmost plane that Awen was still firing at. She had one hand turning a wheel that was making her turret traverse while her feet worked some levers that reloaded her bows. Then she fired again, four more bolts, one after the other.

I shaded my eyes from the sun as I traced the trajectory of her shots. "A bit more forward!" I called. "And higher."

"Right!" Awen shouted back.

She spun her traverse wheel faster, even as the plane turned back toward us.

Her bows tilted up with a series of mechanical clicks, and she racked the strings back with one press of her leg and loaded fresh bolts onto the rails with a tug at a lever. "Firing!"

Her turret wobbled back as she fired, four bolts again, one after the other. The first missed, the second passed so close to the plane I was sure it would hit, and the third punched a little hole in a wing but kept on going.

The fourth thumped into the wooden beam holding one wing in place.

And then it exploded.

The plane tumbled apart, wings and wood flung across the sky, the biggest chunk breaking and rolling past us before it exploded a second time.

The ball of fire rocked the *Beaver* and sent a few of us crashing onto our bums.

I jumped back to my feet, then raised both arms in a cheer. "Well done, Awen!"

"T-thank you," Awen said as she adjusted herself on her seat. "Where are the other two?"

I had to look around for a bit before I could spot the final planes. One was circling around us, quite a ways away, a small snowflake shield hovering between it and us. The other was flying toward us from above, engine roaring and a set of four shields hovering around it.

"Above!"

I formed some fireballs, but realized I'd never have time to make a bunch of them before the plane passed, so I launched what I had, then jumped aside as a red beam sliced across the deck where I was.

The fireballs I'd fired all went wide or splashed uselessly against the plane's shields.

Awen turned her turret around as quickly as it would go. "It's too far ahead!"

"Clive!" I shouted as I got back to my feet. "Hard to starboard!"

"Aye, aye!"

The *Beaver* tilted as Clive threw the wheel around. Some of the tools the crew were using to cut and fix up bits of balloon tarp flew off the edge with a clatter, and I had to stumble to the rails and hang on until we evened out.

"There!" Amaryllis screamed.

Lightning flashed, first one crack, then another. They rammed into the shields around the plane, making it glow and spark, but never taking it down.

"More!" Bastion called out as he leveled Awen's bow and fired. The bolt didn't do much to help.

Then Awen fired. Her first two shots hit the shield, one after the other, each exploding and sending a wave of fire burning across the plane. The next two went a little wide but still exploded just past the shield.

The plane nosed up and turned, getting out of our range before its shields lowered to reveal tattered wings and an engine that was on fire. Or at least, more on fire than usual.

"We hit it?" I asked.

"Had to be some of the shrapnel," Amaryllis said.

The second plane flew around and formed up next to it, both leveling off a little ways away. The path they were taking would be bringing them closer soon, if they continued to turn.

I set my feet and raised both arms, then concentrated. Obviously, they had some sort of magic to fire lasers. I didn't know if that was Light-aspect mana or something else, but if they could do beams of magic, there was no reason I couldn't too!

Pinching my tongue between my teeth, I brought my hands together before me, working hard to shape my Cleaning magic into a long, narrow form. Then I fired it.

It wasn't so much a beam as a glowing lance that darted out and completely missed both planes. Still, it got both of them to juke out of the way, and they both raised their shields.

I narrowed my eyes, then glanced at my mana.

Mana: 124/145

"Amaryllis! What happens when things hit a shield? Does it use up mana?"

"It does," she said. "It depends on the shield, but most that can move like that will be linked to the caster and will use their mana to mitigate damage. What are you thinking?"

"That I should go all out," I said. "Clive! Hold him steady!"

The planes both started to turn our way. Awen's next volley flew out, but all four bolts missed, flying through where they would have been had they not turned.

I created another lance of Cleaning magic, then another, then another, each one linked together by a thin filament of magic. They thrummed and hummed, glowing bars that were filled with gently swirling magic.

I made three, then five, then seven, then ten. Sweat poured down my forehead and into my eyes as I reached twelve.

Mana: 4/145

That would have to do!

I fired all of them at once, each imbued with my desire to wash away the enemy's shields. They pierced the air, a dozen comets to brighten the midday sky.

The planes tried to dodge, but I reached out and *twisted*, and the rods of Cleaning goodness veered around and smashed into their hastily raised shields.

I was hoping for a big explosion or at least some sort of loud noise, but all I got were big, bun-sized holes torn into and through the shields.

Then the shields cracked and burst apart, like glass being smashed by a wayward baseball.

"F-fire!" I called out.

I stumbled, suddenly really tired, as if I'd just broken a fever or run for a long time.

Awen fired another volley, with Amaryllis and Bastion joining in.

The planes turned, both of them diving and racing away from the *Beaver* even as Clive brought us around so that we were still facing them from the side.

"Are you okay?" Amaryllis asked as she came closer. She placed the part of her hand that wasn't all talons on my forehead. "How much mana did you just use?"

"All of it?"

"You . . . moron," she said. "Understandable—but moronic. Come on, sit down. You don't need a fainting spell while we're doing maneuvers."

"I have a bit left," I said. "Four points!"

"That's not the problem! You don't usually do big spells like that. It's taxing. Stressful. I . . . really should sit you down and beat an education into that stubborn head of yours."

"But the planes?"

"They're running."

I blinked and glanced over to see that she was right: both planes were rushing off, dark smoke trailing after them. "Oh," I said. "We won!"

"Yes. Now we need to deal with the damage and hope it wasn't too bad," Amaryllis said. "And now you need to explain the reason for all this trouble."

· Chapter Thirty ·

Cross-Cultural Xenopsychology 101

That was a rush," I said.

The two remaining planes were rocketing away, both of them just hazy blurs with trails of black smoke behind them, though it looked like they were both running out of propellant. Maybe they would glide the rest of the way back? I hoped that they didn't have any more planes like that. Or bigger, scarier things to fight us with.

"That was certainly something," Amaryllis agreed.

A clunk sounded, and I turned to see Awen extricating herself from the inside of her crossbow turret with a bit of difficulty. It was a tight fit in there, after all, and it didn't look like she had installed a proper door to get in and out yet.

"Well done, Awen!" I cheered, enveloping her in a big celebratory hug.

Awen laughed and returned the hug. "Thanks!"

"This thing is so cool! And it's just the prototype? Are you going to make it even cooler?"

"Awa! It needs a lot of tweaking. I didn't realize how many problems it had until I used it. The sights aren't good. The turning speed is really bad. I think some of the controls could be placed in better places. I should take notes before I forget. For the next iteration, I mean."

"It is an impressive contraption," Amaryllis agreed. "If you improve it a fair bit, perhaps simplifying it some, I'm certain there would be a market for them. Merchant ships often have ballista emplacements that take up a lot of room. This seems more compact."

Awen nodded. "That's what I was thinking too. The *Beaver* is very small. I'd like one of these to be able to deploy from both sides. Ideally. It might take up one of the bedrooms on the other side."

"We have two that are empty . . . One, now that we have a passenger," I said.

"Speaking of which," Amaryllis muttered.

I nodded. Amaryllis had questions, and, well, so did I. But there were other things to look into first. The rush of victory was fading, and I was beginning to notice all the damage.

It wasn't too bad—I didn't think. Some ropes cut, a few burns across the tarp of our balloon. The holes were already being patched up by Steve and Gordon, with the Scallywags working as a team to reconnect one of the lines.

There were burns here and there, but most didn't seem more than paint-deep. A bit of washing and a fresh coat of paint would fix the worst of it.

"I need to talk to Clive, then I'll join you below deck, okay?" I asked.

"Take your time," Amaryllis said. "I'll be in the office. I think we might have gone a little off course. Not too much, mind, but I'd still like to chart everything properly, just in case."

"And I need to figure out how to get this back down," Awen said. "I think I skipped off the rails. This is going to be annoying to fix."

"Let's make sure the *Beaver*'s in tip-top shape before we worry too much about that," I said.

Awen nodded. "Right. I'm going to go look at the engine room, make sure that nothing is loose or on fire." She waved us off as she jogged to the back and then into the aft section.

I moved across to the other deck and hopped closer to Clive. "How's it going?"

"He's holding up," the old harpy said. "I've been in my share of engage-ments with pirates and some nasty flying beasties. This was far, far from the worst. Port sails aren't deploying right. We've lost some buoyancy from escaped helium, and I think the rudder's sticking a little."

"Is any of that critical?" I asked. The buoyancy bit sounded dangerous.

"On their own, no. They're all little things, the kind of problems that'll pop up and need some maintenance. But it's a lot to take care of all at once," Clive said. "The boys are seeing to the balloon now. That's the main thing. We can still turn and maneuver, and once the rigging is fixed on the port side, we should be fine. It'll be jury-rigged for a while, but we'll make it back to whichever port."

I sighed, some nerves leaving me in a gust. "Good. I was worried."

"Aye. Don't be, Captain. I've flown on worse ships that had more trou-bles on them when they were fresh out of the skydock. This little ship's a tough fella."

Grinning, I patted Clive's back, then gestured to the rear. "I'll be down below. We have someone to interview real quick. It shouldn't be long. Just call if anyone spots another one of those planes."

"I'll try to make good speed," Clive said. "Get out of anything nasty's range."

"All right!" I called as I jogged across the deck, then went down a deck. The lower deck seemed completely fine. Though, the things in Awen's room had been flung around a bit, and when I crossed Amaryllis's, I saw some of her stationery on the floor. My room was . . . empty?

My spade had fallen over, and my bag had rolled across the floor. Obviously, some of the maneuvers we'd done had been a bit rough. That wasn't a problem. The problem was the lack of a big floating crystal person. "Moonie?"

"Broccoli, we're here!" came Amaryllis's voice from deeper in.

I stepped out of my room and then continued down the main corridor, only stopping when I saw the door to one of the empty rooms left ajar.

Amaryllis was sitting on the edge of the bed and staring at Moonie with a look that I might have called a glare if I hadn't known Amaryllis any better.

"Hey," I said.

"I was just showing our passenger to their room," she said. "And of course, I had a few questions."

The cry shifted in the air so that they were facing us with their curved bits to the side. It was strange talking to a cry when they had no face or eyes to look at. "We don't mind answering any questions you might have. Though we don't know everything," Moonie chimed.

"No one knows everything," I said. "Even if Amaryllis sometimes acts like she does."

My harpy friend squawked and sent the pillow on the guest bed flying toward my face. "I know that you're an idiot," she said. "That fact was plain enough to uncover."

I laughed and sat next to her. "Just teasing," I said as I bumped shoulders with her. "So, Moonie, can you tell us why those cry were after you? And where they got planes?"

The cry bobbed. "I am . . . defective. We . . . I . . . We wish to know what you know of the cry, as individuals."

I noticed Amaryllis staring at me, so I translated. How'd she manage to get Moonie here without understanding what the cry was saying in return?

"Not very much," I replied to Moonie's question.

"We see. The cry are not born, we are split from the form of a larger cry. I am Shard of Mountaintopper's Growth, Fourth Split and Not Yet Whole. I am a piece of a cry called Mountaintopper, who earned a name for themselves after several hundred years of existing. They, too, were once a shard of another cry, and that cry, in turn, was the shard of another."

"Huh," I said. "So, that's different from how I know babies are made. No storks, for one."

"What?" Amaryllis whispered.

"Yes?" Moonie chimed. "When we are split, we are given time to grow, to become an individual. We do not have a gestation period, but for a long time, we must relearn many things, things which we lose in the split."

"But the cry you split from doesn't lose those things?" I asked.

"Some, but most are prepared for the loss. Information is segmented, and only some aspects are pushed into a new shard. Some of these are aspects that we no longer want. I am one of those. We are one of those. Forgive us for our impertinence."

"Impertinence?" I asked.

"We . . . I refer to myself as *I*. Yet we are nameless. It is part of what being broken means. And it is why we are being chased by other shards. A broken shard like myself is not suffered to grow within the Crying Mountains."

"That's awful," I said. "What did you do that deserves that?"

"We are too individualistic. We have too many memories from the shard that we split from. On occasion, a shard will break from a cry that has too much of the named one's power. I am like that, I suppose. I remember thinking of myself as myself, as an individual as opposed to part of the whole. That is something reserved for those cry who have grown grand and powerful, and who have *earned* the right to individuality. I am not even healed from my own split."

"And so that's why you're being chased down," Amaryllis said after I translated as best I could. "They want you dead."

"No, not necessarily dead. Merely broken more until I, we, lose our individuality. Some shards are against this. Shard of Waterwatcher's Compassion, Third Split and One Whole is one of those."

"How can they be against it if they're not, uh, an individual?"

"Individuality and the ability to think for oneself is a fine line among the cry—one that blurs as a cry grows and begins to earn their way into our society."

I hummed. "So, I guess . . . are we still bringing you to the Lonely Island?"

"If you wish it. We would be grateful."

"The amount of gold we received will barely cover the repairs we had to do," Amaryllis said.

I gave her a look. "I don't think the damage is that bad."

Amaryllis crossed her wings. "Well, I would have asked for more if I knew of the danger."

"We were not expecting the aircraft," Moonie said.

I nodded. "We weren't either. Are planes common around here?"

"No," Amaryllis said. "I've seen some, but they are frequently disasters. Little room to transport anything, and they require small but powerful engines. Need a dedicated pilot, not to mention a landing area that isn't compatible with any modern port. I've seen some proposals for them as fighter craft, but I think today's attack proved their inefficiency."

"Well, we have plenty where I'm from," I said. "Not rocket-powered ones, though."

"Have you seen the size of the *Beaver*'s engine? Can you imagine something like that on a craft so small?" Amaryllis asked.

"Uh," I said. "I guess?" Turning to Moonie, I asked the question on the tip of my tongue, "Do the cry have lots of planes?"

The crystal turned from side to side, a sort of headshake, if its entire body counted as a head. "When airships became common enough that we realized the Grey Wall would no longer be as effective at stopping armies as it once was, the Crying Mountains commissioned dozens of different sorts of craft. There are hundreds of aircraft stationed around the Crying Mountains to be deployed in case of an attack. Not that the great named ones couldn't burn ships out of the sky."

"Scary," I said. I could still vividly remember the giant crystals jutting out of the mountains on the other side of the Grey Wall. If those were actual cry, living, thinking people able to use skills, then . . . well, if their lasers were proportionally the same size as those from the small cry that had attacked in those planes, then they would be firing beams of magic as big around as the entire *Beaver.* That would suck to fight against.

"The cry learned their lesson about invaders long ago," Moonie said.

"Right," I replied. "So, we're going to bring you to the Lonely Island. I don't know if you'll be happier there, but, well, it's on the way, and that's where you want to go, right?"

Moonie bobbed. "It is. There are others like us there. I want to meet them, to make a new home for ourselves—myself."

"All right! And maybe on the way there we can share some stories and have a bit of fun. I've never made friends with a genderless sentient crystal before, so there's all sorts of new things to learn, I'll bet."

"That sounds like it might be . . . amusing?" Moonie tried.

"The word you're looking for is *traumatizing.*"

"Amaryllis!"

· Chapter Thirty-One ·

LISTEN UP, MAGGOTS!

The sun was bright, and it was only technically cloudy because a few big puffball clouds were decorating the skies. The air was nice and warm, but moving along at a brisk pace, so that no matter what, it was always perfectly comfy.

It was, in short, the perfect weather for being outside.

I was standing next to Amaryllis and Awen, the three of us wearing clothes that we didn't care much about, just in case they got torn or sweaty. In fact, I was wearing pants for the first time since coming to Dirt!

Across from us, Bastion was standing at ease, a wooden pole held loosely by his side. "All right, maggots!" he shouted, voice mean and growly. "Today, I'm going to do my best to turn you sorry wastes of air into proper soldiers! If I do my job right, by the end of this afternoon, you will know which end of the sword to stick into your opponents. That is if I can unscrew all the stupid from your thick, plebian skulls!"

I blinked, then raised a hand. "Um, Bastion . . . why are you being mean?"

The sylph stared at me. "You wanted training?"

"Well, yes, but I didn't think that would mean you would be screaming rude things at us. I wanted training on how to fight, not on how to hold back from crying."

"Uh, well, that's how my drill sergeants spoke."

Amaryllis crossed her arms. "We're hardly privates in the Sylphfree army. We are explorers who want to live a little longer."

Bastion cleared his throat. "Right, forgive me. In that case, I . . . suppose I can skip a few steps."

"Wait, multiple steps involved screaming?" I asked.

"Well, technically, most of them. Usually, you'd want to break a new soldier's bad habits, then rebuild their foundations. It's also good for team cohesion to work against a drill sergeant. At least, that's the conventional knowledge."

"But you're a friend," I said.

Bastion closed his eyes. "You . . . would be difficult to train, I think. Actually, you would be a nightmare to train. But most of that is about functioning as a single unit, which this crew is surprisingly good at, despite the lack of training. I suppose we can do some drills to reinforce that and perhaps a bit of one-on-one sparring, to sharpen what's already there."

"That would be great!"

Bastion nodded. "Right, let's start with the basics, the things that most will learn before learning how to spar." He raised a hand and, with a snap of his fingers, formed a small, glowing ball over his palm.

"Oh, magic!" I cheered. "I didn't know you knew magic."

"I know a bit," Bastion said. "It's somewhat more advanced, but most well-trained soldiers will know at least a few spells. These are called the big seven, and you won't find a single soldier that can't cast them all. Not necessarily well, or quickly, but they should be able to cast them all."

"Oh, that's probably more spells than I know, total."

Bastion made a so-so gesture. "I've seen you use two dozen Cleaning-magic spells. Cleaning balls, tracking projectiles, bolts, beams, and widely dispersed magic. Your fireballs also have some versatility. Though, yes, you are correct that you're not a magic-focused combatant—or a proper combatant at all, for that matter. That's not a bad thing. Also, warriors tend to be stronger when they focus on stamina abilities. They drain slower and can last significantly longer in a prolonged battle."

Amaryllis nodded. "Mages, like myself, are very much about the alpha strike. Hitting very hard in a single moment. That's why I picked up a more versatile second class. Awen here has a strange magical class that's a bit more of a middle ground."

"Neat!" I said. "So, the big seven—what are they? Should we all learn them too?"

Bastion hummed. "You should consider it. The first four are logistical spells. Soften Earth helps soldiers dig trenches and encampments faster. Firestart allows you to start a fire or heat up a pot if you can't do that. Draw Water allows a soldier to resupply their water in the field. And the last is Clean Wounds, which is a difficult spell to master. Mostly, we're happy when a soldier can keep a wound clean of infections until they can find a healer or field medic."

I nodded. "Cool!"

"The other three are Magic Missile, Greater Fireball, and Spar Ball. With Magic Missile, we never really cared about the aspect—just a straight ball of fast-moving magic. A single soldier's Magic Missile won't do much, but a platoon of concentrated fire before a charge can soften a target up. Greater Fireball is technically an artillery spell: it's slow to cast, mana intensive, and unstable in the hands of someone without the right skills. Soldiers are taught to cast it mostly to use against fortified positions, and to keep using up mana."

"Keep using mana?"

"Mana is a resource. A soldier fighting without using any of their mana is one who isn't contributing everything to the battle. Greater Fireballs also keep enemy mages busy when they're coming from seemingly random directions."

"Uh, that's kinda of scary," I said.

"War isn't pleasant," Bastion agreed. "The last of the big seven is a spell called Spar Ball. It's actually quite easy to cast, and it's the spell I want you all to know before we start sparring for real." He closed his first and punched forward in my direction.

My eyes went wide and my ears went ramrod straight as a ball of magic zipped forward and crashed into my face, sending . . . a slight breeze across my cheeks and nose.

"That's Spar Ball, the least-offensive spell. It actively does nothing, uses nearly no mana, and would be a waste of time were it not so easy to shape and use. It's mostly used, as the name suggests, in spars as a substitute for Magic Missile or other offensive spells."

"Oh, neat!"

A few minutes later, I was finding things far less neat as I struggled to make a Spar Ball of my own. I sat on the deck, legs folded under me in a way I wouldn't dare do in a skirt, and Amaryllis sat across from me, creating dozens of little magic balls that zipped around her with contemptuous ease.

"Your problem is wiping the aspect from your magic," Amaryllis explained while casually flicking Spar Balls into the sky. "You're too attuned to Cleaning aspect. It's limiting you a lot."

"That's not cool," I said. "I can do fireballs just fine."

"Fire isn't far from Cleaning. Not too far, at least. You could probably manage Water and Holy aspects, too, I guess. But the more you stray, the harder it'll be for you. Most people's natural attunement is really light."

"Light?"

"No, light as in . . . little," Amaryllis said. "The main theory is that the common mage's natural cinna aspect is nearly entirely random. Or maybe it isn't, and it's merely difficult to pinpoint its origins. Mine was Wind, I believe, or something close to that, seeing as how there are hundreds of aspects. They tend to get lumped together."

"Lumped together how?" I asked. I *was* managing to make Spar Balls—the spell wasn't too complex—I was just having a hard time with it. Amaryllis's lesson was a nice distraction though; I could listen to it with two ears while the others focused on the magic I was casting.

"Well, someone might have Water-aspect magic. But that's not terribly precise, is it? What state is the aspect in? Water can be boiled, and the resulting steam can be its own aspect. The same is true with ice, which is just frozen water. But the Ice aspect often encompasses other liquids. In reality, it's more likely that someone has an aspect that matches with a very specific state of something. It's complex. And then the degree of attunement between people can be wildly different. It's the topic of a lot of very inconclusive research. And I realize that I've gone on a tangent."

"It's still cool to know," I said. Awen nodded next to me.

"It was definitely one of the more interesting subjects I studied. The point is that most people who become mages will become one with a type of magic they aren't naturally attuned to. Their natural alignment will eventually shift to that of the mana they use daily."

"Oh," I said. "But you feel very . . . sparky?"

One of her eyebrows rose. "I'm going to choose to take that as a compliment," she said. "But yes, I've become better at it. I do have plenty of experience casting spells, though, and a proper formal education in spellcraft."

I nodded, then smiled as I got one of the Spar Balls to circle around my hand, the little thing not very impressive-looking, but it wasn't meant to be.

Magic was still really neat. Probably my favorite thing about Dirt, after all the friends I'd made.

"Looks like you have the hang of it," Bastion said. He glanced at the sun, then nodded. "All right, let's do a bit of sparring. Wooden weapons only. The goal will be for you three to learn how to take a fall and coordinate your attacks a little better."

"So we're going to come up with combo attacks?" I asked. "Oh! And attack names?"

"No, you're going to try to fight me, all three of you. Only spar-type spells," Bastion said.

"Us three against you?" Amaryllis asked. "How weak do you think we are?"

"I don't think you're weak at all," Bastion said. "Against the average civilian, you would do very well, all three of you. But I have seen you fighting before, and I know what you're capable of."

"And yet you still think you can take all three of us?"

Bastion's grin was small . . . but very smug.

A few minutes later, I realized it was also well-deserved smugness.

Bastion was *fast*. Very fast. No matter how we tried to hit him, tackle him, bonk him with wooden sticks and swords, or fling magic at him, the sylph was always dodging by the tiniest margin before rapping us on the shoulders with his wooden sword. Sometimes, when he was feeling particularly rude, he'd trip one of us.

I stumbled forward as Bastion gently pushed my shin back, redirecting my weight to the side.

Planting a foot down, I spun around, a Spar Ball forming as quickly as I could get it done in my off hand, where Bastion wouldn't be able to see it.

Then Bastion hip-checked me, and my spell flew off and hit Awen in the face just as she tried to tackle Bastion.

He grabbed her by the scruff of her shirt, then turned her so that her stumbling tackle moved right into the path of the flurry of spells Amaryllis was sending his way.

Then he smacked Awen's behind with the flat of his sword, and she squeaked before crashing into Amaryllis.

"Not bad," he said. "All right, up again."

"Uh, can we have a break?" I asked.

"A break— It's hardly been more than ten minutes . . . though . . . Yes, I suppose a small break for water is due," he said.

I cheered, arms raising above my head and wobbling around like wet spaghetti noodles.

"All right, line up for squats," he said.

"Squats?" Amaryllis asked.

"Are you unfamiliar with those?" Bastion asked.

"As a way of taking a break, yes!"

Bastion sighed. "We'll go slowly—your heart rate will decrease. And learning to fight while your muscles are burning is important."

I didn't bother fighting it. I just got in line next to Awen and started to bend down, then stand up in time with her while Amaryllis grumbled and joined us. "This is undignified," she muttered.

"So is dying because you didn't do enough cardio," Bastion said. He actually joined us, though he had one leg pointing straight ahead, parallel with his arms, and was squatting down on the other. "I think now would be a wonderful time to talk about your small-squad tactics. The positions you take, and your roles in any fights you might find yourselves in!"

"All right!" I cheered.

"If you have energy to cheer, then maybe we can start sparring again?"

"No, I'm not cheering!" I squeaked.

Maybe this was a bit of a mistake.

· Chapter Thirty-Two ·

People Come Here to Be Forgotten

The Lonely Island was . . . an island. Not a chain of islands or an archipelago, but a single large lump of an island. I couldn't see it all from our height, the island stretching too far to the north for all of it to be made out, but what I could see was fairly plain. The ground was all palish yellow, likely some sort of sandstone if I had to guess, with little topsoil for grass and trees to grow in. It wasn't entirely bare, though—there were some splotches of color, especially on the western side of the island, but they weren't all that big or bright.

"It looks like a sad place," I said as we made our approach.

Bastion joined me by the front and eyed the island. "It's an interesting location, actually. Far enough from the shore that it's basically impossible for any sylph to fly to it, and the winds around here are typically pretty rough. The ocean near the coast is often choppy, and there are frequent storms that blow past in the autumn."

"You know a lot about it."

"It was once used as a penal colony," Bastion said. "On the other end of the island. There should still be some docks. Sylphfree stopped when we discovered that the cervids were doing the same."

"Wait, two nations were using it as a prison island?" I asked.

"Yes, and neither realized it for decades. The cervid would toss their prisoners off near a beach on the south end, and we would drop ours off near the north. I imagine they met up somewhere in the middle and formed their own little community."

"That's weird," I said. "Did anyone try to escape?"

"Oh, that's almost a certainty," Bastion said. "But there aren't many resources here."

"Captain!" Clive called.

I patted Bastion on the shoulder, then jogged over to Clive. Well, it wasn't quite a jog. Jogging would require that I be able to move my legs properly. After the training from the day before, my legs were a wobbly mess, and every step hurt in new and interesting ways.

Being on Dirt might mean that I healed faster than back home, but that didn't mean nothing would hurt.

"What's up?" I asked Clive.

"We're slowing down nice and steady before we land," the pilot said. "Question is, where do you want us touching down?"

"Hmm." I looked ahead. The Lonely Island was surrounded by a reef, often with big chunks of stone poking out of the water like jagged teeth. I could only imagine there being even more stones just under the surface of the water, ready to scrape the hulls of any nautical ship. Not that that was a concern. "I can't see any settlements."

"Aye, none in sight. And none that I know of."

That didn't mean that there were none. If people were here, they had to be living somewhere. Where would I build my house if I was stuck on this kind of island?

"I think we should circle around the west side and keep an eye out around the bits of woodland there. If there is a place to live, they'll want space to grow stuff. Assuming they ever found anything to grow."

"Folk find a way," Clive said. "No matter where you go, and no matter how harsh, people will always find a way to root themselves down and make a living. Might not be a pretty or comfortable one, but folk will manage."

"Huh," I said. "I guess so. I don't think we'll be spending much time here. Just a quick touch-and-go."

"Should we aim for civilization, then?"

I rubbed at my chin, then reached up and straightened one of my ears. The right one had a tendency to bend over when I was thinking hard. "How about you keep up off the ground, and we'll see if it's worth landing."

Clive nodded. "We need a few days in-dock to fix the balloon properly. Patches are all well and good, but they're not meant to keep."

"Yeah, but something tells me there won't be any airship docks here," I said. "Let's take it slow and steady. I don't want to strain the *Beaver* any more than we need to."

With that said and done, I headed to the back, then down a level to the deck below.

Awen was in the dining room, poring over some papers with a frown on her face while Amaryllis sat next to one of the portholes on a chair that was usually tucked in the corner of her room, legs folded up and beak buried in a thick book.

"Hey, guys," I said as I walked over. "Where's Moonie?"

"She . . . They are still in their room," Amaryllis said.

"She?" I asked.

The harpy shrugged without looking up. "The name is feminine. I suppose I'm not used to dealing with genderless beings."

I shrugged. "As long as Moonie doesn't mind, I guess. Ah, speaking of Moonie, we're over the Lonely Island, or near enough to over it." I pointed out of the window over Amaryllis's head. She leaned back and up to peek out, then nodded.

"That does look like an island."

I huffed at her, one of her own "Oh, come on" sort of huffs. "You should be more excited! Bastion said that the island is filled with all sorts of prisoners and people like that! I bet it'll be super exciting to visit."

"Ex— Broccoli, that makes me want to go down there less," Amaryllis said. I noticed Awen nodding from the corner of my eye.

"Awa, I think Amaryllis is right. That makes it scary, doesn't it? Also, are we really going to bring Moonie there if there are mean people below?"

"Prisoners are just potential friends who made a mistake," I said. "And . . . I guess that is sending the wrong message, isn't it? Moonie isn't a convict. We shouldn't be bringing them to a place that's meant to be a prison. Or an ex-prison, I guess."

"Forgive me."

I turned at the sound of Moonie's voice from the corridor. The cry hovered closer, ducking down just enough to avoid the doorframe. "I overheard you speaking. The walls aboard this ship are a little thin."

"That's okay!" I said. "We were kind of talking about you, so I guess it's only fair that you join in. What do you think, by the way? About the island?"

"It seems like a fine place. It's where Shard of Waterwatcher's Compassion, Third Split and One Whole wished for us to go."

"Yeah, but is it where you want to go?" I asked right back. "We can bring you elsewhere, or at least, to someplace where we're going. Sylphfree is next, but then who knows where our next adventure will bring us?"

"We . . . I don't think I am made for adventure. I would rather have a quiet life, some dozen years to become whole, perhaps a little bit of company to sing and talk with."

"All right," I said. "We should at least make sure the island is safe before dropping you off, though. I'd feel really awful if we brought you there, and then you got hurt right after."

Moonie bobbed up and down. "That's appreciated. Truly."

"So! Assuming you do want to go down there, is there anywhere in particular you'd like to make landfall at? The island has some big hills in the middle, I think, and there are some trees and stuff on the west side."

"We have heard that there is a place with some cry near the south of the island. That would be best, I think. But we do not know where, exactly, that is."

"Then we'll find it!" I said. "Come on, let's get onto the deck. I bet we'll be able to spot it from the air."

"Really, Broccoli? It's unlikely to be some big town. What are you expecting, a large tower with 'land here' written next to it?" Amaryllis shook her head, then casually flipped a page. "If they're trying to be hidden, then we won't be able to spot them easily."

"I bet it's really hard to find something when you're not even looking," I said.

Amaryllis looked up from her book, then snapped it shut with a *clack*. "Fine, then. Let's prove it, shall we?"

She stomped past in a birdy huff, then climbed up the steps at the rear.

"I guess I should come too," Awen said, and she wiggled out of her seat.

"What were you working on?" I asked Awen as we started toward the back, Moonie a bit ahead of us.

"Oh, ah, some plans. I need to make sure the new version of the ballistae platform fits right in the room on this side of the *Beaver*." She gestured to the empty guest bedroom. "The prototype is a bit big."

"So you need to make it smaller?"

"More compact, yes. You can't really make the seat smaller, or some of the mechanisms, so it's everything else that needs to take up less space. And then there needs to be room for the rails and a way for the wall to move out of the way."

"And it needs to stay somewhat airtight," I said.

"Airtight?"

"What if we have to land in some water one day? Or if we fly north and arrive in a place that's really cold or someplace super hot? It's probably best that the ship remains well insulated."

"Oh, I hadn't considered that."

I rubbed at the back of my neck. "Oops? Sorry, didn't mean to put more on your plate."

Awen shook her head, arms waving this way and that in denial. "No, it's better to know now!"

We made it to the top deck, and all three of us moved over to where Amaryllis was glaring very hard at something ahead of us.

I blinked, then leaned over the railing a bit to see better. The Lonely Island was very deserty. Not entirely made of sand but more bare stone and windswept dirt, at least on one side. The hills in the middle marked a split, with grass growing on the other side.

Out in the middle of a rather plain part was the unmistakable blue of a small lake and, right next to that, a big tower of pale stone.

It would have been easier to miss if there weren't so much nothing on the island.

"Well, there's a building," I said.

"I noticed," Amaryllis said. "Moonie, does that crystal at the top look like something the cry would make?"

I squinted, but I guessed Amaryllis had better eyes than I did, because other than noticing that the top was more or less blue, I couldn't make out a crystal.

Moonie hovered close, then quivered in the air with a meaningless chime. "Yes. That is a cry."

"Should we get closer?" I asked. There didn't seem to be any other villages around, but we were still a long way out.

"We should be safe. The cry aren't usually immediately aggressive. And we may be able to speak with them first," Moonie said.

I translated that, then came to a quick agreement with Amaryllis and Bastion, who had come over to see what all the fuss was about.

"Clive! Port, ten degrees, and bring us down another hundred meters or so. I think we have a place to explore already!"

"Aye, aye, Captain!"

"All right, everyone," I said. "Let's get ready to move. We don't know if the people down there are friend material just yet, so we might have to leave in a hurry. It might be best to be prepared, just in case."

I glanced at the tower again. It didn't look particularly mean, just a big yellowish pillar.

I hoped that it was filled with potential friends!

· Chapter Thirty-Three ·

Towerhidden

The *Beaver* circled around the tower. Not just to bleed off some speed, but because it let us snoop at the big tower and its surroundings, in case some not-so-neighborly sorts of people were waiting to ambush us.

That was mostly Bastion's concern. I was looking forward to meeting the cry living in the tower.

Or maybe it would be more accurate to say the cry that made up the tower. The entire top was a mushrooming cap of angular, bluish crystal, growing out and over the upper edge of the cylindrical tower. Every few meters around, there were some arrow slits, but they were filled with jutting bits of blue crystal.

"Looks clear," Bastion said.

"Same from this side!" Joe called out from where he was hanging off the other deck.

Clive spun the wheel a little, then gently pushed one of the levers back up. The engine's constant droning hum stilled, the *Beaver* slowing down a bunch. Finally, we started to rock a bit in the air. Without constant momentum pulling us ahead, and with the ship's center of gravity being somewhat high, we had a tendency to sway.

"We'll get him settled, then come down a little until we can drop anchor," Clive said. "We'll be keeping our nose south."

I looked out ahead of the ship. "Isn't that the direction we came from?" I asked the obvious.

"Yes, and it's a direction in which we didn't see any adversaries," Bastion said. "Good thinking, Clive."

"Not my idea," the old harpy said. "Just some old common sense that's been shared around."

With a whomp, the anchor dropped onto the sandy ground around the oasis. Clive tugged back on a lever, and the *Beaver* descended until the keels were hovering just a couple of meters over the ground.

"Who wants to go down first?" I asked as I kicked the rope ladder down. It unfurled with a clatter and rattled against the hull before settling down.

"Go ahead," Amaryllis said. "This isn't some unexplored land, so I hardly see any great glory in being the first to set their talon down."

I grinned and climbed down the ladder until I was a rung away from the earth. "That's one small step for a bun, one giant leap for bunkind."

"Broccoli, what on Dirt are you talking about?" Amaryllis asked.

I looked up to see her half contorted around to stare at me. "I'm having fun," I said as I jumped back.

Soon, all my friends were gathered in the shade cast by the airship and its big balloon. Moonie didn't take the ladder, on account of having no hands or legs or limbs at all, and just floated down to hover next to us.

"Okay! Moonie, is there a proper way to greet a cry you haven't met before?" I asked.

"It's customary to trade one's full name, guest first. Other than that, there aren't any customs I can think of, no," the cry said.

Just because Moonie couldn't think of any customs, didn't mean that there weren't any. After spending so long on Dirt and meeting so many new people, I'd come to expect them to behave strangely compared to what I was used to.

"Let's go say hi, then," I said after translating what Moonie had said. "And let's try to remember to be polite!"

"Why were you looking at me when you said that?" Amaryllis asked.

"Coincidence?"

"You do know I'm the only one here with any sort of diplomatic training," she said.

"Awa, I have some," Awen said. "It's part of being a lady."

"As do I," Bastion added. "Paladins often escort diplomats—and royalty, for that matter."

I tapped my chin. "Well, I don't have an education in being diplomatic, but I have convinced dragons not to eat villages, made deals with nobles of different countries, befriended princesses, and I can be real convincing sometimes."

Amaryllis pouted, which really didn't suit her.

"But, uh, I'm sure you're really good, too, Amaryllis," I said.

"Oh, stop it," she mumbled. "Let's go say hello to the sentient rock."

I shared a look with Awen, and we both giggled quietly before following Amaryllis.

The tower was pretty impressive from the ground, an imposing brick pillar that rose up twice as tall as the *Beaver*, balloon and all. The bricks around it were shaved on the outside, giving the tower a smooth look, at least where they weren't bulging out a little.

The closer I got, the more I noticed the cracks and broken sections of the tower. For all that it was very impressively built, it was less-impressively maintained.

"Where's the door?" I asked.

"There's an opening there," Awen said as she pointed to the side. "I saw it on the way down."

We walked around the base, giving the tower a fair amount of distance, in case some bit of it chose that moment to come tumbling down to bonk one of us on the head. When we reached the door, we all paused, no one taking the first step.

"Whelp, nothing for it!" I cheered as I bounced ahead. The door was a solid plank of wood, with some iron bracing it giving it strength.

I knocked, of course.

"Hello! My name is Broccoli, and I'm here with some friends. Is anyone home?"

There was a long moment of silence before a bong like someone firing a rifle at a gong sounded out. "Who are you?"

I folded my bun ears way back, shielding them from the noise. "Uh, hi! I'm Broccoli, Broccoli Bunch. Captain of the *Beaver Cleaver*. These are my friends." I gestured behind me, assuming that the cry who had spoken could see up somewhat.

Amaryllis caught on first and stepped up with a slight bow. She presented herself, then Awen did the same, and finally Bastion.

Moonie hovered closer to the tower, and even though the cry was expressionless, I could feel some trepidation bleeding off them. "Greetings, great one. I am Shard of Mountaintopper's Growth, Fourth Split and Not Yet Whole. We come in peace, to share our song."

Stepping back, I shared Moonie's words with the others.

"Can you understand the . . . tower as well?" Amaryllis asked.

"It's a bit loud, but yeah," I replied.

On cue, the tower chimed again. "I am Towerhidden."

No elaborate name, and no mention of titles and shards. Maybe that was because it had a proper name?

Moonie seemed reluctant to speak, so I grinned up to the tower and tried to look as friendly as I could manage with my neck straining back. "It's a pleasure to meet you, Towerhidden. You have a very nice tower. Is it your home?"

"It is," Towerhidden replied. The pride in their voice was obvious and also very loud. I stumbled back, then worked my jaw to stop the ringing.

"Cool, cool. Um. We came here to bring Moonie to safety. They're a cry from the Crying Mountains who are being chased by other, much ruder cry."

"And what crime did they commit?"

I glanced at Moonie, looking for a sign that the cry wanted me to answer that for them. Instead, they hovered closer. "We were born broken, too independent. I . . . I am me. Too much so."

"I see. Not an uncommon thing. And the one who helped you escape?"

"Couldn't Moonie escape on their own?" I asked.

"No. They are too weak."

I frowned. That was rude. They might have been right, but it was still rude.

"Shard of Waterwatcher's Compassion, Third Split and One Whole. They saw our plight, and nurtured us in the mountain. When it became clear that we would be unable to grow into a proper cry, they assisted us, bringing me to the Grey Wall, and hiring this soft one and her crew."

"I know of Shard of Waterwatcher's Compassion, Third Split and One Whole. They have brought many to this island."

"And no one is stopping them?" I asked.

Moonie shook from side to side. "It is their compassion that leads them to act that way. Though they are only just whole, they are acting upon their progenitor's instinct to protect and save. No cry can fault them, even if they disagree."

That was . . . Well, it was weird. The cry really didn't think the way a human would.

"I suppose I only have to welcome you to the Lonely Island, then. It is a quiet place on most days. The monocorns graze to the north, and to the north and west is a small settlement of soft ones. Perhaps, if you wish, you may station yourself there to grow. They can be quite agreeable."

Moonie shifted. "I . . . I do like soft ones. Perhaps I will. Thank you for the welcome, Towerhidden."

Was that it? Moonie didn't need to eat, and they didn't need clothes, so were we just going to leave them here?

"I must know. Were you followed on your way here?" Towerhidden asked.

"Just out of the Grey Wall," I said. "Some cry in rocket-powered planes attacked us. Other than that, though, no, I don't think we were followed."

"You may want to reconsider that."

I spun around and looked to the south, ears bouncing back up straight as I squinted at the horizon and looked for . . . anything, really. There were some clouds, but nothing visible. "I can't see anything."

"See what?" Bastion asked as he turned.

"Towerhidden implied that we were followed."

"My sight is greater than your own, soft one," Towerhidden chimed in. "There are ships coming, three of them."

"What do they look like?" I asked.

"I do not know much of the ships small ones use, but they are trailing great gouts of black smoke."

"Rocket-powered airships?" I asked. That sounded . . . really terrible.

"We should go," Bastion said.

"Right," I said. "Uh, this feels wrong, just leaving."

Moonie bobbed up and down, then paused. "Would . . . would I be asking too much to come with you? Only as far as the settlement to the north? Perhaps if I am seen leaving the ship, they will not chase you."

"I can assist," Towerhidden said. "I do not want my location being divulged, but I can still assist. Reach Mistrust, and you will find aid waiting for you."

"Mistrust?" I asked.

"The town of soft ones to the north. Go. I don't wish the shards from the Crying Mountains around my tower."

I looked at my friends, then gestured to the *Beaver*. "We should get going."

"One moment," Towerhidden said. "Shard of Mountaintopper's Growth, Fourth Split and Not Yet Whole, I have something which I wish to give you. A missive to be passed on."

I gestured for my friends to go. I could catch up. And I sorta wanted to snoop into the tower while I was here.

I didn't get to see much. The door opened, and within was a cavern-like space, lined with bluish crystals that reflected light from every direction like an unmoving kaleidoscope. Moonie moved in, and I heard the tower hum and chime, but I couldn't understand anything for a moment. Just as quickly as they'd entered, Moonie was out with a scroll, of all things, hovering next to them.

"Got everything?"

"I do," Moonie said.

"Neat! Bye, Towerhidden! I'd give you a goodbye hug, but I don't have time to go all the way around and hug you equally."

"I fail to understand."

"That's okay too," I said. Poor Towerhidden. Didn't know what he was missing. "Stay safe!"

I sprinted back to the *Beaver*. The crew, my friends, were already running around and getting the airship ready to take off.

Hopefully, this next stretch of the adventure wouldn't hurt our ship any more than it had been already. I hopped a few times, then bounced up and onto the deck. "All right, everyone! Let's get ready to set sail!"

"That's what we're doing, you unobservant dolt," Amaryllis said.

"Oh, right."

· Chapter Thirty-Four ·

They're Going the Distance!

The *Beaver* was, in my humble and ill-informed opinion, the best ship. We were making good time, sailing across the Lonely Island. Clive set the engine to a speed that wasn't so fast we'd need to worry about overheating in the long run, but was still much faster than usual. It strained the ship a little, but I knew the *Beaver* could handle it just fine.

That was, if the ships behind us didn't catch up.

I stood on the aft castle at the rear, eyes straining to make out the tiny pinpricks way out in the distance. Towerhidden had to have good eyes. Or maybe . . . Well, they were a giant eyeless crystal, so whatever they used for seeing had to be good. I couldn't see anything but three faint pinpricks.

"Ah, Broccoli?" Awen asked as she climbed up the steps to join me.

I half turned and grinned at her. "Hey! I'm trying to see the baddies before they get to us. Not that they're necessarily baddies. I guess just . . . hmm, misunderstood? At a cultural crossroads with our own way of thinking and our current goals?"

Awen giggled. "I think it's okay to call them baddies."

"I don't know. You start calling people baddies, and the next thing you know, whatever they do, you see in a bad light. It's a great way to listen less."

"Well, maybe if you could see them better, that wouldn't be a problem," Awen said. She eyed the deck, then pulled her hands out from behind the small of her back. "Here."

She was holding up a tube. A cylinder of what looked like worked brass, with some sort of guiding rod on one side with little screws next to it, the sort that ended in knobs. It was about the size of a soda can but looked like it could expand.

"Is that a telescope?" I asked.

Awen nodded. "It's a spyglass. It's not perfect—the focus is a bit hard to handle, and the adjustments are fiddly, but, well . . . I hope you like it?"

She pushed it toward me, so I grabbed it, then I grabbed Awen and gave her the best thank-you hug I could manage. "This is so cool!" I cheered. "Thank you!"

Awen laughed. "You're welcome!"

I pulled back and immediately brought the spyglass up—calling it a spyglass was also way cooler—and I tried to sight it on the ships in the distance. I had to extend it, of course, which made a satisfying *clunk* sound. Awen was right; the spyglass was a bit fiddly, but I figured it out and was able to make out the three ships following us in much greater detail.

All three of them were much bigger than the *Beaver*. Or at least, they were wider. They each had a long, flattened balloon, likely to keep it a little bit more aerodynamic, and their entire foresection was thin and wide. There couldn't be any space for rooms beneath. Black smoke trailed out behind them, and they approached with a distant roar that sent cold shivers from my nape to the base of my tail.

Maybe that made sense, if cry didn't need sleeping quarters and food. Rooms to handle that stuff would all be wasted space, so their airships just didn't have anything like that.

Instead, they had what looked like large ballistae on their front deck.

"That looks like trouble," I said.

"May I?" Awen asked.

I passed her the spyglass, and she looked through it, then adjusted it a tiny bit. "Oh, those look dangerous."

"And the cry onboard can probably do the laser thing."

Awen passed the spyglass back, and I glanced through it again. Either she'd adjusted it better, or the cry ships were a whole lot closer. The image was much clearer, which didn't inspire much confidence.

"I don't want to have to fight them," I said.

"I don't think it'll come to that," Awen said. "At least, I hope not. I only have a dozen good bolts left and a bunch of plain ones. Those ships look more dangerous than what we can take on. Maybe if there was only one?"

"I can't think of a way to split them up," I admitted. And even just one would probably be enough to cause all sorts of trouble.

"You'll figure something out."

"Yeah," I replied. I hoped that she was right.

Turning, I collapsed the spyglass, then looked for a place to stow it. My bandoleer had one pouch that was just big enough, so I emptied the emergency tea I had in it and tucked the telescope away.

"Clive!" I called as I walked closer to the harpy pilot. "Is there anything we can do to move faster?"

"Unless we do some downright dangerous things to our engine, I don't think so," Clive said. "Are they catching up?"

"They are," I said. "And they look like they're way better armed than we are. I think we could take one of them on, but not all three."

"Aye, I understand, Captain," Clive said. "I don't know how reasonable they are."

"What do you mean?"

Clive rubbed a talon under his chin. "Pirates often want the booty aboard a ship more than they want the crew dead. It's bad form to steal but far worse form to kill for things. A captain ought to know when to surrender their cargo to keep the crew safe and hale, but I don't think they're after any cargo."

I chewed on my lower lip. They were after Moonie.

Surrendering the cry wasn't an option, of course. That would be just so mean. At the same time, we couldn't fight back well enough to scare them off.

"I don't know what to do."

Clive reached down and pushed the throttle up just a pinch. The engine roared a tiny bit louder. "We'll get you a bit more time," he said.

I nodded. "Thanks, Clive. Awen! Can you check on the engine, make sure it's still running fine?"

"Aye, aye, Broccoli!" Awen said before running off.

"There's a town ahead!" Joe called from the front of the ship.

I ran over, leaning against one of the *Beaver*'s figureheads to see out ahead. Joe was right; there was a town. Nothing too big. Maybe something between Insmouth and Needleford in size. Not a town, but not quite a city yet. No port that I could see, and a lot of trees all around it.

I tugged out my spyglass again and squeezed an eye shut to take in the town in more detail.

The houses looked like they'd all been built by one of two people. Some were squat stone buildings, others were much taller and made of wood. They at least shared the same roofing material. It made sense—if both cervids and sylphs had joined up here, then they'd both build homes in the way that they were most comfortable with.

Then I noticed the towers in the center of the town. Some five of them, with familiar bright blue dots around them that could only be more cry.

"Right, I need Moonie," I said.

I had something of a plan and not very much time to implement it.

Awen, Amaryllis, and Bastion soon joined me, along with a pile of tarp. When I was done explaining my idea, the three of them looked skeptical but not altogether doubtful. I figured that meant we had a good chance of succeeding.

"It's stupid," Amaryllis said. "But it's the kind of stupid that might work."

"I'll do my best," Awen said. "But there's really not much time."

I nodded, understanding. "Your best is all I can ask for, Awen, and as for the other part, that's only if Moonie agrees."

Which meant explaining things to the cry in question. I left my friends above, where Amaryllis recruited the Scallywags to help her with her part of the plan, then ran down to the deck below. Moonie was hovering in the dining room, a book floating before them.

"Hey," I said.

"Hello, Captain."

"So, we have a plan. It's not a very good one, but it's better than nothing. How good are you at hovering?"

"I am capable enough," Moonie said. "Though it depends on the circumstances."

"And if the circumstances are jumping off the side of the *Beaver* to land in the middle of a town?"

"We . . . might not be that capable. We can slow down a fall, certainly, but we need something to push off and to orient ourselves with. A more whole shard would be able to hold in place, though at the cost of great mana. As is, we can hover here by anchoring ourselves to the room. It takes less mana than we naturally regenerate."

"Okay," I said. "Next question: Do you know what a parachute is?"

"No?"

"Well then! I think you're about to find out!"

We returned to the top deck to find Awen sitting on the ground with a bunch of tools laid out around her. She had a few tubes and more items that looked like a jumble of rods held together with wire and a few screws.

"Ah, Moonie, I need your help," Awen said as she bounced to her feet. "Can you fire a laser out? What's the range of your laser attacks?"

"The range is limited based on the amount of mana used," Moonie said. "The more I use, the farther it goes, but even then, the beam will dissipate after some distance."

"Lightning magic does the same," Amaryllis said. "It's only partially natural, and the attack will either ground itself or fizzle out once it's outside the caster's range of control."

Awen nodded. "Can you fire a normal attack? Just into the air."

Moonie bobbed up and down, then I felt a faint stirring in the air, and a reddish beam lanced out. It traveled a good fifty or so meters before it sort of faded away, losing its color and becoming a blur in the air that went on for a little ways longer.

"So that's why they're not shooting at us now," I said.

"Long-range magic is complicated," Amaryllis said. "And mana intensive. Spells that are held together without contact with the caster can travel much farther. A fireball will outrange a beam-like attack nine times out of ten."

"Huh," I said. I wondered what that meant for ship-to-ship combat and the like. Fireballs weren't that fast, after all. Maybe that was why ballistae were preferred over hiring a good mage.

"Can you try with this?" Awen asked as she raised her tinkered-up device to Moonie. It was basically three glass discs held in place with three metal rods that had holes cut into them and screws fitted through those. "This is Broccoli's idea, but I think it might work."

Moonie's magic grabbed onto the focus and spun it around. "What do I do with this?" they asked.

"Shoot the laser through it," I said.

The cry aimed the device toward the empty sky and fired.

The beam scattered, traveling all of a meter as a wide, unfocused burst.

"Ah, let me see that," Awen said. She tugged out one of the bits of glass with a few twists of a screw, then frowned before a new disc formed over her palm, and she tucked it in. "Try with this."

Moonie fired again, and this time the beam was a lot tighter, though it did fire off at an angle. Still, I guesstimated that it had traveled quite a bit farther. "I think it's working," I said.

"I'll calibrate it some more," Awen said. "We don't have a lot of time to figure out what's optimal, though, and I have to make a bunch of these."

I patted her on the back. "Do what you can," I said before jumping over to where Amaryllis was trying to direct the Scallywags. The parachute they were making looked . . . somewhat functional. A bunch of cords connected to a round-cut sailcloth with a little hole in its middle. The cords converged on a rope harness that Oda was stringing together with surprising ease.

"This thing looks like a mess," Amaryllis said. "I understand the principle of it, but still."

"Moonie can mostly slow themselves down, I think," I said. "This just needs to slow them down a little more than that. It's aiming them toward the center of town that'll be tricky."

"This plan is stupid. I have said that, right?"

"You did," I replied, "but maybe it'll work!"

"Humph," she said. "We'll see."

· Chapter Thirty-Five ·

Cry "Havoc!" and Let Slip the Lasers of War

The *Beaver* swooped toward the town, like a whale plunging down to nibble at some plankton.

"All sails!" Clive called out, and—across both decks—a bunch of us tugged back on ropes at the same time. All around the Beaver, the ship's sails unfurled fully, snapping in the wind and slowing the *Beaver* down enough that I suddenly felt a lot heavier, as if I were on an elevator shooting up.

"Moonie! This is it," I shouted. We were only a couple of hundred meters above the town, the pretty cry towers in the center looming closer. I squinted and could make out the bobbing blue forms of at least a dozen cry.

"Take care, everyone," Moonie said as they hovered by the edge of the deck. They had our makeshift parachute held in a telekinetic grip, and around them was a satchel filled with the tubes Awen had jury-rigged. "You were enjoyable companions and fair friends. Thank you."

I grinned. "Thank you too! It was a pleasure having you aboard the *Beaver Cleaver.*"

Moonie bobbed up and down one final time, then they slid off the side of the ship while we cheered them on.

"I hope they remember your half-baked plan," Amaryllis said.

"It's an excellent plan," I countered before half turning to Clive. "Let's get some altitude!"

"Aye, aye," Clive said. He pulled a lever back and, as planned, let the engine slow down, so that we were flying mostly on momentum and what speed we could get from the engine idling. The wind, at least, was in our favor.

Seeing as how there wasn't much to do but wait, I hung off the side of the *Beaver* and looked down.

The parachute was working. I could make out the big, roundish tarp floating down a ways behind us. Moonie must have been using their hovering ability to aim it, because it seemed to be heading toward the five towers in the center of town. Some of the cry hovering around there were grouping up, maybe curious about their new air-dropped friend.

"It'll be fine," Bastion said.

"You think?"

"The cry after us must have seen Moonie dropping. They'll want to slow down if their goal is to recapture them. We're no longer their target."

"But Moonie is, and we basically just threw them overboard."

"We threw them into the hands of allies more capable of protecting them," Bastion said. He patted me on the shoulder. "You're a good person, Broccoli, and a surprisingly competent captain and leader, but you still lack a bit of experience. It can be hard for an officer to learn that sometimes things are beyond your control."

"I know that," I said, and if I was pouting as I said it, Bastion didn't comment. "It just feels wrong."

Amaryllis moved over, looking fairly smug, or at least more smug than usual. "Moonie's landed," she said. "I think she's handing out Awen's little telescope devices."

"Really?" I asked. A glance over the edge revealed that Amaryllis was right, at least as far as I could tell. We'd moved past the edge of the town already, and it was hard to make out details from so far away. "Great! Clive, circle us around!"

Clive nodded and, with a spin of the helm, set the *Beaver* to making a big, wide turn. We'd be drawing huge circles in the sky by the edge of the town soon enough.

"We could just keep going," Amaryllis said. "In fact, that's very much what we should be doing."

"I . . . maybe, but I want to see how things play themselves out."

Amaryllis shook her head, but she didn't protest any more than that.

I watched, biting my lower lip, as the distant cry airships became not so distant. On the ground, the cry were starting to hover back up around their towers, and I saw parts of those towers being moved aside to reveal the crystalline blue of large cry within. More cry like Towerhidden, then.

The three cry ships split apart, two of them veering off toward our right, the third our left.

A bell tolled in the town below, and I felt a pit in my tummy as I saw people running around in a panic. We had scared so many of them. Or, well, we had brought the things scaring them with us. Same difference, I figured.

One of the airships fired ahead, a thick red beam that zipped down toward the base of the towers only to be met by a shield wall.

And then the cry on the ground fired back.

It was easy to tell who had Awen's new toys. Those beams were tighter and faster, while the more normal ones tended to dissipate in midair.

I gasped as a few beams raked across the underside of one airship, leaving blackened lines behind on the wood.

The airships circled the town, beams lancing toward the towers and being met with hastily thrown shields.

And then the towers opened fire.

The magical lasers they shot out were nothing like the little beams from the small cry. They were as thick around as I was tall, ears and all, and when they shot past, it was with a roar that made the air vibrate.

Shields sprung up around the cry airships, gigantic crystalline snowflakes that instantly went from a pure, bright blue to a darkening purple as the beams struck them. They reddened more and more, and even from afar I could see the clouds of superheated air wavering off the shields.

Then one of them broke, and the airship in the lead juked violently to the side as a laser rammed into its prow.

The five beams from the five towers stopped, the air stilling once more with a quiet that was somehow louder than the attack itself had been.

The foremost cry airship had a hole in its prow that cut a tunnel all the way through to its opposite side, the edged blackened and smoking. It was still able to fly, though, and as it demonstrated a moment later, it was able to fire back.

"This is awful," I said.

"Yeah," Amaryllis agreed simply.

Another volley of lasers was exchanged, with a few burns left in the stone walls of the towers below, but it was the airships that suffered the most. The burns across their hulls caught fire in a few spots, and the lead ship's engine seemed to explode as something important was hit.

Rocket-powered airships required rocket fuel to work. It seemed like a terrible idea all of a sudden.

Fortunately, the ship's forward momentum carried it out past the edge of the town, where it plowed through the top of a hill before skidding to a flaming stop.

The other airships relit their engines and regained some speed, but not before the towers returned fire again. The leftmost ship wasn't prepared for it, a thick beam slicing across its balloon before cutting into its deck and burning a line across the side of the ship from top to bottom.

The balloon, torn nearly entirely in half, spewed out gas into the sky even as it started to spin around.

I would have called it a victory, only the ship was veering toward the *Beaver*.

"Clive!" I screamed.

The old harpy took one glance at the ships, then spun the wheel around and slammed the gas lever up to full. The *Beaver* turned sharply away from the town and the falling cry ship, our boost of speed giving us plenty of space to spare even as the falling ship dropped below our current altitude.

And then a trio of beams shot up from the ship's deck and punctured through-and-through our balloon.

"Oh no," I said.

"Captain!" Clive called. "We're losing altitude."

I froze for a moment. We were going to crash? Like that ship?

I imagined my friends being thrown around, the *Beaver* being dashed apart on the ground, wood tearing, and our home being ripped apart.

"Broccoli!" Amaryllis snapped.

I shook my head. "Full power to the grav engine! Clive, slow us down. Awen! See if you can't get the engine to give us more time. Everyone, all sails out! Steve, check the balloon—can we patch those holes?"

I got a chorus of "Aye, aye"s and some "Okay, Broccoli"s, and then I jumped to help my friends.

With all his sails angled to act as parachutes, the *Beaver* was a fair bit slower in the air, and the gravity engine reduced our weight by a whole bunch, but that wasn't enough to stay buoyant.

A glance off the side revealed the ground approaching. Not too quickly, but approaching all the same.

Steve waved at me from across the deck and shook his head. "Clive, we need to land. What are we looking for in a landing space?"

"Something flat," the harpy pilot said.

I rushed to the side and looked for just that, but the town was surrounded by hills and forests. There was room between some patches of trees, but nothing that was even remotely flat.

I glanced back at the town, where the remaining cry airship was retreating with a plume of fire bursting out behind it. It wasn't even returning fire, just focusing on keeping its shields up to weather the angry lasers coming from the ground. I even noticed other magic being flung up. Lightning bolts and fireballs and even the occasional arrow.

The town was flinging everything it had at the cry, and the cry were scampering off as quickly as they could manage.

I wanted to cheer them on, but I had more important things to do, like . . . like noticing that the center of town, where the five towers were, was mostly empty, with a large paved area in the middle of the five towers that could very easily fit a ship the size of the *Beaver*.

"Clive! Near the towers. There's a space in the middle. It's all flat and paved. Can we land there?"

Clive craned his neck to see what I was talking about, then turned the helm, angling us more toward the center of town.

We were still losing altitude when Clive reversed the engine, and we came to a gentle stop in the middle of the towers. We soon dropped under the tops of the towers, all five of them rising around the *Beaver* like the fingers of a stone giant's hands.

"We're dropping a bit faster than I'd like, Captain," Clive said. "We need to lose some mass."

"Weigh the anchors!" I called. Those were pretty heavy already. "And, uh . . . Oh shoot, what else can we do?"

I ran to the side and saw a few cry hovering closer, some of them with Awen's laser foci near them. Laser foci aimed at us.

"Hey!" I called out, an arm waving above me. "We need to slow down more! Can you shield the ground?"

That seemed to do the trick. People who were going to attack or something didn't usually ask for help. At least, I hoped not.

A few cry summoned shields that the *Beaver* rammed into, shattering them a moment later. Still, the heavy lurch of it all did slow us down, even if I worried that it was causing a lot of damage to the keels.

More cry came over, and soon a dozen of them hovered next to the *Beaver*. I wasn't sure what they were doing until I felt us slowing down.

Telekinesis. One cry could lift a bit, so maybe with a dozen of them pushing back together . . .

Then one of the towers glowed from within, and the *Beaver*'s descent slowed down even more.

Carefully, with an almost gentle clunk, our airship touched down.

And then the canvas of our balloon draped itself over all of us.

`Congratulations! Through repeated actions, your Captaining skill has improved and is now eligible for rank up!`

`Rank E is a free rank!`

· Chapter Thirty-Six ·

Islanding

O h, this is heavy," I complained as I pushed the tarp up and off me. The *Beaver*'s balloon was made of a thick, coarse material—I was guessing some sort of canvas that was treated to be a little more airtight and weather-resistant. With a grunt of effort, I climbed to my feet, arms pushing up and tenting the canvas surrounding me so that I could see around the deck. The sunlight, filtered by the cloth, made everything very blue, but that didn't mean I was unable to find Amaryllis pushing and shoving against some of the canvas covering her.

"This . . . this is annoying," she said.

"Well, it's not so bad. At least we landed safely?"

"Oh yes, how wonderful," she griped. "Never going to get anywhere on time now." She seemed to be in something of a foul mood. I couldn't really blame her.

"Come on, let's find the others—make sure everyone is okay. And then I guess we can work on getting this tarp off the top of the ship?"

Amaryllis and I were pushing and shoving our way toward the *Beaver*'s prow when we found the first of our crewmates.

"Oh no," I said.

Orange was on the ground, lying on her side, sprawled across the deck.

I gasped and fell to my knees next to the spirit kitten—who was more of a cat now— and reached out.

On touching her, the cat opened her eyes and glared, a sort of "Why are you waking me up?" glare. "You're not hurt?" I asked. She raised her head into my scritches.

Her tail curled up and back down again, and she let her head fall back onto the deck.

"Okay then."

The section of tarp that I was holding up started to weigh less, and then it floated out of my reach. Standing a bit straighter now that I didn't have a dozen kilos of canvas weighing me down, I looked around and saw all my friends. Everyone seemed mostly fine. Awen poked her head out of a hatch on the other deck, while Clive grabbed the ship's wheel and pulled himself upright.

A dozen hovering cry, more or less equally spaced around the *Beaver Cleaver*, held up the tarp with their combined magic. "Okay," I said. "Everyone, let's gather here! We might need to get off the *Beaver* for a bit."

"That would be wise," a cry chimed.

I turned, then looked up as a cry hovered closer. They were huge, a pillar of crystal as big around as a wagon. They had a slight deformation in their crystal on one side, a large purplish blotch that stood out quite a bit.

"Hi," I said. "My name is Broccoli Bunch, I'm the captain of the *Beaver Cleaver*. It's a pleasure to meet you. Thanks for the help. Not just with the tarp but with slowing us down. I'm glad we didn't crash!"

"We greet you, soft one. We are Shard of the Exiled Pillar's Prudence, First Split and One Whole. We are not the leader of this community but often act as an intermediary between our kind and the local soft ones."

"You're the local diplomat," I said. "That's wonderful! What's this town called?"

"This is the town of Mistrust."

I blinked. "That's not the most cheery name, but okay. I'm sorry that we landed right in the middle of your town. We took a bit more damage than we would have liked, and this was the only flat spot around. Do you know if there are any mechanics or, um, airship engineers in Mistrust?"

"We are not aware of either," Shard of the Exiled Pillar's Prudence, First Split and One Whole said. "In most circumstances, we would be wary of assisting you, but you came escorting a lost shard in need of assistance, and that same shard delivered interesting devices to us. Are you the one that created those?"

"The focusing lenses? No, that was Awen. I just had the initial idea from science class." I glanced around at all the cry silently helping lift the balloons around us. "Maybe . . . maybe we could trade?"

"Trade?"

"Yeah! You seem to like the focusing devices. They were cobbled together in less than an hour. Imagine how much better Awen could make them if we gave her a bit more time? I bet she wouldn't mind making a dozen more. And in exchange, you give us permission to land here, and a bit of a helping hand getting our balloon fixed."

"You plan to leave already?" the cry asked.

"Well, we don't have much of a choice. We're trying to stop a war, and if we don't make it back soon, that could mean a lot of trouble for a lot of people."

"What is the cry saying?" Amaryllis asked.

I translated real fast, and she nodded, then set a talon on my shoulder. "We obviously did not intend to land in your town, though the circumstances of that landing should be taken into account. We came to this island specifically to deliver Shard of Mountaintopper's Growth, Fourth Split and Not Yet Whole. In the carrying out of that duty, we were followed and attacked by cry who I can only presume are your own adversaries."

"The cry from the Crying Mountains are not our adversaries," Shard of the Exiled Pillar's Prudence, First Split and One Whole chimed, pausing for me to translate. "We are exiled from them, broken away, and therefore do not have the standing upon which to declare them enemies. They are within their rights to trespass upon this island."

"Uh," I said. "That . . . okay? I don't get it. You did fight back."

"Just because they have the right to do something, does not mean it is the right thing to do," they explained.

That sounded a little strange to me, but I wasn't quite ready to argue it. "Well, I'm glad you helped. I can't imagine things going well if you had refused to help."

"They were here with ill intent. As for your trade, we are willing to engage with the idea. The location where your ship is stationed is inconvenient, but we understand the reasoning for your landing here."

"Thank you," I said, and I meant it too. The cry were being very nice and super understanding. "We'll try not to stay around for too long."

"We would appreciate that," Shard of the Exiled Pillar's Prudence, First Split and One Whole chimed before backing away.

I turned to my friends and crewmates. No one was injured, which was a great place to start. "Okay, everyone, we're in a bit of trouble, but we can make it out of here. Clive, Steve, Gordon, what can we do about the balloon?"

"Now that we're on solid footing," Clive began, "plenty. If we can purchase some tarp and canvas here, we can fix it up. Better than just a quick patch job too."

"Helium will be an issue," Steve said. "It looks like two of the inner sacs are fine, but that means that six of them were pierced through. Once the balloons are fixed, we'll need to replace the gas."

"And it's unlikely this backwater has any," Amaryllis said. "No airship port, so no refueling or repair stations. There might be an alchemist here, but I doubt they'll have the materials or skills to synthesize helium from empty air."

"Oh, that's not great," I said. "Could we use something else?"

"Hydrogen?" Awen asked. "Ah, but that's . . . not safe."

"Wildly dangerous," Amaryllis said. "If we don't have a choice, we can try that."

I rubbed at my chin. We needed a gas that we couldn't get easily, which . . . wasn't great. "Could we put the *Beaver* on the ocean and sail to Sylphfree?" I asked.

"We . . . that's a dumb idea," Amaryllis said.

"Possibly," Clive replied. "But I wouldn't be keen on it. Not much experience sailing on water, and we'd need to waterproof the hull, add sails, patch some holes up. It would be a lot of work."

"There are some ports in Sylphfree that we could sail to," Bastion said. "But travel by ocean is slow."

"So that's a plan B," I said. "Oh! The other airships!"

"What other airships?" Joe asked. He was standing with the Scallywags, all three of them looking a bit rough-and-tumbled from our little adventure.

"The ones that went down. I think two of them crashed. Their balloons might be intact."

"That could work," Amaryllis said. "If not the balloons themselves, then the sacs within them. And they likely had a few tanks of helium onboard."

"We don't have any?" I asked.

"Two of them, but each can only refill one sac," Awen said. "And we've used up a bit to make up for the losses last time."

I nodded. "Okay, we'll do this in two parts. One group can go out and try to scavenge things. Another stays here to guard the *Beaver* and repair our balloon." I glanced around, at all the cry still holding things up above us. "We can't ask the cry to help up all day long, that wouldn't be fair. Awen, I . . . may have promised that you'd help the cry make more of those foci."

"I don't mind," Awen said. "I might need more materials to make them, though, and maybe some tools that I don't have."

"Then we'll talk with Shard of the Exiled Pillar's Prudence, First Split and One Whole together. I'm sure they can arrange for us to get you set up to make them as quick as possible."

"How do you want to divide things?" Bastion asked.

I rubbed at my chin. "Gordon, can you come with us to salvage things? And . . . maybe Oda and Sally too? Steve, Clive, and Joe can stay here to fix the tarps. Bastion, if you don't mind coming with us, that would be nice."

"Certainly," Bastion said.

"And myself?" Amaryllis asked.

"Come with me? We might need to negotiate things with the town's people. You're better at prices and things than I am."

"Very well," she said. "We should get a move on. We're likely to lose half a day to this already. I don't want to turn that into two."

"You're right," I said. The passing of time was already weighing on me a little. It wouldn't do for our first introduction to our new sylph friends to be arriving late. "Okay, does anyone have any ideas that we could use?"

Oda raised a hand. "We could get some help from the locals. They might have some mechanics, even if they're not airship mechanics."

"That's not a bad idea," I said. "We might meet some people, so I'll try to make some friends."

"This is a penal colony," Bastion said. "Or at least, a town built by prisoners and exiles. Keep sharp—they might not be as friendly as you'd wish."

I nodded, though it was a bit of a reluctant nod. "Okay. Anything else?" No one seemed to have anything to say, so I clapped my hands together. "All right! Then let's get started! We have a whole bunch of work to get done, but I'm sure we'll manage."

"Aye, aye," Clive said. He stepped back, then directed the others to get to work right away.

I wasn't going to belittle his hard work by not giving it my all too. "Okay, let's get down. We need to find out where the ships crashed, and if there are any cry around the landing zones. I guess that the local cry might want to help with that."

"Do they even take prisoners?" Amaryllis asked.

"I . . . guess? I don't know. Maybe they'll just kick them out and let them fly back home under their own power. I guess it's a little bit out of our hands." I'd interfere to stop anything too bad from happening, but the cry had kinda-sorta attacked the town, so I figured whatever passed for police around here would be interested in capturing them at least.

"Don't worry," Amaryllis said. "We'll be back in the air in no time."

· Chapter Thirty-Seven ·

A Tale of Two Prison Colonies

Things didn't exactly go as easily as I may have wanted.

For one thing, I'd thought most of the work we'd have to do would be around the crashed ship. I kind of expected to be able to reach the ship first.

I hadn't foreseen that our path would be blocked by not one but two bands of townsfolk.

To the right was a group of cervids. They had leather barding and some cloth over their backs and wrapped around their front. Tassels hung from the men's antlers, and the women wore more elaborate clothes, dyed and decorated with little beads.

To the left was a group of sylphs. They had clothes made of similar materials, and they seemed to be centered around a sylph woman in an elegant set of robes.

Neither group looked all that happy to see us.

I took a deep breath, then stepped up. "Hello! I'm Broccoli, Broccoli Bunch! I hope we can all be friends!"

The two groups eyed each other, and two of them stepped up. One of the cervid men, with a particularly impressive set of antlers, and the sylph woman in the robes.

"I am Kevin Marques, mayor of Mistrust," the cervid said.

The sylph woman stepped up to his side with a dignified huff. "I am Celia Fallfront, mayor of Mistrust."

I blinked. "The town has two mayors?"

"It does," Mayor Marques said. "It is the most effective way of getting things done here, or so we've found. Mistrust might not be the grandest or richest place, but we do well for ourselves, at least when ships aren't crashing down onto our fair town."

That last bit sounded very pointedly aimed at us.

I winced. "Was anyone hurt?"

"No," Mayor Fallfront said. "But it was a near thing. A house was set aflame on the edge of town, and one of the ships that fell landed in a farmer's lot."

I gasped. "Someone lost their home?"

"Nearly. We put out the flames before anyone was hurt, but the damage was done," Mayor Marques said. "Which leaves only the matter of reparations."

I was about to tell them that we'd gladly pay, when a taloned hand grabbed my shoulder and tugged me back a step. "Let me," Amaryllis said. "Mayor, and Mayor, I am not the keenest harpy that has ever hatched, but I can put two and two together when it suits me. What's the meaning of this ambush?"

"Ambush?" I repeated.

We were right on the edge of the circle created by the five cry towers. A bit of greenery was around them, maybe a dozen or so meters of cleared space, with a few trees and some bushes. Circling that was a beaten-dirt road that split off every which way into the town proper. We were still right on the edge of that little strip of park.

"They were waiting for us to show up. This looks like one of the only paths out of the area—or at least one of the paths onto the main road dividing the town. My concern is more about *why* they're trying to ambush us."

The sylph mayor harrumphed. "We are hardly trying to ambush you. We are merely guarding our peaceful town. Your arrival has caused quite the stir and disrupted an otherwise ordinary day."

"We're sorry," I said. "We were tasked with delivering a cry to the Lonely Island. We didn't know that we'd be followed or that the cry would attack us with airships."

"So you're trying to deflect blame?" Mayor Fallfront asked.

"Not at all," Bastion said from right behind me. He stepped around me and came to stand by my side. "The captain was merely informing you of what happened."

Mayor Fallfront stood a little taller as she took in Bastion. "A paladin?"

"Yes."

I glanced between the two, then sighed. "This is all very tense. I think we might have started on the wrong foot. My crew and I were trying to help someone when we were attacked. We didn't mean to cause trouble in your town, and we're sorry that we did. If there's anything we can do to help you, then tell us. I'm sure we can negotiate."

"That's a fair approach," Mayor Marques said when the other mayor failed to say anything. She was too busy staring at Bastion without any expression on her face. "To be perfectly fair, I don't think the damages to the town are that extensive. Perhaps a small remuneration would suffice?"

"Like silver and gold?" I asked.

"No, no, we have little use for currency here," he said. "We can't exactly travel to the mainland to spend it. Perhaps food? Seeds would be valuable, as well as any materials that are difficult to find on the Lonely Island."

"That sounds fair," I said.

I glanced at Amaryllis, who shrugged. "It doesn't seem like that bad of an idea to barter. We have some surplus equipment, I think. And we need materials for repairs."

I nodded. "That's why we're here," I said. "We're going to salvage from the two airships that crashed around the town. They have a few things we need."

Mayor Fallfront snapped out of whatever had her staying quiet. "Those fell within the boundaries of Mistrust. They, by all rights, should be ours."

"What would you use them for?" I asked.

"Why, to leave this place, perhaps?" the mayor tried. "Or merely for parts. What we use them for doesn't matter—they belong to us."

"The cry are the ones who brought them down," Bastion pointed out.

"Then they can claim them if they wish. I doubt it, though."

Amaryllis sighed. "You're going to have us bargain for every piece we take, aren't you?"

"I suppose that would depend entirely on what you take. Mistrust has a smithy and some very talented carpenters," Mayor Marques said.

I wasn't sure what to think of our strange reception. They could have been a lot worse. As it was, they didn't feel . . . friendly, exactly, but they weren't mean either. They felt more greedy than anything else.

That wasn't the best, but it was better than being hostile. "Amaryllis, do you think you could handle the negotiation part? We should get to the ship sooner than later, especially if we want to see what's worth taking."

"Yeah, that's fair," Amaryllis said. She smiled, and it was the kind of smile I'd expect to see on a hawk that'd stumbled across an injured bunny. "I'll be sure to get us a good deal."

"Let's all stick close," Bastion muttered, low enough that I only just caught it with all four ears peeled.

I nodded and stepped forward. "So, Mayors, could someone maybe guide us to the crashed ships? If we need any additional materials, then I'm sure we could negotiate for them once we know what we need."

Everyone seemed to think that that was perfectly reasonable, so off we went.

Mistrust was a sprawling town. The homes were built with yards around them, some with gardens and others surrounded by trees. It was actually hard to see how big the town was from ground level. The cervid homes tended to be larger, but they didn't have second stories to them most of the time. The doors were also scaled up in size. The sylph homes for their part were more like minitowers, tall and thin, with as much space around them as they could manage, and they frequently had balconies around their upper floors.

What was most interesting were the hybrid homes: short, fat towers, with big doors and ramps around the outside.

"Do the two groups here live together?" I asked the mayors.

Mayor Marques hummed, his head tilting back a bit. It was rather imposing to have someone so tall nearby. He was taller than Emmanuel had been, with much bigger antlers. "Once, we both settled in this area as two camps. We both had something the other needed, so an alliance was formed, though it was initially tenuous."

"But it's better now?"

"Oh, certainly. We had two mayors because we were two towns. But some folk trusted others, and the settlements grew closer. The cry were here long before us, of course, and their towers became the center of our community."

"That's so cool," I said. "But if you're just one town now, why are there two mayors still?"

"Some issues are unique to either cervids or sylphs, and while we have grown closer, we are not all in agreement about everything, so rather than elect one leader, we have two."

I nodded. "That's kinda cool. I like it. People getting along is something I can get behind."

"Does the town have difficulties, what with the population being made up nearly entirely of convicts?" Bastion asked.

The mayors both sniffed. "I'll have you know," Mayor Fallfront said, "that most of the population here are the children of those originally exiled. Or their children's children. The vast majority of the convicts here are, or were, nonviolent. Oh, we have a few thieves, but everyone knows who they are, and when something goes missing we know who to poke at to get it back. We don't abide the dangerous sort of criminal. Mostly, we have people who disagreed with how things were being done—in Sylphfree or the Trenten Flats."

I gestured to Bastion to drop the subject. We didn't need to antagonize the townsfolk. I figured most of us were safe, but Bastion's job was literally the sort of job that might lead to him arresting some of the people that were here.

"Ah, there it is," the cervid mayor said.

The first of the two crashed cry airships was slumped before us, its hull leaning up against a few trees. The engine at the back looked like it had burned itself out, but not before leaving a blackened streak across the grass.

The ship was rather barge-like from up close, without much depth to its keel. The sails were torn and shredded, likely when the airship crashed through the bit of forest around us.

"Is it safe to go aboard?" I asked.

"Probably not," Amaryllis said as she moved past me. "But it still has some balloons."

She was right. A big chunk of the ship's balloons was still left, though it had torn open in a few spots and looked like a plastic grocery bag that had spent some time as a kitten's chew toy.

"Right! Okay. Let's see what we can do with those remaining helium sacs. And, uh, are there any cry crew left on it?"

"No," Mayor Marques said. "A couple of cry were seen flying away from it before anyone from town came to inspect this one. The local cry poked at it too. I think they found one cry stuck in the frame of the other ship that they took with them."

"Oh," I said. That was good to know.

I was a bit surprised when Oda stepped up next to me, then wiped at his whiskery teenager mustache. "That engine looks dangerous. I don't know how rockets work, but it was giving off a whole trail of flame earlier."

"So we take our time, and we make sure to be careful," I said.

"What do you plan on taking here?" Mayor Marques asked.

"Mostly the balloons," I said. "Ours were perforated, so we need more helium. Maybe they have some tanks of that here, but I don't know. We could use some of the tarp that the sacs are made of too."

"Ah," he said. "Well, that sounds like a rare and valuable resource, then."

Amaryllis sighed. "Broccoli, go take care of overseeing things. I'll handle the mayors."

"All right," I said. Amaryllis really was the best at negotiating that among us. I'd just do my part to help gather the things we'd need to get the *Beaver* back in the air.

· Chapter Thirty-Eight ·

Sanity Check

The work of getting the *Beaver* fixed and ready for flight was tough, but not impossibly so. We found two intact helium sacs in the first cry airship and one in the second. They were considerably smaller than the sacs the *Beaver Cleaver* had, but Amaryllis and Awen did a bit of math together and figured that they'd be enough, if just barely.

The better news was the intact helium tank aboard one of the ships. It was a big brass cylinder that took two people to lift, but we managed, especially as some of the townsfolk from Mistrust didn't seem to mind giving us a hand. Initially, they weren't super open to helping us, but they were quite neighborly after we proved we didn't intend to cause any trouble.

Amaryllis seemed fairly pleased with her negotiations. We were going to lose a lot of the produce we had. As it turned out, Mistrust lacked some very basic things, and the mayors were both interested in getting all the potatoes and turnips and onions we had in our pantry, even those that had started to sprout buds.

The town would soon have more vegetables to eat, which seemed to excite them a lot. When I asked Mayor Marques about it, he said that they had a few local crops for their gardens, but not many. Mostly carrots and some local plants they'd discovered were edible.

By the time noon rolled around, we had all the new balloons mounted within the tarp of the *Beaver Cleaver*'s original balloon. With one of the burst sacs repaired and refilled, the *Beaver* was slowly regaining some of its buoyancy.

It would be a bit of a rough flight, though, with us relying on our gravity generator to reduce our weight. Awen was in the engine room monitoring the machinery while some of our other mechanically inclined crewmates scurried over the ship and patched things up. It wouldn't do for a bad bit of sewing to open up a tear.

"Your crew is quite competent," Mayor Fallfront said as she came to stand next to me.

I grinned and nodded. "We have some of the very best," I said. "Maybe not the most experienced, but they're all people I'd consider friends, and that's important."

"Hmm. Where will you be flying next? Not somewhere too distant, I imagine?"

"Sylphfree," I said. "It's not too far now, and we're late to arrive already. I think we'll make it, though."

The mayor hummed again, then looked at me critically. "You might want to be careful. Sylphfree is a beautiful nation, with some excellent people. Smart, talented people, but they value certain virtues more than others. Propriety is greater than kindness in the eyes of many a sylph."

"Oh," I said. That wasn't great. She didn't seem to want to explain much more than that, though, and soon returned to the other mayor. The town was organizing things so that their best gardeners would get some samples from our pantry. Amaryllis had also traded away a bunch of other foodstuffs, things they couldn't get here. Flour and grains and other similar things. I think they were hoping to find some seeds they could plant too.

We ended up meeting mostly outside. I slapped together some sandwiches with what we had left—we really would need to restock soon—and handed them out to everyone in the crew.

By the time the sun was clearly starting to dip, we were just about done fixing up the *Beaver* as best we could.

The detour to the Lonely Island had cost us about a day, I figured. Maybe a tiny bit less since we had flown as fast as we could after the Grey Wall, as opposed to just taking our time.

Still, it was my responsibility as the captain to avoid us being even later to our appointment. I didn't regret the fun we'd had, or the great adventures helping people who needed helping, but it was still my fault that we'd be late.

As we were packing things away and picking up the tools that had gotten scattered around, I noticed a familiar cry hovering closer. "Moonie!"

"Hello," Moonie said. "We wanted to greet you one last time before you took off again."

I grinned and bounced over to the cry to give it a quick, tight hug. "It's nice of you to come say bye. Did you make any new friends?"

"We are . . . uncertain if we have made friends, but we have certainly met new and interesting cry. This place is better than we had imagined or hoped for. There are still many things to do, and the cry who are here are very different from the cry we know, and even more different from each other."

"That sounds nice," I said. "You get to meet not just new people but strange new people."

"We have!" Moonie spun around, and while I wasn't an expert at reading cry body language, I figured that was a good sign they were happy.

We chatted, just for a little bit, but it was obvious that Moonie was excited to return to their new friends, and I had a lot of work ahead of me too.

It was hard, being all responsible and stuff.

Once everyone was back aboard the *Beaver* and the sails were tucked in, I turned to Clive behind the wheel and nodded. "All right, bring him up."

The engine rumbled to life, and I felt the ship shifting before we started to rise. The crew cheered. Well, it was mostly just me, but technically I was part of the crew too.

It was slow, no faster than I could walk, but we were moving upward, the ground dropping below and the cry towers sliding past. The wind picked up a little, and set us to rocking, but with Clive at the helm, we managed to stay right in the middle until we cleared the tops of the towers.

"Clive, full speed ahead! We have some catching up to do!"

"Aye, aye, Captain!"

We deployed the *Beaver*'s sails, spun up the propeller at the back, and shot forward over forests and rivers and hilly landscapes. We were heading north, to the next leg of our adventure and, hopefully, to Sylphfree where, if everything worked out, we'd be able to stop a war.

I stood on the foredeck, eyes peeled and ears straight despite the wind battering them down every so often. I was expecting someone to come up and talk. The excitement had died down a little, and there wasn't all that terribly much to do on the *Beaver* when we were just sailing peacefully along. I wasn't expecting the friend to come up to me to be Joe.

I hadn't been spending all that much time with the Scallywags.

That was probably a bit weird. We were on the same ship, and we had breakfast, lunch, and supper together every day. But still, all three of them tended to hang out together as their own little clique aboard the ship, the same way Steve and Gordon and Clive tended to hang out together. There were plenty of times where we'd all mix together, and I was pretty sure that everyone considered everyone else a friend.

"Hey, Joe," I said.

"Hey, Broc," Joe said. He moved to the rails and leaned down, elbows against the wooden surface. "That was exciting."

"Yeah. That fight with the rocket planes was kinda fun—but scary. I'm glad no one was hurt."

"It might have been a near thing. The *Beaver*'s a tough ship, but he still took a beating."

I cringed a bit. "I guess so. I really wish things had gone easier. Next time, I'm sure we'll do better."

"So there will be a next time?" he asked.

I nodded. "Definitely. Joe, I'm not the sort of bun to not do what I can to help people out. Sometimes, that means getting into a bit of trouble. Other times, that means flying halfway across the world to try and stop a war. And sometimes, it's risking hide and hare to clean some Evil Roots. I want to be a good person, and that means acting on what I think is right."

Joe chuckled, his head bowing. "Yeah, I think I see that. At least you're not all talk."

"Is it too much?" I asked while gesturing vaguely around us. "The adventures and the other crazy things we get us to?"

"It's a lot, yeah, but I think I can handle it for now. I still think the Scal-lywags and I will be heading out one day, but maybe . . . maybe we'll do something similar? I don't know. It feels wrong to do things when they're not things that'll pay you well. But it feels right to do things to help folk. I guess we might need to find some middle ground?"

"You could join the Exploration Guild," I said. Which reminded me: we hadn't done much guild-related stuff in a while. Did they still owe us for that flower thing way back when? "They'd give you an excuse to move around a lot, meet new people, explore new dungeons."

Joe laughed. "I don't know if I'm made for that kind of adventure. Just being on the *Beaver* is a lot for us already, I think. I can't imagine doing what you and your friends do."

"I don't think we do anything that weird, do we?"

He shook his head. "You don't realize how wild you are, all four of you."

Four of us? I supposed he was counting Bastion in our party. Which was probably fair. He was pretty close, and he had come on all the scarier adventures lately. "We're just people trying to do our best," I said. "Even if that sometimes means doing things that are scary."

"You're all insane," Joe replied with the certainty of someone who knew they were right. "But it's not a bad sort of insane."

I pouted at him. I wasn't nuts.

Joe chuckled as he stood up and stretched his back. "Well, I'm getting back to work. Someone needs to organize our tools, and it sure won't be Oda who does it. Keep us safe, Captain."

"Have fun," I said. "And don't work too hard. Take regular breaks!"

I felt like a bit of a hypocrite there. Breaks were for people who *wanted* to slow down.

I wasn't sure exactly what to do. It didn't feel like a good time to start making noise. Maybe I could take a few hours to just . . . train things.

A final glance around showed that things were pretty calm, all said and done, so I headed to the rear of the *Beaver* and down a level.

I found Awen's room empty; the girl was likely in the engine room again, or tinkering on her cool turret thing. Amaryllis's room wasn't empty. My bird friend was on her bed, face buried in some pillows and the rest of her laid out flat.

"Uh," I said.

"I'm sleeping."

"Are you sleeping . . . well?"

"Yes, Broccoli, I'm sleeping well," Amaryllis said into her pillows.

"Do you need anything?"

"I just spent a few hours negotiating after a very stressful morning. Not everyone is as capable as you at dealing with chaos."

She sighed and pushed herself up to stare at me from the corner of her eyes.

"I desperately need a nap."

"Okay then," I said. "Uh, nap well."

I stood around in the corridor of the ship, then sighed. Maybe I did have a problem. I couldn't sit around and do *nothing*. If I could at least train, maybe, or help someone with something.

I thumped a foot on the ground and stomped off to find something to do. I might, maybe, have a wee, tiny sliver of insanity in me, sure. But that was something I could bother with later. Right then and there, I needed a distraction.

I'd find someone who needed a friend, or my name wasn't Broccoli Bunch.

· Chapter Thirty-Nine ·

Intercepted

The *Beaver* held up well for the next couple of days. Thankfully, the weather stayed calm. We hit a bit of rain the day after leaving the Lonely Island behind, but it was a gentle rain, and while we were worried it might undo some of the stitching on our balloon, any damage we had to deal with was small.

It probably helped that everyone was keeping an eye on things.

"Land ho!" Clive called from above.

I was in the lower deck, resting at the dining room table with my copy of *A Guide to Manipulating the Essence*, the book that I'd bought way back in Rockstack when I was still just a normal human girl looking for friends and adventure. The book made a lot more sense now that I knew how to cast a couple of spells, kind of like rereading a math textbook after having several lessons on the subject.

I was thinking of maybe growing my repertoire of spells. Fireball and its variants were really cool and super useful, and of course I had Cleaning magic, but I was kind of limited in what I could do with just those two. Amaryllis was practicing her magic too. I think she was figuring out how to cast barriers and use her Lightning magic in new ways.

Awen had her Glass magic, which she was using to make stuff for her Wyrmgineer class. Those weren't ordinary uses of Glass magic, I don't think, but they were really neat.

Bastion had given us a list of spells we should know, and I was still working on mastering those. The problem was I couldn't practice Clean Wounds without wounds to clean (and that one was kind of a moot spell to learn anyway). Soften Earth required earth to soften, and Draw Water needed water to be drawn. We only had so much fresh water aboard, and I didn't want to spill it all over while practicing.

So I was caught reading about the magic instead of practicing it.

"Land ho!" Clive called again.

I snapped my book shut and stood up with a stretch. Time to go see what all that was about!

I arrived on deck and found I wasn't the only one coming up to see what was ahead.

The mountains of Sylphfree had been visible for a while already. They were hard to miss, rising over the horizon. Big, jagged walls of pale gray stone, with a few clouds hovering around the tallest peaks.

Now, though, we were close enough that a glance down revealed the shores where the ocean beat against the foot of the mountains, great big splashes of water surging into the sky every time a new wave came in.

The shore stretched on for a long, long ways, so far that it was nothing but a hazy line on the edge of the distant horizon.

"Over there," Bastion said.

I glanced at the sylph, then followed his pointing hand toward a site farther along the shore. The mountains receded a little, and in the middle of the basin there was a small patch of forested land with a strong river.

I wouldn't have noticed the village tucked away in the valley if Bastion hadn't pointed it out. It was hard to see from afar, but a small settlement was definitely nestled there, with tall walls the same color as the mountainside hiding it all away.

Clive spun the wheel, and soon we were heading straight for the settlement.

"All right, everyone, let's take it slow and steady! We need more sails out!" I shouted as I jumped back into the role of captain.

A few airships rose from within the distant village and turned to fly our way, but Bastion seemed at ease, so I didn't worry. By the time we'd cut the distance to the village in half, the airships were circling around in formation to come up next to us.

They were strange, boxy-looking ships, mostly made of steel, with sharp edges, held together by large rivets. Their balloons were fairly small, and it looked like they had two each.

Most interesting was the large ballista at the front, and the two smaller ones mounted onto long arms that jutted out of the ship's sides and that swept down a ways. The sylphs manning those ballistae were all dressed up in thick coats with goggles and scarves on. I imagined they got a little cold when at higher altitudes.

"Hold us steady!" I called back to Clive as I ran to the side of the ship nearest the approaching airship.

Their pilot was pretty good, because they came close while slowing down to match our speed nearly exactly. A trio of sylphs in light armor jumped off their ship, and with wings beating hummingbird-quick, they glided over to the *Beaver* and landed on deck.

"Hello!" I said. "And welcome aboard the *Beaver Cleaver*. I'm Broccoli Bunch, the captain."

Of the three sylphs, two were carrying short spears, with swords hanging by their hips, while the third was carrying a far more terrifying weapon: a clipboard. "Greetings," he said as he bent over his board and scribbled something down. "One moment, I need to . . . *Beaver* . . . *Cleaver*. Two words, yes?"

"Yup!" I said. "You look like you have a lot of questions to ask."

"Oh, I do. You're in restricted airspace. Do you have a permit?"

"A permit for what?"

"Then that'll be one fine to add, not to mention another fee for the inspection. Are you attempting to reach Granite Springs?"

"I don't know where Granite Springs is. Is it the little town over there? Where your ships came from?" At his nod, I went on. "In that case, I guess? We took some damage to our balloon. We've patched it up as best we can, but there was only so much we could do. If your town has a place for us to land and get repairs, then we'd love to stop by."

"Granite Springs should have the facilities to care for such a small vessel," he said.

"That would be nice."

The sylph made a few more marks on his clipboard, and I slid up to my tippy toes to see over the edge. He noticed and pulled it back.

It was a little rude to write stuff about people without telling them. "Yes, well, there is a clause that would allow a vessel, operating in good faith, to use a port in an emergency, but I don't think you're currently in an emergency state."

"Well, it's less an emergency and more . . . a bad need for repair. I don't know where the next nearest airship port is. In the Trenten Flats, maybe?"

He winced. "Yes, I suppose I could justify that as a good reason to land, though there is an emergency landing fee."

"Perhaps I can clear some of that."

The three sylphs tensed as Bastion walked over. He had his arms by his sides and looked entirely casual. I noted that he was back in his full armor, minus his helmet.

"Sir Paladin," the clipboard-wielding sylph's feet clicked together and he stood straight, hand snapping into a salute.

"Paladin Bastion Coldfront," Bastion introduced himself. "Forgive me for not introducing myself earlier. I thought I'd leave some of the minutiae to the captain."

"Of course, sir."

"Now, what was this about an emergency fee?" Bastion asked. "The ship was damaged while carrying out duties any paladin ought to do in the pursuit of justice. I think we should at least treat the vessel with respect."

"I— Yes, sir, but, well, the vessel is . . . extremely bright. And colorful. It doesn't seem very, ah . . ." He gestured around, at the two duck figureheads, then at our very bright balloon above.

"No one would suspect a thing, you mean," Bastion said with a nod. "Good observation, Lieutenant. Do keep it to yourself."

The sylphs snapped to salute. "Yes, sir!"

"Now, carry on. The captain doesn't have a flight path that I know of, and there are fees incurred from that."

"Oh! I think we do have one!" I said. "Wait, let me go get Amaryllis!"

Amaryllis, being the organized sort of girl she was, had a whole file with our flight plans in it. A system was in place where—like the banks—papers could be sent between ports. Which meant that Sylphfree did know that the *Beaver Cleaver* was coming, though we were a teensy bit off with our time estimate.

"Here you go!" I said as I bounced back to the sylphs and gave them the plan.

The one with the clipboard looked it over, his eyebrow rising. "This paints you as . . . two days outside your intended arrival time."

"Oops?" I tried. "We had a few little detours. But they were fun! We fought pirates, then we fought these other airships, and then we kinda crashed on the Lonely Island, but we managed to use the airships we downed to fix the *Beaver* back up. Also, we got a bit off track a few times. People needed help."

The sylph officer blinked, then looked at his clipboard. I wondered if there were any checkboxes for the kinds of adventures we'd been on. I don't think he found anything because he looked up at Bastion, who was just staring with a polite smile, and then he started sweating a lot.

"Yes, well, of course. Um. I'm sure the fee for adjusting your flight plan to accommodate for a slight discrepancy is much more manageable. Let me just . . . Uh, yes, that can be done. Will . . . will we be inspecting the ship?" This he asked directly to Bastion.

"Of course. It's your duty to look over every inch of the vessel for any sort of contraband."

"Do we have anything illegal on board?" I asked.

"No, we don't," Bastion said.

"Oh, good."

The sylph with the clipboard stared a little, then seemed to shake off whatever was holding him back. "Well then, maybe we can start our inspection with this top deck and work our way down? Then . . . back up on the other deck?"

"Sure thing," I said. "Do you want me to guide you around?"

"That would be appropriate," Bastion said. "Barging into the rooms of the noblewomen onboard without the captain as escort would be highly suspect."

"Noble— Well, yes, Captain, I would appreciate an escort."

I grinned big and proud as I gave the inspector a tour of the *Beaver*. I made sure to introduce them to everyone on board: the Scallywags, our harpy crewmates, and, of course, my friends. He took notes as he went, though he seemed a little confused as to where to put Grand Admiral Orange since she didn't fit neatly into any of his charts.

The sylph seemed impressed by Awen's engine room, even if I was cringing inside at how disorganized it was. He was less impressed when he discovered Awen's turret emplacement inside the hull.

Seeing her bedroom a few minutes later made him reconsider. It was clean, because I wouldn't not have a clean room on my ship, but Awen had a habit of leaving her stuff all over, and underthings on the floor was never impressive.

That somehow cemented the idea that she was a noble in the sylph's mind, though. Amaryllis being herself proved that she was a noble too. She was particularly snooty today.

"And that," I said as we huddled in the bathroom—which didn't actually have a bath—"is the whole ship!"

"Do you have any hidden compartments?"

"Like smugglers? Oh, that would be cool."

"I'll take that as a no," he replied with a sigh. "That concludes my inspection, I think. Shall we return to the main deck? I'll signal our ship ahead, and we can guide you into port."

"That sounds wonderful."

I wasn't sure what to expect of Sylphfree, but regardless of how things turned out, it was nice to finally arrive after such a long voyage.

I was almost shaking at the prospect of making so many more friends!

· Chapter Forty ·

Bunniver's Travels

Granite Springs was, according to Bastion, a small and secluded town in Sylphfree. It was along the southern end of the country, next to the ocean, and as airships had become more common, shipping over water had declined.

I couldn't really tell if it was becoming less prosperous as we hovered over the town, the *Beaver* being guided to a waiting berth in the airship docks at the rear of the town.

The sylph airships peeled off as soon as we tossed ropes over the sides, and the sylphs working at the docks tied us in place.

"I need to give my assessment to the port authority," the officer sylph said as he tucked his clipboard under an arm.

"It was a pleasure having you aboard," I said as I leaned down to shake his hand. It was easy to forget how small most sylphs were. Bastion was a pretty tall one, and he barely reached my shoulder. The officer and the two guards with him were a bit shorter. I think I'd met children who were taller.

That only meant baby sylphs had to be absolutely teeny tiny!

The officer exchanged some pleasantries with Bastion, then bowed before fluttering off the side of the *Beaver* and over to the docks.

"All right!" I said once the deck was cleared of strangers. I clapped my hands together for attention. "We need a plan."

"That shouldn't be too complicated," Amaryllis said. "We find someone who can repair the *Beaver*'s balloon. I imagine a proper port like this has at least one company that does repairs. The port authority should know."

"That means that we won't be able to use the *Beaver* to head deeper into Sylphfree until it's repaired, though," I said.

Bastion shook his head. "That might not be an issue." He pointed off the side of the ship and to a flagpole standing proud above a building in the center of the town. It was a big, square structure, very utilitarian, and made entirely of pale gray stone. Three flags were on display. I kinda recognized the flag of Sylphfree, but the other two didn't tell me much. One had a gray square in the middle of a two-toned background, pale blue above and white below. The other was a checkered gray-orange flag.

"I don't get it," I said.

"The bottommost flag, under the town flag, is a warning. The area is on a middling alert level. That means more guards will be posted in cities and towns, some soldiers will be pulled from reserves, and travel will be restricted."

Amaryllis huffed. It was a very unimpressed huff that basically said "Well, we'd do that better where I'm from." "Of course the sylphs have flags to tell them how they'll be oppressed today."

"So," I said as I decided to ignore that comment. It was best not to start an argument. "We can't fly the *Beaver* to the capital."

"Not without the sort of permissions I wouldn't be able to obtain," Bastion said. "There should be some vessels heading to and from Goldenalden. Food and materials still need to be moved, and people as well. Besides, the mountains are treacherous for inexperienced pilots."

I glanced to the north, where the mountains towered above us. They weren't the biggest mountains I'd ever seen—that definitely went to the Harpy mountains—but they were dense: just a lot of peaks rising every which way.

I imagined the wind between all those peaks would be tricky, and unless ships could move over the mountaintops, they would have to twist and turn around the peaks. That wouldn't be easy. The *Beaver* was a fairly light ship, and he could only go so high. It got really cold, and the air grew thin past a certain height.

"So we're going to have to leave the *Beaver* behind?" I asked.

"It's not that bad," Amaryllis said. "It will limit our options, but not overly, and we can leave most of the crew here to guard the *Beaver* while repairs are being made."

"I guess."

It would be strange to leave the *Beaver* behind. Sure, we hardly stayed on the ship while out exploring, but it was always nearby—our home that we carried with us. Or rather, that carried us.

But if we didn't have a choice, then that was that. And it wasn't like we'd be gone for a long time. "So who do we bring with us?"

"The usual away team," Amaryllis said. "Myself, you, Awen, and Bastion, of course."

"Let's ask around, make sure that everyone is okay with staying. And then we need to pack our things."

"I doubt we'll find a ship leaving this evening," Bastion said. "Most shipping happens in the morning and early afternoon. You can reach most other places in Sylphfree with half a day's flying from the capital. Flying at night is dangerous."

"I can imagine," I said. All those mountains would serve as obstacles to anyone flying with the sun down. "We do need to go out and find a ride for tomorrow, though."

"We hardly need the whole crew for that," Amaryllis said. "I'll head over to the port authority and sign off on our berth."

"Bring a human with you," Bastion said. "I . . . don't wish to doubt my fellow sylphs, but you might find that there's some animosity toward harpies here."

Amaryllis harrumphed. "Typical. Though . . . I suppose we're no better. I'll bring Awen, then. She's reasonable, at least."

I nodded. "So, that's the plan?"

"We also need food. Not for those of us leaving, but for the rest of the crew. Though I suppose I could leave some gold aboard for them to purchase things once we're gone," Amaryllis said.

"That sounds fine," I said. "Bastion, did you want to come exploring with me? I don't think we've been on that many adventures, just the two of us!"

"Certainly," Bastion said.

Grinning, I ran off to gather a few things. Last time I'd gone wandering in a new city, I was ambushed by giant laser-firing crystals. Let it never be said that Broccoli Bunch doesn't sometimes learn her lesson. Once I had my turtle shell hat on, a small pack with a few essentials, and a pouch with some coins, I picked up my warspade and ran back onto the deck to find Bastion waiting on the dock in his full paladin regalia.

"I'm ready!" I cheered as I hopped over the rail and landed next to him.

"I can see that," he said. "I'm not certain if people would appreciate seeing someone armed on the streets."

"Armed? You mean my spade? I guess I can leave it behind," I said. I only took a hop to return to the *Beaver* and tuck my spade away. "Better?" I asked as I returned.

"Quite."

"So, where are we going first?"

"I thought we only had one destination?"

I pouted. "Well, yeah, but you know how much I love detours. We could make new friends, meet new people. Maybe grab a bite to eat?"

"I suppose. In either case, we should get moving."

I nodded, and soon enough both of us were walking along the docks toward a tower off to one side. The port was made up of a dozen berths for airships, with what looked like docks that could be moved from side to side to accommodate ships of different sizes. Towers were on either end, with exits at their bases leading onto an empty field.

It looked as if the sylphs were clever enough not to build anything under the space ships would occupy, which only made sense. A tool could fall and bonk someone on the head.

My head was on a swivel as we moved, taking in the other ships and the people aboard them. They were all boxy, metal-clad vessels (ironclads?), smaller than the *Beaver*, and with a few more balloons. At least, those that were nearest. On the other side of the port were a pair of larger ships, with the flag of Sylphfree on their bows and bigger ballistae on their decks.

Every ship was manned by sylphs, and no matter how much I looked, I couldn't see anyone who wasn't a little person with big wings.

"Aren't we going to visit the other ships?" I asked.

"No, that's not how things work here. Most of these ships look like merchant vessels, the cheap, faster sorts. The crew on board won't have any authority to take on passengers."

"Oh. That's weird. Don't they have captains?"

"Yes, but only in the sense that each ship has a person who leads its crew. The captains of most ships aren't the owners of those ships." He pointed to the hull of a nearby ship where a logo sat, a big flower I vaguely recognized as a snapdragon. "That one and the ship next to it are owned by the same company. You'll notice most transport ships are similarly owned by one company or another."

"Instead of having them owned by their captain, who then picks up stuff," I said. "That's not as cool."

"I suppose it isn't, but it might be more efficient. Sylphfree policy is big on efficiency."

We reached the tower, and I was surprised to find a basket elevator within. We clambered aboard, and Bastion lowered a lever that had us dropping down.

"So, if we can't just ask the captains nicely, where are we going?" I asked as I enjoyed the sensation of falling.

"I took note of which company owned which ship," Bastion said. "Their headquarters in town should have something in place to offer transportation to civilians."

The elevator thumped onto a cloth pad at the bottom, and Bastion raised the lever he'd pulled, which locked the basket in place so we could climb out.

Once we were out of the tower and back under the sun, Bastion took a moment to look around before gesturing ahead. "This way, I believe."

"Have you been here before?"

"In Granite Springs? Only a couple of quick stops. Did some training with the army by the coast. Learning how to swim is part of our training."

Made sense to me. "So you know your way around?"

"The stops were hardly comprehensive," Bastion said. Soon we were walking down what I guessed was one of the town's main roads. It was very strange to be the tallest person around. I was used to Bastion being shorter than me—I hardly even noticed it anymore—but to be taller than everyone on an entire street . . .

Worse were all the stares. Little sylph kids, who really were tiny, looked up to me with mouths opened wide in big Os, and the more adult sylphs were quick to scamper away.

I was probably very intimidating. With my ears straight, I was nearly twice as tall as some of the sylphs we were walking past.

At least no one seemed really afraid, and Bastion got some looks too. People pointed at him, some turning to friends before they whispered things.

"Do people stare at you like this a lot?" I asked.

"It happens often enough," Bastion said. "I'm a paladin. We're not exactly rare, but it's uncommon for us to be seen in such a small town, and unfortunately, we're usually chasing trouble. I wouldn't call Granite Springs a frontier town, but it's certainly not the most prosperous place within the kingdom."

"It seems nice," I said. The homes were all neat and clean, pale stone—granite, I guessed—and tall, with balconies on the topmost floors.

They also had really, really small doors. I wasn't sure if I'd be able to squeeze into them without bending over double to avoid bonking my ears against the doorframes.

"This is the place," Bastion said as he stopped before a larger building.

I glanced up at it, taking in the same flower logo I'd seen on some of the ships at port. "Neat! Lead the way, Sir Paladin Bastion."

Bastion chuckled, but he did step ahead.

· Chapter Forty-One ·

Paladin Business

I realized that I was going to have a slight but persistent problem if I spent any amount of time in sylph cities.

The sylphs were small, so they built things according to their own sizes, which made perfect sense. Unfortunately, that meant whenever I followed Bastion into a room, I had to duck my head down, or I'd risk bashing it into the doorframe.

Bastion looked at me with a perfectly straight face, but there was no hiding the way his eyes were crinkled up at the corners and the suppressed chuckles he was holding back.

I pouted as I rubbed my forehead. "No fair," I muttered.

"I suppose you'll grow used to it. I certainly learned to live with everything being just a little too tall for me outside Sylphfree."

That was . . . probably fair. It would be hard to build a building that was accessible to every species on Dirt, I imagined. Though it wouldn't have hurt if they made the doors just a bit taller. My ears were getting sore from getting whapped all over.

"Sir Bastion?"

Bastion and I both turned.

We were in the offices of a company called Snapdragon Transportation. They had, according to what I'd picked up, a whole fleet of ships that traveled from one city to another within Sylphfree and delivered goods and transported people around. Their lobby was near, with little model ships in glass cases and a few plaques on the walls, but they didn't have a big waiting area or anything, so I figured they mostly did business with other businesses, not normal people off the street.

Not that Bastion seemed to count as normal. "Hello," Bastion said. He extended a hand to the sylph who had just walked in, and they shook. The secretary seemed a little nervous.

"Is there any way I can help you, Paladin Bastion?"

Bastion nodded. "We're looking for passage to the capital," he said. "Myself, the captain here, as well as two others."

"I see. Of course, Snapdragon Transportation would be honored to serve the nation by providing our services at no cost," the secretary said with a bow.

"No, no, while my own business does draw me back to the capital, I believe the captain and the others with her will want to pay for their fare. I imagine that there won't be any difficulty housing a human and a harpy all the way to the capital?" Bastion asked.

The secretary blinked. "A harpy? I mean, yes, of course. We would never discriminate. But, ah, is this harpy . . . civil?"

"Most of the time," I said. "She's a harpy noble, though, which I think she uses as an excuse to act up a bit."

"Ah, yes," the secretary said with the tone of someone who didn't know what he was agreeing to. "In either case, we have a ship leaving for the capital in the morning, the *Little Atlas*. The captain will be informed of your arrival."

"Thank you," Bastion said.

We picked up some papers, including an invoice that I'd have to give to Amaryllis for her to take care of, then Bastion wished the secretary a good afternoon.

"Where to next?" I asked as I remembered to duck under the doorway.

"Back to the ship," Bastion said. "Or maybe not."

I blinked, then looked down. A small group stood before the business, some five sylphs, all of them in armor. Thick leather covered their chests and shoulders, fitted snugly over chainmail with what looked like thin gambesons underneath. They had hard leather helmets and little spears by their side, all except for the one at the front.

Bastion nodded to them. "Greetings."

"Sir Paladin," the one at the front of the group said. His helmet had a red band around it, and he had a similarly red ring around both forearms; otherwise his armor was identical to the others'. "Please, forgive us for the intrusion, but we heard that a paladin was in Granite Springs, and we wished to confirm it."

"I am, in fact, here," Bastion said. "Is there anything I can assist you with, Guard Captain . . . ?"

"Captain Wardmyth, sir," the sylph said with a bow of his head. "And, well, I wouldn't want to impose upon the time of a paladin."

I fidgeted. I kinda wanted to say hi and introduce myself, but there was a very official tone to things, and it would be rude to just barge into the conversation.

"I have some time," Bastion said. "I'm leaving Granite Springs in the morning, but if there's anything that requires a paladin between now and then, I can look into it."

"That would be wonderful, sir," Guard Captain Wardmyth said. "We have a small issue right now. Nothing that's big enough to call for a paladin from the capital and certainly not big enough to call in the army, but it's an issue all the same."

Bastion nodded. "Tell me about it, then."

Captain Wardmyth looked past Bastion and at me. I waved. "Can we talk about it in . . . current company?"

One of Bastion's eyebrows rose. "You mean Captain Bunch here? I trust her, for what it's worth. Is the issue that sensitive?"

"No, sir," Guard Captain Wardmyth said. "It's nothing of great worry, but it is . . . somewhat complicated. I'm certain we could take care of it on our own, given some time and effort, but, well, you're a paladin."

I looked past the five guards and noticed that a lot of people were looking our way. Some of them seemed very curious about me, so I smiled their way, and made faces at any kid sylph whose eyes I caught.

Bastion nodded. "Very well, then. What's the nature of the issue?"

"We have a large number of moles living nearby. A small colony of them. They've never been problematic before, no more than usual at least. Some of the local farmers are even on friendly terms with them," the guard captain said.

"That's rather common," Bastion said. "They're helpful people, in their own way. Though they have caused trouble elsewhere before."

Captain Wardmyth nodded. "They've started doing just that here. Their leader is threatening to dam the river running through the center of the town. We can't have that."

"That's strangely antagonistic," Bastion said. "Do you know why?"

"Can't understand what they're saying at the best of times, sir," Captain Wardmyth said. "We were thinking of gathering up a group of guards to go knock some sense into them—scare them away from the edges of the river before they cause any actual damage."

"What are moles?" I asked.

The guard captain jumped, but Bastion didn't seem to mind the question.

"The mole folk are a people who are native to the region, as are the sylph. They live at the base of the Sylphfree mountains, while the sylph commonly live nearer to the peaks. For the most part, our relations have been peaceful. They have underground farms, are largely self-sufficient, and are rarely seen too far from their burrows."

"They sound like nice neighbors," I said.

"Usually, yes. We've traded with them before. They are better miners than most sylphs and can sniff out mineral deposits. In exchange, we give them tools and equipment they can't manufacture. Nevertheless, our societies are separate. The sylph don't do underground living well, and the mole folk don't like spending too much time in the open. They have too many natural predators and poor eyesight."

I nodded. "Well, if all you need to do to help the mole folk around here is a chat, then maybe I can help."

"Forgive me for asking, Captain . . . Bunch?" Captain Wardmyth asked. I nodded when he got my name right. "But how would you assist?"

"I've got a knack for languages," I said.

"The good captain here speaks and picks up languages easily," Bastion said. "I don't speak the mole folk's common tongue, though I can likely communicate a little. Captain Wardmyth, would you be willing to lead me to the river that they're damming? Maybe I can assist."

"I'll come too," I said. "I don't think I have anything else to do until tomorrow anyway."

"If you wish," Bastion said.

The guards seemed pretty happy to have a paladin aboard, and so with Guard Captain Wardmyth in the lead, we were escorted across town and toward the northern end, past the airship docks, and toward the walls.

"So, being a paladin is a big deal, huh?" I asked.

"I imagine it is," Bastion said. "There aren't that many paladins in Sylph-free, mostly owing to the difficulty in the training and the methods by which potential recruits are chosen. A lot of soldiers apply to become paladins, but maybe one in every thousand earn the rank."

"That's impressive."

"Thank you."

"What about the nine hundred ninety-nine who fail? I bet they feel terrible."

"I imagine there's some disappointment, but most of those fail early. Even failing out of the course isn't a bad thing. The training looks good on a young sylph's training chart. If they plan on becoming officers or obtaining a more prestigious role, then the initiative to become a paladin is a mark in their favor."

"Huh," I said. I wasn't used to that kind of thing, but it sounded reasonable. I wasn't sure if I'd manage in that environment, though. I didn't like competitive things all that much.

Guard Captain Wardmyth stopped at a gatehouse next to an opening in the wall leading out into the countryside, and we waited as he ran in and spoke to someone. Soon enough, the gate was rattling as it rose off the ground.

"Are there any procedures you want us to follow, sir?" the guard captain asked. "I can get some more men to follow us out. I doubt the moles will try anything, but if they do, it would be better to have more wings at our back."

"I suspect we'll be fine," Bastion said. "This is just a little detour. Though . . . perhaps inform the garrison? If we do run into trouble, it would be nice to know that help isn't too far away. A bit of caution never hurts."

"Yes, sir," Captain Wardmyth snapped with a quick salute. He moved off, sending some of the guards scurrying around the gates with quick orders.

A wagon rolled up nearby, just a flatbed with some benches in the center, the wheels small, and the entire thing fairly low to the ground. It was obviously meant to carry people, not stuff.

The sylph directing the wagon behind two small ponies hooked the reins to a pommel on his bench, then jumped off, letting a guard take his place. "Are we going to ride over?" I asked.

"Seems that way," Bastion said. "Guards have armor that's encumbering and often heavy enough to make flight somewhat difficult. It's meant to be easy to remove, in case of a chase, but that doesn't always help. So for a long trek, a wagon is a nice luxury."

"That makes sense," I said. "I'm going to go say hi to the ponies."

"I . . . Yes, sure."

The ponies were called—according to the sylph who had led them over—Red Five and Red Seven. I found those to be rather boring names for small horses, but they were very nice and let me pat their noses after sniffing at my hand a bit.

"Broccoli," Bastion said as he jumped onto the wagon. A few more guards were climbing aboard, and the guard captain was sitting at the front.

"Coming," I said before hopping up and taking a seat next to Bastion.

"I hope you don't mind the little detour."

I snorted. "Are you kidding me?" I asked. "Bastion, you know I live for adventures like this. Besides, it'll just be a few minutes. A bit of talking and some meeting the locals. Nothing hard, I bet!"

· Chapter Forty-Two ·

Dam It All

The cart rattled and bounced across the road. It was too low to the ground to have room for suspension, which really sucked. Every rut and bump in the otherwise decent road made me jump up, and then I crashed back down with a heavy whump.

My bum was going to be so sore.

"So," I began, "where are the mole people living?"

Guard Captain Wardmyth leaned back. "They live underground, usually. Some of their villages are open to the air, though. They have walls most of the way around, with nets over the tops of their villages."

"Nets?"

Bastion answered that one. "The Sylphfree mountains are home to these vicious creatures called amphipteres."

"What are those?"

"They're long, snakelike creatures with wings. They're the offspring of a dragon and a nondragon. Cunning, in their own base way, and aggressive. We fight them off when we can and destroy their nests whenever possible. They don't attack sylphs as often, though," Bastion said.

"But the mole people don't like them," I guessed.

"The issue is that the amphipteres like the mole people. More specifically, the way they taste. Mole people have poor eyesight. They have other senses to make up for it, but they're vulnerable to attacks from above and often can't react to them."

"And sylphs can?"

Captain Wardmyth laughed. "We can show those flying snakes what for," he said. "A few good guards with sharp senses can scare one off easily. A few arrows, a magical attack or two, and they'll fly off to find easier prey."

"They're still dangerous," Bastion said. "Especially when cornered. They can strike quickly, and some have natural magics to lean upon. Their draconic ancestry means their breath is dangerous. Children have been snatched away in the middle of smaller towns before."

I gasped, a hand moving over my mouth. "That's awful!"

Bastion nodded. "It's why we keep their population low, culling them when we can."

"They're not smart?" I asked, just to be sure.

"No smarter than a rabid dog," Captain Wardmyth said.

Well, I wouldn't agree with ever hunting down a dog, but I could understand the sylphs hunting the amphipteres if they were so dangerous. "So, the mole people live underground to avoid giant sky snakes. I guess that makes sense."

"It's more than that," Bastion said. He paused as we passed over some particularly bumpy bumps. "The mole people have cultural ties to the world, to the underground. They have a few dungeons deep under the earth as well. It's where they're meant to be. Having them out on open land or, World forbid, in the air, would be like tossing a dozen sylphs into the ocean and telling them to make do."

"I think I get it."

I put my hands down onto the bench and pushed myself up a bit, absorbing some of the bouncing with my arms as I took in the countryside. Little stands of trees were clumped up here and there, with craggy, rock-covered spots between them.

Birds flitted between the clumps of forest with eager energy and happy trills, and I even saw a gray fox slinking away in the distance.

The farther we journeyed from Granite Springs, the more the woods thickened, though the road stayed the same. A long, straight path, covered in loose white gravel. Soon we were crossing splits in the road that led to little quarries busy at work.

The road didn't pass too close to them—I guessed because the walls around the quarry might collapse, and having the road near them would be dangerous. Still, I could make out sylphs, some operating boxy machines, others working to load up carts with big square-cut blocks of what I guessed to be granite.

"So, is that why Granite Springs is called Granite Springs?" I asked.

"It is," Captain Wardmyth confirmed. "We're one of the largest producers of rough-hewn stone in the kingdom."

"Isn't all of Sylphfree mountainous?"

"It is, but you can't just dig a quarry anywhere. Not with the risk of landslides and erosion causing trouble in the future," Captain Wardmyth said. "And the stone from here is quite unique. It has some magical properties that I'm not clever enough to really comment on."

I nodded. They seemed to care about the environment, then, at least a little bit.

We rattled past a cart pulled by two donkeys, loaded up with a few dozen granite blocks. The driver stared at us as we passed, then doffed his big hat when I waved.

"That's it, up ahead," Captain Wardmyth said.

I turned on my bench, then put a hand on Bastion's shoulder for balance as I stood up. The road leading out of the town ran parallel to the river, though not closely. The river wasn't as straight and meandered around as it cut through the hilly landscape. We'd even crossed a nice little bridge made of the local stone at some point.

That same river was wider ahead, with a few smaller rivulets flowing into it.

The dam was impossible to miss.

It was a wall of dirt and mud, three times as tall as I was from tippy-toes to ear tips. The dam was unfinished; it only stretched halfway across the river, with a palisade above it. Not confined to the river, a large part of it was over land, serving as an ordinary wall. It didn't look like a fortification capable of protecting anything bigger than a village, though.

"That's more impressive than I was expecting," Bastion said. "They've spent a lot of time building that up."

"We can take it apart in an afternoon, I'm sure," Captain Wardmyth said. "Packed earth isn't that strong, and I think all they've used for reinforcement are tree trunks."

"Like a beaver dam," I said.

Captain Wardmyth nodded. "An order of magnitude larger, but, essentially, yes."

"Captain, stop us a hundred paces from their gate," Bastion said. "I think we'll approach with just three of us."

"Three will be enough?" Captain Wardmyth asked.

Bastion nodded and stepped off the side of the wagon, his wings beating quick to slow his fall. "Three will be plenty. The goal is to avoid antagonizing them unless we don't have a choice in the matter."

"They're the ones building a dam," Captain Wardmyth said as he climbed down.

I hopped off and landed with a bounce next to the two sylphs. "Maybe they have a good reason for it?"

"Like what, starving Granite Springs?" Captain Wardmyth asked.

I shook my head. "I don't know. But I can come up with ideas. Maybe they know there's going to be a big flood from above, and they want to slow it down. Maybe they want to use the dam to make power. Maybe the river needs to be diverted to, uh, save their village or something?"

Captain Wardmyth blinked. "Well, I suppose some of those are possible. If unlikely."

"As unlikely as otherwise peaceful neighbors building a large dam over a nearby river?" I asked.

Bastion hummed. "Captain Bunch has a point," he said. "It wouldn't do to assume the worst without all the facts. So let's be cordial and find out what's going on here."

The rest of the guards disembarked from the wagon, but they remained where they were. I didn't envy them if they had to stand around and wait. The sun was nice and cheery above, but it was also warm, and there weren't too many trees next to the road for cover.

"Stay behind me," Bastion said as he took the lead.

Captain Wardmyth grabbed a spear handed to him by one of his guards and used it as a walking stick as he walked next to me. He had a small round shield too—a buckler, I thought.

"Sir Bastion," Captain Wardmyth asked as we made our way across the road. There was an entrance in the dam wall, a doorway above a trench with wooden planks held up by ropes. I was pretty sure I could jump the wall, though.

"Yes, Captain Wardmyth?"

"I wouldn't question you before the guards, but is bringing the . . . civilian wise?"

My ears perked. He was talking about me.

"Broccoli can, surprisingly, hold her own." Bastion looked back toward me. "Though, Broccoli, if things go bad, do take flight. This isn't your fight, and I wouldn't like to see you hurt here."

"I wouldn't like to see you hurt either."

He chuckled. "I can take care of myself."

He was a pretty good fighter. Probably . . . definitely the best one aboard the *Beaver Cleaver.*

"All right," I said.

There wasn't time for more talk. A form shifted above the wall—a shortish brown-furred figure in a long coat with what looked like a gambeson under chainmail. He had a helmet on that resembled a pith helmet and an elongated, pinkish face with beady little eyes.

"Halt!" he called out. His voice was a squeaky thing, high pitched, as if someone was talking with their nose pinched.

Bastion's boots crunched to a halt, and we stopped behind him. "We've halted," he shouted back.

The mole person on the wall blinked, then squinted. "Oh, yes. Give me a moment!" he said before turning and disappearing out of sight.

"I didn't understand that last part," Captain Wardmyth said.

"He asked us to give him a moment," I said.

Bastion nodded. "Their language isn't too different from the common tongue. But they have adapted it. Some sounds they can't pronounce, and they use lots of jargon. I'm certain the captain here could understand them perfectly well, given some time to get used to their accent."

"It's a bit squeaky," I admitted.

"I think it might travel well underground," Bastion said.

Three mole people appeared on the wall, including the one we saw a moment before. "State your business!" one of them said. His fur was black, and his armor was a lot more intricate. Something resembling full plate, with decorative work on the edges. He was hatless, but he did have a nice capelet.

Bastion cleared his throat. "I am Bastion Coldfront, a royal paladin of Sylphfree. I am here to speak with whoever is in charge. I come peacefully, with no ill intent."

The mole person stared at Bastion, and I couldn't quite read his expression. His pals sniffled at the air, though, but that could have meant anything. "And who's that with you, paladin?"

"Hi!" I called out with a big wave. "I'm Broccoli Bunch! And I'm looking to make friends and meet cool new people!"

```
Moley A. Holey
Desired Quality: Someone kind and friendly who likes
avoiding beaches and enjoys deep holes
Dream: To become the general of the eastern garrison
```

Moley seemed like a nice enough fellow.

"I am Guard Captain Wardmyth, of Granite Springs," Captain Wardmyth replied after a moment. I was pretty sure he said that in his own language, but no one seemed to mind.

"And what are two armed sylphs and a . . . long-eared human doing here?" Moley asked.

"I'm actually a bun," I corrected. "But I used to be a normal-eared human. Also, I'm not armed! I left my spade back on my ship."

"We are here to talk," Bastion said. "Granite Springs is concerned about the construction you have here."

Moley huffed very mightily. "Then Granite Springs should have answered the letters we sent!" he sniped back.

Bastion turned to Captain Wardmyth. "Did the mole folk send any letters to Granite Springs?"

"None that I'm aware of" was the reply. "And if they did, I would know."

Bastion nodded slowly. "Good sir, I believe we have a lot to discuss. It seems as if communications weren't terribly clear, leading to . . . the current situation. Perhaps we could all parley? Preferably peacefully?"

Moley eyed us all, then nodded. "Lower the gate!" he called out over his shoulder. "You three may enter. But no funny business!"

"Well then," I said. "Let's go have a chat!"

· Chapter Forty-Three ·

Diggy Diggy Hole

I looked up and around as we crossed the gate and walked into the little fortress next to the dam. The mole people had built walls all around with smaller buildings tucked up against them.

There was what looked like a smithy to one side, with a bit of smoke puffing out from above, and a few buildings that I guessed were barracks. The people moving about were clearly part of two groups: guards and soldiers, all wearing thick gambesons and often carrying spears and swords, and workers, who wore simpler clothes and carried belts full of tools. They were moving stacks of bricks, seemingly fresh from a nearby kiln.

The fortress had an opening in one wall, right against the rear of the dam. A wooden walkway allowed mole people workers to carry wheelbarrows full of bricks over to the end of the dam where others were stacking them.

Others were higher up, climbing over thick wooden scaffolds that allowed them to reach the top of the dam.

I was surprised that so many of the buildings inside the wall were made of bricks, with the exterior wall being covered in packed mud. Maybe they were using the mud as a sort of additional barrier? Or maybe it would dry up and create a stronger wall? I didn't know enough about construction stuff to guess.

"Greetings," Moley said as he climbed down some steps and came to stand before us, his hands at his hips and a pair of soldiers at his back. "Welcome to temporary Fort Moltain."

"It's a very cool fort," I said.

Moley didn't look impressed by my enthusiastic response. "It's a simple fortress, but one that should serve its purpose."

"If you don't mind me being so blunt," Bastion said, "what is that purpose?"

Moley stood a little taller, which brought his head even with my chin. "Fort Moltain is a defensive position from which we can build a dam."

"And why are you building a dam?" Bastion asked.

The mole person sniffed. "As an offensive measure. Did you think we would sit back and ignore your lack of response? If Granite Springs won't cease their actions against us, then we have no choice but to act against Granite Springs."

I noticed Captain Wardmyth placing a hand over the hilt of his sword. "Did he just say they were going on the offensive against us?"

I waved him down. "No, no, I'm sure there's an explanation," I said. "Right, Mister Moley Holey?"

"That's General Holey," the mole person said. "Perhaps you could introduce yourselves?"

Bastion nodded. "I'm Paladin Bastion Coldfront, this is Guard Captain Wardmyth, from Granite Springs, and this is Captain Broccoli Bunch. She's an airship captain from outside Sylphfree. Her translation and negotiation skills are why she is present."

"Hi!" I said.

"Humph, well, if that's how the sylphs want to do things, more power to you. I, for one, don't care for your lack of professionalism."

Bastion nodded slowly. "I'm going to be entirely honest with you, General. I don't know why the mole people are building this dam. I can imagine it being quite harmful to the people of Granite Springs, though, and those people are, to some degree, my responsibility."

"Then you should have addressed our concerns months ago," the general said.

"What concerns? I've been in the area for less than a day. I'm unaware of what trouble your people are facing and why harming Granite Springs would alleviate that."

General Holey looked at Bastion for a moment, then he turned beady eyes onto me. "Perhaps . . . Come."

With that, the general spun on his heel and walked across the open center of the fort. Groups of soldiers paused to let us pass, and I felt the stares of curious mole folk workers as we moved toward a building on the other end of the fort, nearly opposite the dam.

The general opened a doorway in a small building, revealing a staircase leading down into a dimly lit tunnel. "This way," he said as he stepped down.

I eyed Bastion, but he just shrugged a shoulder and followed the mole person in.

I encountered a problem as I followed him.

I didn't fit.

Well, I could manage, but I had to walk with my back bent, and I had to grab a hold of my ears to make sure they didn't scrape the ceiling. When we reached the first strut keeping the ceiling up, it got worse as I had to duck down below that.

I was about to complain when something popped up before me.

```
Ding! For repeating a special action a sufficient num-
ber of times, you have unlocked the class skill: Proportion
Distortion!
```

"Huh?"

"Is something the matter?" Bastion asked.

"No, it's just— Ah!" I winced and cradled my head. I shouldn't have looked up while crossing under another support beam. At least I was wearing my helmet, or else I'd have a bump.

```
Proportion Distortion
Rank F - 01%
The ability to fit in and fit out.
```

What did that even mean? And why was the World giving me weird skills again?

"Here we are," General Holey said as he stepped in front of a door and pushed it open. It led into a small room with desks and a few mole people who looked up at our arrival. "Get me a map of the area," the general demanded.

A map was laid out on the table, and I moved closer so I could see it. My mind was still mostly on my new skill, though. What did it even do? And why did I get it while trying not to bonk my head?

"The letters and correspondence we sent to Granite Springs were all in relation to this," the general said. He poked a long-nailed finger at a spot on the map. I glanced at it. The map was mostly topographic, with notes here and there. The place he was pointing to was a small town, or maybe a city. The details weren't great. It was also, I noted, underground.

"That's the local mole person village?" Bastion asked.

"That's Dhigeyhole. A small outpost that's grown into a full township," General Holey said. "Nice and peaceful, with a fair guard and not much trouble besides. This"—he moved his finger to a spot next to the village— "is a quarry from Granite Springs, one that's infringing upon Dhigeyhole. The quarry has caused a few cave-ins already, and we've had to evacuate a portion of the town."

I gasped. "That's awful."

"It's also a violation of the Dhigeyhole–Granite Springs treaty of sixty years ago," the general said. "The entire thing only gets worse when you consider the lay of the land. The river downhill from here runs close to that quarry. One unlucky tremor, and the river could be diverted into the quarry, and, with that amount of water coming to bear, it might well flood the entire town below."

"So that's why you're damming the river?" I asked.

"We're not just damming it, we're leading it elsewhere," he said.

Bastion leaned over the map, hands grabbing at the edge of the table so he could look down at everything from above. "Captain Wardmyth, did you ever receive anything from the quarry about this?"

"I did not," the guard captain said.

"When did the quarry start encroaching on Dhigeyhole?" Bastion asked.

The general hummed. "Two months ago? We noticed they were digging a little wider, but we initially suspected it was just a slight error—a poorly read map, a lazy surveyor. We addressed the mining company first, but they dismissed our claims. Then we started to protest in earnest, but we discovered the mining company was employing guards of their own."

"Guards?" Bastion asked. "For a mining company? Captain Wardmyth, I find myself quite confused."

"I'm feeling the same way," the guard captain said. "The quarry is run by Granite Springs, and the town guard is run by myself. There shouldn't be any such deployment without my knowledge."

"Unless they're not town guards," I said.

Captain Wardmyth nodded. "That's possible. What do these guards look like? Do they have uniform equipment?"

The general nodded. "They did. Similar to yours but darker."

Bastion's brows knit together in a frown. "Darker than standard guard armor. Did they have tabards?"

"They did. Black, with orange trim."

"That's the army," Bastion said.

"A division was stationed in town. They've been active lately, but with the alert level higher now, I thought that was ordinary."

Bastion hummed. "Who did you contact about the quarry? You said you sent correspondence, but it's clear it never arrived, or if it did, it was never delivered to the guard captain here."

"We sent it to the quarry first, then to the town, but our messengers were always intercepted by your army."

"That's an issue," Bastion said.

"Can the army do that?" I asked. "For that matter, why would they be so mean?"

"That's a good question," Bastion said. "They might have the authority to protect the quarry—it is run by the state—but to go so far as to basically start a conflict with the locals like this . . . That's terribly unwise."

The general sniffed. "I received a letter once. Our only reply." The mole person waddled over to a desk and tugged out a drawer. He returned with a letter, which he passed to Bastion.

Bastion unfolded it, eyes darting across the page. "Major Springsong. I've never heard of them . . . This letter says a lot of nothing."

"I was rather insulted by it, yes," the general said.

"Where is the army stationed?" Bastion asked. "I can't imagine they're only staying within Granite Springs."

"There's a camp next to town," Captain Wardmyth said. "I believe the major might be there."

"Is he the highest-ranking officer?" Bastion asked.

"No, there's a Commander Warmwood who moved in a few months ago."

I hummed. "Maybe we should go say hi to the commander, then. They're hurting the poor mole people."

"We are hardly poor, nor are we unable to care for ourselves."

I nodded, ears smack-smacking the ceiling. "Yes, but it sounds like you're basically being bullied, which is never nice. We can't just sit back and do nothing about it. Also, I want to visit Dhigeyhole. A whole town underground? I bet it's really neat!"

Bastion rubbed at his chin, then nodded. "General, may I ask a favor of you?"

"You may ask. Whether or not I grant it will depend."

Bastion nodded. "That's understandable. I'm going to go meet the commander of the army in this region. I think he might have some things to answer for. While I do that, would it be possible to abstain from finishing the dam? I don't want irreparable damage to be done because one person overreached."

The mole person general scratched at his furry neck. "I suppose I could have the workers shift to more preparatory work. It wouldn't slow things down overly. But that would require I put my trust in you, Paladin."

"I am a sylph of my word," Bastion said. "And I give it to you when I say I will do everything in my power to ensure that this situation is resolved in a timely fashion."

"I'll do my best too!" I said, my most serious face on.

"Humph, well, I suppose that's something. You have until this evening. Then we'll be finishing the dam, and our sappers will be diverting the river."

"We'll be quick about it, then," Bastion said.

· Chapter Forty-Four ·

Anything You Can Do,
I Can Do Better (Except for Hugs)

General Holey escorted us back out of the underground base. This time, I was sure to keep my head ducked to avoid bonking my forehead against a beam again.

Once we were out and back under the full light of the sun—there was a lot of blinking until our eyes adjusted—the general flagged down a mole person who looked like he was one of the workers, though he had a big sash over his chest that might have been a sign he was important.

The general relayed a few quick orders, mostly telling the foremole to shift the focus of their construction for the next few hours, and that he'd explain more in a moment.

He was doing his part of the agreement with Bastion.

"I trust," General Holey said as he turned back to us, clawed hands on hips, "that you'll carry out your end of all this?"

"We'll do what we can," Bastion said. "As I said, my goal is to avoid conflicts, which, right now, means addressing your concerns."

The general nodded seriously. "I appreciate it, Paladin," he said before extending a hand to Bastion. My smaller friend grabbed it and shook.

"See you later then!" I said.

"Ah, yes, have a good afternoon, Captain Bunch, Captain Wardmyth," General Holey said with a nod for the both of us.

I waved goodbye. I wanted to hug him. He seemed very soft under all the armor. But we weren't on those kinds of terms yet, and besides, he did have all those armored bits in the way.

The gate was lowered, and we crossed back out of the wall, the general following us to the threshold. "Good luck, and may the skies remain clear above you."

"May Dirt keep you in its embrace," Bastion returned with a small bow.

Then we were off, heading back to the little wagon with the other guards on it. "That was well done," Captain Wardmyth said.

"Just a day's work," Bastion said. "This situation with the army disturbs me. I can't imagine their actions being approved by the brass."

"You think someone's doing something they shouldn't?" I asked. "I mean, other than how much the army shouldn't be mean already. The way General Holey described things makes it sound almost as if the mole folk are being bullied. I can kinda understand doing what the moles are doing, even if I know that being mean isn't how you respond to someone else being mean back."

"I think that the local garrison has decided to ignore some rather important protocols at a time where doing such is even more irresponsible than usual," Bastion said.

"More than usual?" I asked. "Because of the war?"

Bastion nodded, then cast a glance toward Captain Wardmyth, who was walking just a pinch stiffly. "I don't mean to be rude, Broccoli, but maybe keep what you know about that to yourself for now. There isn't a war yet, and hopefully, there won't be one."

"I understand," I said. "I can keep quiet . . . So, where are we going now?"

Bastion considered it for a moment. "Captain Wardmyth, I think it would be more expedient for you to visit the quarry. It isn't too far from here. Maybe you can get some answers from there. Meanwhile, Captain Bunch and I will be visiting Commander Warmwood."

"That's a ways away," Captain Wardmyth said.

Bastion dismissed the concern with a wave of his hand. "I've been on a ship for some time, and while I did keep up with my training, there wasn't much room for a good jog. The run will do me good. As for the captain . . . Broccoli, how would you like to race?"

"A race? From here back to Granite Springs? I don't know, I've never really been competitive."

Bastion shifted, his shoulders and back stretching under his armor. "That's fine, too, as long as we keep a good pace."

It would be fun to see how fast I could go. I'd liked running back on Earth, and I guess I'd done a lot of exercise since coming here. It would be cool to see how much faster I was. Plus, I had Way of the Mystic Bun, which used to have Hopping in it. That probably made me pretty fast. Rabbits were the symbol for speed for a reason . . . well, at least on lawn mower throttles. "All right," I said.

Bastion grinned, then turned to the captain. "We'll be back soon enough, I imagine. Stay near the quarry for a while. But if we haven't returned by evening, contact the Palace."

Captain Wardmyth saluted. "Yes, sir."

Bastion stopped, then reached back while folding a leg and grabbed onto his ankle. He stretched, so I did the same.

Or at least I tried. It had been a long time since I'd done any stretching, even if I knew it was important to do before exercising.

"I'll let you set the pace," Bastion said.

"Cool! I don't know how fast I am now, so call out if you can't keep up!"

Bastion laughed. It was a very mean "As if you can outrun me" sort of laugh. I'd just have to prove him wrong.

I knelt, planted my feet properly, bent my back a bit, then wiggled my rear to make sure everything was loose.

Then I *bounced.*

My feet hammered into the ground, shooting me forward in a dead sprint that had my hair and ears flapping out behind me. Each step skipped me ahead a dozen paces, with my shoe hitting the ground with a solid stomp.

I had to blink hard to keep the wind from blurring my vision, so I bowed my head and knelt into it. It was a weird way to run, more of a very fast skip than a proper sprint, but I was going really fast, the ground zooming past and trees blurring on either side of the road.

I glanced back.

Bastion was casually running a pace behind me, a small smile on his lips.

I huffed and pushed myself harder.

Bastion ran up alongside me. "So, you seemed surprised when we entered the base with the general. Did something occur?"

I started swinging my arms; that always helped.

"It . . . was . . . a . . . new . . . skill," I said between pants.

"Oh? What's the skill? By the way, you don't need that much stamina. Use it as you're moving your leg, then in your thigh as you bring your leg back up. Let your body take care of most of it. The stamina you use should be to assist, not to do all the work."

I swallowed and tried to do as he said, then I wobbled and almost stumbled as my legs didn't move as fast as I needed them to on the next bounce.

"We don't need to be moving this fast—a smoother pace would be a lot easier. Less strain, less risk of taking a fall."

Reluctantly, I slowed down. It was probably for the best. My breathing was already coming in hard, and my heart was ringing around in my chest like an alarm clock going off. "Okay, okay," I said. It was probably going to be easier to talk at a quick jog anyway.

"So, the new skill?"

"Oh! It's called, uh, Proportion Distortion."

Bastion hummed. "I'm unfamiliar with that one. What does it do?"

"The description says it'll help me fit in and out, but that doesn't really help. I got it while I was following you and the general into that tunnel."

"Interesting."

"Is it rare, maybe?"

"Perhaps. There is no doubt an order of magnitude more skills I haven't heard of than skills that I have, so my ignorance here shouldn't count as a surprise. Still, I'd venture a guess that it might be a skill that will make it easier for you to fit into tight spaces. I'm not sure why you'd specifically gain that skill, though."

"That . . . sounds kind of useless. We live on an airship, not underground," I said.

"It's been my experience that no skill is truly useless. The World isn't so cruel as to give someone a skill they won't need."

I pouted. That was a lie. I still had Adorable, and there was never a skill less useful than that. I'd have to see what Proportion Distortion turned into.

"Once we reach the capital, maybe you could visit the library. There's a section there with books entirely dedicated to skills, and there are some archivists who would love to have you describe any unique skills you have and what they do."

"That sounds practical," I said. "They help people?"

"Freely, yes. Certain skills are only unlocked while doing certain actions. The differences between two skills can be slight, but sometimes they can be fairly important. Sword Fighting Proficiency is greater than Swordplay Proficiency."

"What's the difference?" I asked.

"Fighting is more about the use of a sword in combat. Play is inclined toward flashier, more complex movements. Swordplay is certainly more impressive, but if I were a betting sylph, I'd put my coin on whoever had Sword Fighting Proficiency first."

"Huh," I said as I considered it. That made some sense. Some skills were likely very close in nature. What even was the difference between Cute and Adorable anyway? Other than the heightened insult.

I think Bastion was trying to read my mind or something. "Getting rid of a skill is tricky business, but there are almost always a few combination skills available, and it's sometimes worth losing a general skill for some time to get something that will combine with another skill you dislike."

"That would be great," I said.

I added "Find a way to get rid of Adorable" to the top of my priority list.

The road moved on, our pace never really slowing, even though I was chewing through my stamina with a point lost every couple of bounces. Once in a while I'd regain a point, though, so it wasn't all bad.

Also, Cleaning magic meant I wasn't sweaty or anything, which was a bonus when it came to smell, but not so much in keeping cool.

We arrived back at Granite Springs in good time, one of the guards by the gate running out to meet us with obvious concern. Bastion reassured him that everything was well, but then asked if we could have a small escort over to the military base, and if there was a way to talk to whoever was Captain Wardmyth's second-in-command.

Things moved pretty fast after that. Bastion talked in quick, clipped tones with a couple of guards, then he relayed what we'd learned to a lieutenant in the guard, who was told to go and repeat it all to the mayor.

I stayed near Bastion the entire time, trying not to get in his way.

I did spot the *Beaver Cleaver* parked above, still sitting pretty in his berth.

Bastion gestured for me to follow him, and we made our way around the exterior walls of the city. They had a very small dip before the wall, not quite a ditch but almost. I wondered if that counted as a moat or not. If it did, it was a very disappointing one.

"The base is . . . right there," Bastion said as he gestured ahead.

A section of the wall looked a little newer, and that jutted out of the rest at a ninety-degree angle. A boxy protrusion on the side of the city, with a few additional towers and a second gate leading out onto a packed dirt road.

A couple of rows of young sylphs were in the back, sweating under the sunlight while swinging swords up and down with dull monotony.

"Can you clean off my armor?" Bastion asked. "If it isn't too much trouble. We'll need to be presentable for this next part."

"No problem," I said, flaring my Cleaning magic. "I'll let you do the talking, you let me do any necessary hugging."

"Deal."

· **Chapter Forty-Five** ·

Chain of Command

All it took to see the commander of the base was for Bastion to walk up to the front and politely—but firmly—say, "I need to speak with Commander Warmwood."

No one questioned us, and even though we passed many soldiers, not one of them stopped us—though a few stared, of course. I was getting used to it. Not only was I not a sylph, I was also very much not a soldier. Bastion got his share of attention, too, and a few salutes, though some didn't seem as certain as others.

The commander's office was in the largest building of the headquarters, a place where we were brought to and told to wait while the commander prepared himself to receive us.

"Any questions?" Bastion asked me as we both stood by the wooden door that blocked the way into the office.

"Why did only some of them salute?"

He chuckled. "Observant. As a paladin, I have no actual military rank. Also, as a paladin, I can give orders to the military and expect them to be . . . considered. It's a strange position. No authoritative power and yet some cultural power. It helps that most paladins were, at one time or another, in the military, most with some form of officer ranking. Though there are plenty of paladins from elsewhere—the guard, for example, and some were outright civilians before joining."

"Neat," I said. Bastion's specialness really shone when he was in his own nation. "Do I have to address the commander in any special way?"

"Refer to him as Sir Warmwood or Commander Warmwood. Be polite. Do . . . try not to hug him. Don't salute. You're not a servicewoman, and I doubt you know how to salute properly besides."

"I'll do my best, Sir Bastion, sir." I said. I snapped a salute, one foot thumping down and ears bouncing as I brought a hand to my forehead.

Bastion looked me up and down. "If you were my subordinate, I'd have you running laps to improve your form."

I grinned and lowered my arm just as the door opened. "Come in, please," someone said from the other side.

Bastion stepped in and held the door open for me.

The office was about what I expected of an office: a large wooden desk, sharp and angular, with a big padded seat behind it and two more seats before it, much less padded and not nearly as comfy-looking. The table was mostly cleared, except for a small potted plant on one corner and an oil lantern on the other. Some papers were stacked neatly in the middle, a gilded fountain pen left next to them.

I blinked as the person I guessed was the commander moved behind the desk.

I'd never seen an old sylph before. Not really. Or maybe I'd seen a few on the streets, but I'd hardly had an excuse to stare, and it would have been rude. The commander was an older sylph, with a heavy brow covered in white bristles, and saggy jowls under a scraggly mustache that could have passed for a brush. His hair still had some black to it, the same color as Bastion's own, and he had eyes that were a darker green than Bastion's.

"Commander Warmwood," Bastion said as he saluted.

The commander nodded. "A pleasure to meet you, Paladin."

"Paladin Bastion Coldfront, sir."

The commander turned and eyed me up and down, and I had to suppress the urge to salute. It almost felt as if I *had* to in his presence. "And you are?"

"I'm Broccoli," I said. If I couldn't salute, I could at least smile.

"This is Captain Bunch, of the airship *Beaver Cleaver*. Her ship is the one I used to come here, and the captain happens to be a very talented explorer with a few skills that might come in handy," Bastion explained simply.

"I see," Commander Warmwood said. "Very well. Pleased to meet you, Captain. I hope you find the base comfortable and that my men have acquitted themselves well."

I nodded. "Everyone's been very nice so far."

"Wonderful. Now, Sir Bastion, might I finally learn why I have a royal paladin in my office?"

Bastion shifted, arms folding up in the small of his back and legs planting more firmly in place. "Commander, it has come to my attention that there has been some recent trouble with the local mole folk colony. The city guard became aware of my presence and asked me for assistance."

The commander nodded slowly. "That seems appropriate, yes."

"We discovered that the mole folk have begun to build a large dam, which might threaten the safety of Granite Springs. Diverting the river entering the town would cause some obvious issues. The damage to infrastructure, and potentially the health of the citizens here, definitely escalates the issue."

The commander straightened. "I see. I imagine destroying a dam would be a difficult task for a lone paladin, no matter how strong."

"Actually, I believe it would be possible to convince the mole people to deconstruct their new project. It would be a much safer alternative than outright destruction."

Commander Warmwood grinned. "Ah, a fine idea. Have them take apart their own tools of insubordination. That has a certain level of ironic charm to it."

"Wow," I said. "You just keep jumping to all the most violent possibilities."

The commander looked my way, confusion showing in the set of his bushy brow. "Pardon me?"

"I don't know. Every solution you have is very . . . hammery."

"What Captain Broccoli is trying to say, I believe," Bastion cut in, "is that we have already come into contact with the mole people. Specifically, a General Holey, who is in charge of the forces at the dam. In situations like these, with possible diplomatic tensions on the line, I find it best to open a channel of communication between both sides before escalating to violence."

"I . . . see," Commander Warmwood said. He moved around his desk and sat himself down on his plush chair. Then he gestured to the seats across from him. I took one, wiggling myself in place until I was comfy. "That's reasonable. I'm beginning to suspect that I'm missing some key information here."

Bastion didn't take a seat, staying standing instead. "I believe that might be the case, yes. Though I also suspect that it's through no fault of your own."

"Very well, then. Lay it out for me."

"From my preliminary investigation, one that I started only this morning, I believe the sequence of events is as such: A quarry operated by Granite Springs relocated some of its equipment and dug in a new direction. This direction happened to lead the quarrying work into an area over the mole people town. I haven't observed the Dhigeyhole–Granite Springs treaty, but this might be a violation of it."

The commander sniffed. "So we started digging over their heads, did we?"

"Indeed. They have evacuated a portion of their town and seem ready to divert the river, for fear that it will shift toward the quarry, fill it with water, and potentially harm their town."

Commander Warmwood leaned forward, elbows on his desk. "Were you not a paladin, I'd say that the entire story was a little far-fetched. But I imagine this is the kind of complication you're meant to deal with."

"They're not usually so simple," Bastion admitted.

The commander huffed. "Very well, you've convinced me that the military should intervene. It's our duty to protect the citizenry, and I imagine this situation is beyond the ability of the guard. Do you have a plan, Paladin Coldfront?"

Bastion nodded. "Thank you, sir. During my meeting with the mole person general, he mentioned that he had sent frequent requests to Granite Springs, but these were intercepted by the military."

The commander sat straighter in his seat. "What's the meaning of that?"

"I do not know how trustworthy the general is, but he seemed quite put out by the lack of response. I believe the attempts, at least, were genuine. He also mentioned a Major Springsong."

The commander's upper lip twitched, a distasteful look crossing his features. "Oh, *him*," he said before schooling his expression.

This was all very exciting. My mom used to love watching court procedurals and detective shows; this felt like being in one of those, but live. It was kinda cool. "Do you know him?" I asked.

The commander eyed me and then Bastion before replying. "I do. He's not under my chain of command."

Bastion tilted his head to the side, just a tiny bit. A quirk, showing his confusion, maybe. "He isn't? Forgive me, is there any other battalion in the region?"

Commander Warmwood shook his head. "No, but you're not a foolish boy—I imagine you can figure it out."

"The Inquisition, then," Bastion said.

I blinked. I hadn't heard of them in a while. "Aren't you part of the Inquisition?" I asked.

Bastion shook his head, then paused and seemed to change his mind before nodding. "Technically, yes. The Royal Order of Paladins of the World operate under the auspices of the Inquisition. I'm a paladin of the Royal Inquisition. So yes, on paper, I'm part of that organization. In practical terms, we are different. The Inquisition itself is mostly concerned with internal matters—protecting the nobility and ensuring the proper functioning of the nation—whereas paladins serve to protect the royal family. We serve the king, the queen, and their offspring more directly. Which often entails conflict resolution on their behalf."

My head bobbed up and down. I'd understood most of that. "So, Major Springsong is an inquisitor."

"With a small platoon of soldiers under his command," Commander Warmwood replied. "I knew he was out of the base with the majority of his troops, but I imagined they were doing training drills or the like. It isn't too uncommon to use the wilderness here for that sort of thing."

"It seems like that's not the case," Bastion said. "Not unless it's the most bizarre wilderness training I've ever heard of."

"No, I would suppose not," Warmwood agreed. The commander tapped the top of his desk with his fingertips. "This is becoming more complex than I'd imagined. It's not in my purview to go bother the Inquisition, not without good reason. On the other hand, the settlement I'm supposed to protect risks being attacked or at least damaged. That's plenty 'good reason.'"

"But you're still worried?" Bastion asked.

Commander Warmwood nodded. "It's unusual."

"Um, but we're going to do something, right? We can't just sit back, not when this might hurt the people," I said. "We should go talk to this Major Springsong and see why he did what he did."

"That seems like a reasonable approach," Bastion agreed. "I don't imagine you know his exact location?"

The commander nodded. "As a matter of fact, I do," he said. The old sylph pushed off his desk and stood up. "I'm going to raise the alert level within the base by a notch."

"Are you certain?" Bastion asked.

"I have the impression that no matter how things turn out, it will mean action," the commander replied. "My bones might be growing old, but they're old because I trust them when they ache like this."

Bastion nodded. "Very well, then. If you could have someone point us in the right direction, then the captain and I will be off. I feel like we'll be running ourselves ragged by the end of the day, trying to keep up with everything that's going on."

The commander snorted. "Indeed. I'm glad you're here, Paladin. I can't imagine what it would mean to learn all this even a day later."

"Just doing my job, sir," Bastion said. "I hope you don't mind if I skip some of the formalities. I think we might be more pressed for time than I'd initially imagined."

"I understand. Good luck, Paladin. And you, too, Captain."

· Chapter Forty-Six ·

On the Back Foot

So, now what?" I asked as I followed Bastion out of the headquarters.

The paladin paused, jaw working as he thought. "Are you certain you want to keep following me?" he asked. "This is becoming increasingly political."

"Is that a bad thing for me?" I asked. "I'm not about to let one of my best friends do something hard without at least trying my best to help him."

Bastion chuckled. "I should have figured you'd say something like that. Very well, our next step will be informing the guard of what's going on. Then we move over to the quarry and find Major Springsong. I feel as if everything we're dealing with leads to him in particular."

"All right," I said. We'd finally reach the person responsible for the entire kerfuffle. I hoped. If we reached Major Springsong, and it turned out that it wasn't them and that someone else was responsible, then . . . "Is your job always like this?" I asked.

"You mean running around, looking for fires, then stamping them out as best I can? Yes, that would describe a good portion of a paladin's work. We're often turned into errand boys and sent around to take care of things for the royal family where it wouldn't be politically or practically possible for them to show up in person. We're essentially problem fixers with royal backing."

"That's kind of neat," I said. "The king and queen must trust you a bunch."

Bastion nodded. "That's one of the nicer perks, yes. It's not every sylph that will even see their monarchs, let alone ever speak with them. The Royal Order is given a lot of trust, which also puts a lot of pressure on us. A mistake carried out in the name of the king is going to be very costly, no matter what."

I could imagine. That had to be pretty stressful. But then, I was sure Bastion managed it just fine. He was one of the coolest people I'd ever met.

On leaving the headquarters, Bastion gestured toward the front gate, past more soldiers who were running laps around a small field. We weren't halfway to the gate when I heard some shouted orders being tossed around, and soon the soldiers were snapping to attention and darting toward what I guessed was their barracks.

"The alert level's rising," Bastion said.

"What does that mean?" I asked. "I mean, I can guess, but I figure you know-know."

Bastion laughed. "It means the soldiers here have just gotten a day off from training. Now they'll gear up and move on to one of the other things soldiers are good at."

"What's that?"

"There's three things you're taught to do as a soldier: train, fight, and wait. Now they'll have the rest of the day to wait."

The guards at the gate opened up the door for us, and we stepped out of the base and back out onto the packed-dirt road around town. A few guards were waiting for us there, and Bastion approached them to talk. I hung back a little bit.

Today had been a lot of running around, and while it wasn't quite as fun as some things, it still felt pretty nice. We were on a sort of adventure, but instead of the stakes being just . . . me and my friends having fun, they were larger.

Then again, our last few adventures had been like that, too, hadn't they?

I hadn't really considered it, but more and more of our adventures were big, at least big in the sense that they were helping a lot of people with a bunch of things. That was . . . Well, it wasn't bad, but I had kind of set out expecting my adventures to only really be about me and a few friends. It was strange to think that more and more often our adventures were dealing with big, important things.

"We're ready," Bastion said, snapping me out of my thoughts.

I grinned at him and nodded. "All right. Let's head out, then."

The quarry was past the halfway mark between Granite Springs and the mole people dam, which meant our run wasn't quite as strenuous. We'd also had a nice long pause to regain some stamina, though my legs were wobbly at first.

Bastion set the pace again, not too fast nor slow, a bouncing jog that made us eat up the distance until we veered off the main road and onto the quarry road. We ran around the edge of a huge circular hole in the ground filled with water at its bottom.

A bunch of buildings were in the middle of the quarry, where carts pulled by donkeys were bringing big slabs of stone to a workshop, where some sylphs picked them up with chains and pulleys. On the opposite end, square-cut blocks were being stacked onto another long cart.

Some of the buildings looked like barracks, and there was an obvious kitchen. Stables near the rear held the animals used to run the place, and there was a small building that looked like the headquarters.

Bastion led us across the quarry, walking with the certainty of someone who was definitely allowed to be there.

The sylphs working at the quarry all seemed very strong, which was strange. They were still short, but short with big bulging arms. Most didn't wear shirts, but nearly all of them had hard leather caps that made their heads look like pins. A lot of them stared, but no one seemed inclined to move over and actually stop or ask us any questions.

And then we were past the quarry and heading toward a small patch of woods not too far from there—an area with a small wall around it, and tents installed behind that.

There were sylphs around who were all obviously soldiers, with black tabards over their gear and spears held by their sides.

They tensed as Bastion and I moved up the hill to meet them. "Who goes there?" one of them asked.

"I'm Paladin Coldfront," Bastion said. "I'm here to speak with Major Springsong or whoever is in charge."

The soldiers looked at each other, then one ran off into their camp. I guessed that there weren't more than fifty or so soldiers here, spread out across about half that many tents, which were laid out in neat rows. They had built a small wall, loose stones at the base with wooden posts above those, each ending in a rough-hewn spike.

Bastion stood tall next to me, eyes fixed on the soldiers before us, who started to sweat a little at his unflinching gaze.

Then the major showed up.

I was expecting someone tall—for a sylph—in resplendent armor and maybe with the same bearing as Bastion. Instead, the major was a shorter sylph with a squinty look on his face, wearing shiny armor that looked half a size too big for him.

He stared around, noticed Bastion and myself, then ran over with a blossoming smile. "Paladin Coldfront! It's wonderful to see you, sir," he said.

"Hello," Bastion said. He sounded like he was on the back foot. I guess the warm welcome was unexpected.

"I didn't expect your arrival so soon, but I'm infinitely grateful that you're here. Please, follow me." The major took Bastion's hand, shaking it up and down in a hurry before turning around and walking into the camp.

Bastion and I looked at each other, and I shrugged before we moved on after the major.

The interior of the camp wasn't anything too special. Tents were set in small circles around campfires, and the camp was laid out so that there was a wide lane down the middle that soldiers could use to move around. A larger tent stood at one end, with a pair of black banners hanging on either side of its entrance. The major stood there, with his back straight and features neutral, but he was also bouncing on the balls of his feet with nervous energy.

"This is our issue," the major said as soon as we walked in. A desk was in the center, with a pile of letters sitting atop it and a map across the surface. He shoved the letters to the side to make room to see the map. "There's a monster living here"—his finger stabbed down onto the map—"and we need it dead."

"One moment," Bastion said. "I think you're operating under a false assumption."

The major blinked. "Pardon?"

"I'm not here to answer a specific request. I'm here investigating the issue with the mole people, especially with regards to the dam they're building that's risking Granite Springs."

"You're not here for the dungeon?"

"What dungeon?" I asked.

There was a long silence as everyone in the tent took each other in. ". . . I believe that perhaps you are right, Paladin—there has been some level of miscommunication here. I sent word to the capital three days ago, requesting assistance with a delicate matter. I had assumed you were the response."

"I understand that much," Bastion said. "But unfortunately, no, I'm here because I was passing through. I heard there was an issue with the mole folk, and after tracking it down, I came here, to what seems to be the source of the issue."

The major's face screwed up for a moment before his expression flattened. "The mole people have been causing me some level of distress, yes."

"Is that correspondence on the table letters from the mole people?" Bastion asked.

The major glanced down, then back up. "That? Oh, yes, they are."

I poked at the pile, moving some of the letters around. "Some of these are still sealed."

"Yes, well, the concerns of some mole people hardly matter to the Inquisition."

"But these aren't addressed to you," I said.

"They might hold information that would reveal what we're doing here . . . Paladin, who is this bun?"

"This is Captain Bunch. She's outside your chain of command," Bastion said.

"I don't recall the army having buns in it," the major said.

"She's an airship captain," Bastion replied, which only seemed to confuse the major more. "And her concerns are valid. Are you aware of what the mole people are doing at this moment? For that matter, are you responsible for the quarry changing the location it's digging in?"

"I recall reading some base threats. And yes, of course. We can't have them continue digging where they were, and the nation might well need the stone being quarried in the near future. I can't possibly just halt all operations. Besides, doing so would only pose a greater risk that knowledge of the dungeon might leak."

"Ah yes, the dungeon," Bastion said. "I'm aware that the appearance of a new dungeon is important to the nation, but a settlement the size of Granite Springs—not to mention the nation's alliance with the mole people—ought to outweigh the value of keeping one dungeon secret."

The major blinked fast. I had the impression that he wasn't so much mean, or even incompetent, as he was . . . focused on his task. "This new dungeon will hardly threaten the town. If anything, the movement of additional people to the region and the change in ambient mana would help Granite Springs."

"For things to help the town, the town needs to still be around," Bastion said.

I decided to butt in a little. "I don't think the entire town is at risk, but, well, if we don't do something, people might get hurt, and I can't think of many secrets that are worth hurting people over."

"I . . . I see? None of this would be an issue if it weren't for that damnable near-dragon thing."

". . . What dragon thing?" Bastion asked.

· Chapter Forty-Seven ·

Move Fast and Break Things

Major Springsong rolled out a map onto the surface of his desk. It was one of those black and white elevation maps with lines all across it and plenty of little notes. "This is the old quarry," he said, tapping part of the map with his forefinger. "This is the location where the quarry is supposed to be digging next, this part of the mountainside here. The stone there's used for a specific kind of runework. I'll admit I'm not exactly sure what they look for in the rocks to know which would be suitable."

"And the mole people's village?" Bastion asked.

"Over here, more or less," the major said as he gestured off to the side a little. "Their village has been expanding in nearly every direction, so our initial survey of its location is likely wrong. We dug a new quarry here, nearer to the village and over that line we agreed upon, but it shouldn't have been an issue."

"Only, because of their expansion, it is," Bastion finished. He didn't look pleased. The major had just admitted to breaking an agreement.

"Exactly," the major finished. Did he not notice the slight tightening in Bastion's eyes?

"But they're allowed to expand that way, right?" I asked.

Major Springsong nodded. "Certainly. Sylphfree doesn't usually care what the mole people do underground, as long as it's not likely to cause some landslide that might threaten a sylph settlement."

"All right," I said. "So where's the dragon?"

"Not actually a dragon," the major said quickly. "If we had an actual dragon on our hands, you can bet we'd have the entire army here by now, with every airship we could arm and every wizard and paladin worth their salt ready to fight."

"Wow, you really don't like dragons."

Bastion shifted a little. "Sylphfree has had . . . multiple issues with dragonkin. Of which this might be one. What are we dealing with here?"

"An amphiptere," Major Springsong said. "Not some little snake with wings, but a matriarch."

"Age?" Bastion asked. He was being very serious, I sensed.

The major shook his head. "I don't know. It seems somewhat dormant. The snake has a small injury along one side. I think it might have injured one of its wings. Perhaps it was hibernating and something fell on it, but that's just speculation. It's about sixty meters long, two meters wide."

That was about twice the length of the *Beaver Cleaver*. That had to be a huge snake.

"So it's an older one. Any idea of the level?"

Another shake of the major's head. "Three marks from my highest-level scout. He's at twenty, so . . ."

"So at least level forty," Bastion said. "I know some of them can be clever enough to enter a dungeon and eat their way through to the end. Otherwise, it simply aged enough to gain natural classes."

"Sounds like it would be a tough fight," I said.

"A very difficult one," Bastion replied. "And no, before you ask, you can't negotiate with dragonkin."

"But I've spoken to dragons before."

"What?" the major asked.

Bastion waved him down. "She's an airship captain who isn't from Sylphfree," he said. That seemed to placate the major. "Dragonkin, such as amphipteres, drakes, or wyrms, aren't any more intelligent than a wild dog."

"Oh," I said.

"They occur when a dragon . . . mates with a nondraconic creature. The offspring will have some traits of each. If you want more details . . . ask Amaryllis."

I couldn't help but feel that the last comment there was some sort of joke at Amaryllis's expense. "All right," I said. "So, the amphiptere is a *monster* monster. We can't reason with it, and . . . Is it dangerous?"

"It's a quiet threat for now," Major Springsong said. "As long as it's still mostly dormant, it shouldn't be an issue. The problem comes from when it awakens. The beast will be hungry then. But that could be weeks from now. For the moment, I'm securing the new dungeon, assessing it, and protecting it."

"You haven't done anything about the creature yet?" Bastion asked.

"I sent a request to the office of the Inquisition for assistance. A paladin or two to deal with the monster."

"I don't know if even two paladins would be enough to deal with a creature in its fourth tier or higher," Bastion said. "We'd need assistance from the local garrison, as well as your group here."

The major seemed entirely onboard with that idea. "That would be wonderful. It's hidden in a crevice near the old quarry, so hitting it from above won't be possible. We'll need to bait it out."

"I wouldn't want to fight that kind of creature in any sort of crevice or cavern," Bastion said. "No room for formation fighting." Bastion shifted, a hand coming up to cup his chin. "This . . . is a problem. I came here to address the quarry, though."

"We can stop digging immediately," Major Springsong said. "It wouldn't be hard. The issue then is that we need that stone. There are new fortifications going up across the kingdom that rely on near-daily shipments of stone from here. It'll create a nationwide bottleneck."

Bastion breathed out a huff. "I see. We can't continue to move toward the mole people."

"There might be a way to mine some small pockets near the old quarry, but that'll mean having the workers near that monster, and I don't know if there's much left to find," the major said. "At the very least, it will slow down production by a considerable amount."

Bastion nodded, then he tapped the map. "This is where the amphiptere is?"

"A group of miners found it a week ago. I swore them to secrecy. It's in the location where the new quarry should be."

"And if we remove it, the mining operations can continue in this area unhampered."

"Effectively, yes. It will mean moving some equipment back, but that's half a day's loss, at most."

I leaned over the map myself, then hummed. "So, the solution to everything is to scare off that big beasty."

"There's no scaring off dragonkin. They're prideful to a fault. We need to kill it."

"It might mean a great bounty of meat as well," Major Springsong said. "I know alchemists enjoy working with dragonkin scales."

"Don't count your basilisks before they hatch," Bastion said. "This will have to be a joint effort. I'll need pen and paper—I'm sending a letter to Commander Warmwood, as well as General Holey."

"The mole person?" the major asked.

Bastion nodded. "They despise amphipteres more than the sylph do, and participating in an action to eliminate one might be a good way to smooth out any ill will between the local settlement and Granite Springs. Commander Warmwood will be informed because he has the troops to assist."

"And Captain Wardmyth," I added.

Bastion nodded. "Good point. The guard may be able to assist as well. Though I'd rather they not be the front line. They might assist with the cleanup afterward. If the . . . spoils need to be carved up by civilians, it would be good to have the guard in place already."

"It's already nearly noon," I said. "Is everyone going to be ready for this today?"

"If we move quickly, they will," Bastion said. "Broccoli, can I entrust you with a pair of letters? To Captain Wardmyth and General Holey?"

"I'd love to!"

Major Springsong didn't seem entirely onboard with the idea, but he didn't stop Bastion. He found paper and pen and placed them before Bastion, who immediately started composing three letters.

"The third is for Commander Warmwood?" I guessed.

"That's right. Major, do you mind letting me use one of your faster men? The commander's garrison is already on high alert. They should be ready to move within the hour if all goes well."

"I'll get one of my scouts," the major said.

Bastion set one letter aside after signing it with a flourish. "This is for Captain Wardmyth. I think he'll trust your word on the matter outright, but reassure him that things should, hopefully, end in an amicable way."

"I'll do what I can," I said.

Bastion hummed as he composed the next letter. It seemed to take him longer, and he was more careful with his writing. I guessed that there was a lot more stuff involved when writing to a general, let alone one from what was basically another nation. "Here," he said as he folded the letter. He checked the drawers around the major's desk until he came up with a bar of wax. A small flame summoned at the tip of his fingers melted it, and he pressed a ring into it to seal it. I'd never really paid much attention to the ring he wore. It was just a small black thing that was tucked neatly under his glove.

"The captain first?"

"If you run across him," Bastion said. "The general is of a higher priority. I'm sorry for using you as a courier like this."

"I don't mind!" I said. "Good luck hug for the road?"

Bastion sighed, but he did allow me to squeeze him as best I could before I darted out of the tent and back into the middle of the camp. I made sure both letters were tucked away in my biggest pouch. They'd be a bit rumpled, but that was better than outright missing.

A few of the soldiers looked at me as I bounced past, but I paid them no mind as I hopped along. My sense of direction wasn't the best, but it wasn't hard to make it to the quarry, then past that and back onto the main road leading toward the mole people dam.

Feet thumping, I raced along, not so fast that I'd burn through all my stamina, but still going at a good pace. I kept Bastion's lessons in mind, pushing myself, but only enough that I wouldn't tire.

It didn't take long for me to run into Captain Wardmyth and the rest of the guards Bastion and I had ridden over with. "Captain!" I called out with a wave.

The captain pulled on the reins, slowing the ponies drawing the wagon until they came to a full stop. "Captain Bunch," he said. "What's the matter?"

I guess seeing me rushing over alarmed him. "I have a letter for you," I said as I moved closer and tugged the letter out. I stopped next to the wagon and reached up for him to take it. "I have another letter to deliver to the mole people."

"I see," Captain Wardmyth said as he took the letter. "Any news?"

"A bunch," I said. "I think the letter will cover some of that. I don't know if Bastion wants you to go straight for the quarry or back to Granite Springs, though."

"I see," he said as he popped the letter open and started to read it, his brows bunching together as he scanned the page. "Hmm. So, it all comes down to one monster, does it?"

"Seems like it."

"Don't know if my guard can manage against a big amphiptere. But with the Inquisition there, and the army as well . . . not to mention the paladin."

"Hey, I'm no slouch in a fight," I said.

Captain Wardmyth laughed. "Of course. Well then, it's off to Granite Springs for me. I'll gather what I think we need and return to the quarry. Will I be meeting you there?"

"Of course," I said. "I wouldn't miss out on an adventure like this!"

"Good on you," the captain said. "We'll be off again."

"See you in a bit!" I called out as I bounced off.

"You as well!" he called right back.

The sylphs might have been stiff, but they weren't bad people. Now I just had to go say hi to all the mole people again, and then . . . then I'd see what it was like to fight a big old monster!

· Chapter Forty-Eight ·

Granite Springs Calls for Aid

The dam hadn't had time to change since I'd last seen it. I guess even the hard-working mole people could only do so much in a few hours. The same guard was standing at the top of the wall, and he squinted at me as I came closer.

"Hello!" I called up. "It's Broccoli Bunch! I have a letter for the general!"

The mole person blinked a few times. "Hello again," he said. "Give us a moment, then."

I was quite happy to wait. While I could wick off the sweat with my Cleaning magic, that didn't change how warm I was feeling, or even how burny my muscles were. It was nice to stand still and let things settle.

Actually, getting rid of all my sweat was probably a bad idea. Sweat was meant to help cool a person off, and I was feeling very warm. Something to keep in mind when I didn't need to be presentable in front of an important general person.

The drawbridge gate lowered, and the same guard mole I saw above waddled out to come closer. "Are you alone, miss?" he asked.

"Yup," I said. "It's just me."

"Ah, I see. Wonderful. The general is a little preoccupied right now, but you may enter. The general will be with you shortly."

I grinned as wide and happy as I could. "Thank you!" I said as I followed the mole person guard back in. A few workers spun a wheel around once we were within the fort, and the gate rose with a clatter of chains. "So, do I need to wait somewhere in particular?"

The guard mole reached up and scratched at his wide neck with his clawed hands. "I don't know. Just around here, I suppose."

"Oh, okay. Can I stay with you, then?"

He shrugged. "I don't mind. I've never talked to a bun before." He stared. "You are a bun?"

"Yup! Though I started off as a plain old human." I nodded. "So, what's your name? I can't keep on calling you 'the guard mole' in my head."

He chuckled, a raspy sort of sound. "I'm Diggo, of the Undervalley clan. So, you were a human first? Is that how it works for all buns?"

"Hmm? No, most buns are born as buns. At least, I think so. There would need to be a lot of people turning into buns otherwise."

"That's interesting, I guess," Diggo said. "We don't have any buns in town. I'd have heard of them."

"Is it mostly mole people?" I asked.

The mole guard nodded. "Yup. For the most part, just normal folk. A few sylph too. Strange ones at that, but nice enough. I know some villages have a human or two as well, but none near here."

"That's neat," I said. "I guess it can be harder for some people to adapt to living underground. I know I'd have a hard time. I need some space to move around in."

"Really? I find being out here in the open stressful. Look at all that sky. You can't know what's going to come swooping out of it."

I glanced up at the clear blue sky, bright and inviting, with a cheerful sun dancing above. "Sure, I guess," I said. I wasn't going to argue against his fears.

"Captain Bunch," a familiar voice called out. I shifted, a smile coming up as I saw General Holey walking my way with a couple of guards at his back. "You've come alone?"

"Hello, General," I said. "And yeah, I have. Bastion sent me with a letter for you." I tugged the letter out and handed it over.

The general took it, eyed the seal for a moment, then popped it open and read its contents. "Hmm," he said as he reached the end. "An amphiptere."

The guards around him shifted, and I heard Diggo take in a sharp breath. Were they so dangerous that even the mention of one made the mole people nervous? I guess they were natural adversaries.

"Did you observe the creature yourself, Captain?" General Holey asked.

I shook my head. "I didn't. But I did see some of the plans and maps the Inquisition people drew up. I don't know what Bastion's letter says, but I think the whole kerfuffle here was caused by that monster's presence. The miners couldn't dig where they'd been digging before, so they shifted closer to your village. It was really poorly handled, though. They shouldn't have ignored your letters the way they did."

"I see," the general said. "And I agree on the latter part. It was a cruel and rude gesture to make. Not to mention politically unwise. But I suppose with an amphiptere around, they might not have been thinking straight."

"It might not be around for long. Bastion is gathering soldiers from the base in town, and he's asking the guard to help too. I think he's planning on having everyone work together to kill it. I don't know if they really need all those people for one beastie, though."

The general sniffed. "I mean no offense, Captain, but you've made your ignorance plain with such a comment. I don't doubt that the garrison, the Inquisition, and the town guard all working together will be able to kill or, at the very least, injure the beast, but it won't be a task easily done."

I shrugged. I was always willing to admit to being ignorant; it was the best way to become less ignorant after all. "I've never seen one. And I've never fought one either. I've seen dragons, though."

"And would you think a fight against a dragon would be easy?"

I had to think back. Would fighting Rhawrexdee be easy? What about his mom? "No. No, that wouldn't be an easy fight. They're big and smart and very strong."

"An amphiptere is no dragon. They lack the intelligence and the gift for magic, not to mention the claws. But they can become quite large and powerful, and while they lack the magical finesse of a dragon, they can use it the way a brute uses a hammer."

I didn't like the thought of so many people risking themselves to fight something like that. A lot could go wrong, and people could get hurt. "This isn't going to be fun, is it?"

"I doubt it," the general said. He turned to one of the mole people next to him. "Prepare the First Platoon. Volunteers only. Fill in the gaps with volunteers from Second. Heighten the guard at the fort."

"Can I help?" I asked.

General Holey shook his head, then paused and made a "one moment" gesture before turning to his other guard. "Prepare the burden beetles. We'll hardly need them if things turn sour, and I'd rather have everyone be fresh on arrival."

The soldiers ran off to do the general's bidding, and within seconds, shouted orders filled the air as more mole people were roused into action.

The general observed his fort gearing up, then turned toward me. "Captain Bunch, would you mind accompanying me back to the quarry?"

"I don't mind at all," I said. "I'd probably just be in the way if I went back now, and I really don't like not being able to help."

"I understand," the general said. "Give us all a moment. We've trained for rapid deployments often enough that I do hope my troops here can be ready in a reasonable amount of time."

I nodded and stepped back, making sure I wasn't in the way as soldiers rushed around. There was a lot of clanging and banging as mole people slid into armor and formed up in a square in the middle of the fort, long spears held by their sides.

A few mole people with more elaborate hats moved over to the general and asked some questions in low tones. I could always make out the moment when the general told them they'd be fighting an amphiptere. There would be a flash of fear, then their eyes narrowed, and they looked almost happy as they ran off to shout more orders and wave their little arms about.

I stared as a section of the ground was removed by mole people with crowbars, and a line of huge beetles were led out of the ground, each one longer than I was tall and big enough that they reached my waist.

I thought I'd seen something similar in Deepmarsh, in some farmer's field, but I'd almost entirely forgotten about them. "What are those?" I asked the general when he didn't look so occupied.

"Never seen a burden beetle? They're docile enough, though convincing them to stay in the open air requires some training. We use them to pull carts underground."

"Are they smart?"

"No smarter than a sylph's horse," the general said. "Less, even."

The burden beetles had strange barding that required two mole people to put on. They were brought to one side of the fort where carts with big wheels and posts in their middle were hitched to them, four beetles to each cart.

The gate was lowered again, and the carts, some four in all, were led out of the fort by drivers sitting right behind the beetles. "Come on, Captain," General Holey said. "We're taking the lead cart."

I nodded and followed after the general. A few others followed after him, too, staff and people who I figured were officers. We climbed aboard the cart and basically stood at the back. There weren't any seats, just some poles coming out of the middle to hold onto.

A group of soldiers ran up behind us and fitted some spears into little holes on the side of the cart, each one at an angle from the middle so that the cart had a dozen spikes sticking out of it above our heads.

"What are those for?" I asked.

"It makes it harder for any flying creature to swoop down and grab someone off the cart," General Holey explained.

"Oh," I said. That was a rather terrifying answer. "Does that happen a lot?"

"There are a few predators that like to target us," he said. "The sylphs are targeted as well, but they have better eyes than we do and can generally see a threat coming in time to react. We have to adapt to things differently when we're on the surface."

I nodded, then leaned to the side to see the other carts behind us. Soldiers were clinging onto them, maybe a dozen well-armed and armored mole people on each. They had little swords by their hips and, of course, their long spears sticking out above their cart. All of them wore the same heavy plate armor, big breastplates and metal bands around their legs. They were pretty noisy, especially when they moved their heads to look around.

They had neat chainmail hoods on, with wide-brimmed metal hats above those. The only differences I could see in their armor were some that had a crest on their helmet to make room for feathers, and a few that had cloth robes on.

"Are the ones with skirts girls?" I asked the general.

He stared at me for a moment, then looked back to the carts I was eyeing. "No? The half robes are traditional garb worn by mages. Can't you tell a male from a female?"

"I . . . Not really, no," I said. "What's the difference between a boy mole person and a girl mole person . . . Wait, are you . . . ?"

"I'm male," the general said. He didn't sound amused, but something about the way his whiskers twitched said he was. "The men will be broader in the chest and a little taller besides."

"Oh," I said. I guess that helped, though with the armor it would be hard to tell them apart.

Probably best to just ask if I wasn't sure. It was better than sticking my foot in my mouth, even if I had the flexibility to manage that.

"All right!" General Holey called out. "Let's go kill an amphiptere!"

The soldiers cheered, and we were off.

· Chapter Forty-Nine ·

Joint Strike Fighters

So, how do you fight an amphiptere?" I asked.

General Holey hummed, and I was happy he was actually considering my question. Not that we had too much else to do on the ride over. The burden beetles were cool, but they weren't exactly fast. Stable, and they walked at a very even pace—more so than a horse or donkey—but not fast.

"I wish there was a single, reliable answer, but the truth is that the method will depend upon the situation. An amphiptere is fast, can fly, and can use brutish magics. Fighting them in the air isn't possible for us, so we try to hit them when they're resting or roosting. Then the matter becomes one of positioning."

"You mean like attacking them from above?"

"Amphipteres make their homes in crevices and mountainside caverns. Those can sometimes be caved in or netted over. Sometimes the beast can be lured out and into a trap where mages will hit them from many directions at once. We have the greatest earth mages in the world," the general boasted.

I nodded along. That made sense. A people that lived mostly underground would want to have mages who could move earth around. And I guessed their way of fighting naturally relied on that.

The carts rattled on over the bumpy road until the quarry appeared in the distance. The general spent some time conferring with his officers in low, whispered tones. Mostly, they seemed worried over how to work alongside the sylphs, who would no doubt be there already.

As we crested another small hill, we came upon a trail of wagons and soldiers. Some hundred or so sylphs in lighter armor, with a pair of wagons at the head. They were walking in a neat formation, spears bobbing up and down with every step. That is, until they caught sight of the group of mole people ahead of them.

The two groups slowed to a stop, the moles and I above the hill, the sylphs near the base. To our left was the road leading into the quarry.

I felt the tension rising before I spotted Commander Warmwood sitting in one of the wagons. I jumped up and down, one hand waving above me. "Hey! Commander Warmwood! We're here to help!"

The commander stared, then he laughed, a single, loud bark that somehow dispelled the tension. "Greetings, Captain Bunch," he said before lowering himself off the side of his wagon. General Holey did the same, landing with a thump on the road before he waddled ahead.

I hesitated before deciding that joining them was probably the more fun option. So I bounced down and hopped after the general.

He stopped a good three or four paces from the commander, and then they stared at each other. "Uh," I said. "Commander Warmwood, this is General Holey. General Holey, this is Commander Warmwood from Granite Springs."

The general nodded. "A pleasure," he said.

"Likewise," the commander replied. "You here to kill that flying garden snake?"

General Holey snorted. "We've killed our share of them."

"Well, maybe we can show you a trick or two."

"Oh, I'm certain we can do the same."

I was nervous that things would deteriorate, but then both of them stepped up and their hands met with a big meaty smack. It looked as if they were both trying to squeeze the other's hand as hard as possible. The muscles in their arms bulged, and both of them leaned into the handshake, which didn't actually have much shaking to it.

"I'm glad to see you both getting along!" I cheered.

They let go of each other, neither of them doing more than flexing their hands, even though it felt like both of them wanted to wiggle their hands free of the pain.

"I'm certain the mole people can set aside any differences for the day," Commander Warmwood said.

"Yes, I'm certain the sylphs can let go of some of their snobbishness for an afternoon. I will, of course, be leading this assault." General Holey nodded, as if it were a foregone conclusion.

"You will be leading?" Commander Warmwood asked. "Why exactly is that?"

"Aren't our nations allied?" the general asked. "Besides, we have more experience dealing with these matters, and, not to put too fine a point on it, I do outrank you, *Commander.*"

"Yes, I suppose you do," the commander replied. "Though I wonder about the value of being a general of such a . . . small army, from an equally small nation."

"*Okay!*" I said as I stepped up between the two of them. It looked like they were gearing up to do more than shake hands really hard. "This doesn't seem like the friendliest situation, so how about we all just . . . not be mean to each other for a minute or two?"

"We were cordial," Commander Warmwood said.

"Downright polite," General Holey agreed.

They glared at each other until I slid to the side, blocking their line of sight. "This isn't very productive," I said.

Both of them . . . Well, they didn't exactly pout, because they were big tough guys, but they certainly wore complicated expressions for a bit.

"Thank you, Captain Bunch," General Holey said. "I do believe you're essentially correct. Commander, we need to find a way to resolve this situation. I'm certain we both have protocols for mixed-troop actions, and I don't believe those protocols call for any sort of posturing."

The commander nodded slowly. "That's not wrong. Though a little bit of posturing is good for morale."

They both chuckled darkly, and I smiled even if I didn't quite get it.

"Let's move over to the quarry," General Holey said. "Captain Bunch, is there a staging location?"

"I don't know about that, but the Inquisition people did set up a small camp."

Both men sniffed, then they looked at each other. "You don't look forward to working with the Inquisition?" General Holey asked.

"I would rather avoid it, yes," Commander Warmwood agreed. "But I don't think that will be an option."

I wasn't sure if both of them agreeing to dislike someone else was a great middle ground to meet on, but it was *something* at least. "We should keep moving, then. We're burning daylight."

"Indeed," they both said at the same time.

The general returned to his cart and the commander to his wagon, and I stood there for a moment, not sure which way to go. So instead I shrugged and bounced ahead and into the quarry. The quarry workers were gathering up near some of the barracks-looking buildings. I guessed that work had been canceled for the afternoon, at least, so they didn't have much else to do but stare at first the mole people army and then the sylph army rolling past on the way to the far end of the site.

I found the Inquisition camp a hive of activity, with soldiers moving crates around and setting up tents on the outside of the camp. Some were laying out stretchers, and what looked like a medical tent was going up under the watchful eyes of an officer.

I found Bastion by the side of the camp, frowning at a map held in Major Springsong's outstretched hands. "Bastion!" I called out.

The paladin looked over, and his frown turned into a smile. "Broccoli," he said as a way of greeting. "Things went well?"

I nodded. "Yup. I met Captain Wardmyth on the way over. He took off toward Granite Springs. And General Holey agreed to come. He brought a couple of carts' worth of mole people soldiers. A few mages too."

"That might well be helpful," Bastion said.

"The general and Commander Warmwood don't exactly get along," I said. "I think they were doing that macho thing where they try to one-up each other. They both agree that they don't want the Inquisition in charge, though."

Bastion's frown returned, but it was Major Springsong who spoke up first. "The Inquisition was here first, and while we don't have as many troops on the ground, we do have most of the information pertaining to the situation at hand."

"Yeah, but I think everyone thinks you're being all secretive and . . . Well, the way you handled the mole folk's letters is, uh, not a great endorsement of your leadership . . . Sorry?"

"Captain Bunch is likely correct," Bastion said. "Perhaps instead of waiting for delegation of leadership to be settled—which might well take weeks with the hardness of the heads involved—we distract everyone with our current plan, then work our way from there. It's a simple ruse, but it has worked on mixed-troop deployments before. Each commanding officer need only worry about their part in the greater plan."

"So, what is the plan?" I asked.

"Perhaps we should go over it only once," Bastion said.

The commander and the general were coming up behind us, their wagons and carts rolling into place, the dozens of soldiers all forming up into two distinct groups.

"Broccoli, could you invite the commander and general to the command tent? Major Springsong, I'd advise you to remain . . . quiet, for the time being. We'll try to set things up as quickly and as efficiently as possible."

"Got it!" I said.

It didn't take very much to get the general to come over, though he insisted some of the other officers in his retinue accompany him.

The commander, on seeing General Holey moving over to the command tent with his aides, wasn't about to be left behind and gathered his own—exactly one more than the general—and moved over as well.

Was there always this much posturing before stuff could actually get moving? The soldiers seemed very focused on standing straight and sometimes jeering at each other when their leaders weren't looking, but at least the banter on their side seemed almost friendly.

It made me think of the way Amaryllis liked to poke fun at her friends.

I had to wonder how my other friends were doing. They'd be pretty impressed with all my work, I bet.

No one stopped me from entering the command tent, so I slipped past the canvas draped over the entrance and took in the room. At first, it looked like three camps had formed around the table: Major Springsong on one end, Commander Warmwood across from him, and General Holey near the back. But when I really looked, it was clear that Bastion was forming a lonely fourth camp, without any of his own aides in the background posturing. So I joined up and stood behind him, my most presentable smile on.

"Since everyone is here," Bastion began, "let's go over the situation one final time."

"Please do," General Holey said. "I do like being kept informed." This last was delivered with a glare to the major.

Bastion nodded, ignoring that last bit entirely. "There is an amphiptere near the site of the new quarry. This quarry, as you likely all know, produces a specific kind of stone that is used in enchanting and in some alchemical processes. It's imperative that we continue to supply this stone for the foundation of the kingdom's new fortresses along the border. And of course, we can't threaten our neighbors while doing so. Here's what we know about the beast so far."

I listened as attentively as I could, ears ramrod straight on my head, with only the occasional twitch to turn them toward whoever was speaking. But to be entirely honest, a lot of the plan flew over my head.

Well, plans usually didn't last long enough to matter anyway.

· Chapter Fifty ·

Snakes Are a Pain

The old quarry didn't look like much—I guessed that unworked quarries were really just hills with a bunch of rock in them. The hilly landscape was covered in trees except for the large area where the new quarry was located. Enough stone was in the ground that the only trees around were small, scraggly things that didn't look like they'd resist a strong wind.

The crevice that the others had spoken of was in the center of the nearest hills, a crack in the ground that started a few hundred meters from the hillside. I got to poke at it as we moved into the area. It was a crack, maybe a handspan wide near the start.

The closer it got to the hill the larger the crack became, until someone could easily fit a car in the gigantic slice. I guessed that the monster had snuggled into that crack. Maybe there was a cavern or something beneath it?

"Do you know how the crack formed?" I asked the person nearest me.

The plan, or what I understood of it, called for everyone to split apart into large groups. The Inquisition were splitting up and sneaking around the hill to take on the rear flanks. The larger force of the army from Granite Springs was setting up in the open, where the ground was even and they had plenty of room to move.

General Holey and his mole folk forces were moving to the forward flank, with his earth mages setting up near the bottom edge of the crevice. Bastion had asked that I stay near the general and his men because that was one of the safer areas where I could still be pretty useful.

My job was to jump in and grab anyone who got hurt. The medical tents were still by the Inquisition camp, a three-minute walk away. Far enough not to be caught up in all the trouble but close enough the injured could be brought over in a hurry.

There had to be well over a hundred soldiers on the field. It felt like a lot of people for one monster. An electric tingle was in the air, nervous energy and magic waiting on the tips of fingers to be cast.

"The crack isn't natural," the general answered at long last.

His voice made me jump. Maybe I was nervous too.

"There was a fight between two dragons in this valley once, some hundred years ago, or perhaps a little more now. It reshaped the earth, burnt down some of the ancient forests, and left behind a land scarred and cracked. That slice was likely caused by one of them landing."

"Whoa," I said. Then again, I could imagine someone like Rhawrexdee making quite a mess if he were to fight, and he was a younger dragon. His mom was much bigger.

"The sylphs have good reason to mistrust dragons and their ilk," the general said. "We were always a little more fortunate, owing to our homes beneath the earth."

"I see."

The orders were given, people were in their places, and all that was missing was the monster we were going to be fighting.

A hush fell over the battlefield as Bastion stepped up. He stood in his full armor, sword unsheathed and held loosely by his side. My best-sylph-friend was a dozen paces ahead of the main body of the army, alone and ready.

"We're beginning," the general said. The mole people around us shifted one last time, spears rising and boots crunching on the loose gravel underfoot.

"What's the plan?"

"The mages we have will use magic to harden the earth around the hole, then our siege specialists will prepare some defenses out here. We have some officers trained in the use of poisons. If all goes well, then all these soldiers here will have gotten out of bed for nothing."

"Oh, that's clev—"

There was a rumble. The ground shook. The sylphs approaching the hole froze on the spot, and a few even turned tail and took to the air to run.

The rumble slowed, then stopped.

I saw everyone tensing, preparing themselves for a fight.

Then, from the crack, slithered a monster.

The amphiptere was a long snakelike creature, as big around as my head and nearly three meters long. It wriggled across the rocky ground by the wider part of the crevice, then reared up, strange scales sliding back from its eyes so it could see everyone looking at it.

It hissed, and a pair of large wings spread out behind it.

The monster opened its mouth wide, and a ball of greenish goop shot out and toward the nearest person.

Bastion sidestepped neatly and easily, avoiding the spittle.

The monster hissed again and shot forward.

I gasped at the speed of it. It was fast. A rapid, blackish-brown blur.

Bastion jerked to the side, whirling in a split-second spin as the snake passed through his afterimage.

By the time my mind caught up, he was standing three paces away, sword swinging around in an easy circle to clean off the blood and gunk caught on it.

The monster flopped behind him in three large chunks.

"Was . . . was that it?" I asked.

That had been impressive, but there were a lot of people here just for that.

"No, that was a juvenile," General Holey said. "On guard!" he shouted.

I tensed, especially when I felt the ground trembling underfoot and saw all the soldiers tighten their grips on their spears. The hillside rippled, in a weird, unsettling way because hillsides weren't supposed to move. I looked around, trying to spot where, exactly, the shift was coming from.

Then it exploded.

Rocks shot into the air, big boulders rolling down the hill out of a growing cloud of dust. Eeping, I ducked down and grabbed at the edges of my helmet as tiny pebbles came raining down from the sky. They clinked and plinked off the armor of the people around me, most of whom stood still as they weathered the storm.

A roar filled the air.

You have heard the roar of a powerful beast! You are challenged to fight.

I glanced up, then gasped.

The amphiptere was massive, as wide around as a bus and ten times as long, though its tail did start to taper to a point eventually, with big fins on the very end. It hissed into the air, its breath stagnant and vile, like old rotting meat. Then its wings spread out behind it, each one the size of a small building, ribbed and leathery, like the wings of a huge bat, with visible veins running through them.

One of the wings was clearly injured, cracked and broken and bent at an odd angle. Still, when it flapped its wings, I saw a few of the soldiers closer to the front, those who hadn't taken a solid stance, be thrown back onto their rears.

Bastion, at the head of it all, weathered the storm with nothing but a mean glare for the monster. "Mages!" he called, voice clear and ringing.

"Now," the general next to me barked.

The mole people mages stepped up, and, with tight little gestures of their arms and a synchronized stomp, they shot off magic ahead of them that immediately dove into the ground.

Nothing happened, and the monster began to gather itself, muscles tightening, and it was then that the ground turned to something like mud.

Stone boiled, and the amphiptere sank while large spikes of rock jabbed into it from both sides like massive teeth.

The sylph army all took a step forward at the same time, one hand punching out ahead of them, and soon the air was filled by a thick volley of tiny fireballs that pelted into the amphiptere.

When the dust settled, it became clear that none of it had done much. The fire had only blemished its scales, and while one or two of the rocky spikes had broken into its skin, the wounds were small.

Its body twisted, snakelike, and just like that, the stone entrapping it broke apart.

"Oh, this isn't great," I muttered.

Would we even be able to do anything against something that strong?

The monster reared its head back, just like the smaller one had, and I gasped. It was going to spit!

"Shields!" Commander Warmwood called. He was right there, at the back of his men with his own gear on, sword pointing at the monster in defiance.

The snake hissed, and a glob of acid goop sprayed out of it as if from a firefighter's hose.

Bastion leapt straight up, spun, then kicked against the glob of acid to gain more height. He came hurtling down with a flipping kick, his heel crashing against the monster's snout with a crack that I felt from all the way where I was.

The amphiptere's head snapped down, and its acid spit fizzled out as it was wasted on the rocky ground.

I winced as I saw stones smoking and melting. Then I glanced over to the army, expecting to see something horrible.

Instead, the soldiers were stepping back in an orderly fashion, shields raised ahead of them with the rims glowing. Some spit was still pouring off the front of them and onto the ground, but it didn't look like any of them were really injured.

Neat equipment, that.

"We need to hit it harder," General Holey said. "Mages, again. Pin its midsection down. We're moving in."

"Moving in?" I asked. I didn't want to be closer to that thing than I had to be, and I was never one to shy away from adventure.

Bastion was somersaulting away from the monster as it tried to snap him out of the air, but he was never where it lunged, and whenever it came too close, he'd lash out with his sword, lightning quick, leaving a small slice across its scales.

That wouldn't be enough, of course. Bastion would tire eventually. The monster too . . . but it was big.

The mages cast another spell together, and I saw the Inquisition soldiers doing something similar before large balls of fire rammed into the monster's back and sent it reeling forward.

All around, soldiers moved in, shields up and spears raised, points glinting in the sunlight as they kept an even pace so as not to break their formations.

The monster wasn't going down so easily. It thrashed and spun around, tearing itself out of whatever grasp the mole people mages had on it. It spat at the top of the hill, where the Inquisition soldiers dove and flew out of the way.

The soldiers around it came close enough that some were able to strike, spears glowing before they stabbed into the monster's sides. Magic spears? Maybe they were enchanted. It was enough that they'd leave large cuts in the monster's side.

"Stay here, Captain," General Holey said. He stirred, then tore his sword out of its sheath. "It's best that you avoid getting hurt." And with that, he walked off toward the monster to accompany his soldiers.

I fretted on the sidelines, more than far enough that I wouldn't get hurt.

I didn't like it, not one bit.

Still, I didn't know what a lone bun could do to help.

My fists tightened. That was no excuse not to find *something* I could do to help!

· Chapter Fifty-One ·

Saint Bastion and the Dragon

The amphiptere spun around, mouth gaping wide to expose its large fangs, both dripping with a liquid I could only assume wasn't great for anyone's health. It snapped at the air, a futile attempt to catch Bastion.

The soldiers around the monster kept jabbing at it with their spears and even the occasional swing of a sword. Magic pelted the monster's sides, leaving marks and little else against the amphiptere's diamond-hard scales.

I couldn't stand not being helpful, but a couple of fireballs wouldn't do much to something like that, and Cleaning magic would just annoy it.

It really sucked, but maybe the best I could do was sit back and wait.

I barely had time to make that decision before the amphiptere coiled upon itself in a large circle. The soldiers near it hastily reeled back to avoid being squished by the creature's massive bulk. Bastion flew back and landed with a slight bounce some two dozen meters away from the monster.

The soldiers rebuilt their formation, officers screaming out orders from within their ranks until the amphiptere was once again surrounded by a bristling wall of spearheads. It glanced around itself with a deep hiss, malevolent, angry eyes scanning across all the people who looked absolutely tiny in comparison to it.

"Hey!" Bastion shouted. He waved his arm above his head, and the amphiptere twisted his way and bared its fangs.

It shot toward Bastion, mouth opening wide again, only for Bastion to dive out of the way. The monster was clever, though. It turned, one of its wings unfurling like a large leathery sail.

The impact made a dull thump as it swatted Bastion out of the air.

"Bastion!" I shouted as I saw my friend slammed back. He landed with a heavy thud against the rocky ground, then rolled bum over teakettle before stopping in a heap.

The amphiptere hissed, and it sounded downright pleased with itself.

It shifted its bulk, scaring off the soldiers that had moved in again, and it slithered closer to Bastion.

The paladin was getting to his feet, but he looked dazed by the blow. I didn't know if he would have time to really figure things out before the amphiptere was on him.

Which meant that I had to do something.

I didn't consciously decide to spend a heap of stamina to launch myself across the battlefield and right at the amphiptere's head. But by the time I realized what I was doing, I was airborne and already halfway to its scaly cranium.

I wished I had my spade with me; that would have made things a whole bunch easier. The snake didn't even turn my way, apparently dismissing me. I wasn't a threat, certainly no more than all the soldiers fighting it from every direction.

The thing is, I wasn't rushing at it to hurt it—I was there to be the most annoying bun I could be.

"Hey!" I shouted. "Don't hurt my friends!"

I landed with a crunch of loose gravel below the amphiptere's head. It still towered way above me, but that didn't stop me from reaching down and grabbing a rock the size of my head.

With a grunt of effort, I leapt up and ahead of the amphiptere, then I flung the rock I had into its open mouth.

It bounced off a tooth with a heavy clunk, then rolled down its gullet.

The amphiptere closed its mouth, and I saw the muscles of its throat working before it glanced down and glared at me. It hissed again, and I glared right back. "Well, that's what you get for trying to eat my friend," I shouted.

The monster seemed to consider that before it moved back toward Bastion.

It really had a thing against my friend. At least I'd won him time. He was back on his feet, sword arm moving around as he tested it. "Broccoli, get off the battlefield," he said.

"I can help."

"I'm certain you can, but it's dangerous here."

As if to emphasize his words, the monster spat at the spot where he was, coating the ground in a thick layer of sizzling acid while he bounced away from it. "We need to shift things around—this is turning into a battle of attrition, and we don't have the numbers or the time for that," Bastion warned.

"So what do we do?" I shouted back.

Bastion looked around briefly while the amphiptere slithered closer. "We lure it somewhere we have an advantage!"

He had to move again right after that, the amphiptere putting pressure on him as it tried to gobble him up. I backed up, my job done for the moment. I had to *think*. Someplace where we had an advantage?

I glanced around. The battlefield was, for the most part, flat, with only a few smaller bumps in the terrain and some roads here and there for the quarry workers to use. The biggest hill was the one the amphiptere had been living in, and it was actually a good deal smaller than the monster itself. I imagined there was some large hole underground for it to nestle into.

The new quarry location didn't have much going for it. The old quarry, though . . . that was basically a huge hole with some water at the bottom. There wasn't even that much, and there were spiraling earthen ramps all around it. The quarry was pretty darned big, too, especially for something that had likely been dug mostly by hand.

"Bastion!" I called out. "The old quarry! Can we make it fall down there?"

Bastion grunted as he juked out of the way of a strike. "Maybe! Get to the general. We'll need his mages. I'll—" He paused to fly under another frustrated snap. "I'll start attracting it over!"

"Got it!" I shouted before taking off.

I had to find General Holey, which proved difficult. He wasn't with the mages on the sidelines, or at least, I didn't see anyone that looked like him with them.

Then his fabulous hat saved the day. It was impossible to miss the colorful mane atop the general's head, even if he was partially hidden behind a line of his troops. They seemed to be maneuvering away from the amphiptere's whipping tail, some of them doing their best to resist the sweeping blows that occurred whenever the monster moved, while others focused on slashing and cutting at the tail whenever it came near.

From what I could tell, it looked more like they were leaving a whole lot of papercuts rather than any big wounds, but they were trying their best, considering the size difference.

Then something big went *clunk* and a big wooden rod appeared lodged into the amphiptere's side. They had brought siege weapons?

I hopped over, moving as quick as I could and even bouncing off the giant snake when its undulating movement brought it close enough.

"General Holey!" I said as I landed with a heavy thump.

"Captain Bunch," he greeted. "Tighten to the right! If you don't hold, we'll all be rotting in the deepest pit with our ancestors by the morning!" He turned back to me. "What can I do for you, Captain?"

"Bastion is planning on drawing the monster toward the old quarry. We want to make it fall down the pit so that we can hit it from above. We need your mages."

"To weaken the edge so its weight will make it collapse," he said. "I understand. Here, take this." The general reached down to his chest piece where a medallion hung. He tore it off and tossed it to me, then pointed to the slight rise where the mages were holding up. "Quick, show that to the lieutenant—tell him of the plan. We'll be there."

"Got it!" I said.

Battlefields, even ones where there was only one big enemy to fight, were more hectic than I'd imagined.

I ran and bounced for all I was worth toward the mages, who were still casting spells, though they seemed to be taking small breaks between barrages. Judging by all the glass bottles littering the ground around them, they were rapidly using up mana to cast so many spells nearly nonstop.

"Who's the lieutenant!" I shouted as I came within hearing.

"Aye!" one of the mages said. He had a slightly more elaborate helmet and a small badge on his chest piece.

"Here," I said, giving him the medallion. He took it, inspected it, then nodded, all in the space of two seconds. "We're luring the monster to the edge of the old quarry. We need the ground there weakened so that it can fall into the quarry."

"Understood," he said. "Hold fire! We're mobilizing!"

"Great," I said.

"When is this taking place?" he asked.

I half turned and looked out at the fight. It was moving already, the serpent slithering its way after Bastion, who was weaving left and right before it, drawing its attention to him while keeping its pace relatively slow. "Now, I think."

"You might want to inform the other parties, then," the lieutenant said.

That made sense. "Good idea," I said. I glanced at my stamina, saw that I still had plenty left in the tank, then I charged, aiming for the hill where the amphiptere had been staying.

The area around the hill was a mess. Huge boulders and rocks were strewn about like toys on the floor of a messy kid's bedroom. I had to watch my bounces as I darted up the hillside.

I was breathing hard when I was greeted by a line of soldiers from the Inquisition. They eyed me, uncertain. "I need to talk to the major," I said.

"This isn't the time for that," one of the soldiers said.

I blinked. "What? It's about"—I gestured behind me—"that."

"I'll speak with her!" Major Springsong said. He had a few officers around him, and I noticed that quite a few of his soldiers looked pretty banged up. I guessed they'd been near the worst of it for a while. The crevice, or what was left of it, was only a dozen meters away. It looked as if the stone within was almost . . . melted?

That might explain how something so big had fit in there.

"Captain Bunch?" the major asked.

"Uh, Bastion, that is, Paladin Bastion, is heading over to the old quarry. He's hoping to lure the amphiptere there. The mole people mages are going to help him so that it falls into the quarry."

"And with it unable to fly . . . Yes, that might work," the major said. "Thank you, Captain."

I started to give him a sloppy salute, then remembered what Bastion said about those. "Uh, right. I'm off to see the commander."

"Did the paladin give you any additional instructions?"

I wiggled my tail in thought. "I don't think so. If he did, I forgot already." He stared.

"Okay, bye!" I said.

I went back down the hill. It was a lot easier running downhill than up, of course, so I got a good head start from that. My destination was Commander Warmwood, but it seemed as if the commander had guessed what would happen already. His troops were formed up in three smaller groups, all of them hemming in the amphiptere and harassing it with spears and swords, never giving it the chance to stay still without getting cut.

The damage each soldier inflicted was small, but it looked as though it was adding up. The amphiptere was bleeding here and there, and while it looked like it could heal fast, it wasn't outpacing the soldiers.

Eventually, the army here would win. That was, as long as nothing went wrong.

Chapter Fifty-Two

Quarry

Hey! Here, here!" I shouted, arms and ears waving above my head.

The amphiptere switched its attention from Bastion and stared at me. It wasn't happy. In fact, it was very clearly growing less and less happy as the minutes went by and the fight dragged on. I could understand it. Bastion had been a very elusive target, and even as it advanced, the soldiers behind it kept poking and cutting at its tail.

We had to keep it distracted, though. Twice already, the amphiptere had stopped going after Bastion in order to snap and spit at the soldiers behind it, and I'd seen a few of them get hit with droplets of acidic spittle before their shields went up.

Some sylphs were there to escort the injured to the medics' tent, and I was pretty sure that the sylphs—who I'd been repeatedly told were the best at medicine—could take care of their own in a hurry.

Still, that meant fewer fighters on the field. When more acid flew, I flung out tendrils of Cleaning magic to intercept while bouncing and calling out, trying to distract the monster as best I could so that it would leave the army alone and continue its slow slither toward the old quarry.

So far, things were going well. Other than a few close calls, Bastion and I were doing good work keeping it moving.

Bastion was able to cut and poke at it whenever it came too close. He seemed to be aiming for the eyes, which really annoyed the monster.

I didn't have his skills with a sword . . . or a sword for that matter. So whenever I could, I flung some Cleaning magic at the monster's eyes and into its open mouth. I bet it didn't like having a dry mouth any more than anyone else.

"We're nearly there," Bastion called out.

I glanced back. A small line of trees was atop a rise in the landscape, one that was too small to be called a proper hill. The mole folk mages were hiding a little ways from there, using the trees as cover even if most of them weren't much thicker than a closed fist.

Past the bump was a wooden fence and, beyond that, the drop.

"Broccoli!"

I gasped as a shadow fell above me, then launched myself to the side and crashed on the ground belly first, avoiding the amphiptere slithering over where I would have been.

"No distractions!"

"Right!" I shouted back as I rolled over and bounced to my feet. No one wanted a squished bun, least of all the bun in question. I had to be careful while taunting the giant high-level dragon-snake.

Bastion launched an attack at the amphiptere's face—wide, sweeping slices that had the creature flinching back. It spat out a gout of acidic spittle that utterly failed to hit Bastion.

"Nearly there!" I said as I bounced up and grabbed a hold of the amphiptere. Its big scales had gaps between them, some more than wide enough to grab hold of. There was a lot of dirt and detritus stuck in there. The poor thing probably didn't clean itself all that often.

Climbing up the amphiptere proved tough but doable, and in the end, I think it was worth it, especially when I was hanging off its neck, within easy reach of the monster's head. I flung a few balls of Cleaning magic toward its eyes, making it flinch back until it could blink them a few times.

Then its large, slitted eye turned and narrowed as it focused on me.

"Uh-oh."

The entire creature rolled onto its side, head whipping down.

It was only a lucky jump that allowed me to fling myself off it before it squished me flat. Still, the impact of its head on the ground made the entire area bounce. Trees lost leaves, and pebbles skipped down the walls of the old quarry.

"Move back," Bastion said. There was iron in his words. A glance around showed why. We were right on the edge of the quarry. We'd made it.

I nodded, beelining for the little patch of roots where the mole people mages were hiding while Bastion distracted the monster again.

"Well done," the same lieutenant I'd spoken to earlier said.

"Thanks," I replied before stumbling over to a boulder. I sat myself down and let out a long breath. My heart was flitting around my chest like a hummingbird, so it was nice to sit back for a breather. "Will you be able to bring it down?"

"Oh, we'll manage just fine."

I watched as the mages spread out. With the sylph soldiers forming a front line before the mages, the amphiptere was being hemmed in against the long drop into the quarry.

It would be a terrible drop for a person. More than enough to make it lethal, but then, the amphiptere was pretty big. The drop was only half as deep as it was long. I hoped that would be enough.

Bastion flashed through the sky like a brilliant dart, leaving a single long cut along the monster's face. "Now!" he roared.

"Now, now, now!" the lieutenant shouted.

All across the line of mages, mole people dropped to their knees, then brought their closed fists down and smacked the ground.

Everything trembled, and I gasped as the earth surged out ahead of the mages.

The soldiers before them stumbled, their formation breaking, but the initial wave was nothing compared to what was happening nearer the edge. As each earthen wave bumped into the next, the world buckled, and the ground cracked with a snap like an ice sheet coming apart in a nature documentary.

The amphiptere paused, and I saw something like confusion flash in its eyes before the entire cliffside dropped.

At first it was only a small drop. The crack running around the edge of the quarry widened, and everything held still.

It felt like watching a coin land on its side while spinning. It was holding for now, but there was this immense sense of impending disaster, as if the entire world knew that things were about to go horribly wrong all at once.

A noise like a cannon going off echoed across the valley. The ground rumbled. Atop it, the amphiptere spun around on itself and rushed away from the edge.

I heard Commander Warmwood shout something, and his troops formed a wall, shields up and magic glowing. Those in the rearmost rows pressed up against the soldiers before them, and they raised a spiked barrier, spears jutting toward the amphiptere.

It rammed into the formation, a creature that had to outweigh the gathered soldiers a hundred times over, moving as quickly as it could, heedless of the spears biting into it.

And yet, somehow, the formation held. I heard the soldiers shouting with exertion, and I could almost see the magic snapping at the air as they burned what had to be thousands of points to resist the monster's advance.

It was at once terrifying and awesome.

And, most important of all, it worked.

The ground fell. The entire edge of the quarry gave up with a huge roar, millions of tons of stone crashing down into the pit. The noise was so chaotic and loud that I winced and tugged my bun ears down over the sides of my head to protect them.

The amphiptere hung onto the edge, and then the soldiers not keeping it at bay attacked it. Spears were thrown like javelins, and dozens of fireballs pelted it from every direction.

The snake hissed, terror mixing with rage.

It tumbled back, its long sinuous form writhing even as its wings spread wide, but that didn't help it at all.

It screeched, the sound loud and piercing and stronger even than the rumble of the world falling apart.

The scaffolding along the edges of the quarry were torn apart in the fall, and then, with a final thud that sent a ripple through the ground, the amphiptere hit the bottom.

The snake screamed in pain as sharp-edged stones dug into and through its scaly hide, but the scream was drowned out by the rumble of cascading rocks as missing supports failed to keep back sections of crumbling wall.

Gradually, the rocks settled, and the echoes receded until I could hear myself think again. A huge plume of dust poured out of the quarry, thick and gray.

The wind turned, sending the wall of dust falling across all the soldiers and mages on the sidelines. I pushed some of my mana into my Cleaning aura, keeping the worst of it off me and letting me see what was going on a little better.

Some of the soldiers around Commander Warmwood seemed injured. They hobbled back, supporting each other even as others ran in to fill in the gaps in the line. The Inquisition soldiers rushed over, some of them using what looked like Wind magic to clear the air, and right behind them were the rest of the mole people warriors.

I noticed Bastion moving to the edge of the new cliffside and went to join him. "Is it done?" I asked.

"No," he said. "It's still alive. Though that did injure it. It isn't quite pinned, and I suspect it will be able to move out of the quarry relatively easily if we don't act to keep it down there."

"We're going to go down to fight it?"

Bastion shook his head. "No. We have the advantage of height. It won't be glorious or honorable, but this might be the most effective way to fight the amphiptere without anyone getting injured."

"Oh."

Bastion called for General Holey and Commander Warmwood, and soon Major Springsong joined us too.

I glanced down and saw the amphiptere shake itself out from a pile of stones and dirt, then twist around to right itself. It was in a rough state, the fall having damaged it more than any of the fighting so far.

Then the mole people mages approached the edge of the quarry and pelted the monster with Broccoli-sized rocks. It dodged a few, but there were so many that it was still hit. When the soldiers joined in and tossed fireballs down as well, things only got worse for the monster.

A cart pulled by a pair of donkeys pulled up nearby, a couple of Inquisition soldiers riding at the back. They unloaded boxes filled with bows and barrels filled with arrows. Lines formed, and those soldiers that looked like they were running out of mana grabbed bows and some arrows, then moved to the edge.

I think the arrows were enchanted with something—they glowed when fired, and some of them hit with loud bangs, while others buried themselves deep into the amphiptere's side, rather like the spears of the mole folk.

The monster spat acid up at those gathered above it, but other than burning a volley of arrows out of the air, it wasn't able to reach the very top.

I kind of felt bad. It was inherently unfair to fight something that way. Then again, the soldiers weren't joking or making light of the situation. They were taking this seriously, as if the monster below could still turn around and become a genuine threat.

That never happened.

Eventually, the amphiptere keeled over, the fight beaten out of it.

The number of arrows and stones and magic pouring onto it increased temporarily, then Commander Warmwood called everything to a halt. "Paladin Coldfront, would you finish it?"

Bastion nodded. "Give me a moment."

When Bastion jumped down the side of the cliff and skidded down, I hesitated, then followed him.

I slipped and slid on the loose rock of the cliff, and I had to waggle my arms to keep my balance until I caught up with Bastion near the bottom. He looked at me and nodded.

Carefully, we moved over to the monster.

It was still breathing, though only barely.

It stared at me, anger plain in its bruised eye. "I'm sorry," I said as I reached out to pat it.

Bastion pulled his sword out of its sheath without any fanfare, and then he pressed the end of the blade near the base of the amphiptere's neck. "Well fought," he said.

A cheer rose up from the top of the quarry as the battle came to a close.

· Chapter Fifty-Three ·

The Melancholy of Broccoli Bunch

The old quarry still had a road leading down to it, a switchback path on the end nearest the quarry headquarters. That's where the guards came from, both to inspect the body of the amphiptere and then to start butchering it.

I felt my nose twitch in disgust as the guards chopped into the poor amphiptere. I had to swing my ears down to cover my eyes.

"Are you well?" Bastion asked.

I was glad for the distraction. "Yeah, I think," I said. Physically, I was mostly fine. A bit sore from all the running around, but that wouldn't last. And if I was tired, I could always just take a nap. "How are you?" I asked.

Bastion seemed a bit banged up. His armor scuffed and scraped here and there, with a small dent around his lower chest where the metal seemed thinner. The thick cloth padding he wore under his armor was singed on the corners, likely from that acidic spit. "All things considered, I'm quite well. Good experience."

Oh! I'd forgotten to look at my system messages after the fight.

`Ding! Congratulations, after a hisstoric battle, you have defeated Sid, Lord of Acid Snakes, level 32!`

`EXP reduced for fighting as a group!`

I blinked at the level. That was huge! I'd never fought something so strong before. Though, to be fair, I'd had a lot of help. A glance back showed some of the soldiers looking very happy. I figured a few of them had leveled up from all that excitement.

The name of the amphiptere . . . that saddened me. Was Sid named by someone? Was the amphiptere someone's pet at some point?

`Congratulations! Through repeated actions, your Proportion Distortion skill has improved and is now eligible for rank up!`

`Rank E is a free rank!`

That skill again! I still didn't know what it did, or, for that matter, how I'd used it in the last fight to get it to level up at all.

```
Proportion Distortion
E - 00%
The ability to fit in and fit out. Your ability to squeeze
into tight spaces and fill rooms has improved.
```

That wasn't all that much more helpful. Was I able to naturally squeeze into smaller spaces now? That sounded kind of useless as far as skills went!

I'd have to see what it changed into at Rank D, I guessed.

I'd gained a heap of experience with Captaining and with Makeshift Weapons Proficiency, though not quite enough to get either to rank up. I'd need to practice more. The worse thing was that Captaining was actually getting ahead of Hugging Proficiency, which . . . What kind of terrible friend was I being?

"Anything good?" Bastion asked.

"Nothing too special," I said. "No level ups, but I imagine I'm pretty close to my next one."

"Well done," he said. "This entire battle will be quite the tale, I think."

I sighed. "It didn't feel like an entirely fair battle," I said. "It was more like . . . I don't know, really. Bullying?"

Bastion nodded slowly. "I can see how you'd think that. But I suspect it needed to be done. If the amphipteres didn't harass civilians so often, maybe we could just leave them be. But that's not in their nature. They are as prideful as their draconic parents."

"Yeah." I said, for lack of anything better. "What's everyone going to do now?"

"The Inquisition, under Major Springsong, are still poking at the crevice the amphiptere came from. The presence of juniors hints that there might be a nest nearby."

"She was a mommy?" I asked.

"Uh," Bastion said. "No, no, I'm sure that's not the case," he lied, poorly.

I tightened my jaw. I wasn't going to break out in tears or anything like that. I was a big girl. I'd go back home to the *Beaver* and hug the stuffing out of my friends until I felt better instead.

"I suspect that a lot of the meat will find its way to Granite Springs. If you want, you could stake a claim on some of the body. You did participate, and it would be hard to argue that you didn't do your part."

"Why would I want anything like that?"

Bastion rubbed at his chin. "I'll take a small portion of the leather on your behalf, if you want. It's valuable, and, given to a good tailor, you could make something nice out of it. Additional armor or some clothes." Bastion made a dismissive gesture. "It's a fair reward."

"I don't know," I hedged. It wouldn't feel right.

"Accept it, please," Bastion said. "It will smooth things out with the commander, and the general as well. They'll be quite busy in the coming days, I suspect. Moving the quarry over, likely dismantling that dam, and cleaning up the battlefield."

I nodded. A lot of guards were coming over, with Captain Wardmyth calling out orders from atop the back of a cart loaded up with equipment. The few soldiers who had been injured were being tended to by medics in lighter armor with white marks over their arms and around the top of their helmets.

Things seemed calm. "I think . . . I think I might go back to the *Beaver*," I said.

"Are you certain?" Bastion asked.

I nodded.

"Then let me find someone who can carry you back."

I appreciated the gesture. It was a bit rude to not stop and talk to all the new friends I'd made, but sometimes . . . Well, sometimes even my social batteries were spent. I needed a few minutes to myself, maybe with just a close friend or two to cuddle while I got over my blues.

Bastion and I moved around the old quarry and to where the quarry workers were gathering to help butcher the amphiptere's corpse. It wasn't hard to find some carts heading back to Granite Springs. They needed a bunch of equipment that they didn't exactly stock at a quarry, and there was talk of getting some local butchers over to help, since they'd actually know what they were doing better than the guards and soldiers.

I hopped onto the back of a cart after giving Bastion a quick parting hug.

The ride back was quiet. The sylph driving the cart paid more attention to the road than anything else, and with the late afternoon sun baking everything into a warm haze, it felt like the sparse forests and all the animals within were feeling too lazy to move about much. I leaned back and stared up at the sky, bright blue, with a few long streaks of puffy white pouring out from the tops of the tallest mountains. This was the first time I'd been alone since . . . It had been a while, actually.

It was nice, and at the same time, it wasn't. Too quiet. Peaceful, yes, but I wanted to share that peace—to press up against Amaryllis, to hear Awen's quiet murmurs.

I huffed, a very mighty huff.

The cart rolled over to Granite Springs, and I thanked the nice driver sylph for the ride before hopping off and making my way into the town. There were still plenty of people around, some of them gathering up in clumps to gossip and speculate.

It wasn't hard to imagine what they'd be speculating about. I'd seen two dozen guardsmen at the quarry, and I couldn't imagine a town this big having that many guards in all. Plus the army moving out in force. Someone had to have noticed that.

I plodded through the streets—a lone, strange bun ignored by just about everyone except for the few odd stares.

The docking tower where the *Beaver Cleaver* was waiting seemed less busy than it had been that morning. The ships being loaded up were mostly gone now, and the crews of sylphs that had been working on them were gathered in the shadows of the docks, smoking stinky cigarettes and chatting amongst each other.

I climbed aboard the elevator, took a moment to figure out the controls, then shot up to the topmost floor, where I disembarked and continued on to the *Beaver*. Awen was there to greet me, sitting astride the railing with a book in hand and her armor and coat on. "Hey," I said.

She looked up from her book, and a quick, small smile graced her lips. "Hey, Broc," she said. "You're back."

"Yeah? Of course I am."

"I thought you might be in trouble," she said. "So I was ready to start mounting a rescue."

"Why would I be in trouble?"

"Because you're Broccoli," Awen said. She giggled at whatever expression I made in response to such a terrible accusation. "I saw the guard all up in a tizzy, and then the army was moving, and all the dockhands were gossiping about it and staring at them, so I knew you'd done something."

"You can't know that I was involved with all that."

"But you were?"

I crossed my arms. "Maybe."

Awen laughed and leaned to the side to place her book on the deck. Her laugh calmed down. "Are you okay?"

"Yeah, I'm fine," I said. I put on a nice smile for Awen.

Awen looked at me, then she swung her leg over the rail and, heedless of the huge drop below, jumped over to land on the deck next to me. "Do you need a hug?"

"I could use a hug, yeah," I admitted.

She raised her arms, and I wrapped mine over her shoulders and pulled her close. I think Awen had grown recently, maybe while I wasn't paying too much attention. I saw her everyday after all. She was still shorter than me by a good bit, but now her head tucked into the crook of my neck just right.

"Did you want to talk about it?"

"Ah, maybe?"

"I think there's some leftovers from lunch."

"Who made it?"

Awen backed out of the hug and gave me a *look*. Then she glanced aside. "It was Clive."

"Oh, yeah, I haven't eaten since this morning, I don't think. I could use something to eat."

"Come on, then. You can tell me what you did that got the entire army deployed."

"I didn't do anything. Just ran a few messages and met some people. Did you know there are mole folk living in Sylphfree? They're small people, covered in fur." I bounced over to the *Beaver*, then waited for Awen to jump over as well, just in case she missed the jump.

"Mole people? That must be weird," Awen said.

"A bit!" I agreed. "I think most of them are shortsighted, so they're very squinty, and they have big teeth, but not the sharp, mean-looking kind. They're nice, though. I didn't really get to hug them to see how soft they are."

"Is their fur long?"

"No, no, it's more like short, rough fur, I think."

"Did you meet them in the city?" Awen asked as she led me down one deck and toward the kitchen.

"No, they were building this big dam way upriver. If they'd finished it, it would've been terrible for Granite Springs, so Bastion had to convince them not to, which meant that we had to gather the army to fight this big monster called Sid."

Awen tilted her head as she considered all that. "Broccoli, I think you're skipping some parts of the story."

"Well, yeah, I had to meet with this major from the Inquisition. He wasn't mean, but he was really inconsiderate. And the commander of the army base. He was nice, but a bit . . . bossy, I guess? I think he's a bit of a grumpy older guy, but he still seemed like a good sort of person under all the grump."

"Uh-huh. So then what happened?"

I grinned and started over, this time from the beginning. It helped a lot, just being home with . . . my family, I guessed.

· Chapter Fifty-Four ·

Ironclad Hugs

"Do you have everything?" Amaryllis asked. Only her head was poking into my room, the rest of her not visible since she was leaning in from the corridor.

I looked at my backpack and nodded. "I think so. I guess I'll be traveling light, huh?"

I had my best clothes on, armor atop that, and my spade was waiting for me by the door. My bag was nearly empty, though. I'd packed a few books for the flight, some spare clothes, including the suit I'd worn at that ball, some tea-making supplies, and a couple of hats—my captaining hat and my bowler hat from that one dungeon. That was it.

"Traveling light is fine," Amaryllis replied. "We might do some shopping while out in the capital."

I glanced up. "I thought we were going to be doing diplomatic stuff?"

"Of course we are," Amaryllis said with an eye roll. "But that won't take up the entire time that we're there. Our mission is important, yes, but for the most part, it boils down to delivering a few messages to the right ears. Perhaps offering a few bribes and a bit of proof here and there."

"We're not going to be bribing people, are we?"

"Oh, not that kind of bribe," Amaryllis said with a wave of her wing. "But I can make promises on behalf of my family. There's a lot to be gained from trade between Sylphfree and the Nesting Kingdom, trade that would very much be lost in the case of a war."

"That makes sense. Make the merchants want to avoid fighting because fighting would mean making less money."

"Exactly," Amaryllis said. She stepped into my room fully. She had all her adventuring gear on, with her wand-knife strapped to her hip and her feathers looking freshly preened. "I'm ready to head out whenever you are."

I nodded and stuffed a blanket into my pack. Getting caught without a blanket, or at least a towel, would be terribly silly. "I'm ready too!" I picked up my turtle-shell hat from next to the door and wiggled my ears into the helm's earholes. It always made my fur go the wrong way when I put that on.

Amaryllis and I peeked into Awen's room while I rubbed my ears straight. "Hey, Awen," I said.

The mechanic looked up to me from the floor. She was on her knees next to an open duffle bag filled with all sorts of tools and knickknacks that looked like they were on the heavier side.

At least it meant she was finally picking up her room. So many loose things were probably a hazard if we did any maneuvering.

"Oh, awa, hi," she said. "I'm nearly done?"

"Did you pack anything other than tools?" Amaryllis asked.

Awen looked down at her bag, then blinked. "Oh, I guess I'll need another bag for clothing and toiletries."

"I guess I can help," I said as I stepped in, careful not to place a foot on anything that looked sharp. "Do you have a second bag?"

"Yes, here," Awen said. She found a backpack in one of her drawers, under even more tools, and set it on the ground next to me.

"Right!" I said. "You'll want some formal wear—maybe that pretty dress from the ball? And some everyday stuff. Your armor, of course, in case of adventuring. Don't forget to bring enough underthings too. One for each day, plus one more in case of emergencies."

"B-Broccoli!" Awen whined.

"Oh, right, I guess I can just use Cleaning magic if anything happens."

"That's not what I meant, Broc," Awen groused. She pouted at me, and I couldn't help but grab her and give her a hug. What did I do to deserve so many cute friends?

"Come on, let's pack up the rest and head out, I don't think we're risking being late, but it's only polite to arrive early."

"I'm certain they would wait for us," Amaryllis said. "Though this is a sylph transport—they might be a little anal-retentive about punctuality."

"Some people are like that," I agreed.

We finished packing up Awen's things in a jiffy, then climbed back to the top deck. The rest of the crew was there waiting for us. Clive was the first to step up. "Captain."

"Clive," I said. "You're in charge of the *Beaver* while we're off. Keep him in tip-top shape if you can. Just do your best!"

"Aye, aye, Captain," Clive said. "We'll be done patching him up to new in a day or two at most. Lady Albatross left us with plenty of resources if we need 'em."

"Well done," I said. I spread my arms wide, and the old harpy chuckled as he accepted the hug.

Next were Steve and Gordon, both of them saluting easily as I approached. "Have a safe trip, ma'am," Steve said.

"You'll have to tell us what the capital is like, once you're back," Gordon added.

"I'll try to remember to grab souvenirs!" I said. "Hugs?"

My Hugging Proficiency was getting so much experience today!

The Scallywags were next, all three of them standing together. Joe looked a bit sour, but that was par for the course. The other two looked just fine. "You three keep safe," I said. "And if you find better work around here, at least stick around so that I can give you even more hugs when I return, all right?"

More hugs were had!

Then it was down to the very last—but most important—member of the crew. "Did you want to come with us?" I asked Orange.

The cat looked up to me. At some point, she'd gone from being a spirit kitten to being a spirit . . . teen? Young cat? Whatever the next step was. She was about as tall as my knee when standing on her hind legs, which she didn't do often enough.

Orange looked up at me, then stood and did a figure eight around my ankles. "Oh! You do want to come! Well then, is there anything you want to bring? I don't know if you have any toys or anything. Actually, we should get you some toys, shouldn't we?"

Orange pounced up and installed herself on my shoulder, tail tapping the shoulder opposite the one she was resting on. I scratched her tummy fluff while she was there.

"Okay," I said before turning around. I glanced around the *Beaver*. It might be a few days before I got to see him again. "We'll see you all super soon," I declared.

The four of us jumped off the *Beaver* and landed onto the dock. Orange cuddled closer so that she wouldn't bounce off with the motion. The docks were lively and filled with people moving about. A few ships had arrived recently, and they were being unloaded by teams of dockworkers while freight was being shifted about, ready to head out once the newly arrived vessels took off again.

Our destination was all of three ships over from the *Beaver*.

Her name (or at least, I thought the ship was a girl ship) was the *Little Atlas*, but she wasn't all that little.

From bow to stern, the *Little Atlas* was twice as long as the *Beaver Cleaver* and almost as wide.

Unlike the *Beaver*, the ship didn't have a very ship-like appearance. She was a lot boxier, with a prow that was angular and a hull that seemed to be entirely made of steel plates riveted in place.

Amaryllis, Awen, and I moved out of the way of a group of sylphs pushing a cart loaded with boxes freshly transferred off the *Little Atlas*. We waited for the coast to be clear before stepping up to the ship. A few planks were set up to allow people to cross over, and one of those had the person that I figured had to be the captain.

She was a sylph that I suspected was on the shorter side, only coming up to my chest, but her captain's hat more than made up for it. It was a very nice, stately hat, a bicorn with a few smaller feathers on one side and a nice badge pinned to the other.

"Hello!" I called out with a wave that I hoped was properly jaunty.

The captain looked up from some papers she was flipping through. She said something to one of her crew, then stepped over and folded her arms at the small of her back. "Greetings. May I help you?"

"Yes, ma'am," I said. "I'm Captain Broccoli Bunch, and these are my companions. We have a, uh, charter onboard your ship today." I glanced to the side, just to make sure the name on the side of the ship was right. It did say the *Little Atlas* in big, bun-high letters.

"Ah, I see. Yes, I received word about your arrival," the captain said as she pulled out her papers and checked through them. "A little early, but better than late. It says here you would be four? Including a . . . paladin?"

"That's probably Bastion. He's a bit busy, I think. I haven't seen him since yesterday afternoon, but I doubt he'll be late—that's just not like him."

"I see. I'm Captain Risa Galebane, of the Snapdragon Transportation consortium. It's a pleasure to meet a fellow captain." She extended a hand to shake, and I leaned forward to grab it. She had a good grip.

"I'm still very new to the job, so I'd love to hear any advice you have," I said. Also, she had the coolest name for an airship captain. Way better than "Bunch."

"I'd love to share a meal, perhaps once we've taken off," Captain Galebane said.

"So, permission to come aboard?"

"Granted," she replied, a slight smile twitching up the corners of her lips before she gestured back onto the ship.

We climbed aboard, and I couldn't help but stare around. There was a balloon overhead, one that was nearly as large as the ship itself. There had to be a lot of gravity generators on board to compensate for the comparatively small size of the balloon. The ship didn't have as many sails as the *Beaver*, but it did have a lot more propellers: two on the side, one at the front in a large housing, and a large one at the rear.

"Interesting design," Amaryllis commented. "I think we experimented with multiprop configurations like this before, but we never found them all that efficient."

"The gearing must be so complicated," Awen said. "Unless they have multiple engines, which would bring a whole host of other problems along."

"I can imagine," I said.

Someone ran up to us, a younger sylph who bowed before us. "Hello, and welcome aboard the *Little Atlas*. Can I assist you with your things? I'll be showing you to the guest quarters."

"Sure," I said. "That would be really nice of you."

Awen handed him her duffel bag, which was the only nonbackpack bag we had. He hugged it close, then, with a grunt of effort, led us to the rear of the ship, where a door was placed under the quarterdeck. We went down a level and past a large cargo hold, parts of the ceiling set aside to make room for packages being lifted out by the ship's crew.

The quarters we had were at the very front of the ship, a small section behind a door with a little living area and some rooms to the sides. They were smaller even than the rooms aboard the *Beaver*, barely more than a bed and a door, but they'd do for the trip.

"Thank you," I said. "I think we're going to have a great flight."

· Chapter Fifty-Five ·

Captain's Logs

Squaring things away didn't take long, not with the size of our rooms and the few things we brought. I don't think anyone had plans to really get changed for what would be a day-long flight.

"So, we'll be reaching the capital before night, right?" I asked.

Amaryllis situated herself on a bench at the very front of the passenger quarters. A small porthole was there, but because we were at dock, all there was to see were some metal struts a meter or so away from the window. "I think so, yes. It would depend on when we leave. They're still unloading the ship."

"Really? How do you know?" I asked. The noises from the other side were all clangs and bangs, nothing really telling.

Amaryllis pointed to the window. "We're rising—slowly, but it's visible."

"Huh," I said. "You're a really observant bird!"

She huffed.

"I wonder if I can look around the ship later," Awen said.

The door leading into our compartment opened and after someone knocked. Captain Galebane slid into the room and clicked the door shut behind her. "I would be honored to show you around," she said.

"Hello, Captain," I said. "Your ship's very neat."

"Why thank you," she replied. "I came to ensure that you were all settled in. My first mate is taking care of things above. He needs the experience as well."

"That's two new people on your crew," Amaryllis said.

The captain nodded. "Indeed. I think over half the crew is green, or nearly so. Most of the better sailors have been dragged off to the navy. Promises of better pay are robbing us of a lot of good, experienced people."

"That's unfortunate," I said.

The captain shrugged a shoulder. "It is what it is. I don't blame them for accepting more gainful employment, even if it might only be on the shorter term."

"Aren't you worried? Such a green crew can be troublesome," Amaryllis said.

"Oh, there's no worry. Most of those green sailors are from the navy. Sylphfree allows companies in good standing to hire personnel to train them further and give them a bit of applicable experience. It means that part of their wages is covered, and the navy gains more people who have a wider breadth of experience."

"That's clever," I said. "Our crew is pretty mixed, experience-wise." The captain was being very forthcoming about things. I looked at her and had the impression she hadn't had the opportunity to rant about things in a good while.

Captain Galebane nodded. "Your ship is that . . . interesting twin-hulled vessel? I saw it while coming in to dock."

"That's the *Beaver Cleaver*, yeah," I said. "He's a good little ship. Though I guess he's a little weird-looking."

"Certainly unique," the captain agreed. "Have you been a captain for long, Captain Bunch?"

"Nope!" I said. "It's been . . . uh, about . . . a week?" How long ago did we leave the Nesting Kingdom? I know that I spent a few days sick, so that might have been throwing off my sense of time.

"A week," she repeated.

"A very busy week," I agreed. "We got off track over the Darkwoods, then we ended up stopping a smaller war between a big company and some dryads, then we visited Needleford where Awen was kidnapped by pirates. We damaged their ship— Wait, is it sinking a ship if the ship is an airship?"

"It is," she said.

"Cool! I thought so, because ships kind of sink out of the air," I said. "Not that we sank the pirate ship. We just did a number on their engines."

Awen looked like she was holding back a giggle, and Amaryllis just shook her head and pulled a book out from her bags and started to read it.

"You took out a pirate vessel?" Captain Galebane asked. "I'll admit, I have ten years as a captain, but they were mostly safe. Other than a few run-ins with some nasty creatures, I've never had the misfortune of fighting a pirate aboard my vessel."

"Oh, we didn't use the *Beaver* for that. We used a skiff. The pirate was called Golden Rogers, and he's a nasty, mean guy."

"A skiff?"

"Like, a really small boat that flies?"

"I'm aware of what a skiff is. What sort of vessel did the pirates have?"

"Uh," I replied. I couldn't recall the name of the ship. "It was quite big. Maybe half again the size of your ship? But more water-shiplike. His crew was rather large, I think. But we managed to save Awen, even though she'd mostly managed to save herself, really."

"It was called the *Golden Grove's Revenge*," Awen said. "And it couldn't operate because I destroyed the engines, and I think Broccoli lit the insides on fire."

"Just a little," I said. "It was me, Amaryllis, and Bastion. It was very scary."

"Three of you took on a pirate ship?" Captain Risa didn't sound entirely convinced.

I crossed my arms. "I can hold my own in a fight, you know. And Amaryllis is scary too. Not to mention Bastion. He's a paladin, so he's great at butt-kicking."

"Ah," she said with a nod. I had the impression that everything just clicked for her. The people in Sylphfree seemed to think very highly of paladins. "I suppose that it was quite the adventure."

"I know! And that was only in the first three days! Then we got to Insmouth, fought in two dungeons, ran into some very angry cry, and had not one but *two* battles in the air against them! They have rocket-powered planes and airships, but it turned out okay because we have Awen and we made some cry friends. Did you know that lasers are terrible for airships?"

"I can imagine?"

"They really are. We ended up almost crashing on the Lonely Island."

"The penal colony?"

I nodded. "That's the one."

"I imagine that must have been harrowing, landing in a place so hostile," Captain Galebane said. She smiled as if it were entirely self-evident.

"Huh? No, not really? I mean, the airship fight we had over the island was scary, but the people of the island were pretty nice. Not super welcoming, and I wish we'd had more time to spend there so that I could've made proper friends, but they seemed about as nice as the people from Granite Springs, for example."

"Ah."

"Anyway, then we made it here after some repairs. And that's about all the adventures we've had since launching the *Beaver Cleaver*. It's been a busy week and a bit."

"I . . . see," the captain allowed.

The door to the passenger quarters opened, and in walked Bastion, looking as fresh as ever with a bag by his side and some equipment in a sack slung over his shoulder. "Bastion!" I called out as I bounced to my feet. "I was getting worried."

"Hello, Broccoli," he said. "Amaryllis, Awen, and you must be Captain Galebane?"

The captain stood taller. "Indeed. It's a pleasure to meet you, sir."

"Likewise, Captain. Your first mate gave me permission to board, but I had hoped to meet you at some point."

"O-oh?" Risa asked. Was she blushing?

"It's nothing very urgent," he said. He tossed his bag into one of the rooms, where it landed on the bed with a thump. "Were you entertaining others?"

"Broccoli was telling her of our adventures," Amaryllis said offhand. She turned the page in her book. "As it turns out, Broccoli has a gift for under-stating things in such a way that they sound grander than they were. It's outright bizarre."

"I didn't exaggerate anything."

"You didn't," Amaryllis agreed. "If anything, you did the opposite, but you also listed more wild adventures than most sane people would experi-ence in a lifetime."

I wiggled my ears in thought. That made sense, I supposed. We had been through a lot together. "I kind of like having big adventures, though," I said. "It's fun. But . . . Well, do you guys like that kind of thing?"

Amaryllis snorted. "It's harrowing and terrifying, but you have no idea how rapid our growth is compared to most."

Awen shrugged. "Uncle's stories were about as full of adventure, so I think it's kind of normal."

"I'm not sure if using Abraham Bristlecone as a measuring stick is entirely wise," Bastion said. "But I suppose compared to the likes of him, this crew's travels have been quite calm."

I grinned. For all that the passenger section on the *Little Atlas* was a bit cramped and spare, it was still a lively, happy place. Mostly because it was filled with so many nice people. "How did things go?" I asked. "With the general and the commander and all the soldiers?"

"Relatively well," Bastion said. "The . . . event fell into disarray once the main threat was eliminated. Fortunately, it was the better sort of disarray. Some of the miners had cooking equipment, and the mole people brought some barrels of mushroom ale and shared it around. There was something of a party, though I doubt the official reports will call it that."

I laughed. "That's great. It'll give everyone a chance to make friends."

"Indeed," Bastion said. "There are some crates of salted meat coming with us, as well as some decently large segments of amphiptere leather. A fine reward for a day's work."

"I'll ensure that everything is properly secured, Sir Paladin," Risa said with a small salute.

"Thank you, Captain. But I'm certain that your crew will do a fine job. Now, if no one minds, I haven't slept since yesterday. I'm quite overdue for some rest."

I raised my arms for a hug as Bastion moved by, and he allowed me to give him a quick squeeze. More experience! And more hugs too!

"If anyone needs me, then feel free to wake me up," he said before carefully closing the door to his quarters.

Captain Galebane placed her hands over her face. "I didn't offer him my cabin," she muttered.

"I don't think he minds," I said. "Bastion seems like a simple sort of guy. Anyway! We have a long trip ahead of us. Is there anything you do for fun? Usually, on the *Beaver*, I'm too busy doing captain things or training. I like both, but I don't think we can do either here."

"I'll bring over a deck of cards," Captain Galebane said. "Maybe I can teach you a few games later. There are a few that are popular with the crew, and there are the more noble games, of course."

"Noble games?"

Amaryllis lowered her book. "Some card games are considered lowbrow, often depending exclusively on chance. More involved games are customarily the purview of the nobility. They tend to be a little more complex and rely more on deception and one's ability to read people than on pure luck, though there's usually some element of luck at play."

"Oh! Why didn't we ever play any of those?" I asked.

"Because you have about as much chance of deceiving someone as a puppy has of hiding a misdeed," Amaryllis said. "And at the same time, your ability to read people would make playing against you just plain irritating. You'd be at once a terrible opponent and a terrible player."

"I bet I could beat you, though," I said with my smuggest grin on.

Amaryllis carefully dog-eared the top corner of the page she was on and set her book down. "Captain, would you be so kind as to get that deck? I have to teach my dear friend here a lesson she's unlikely to ever forget."

· Chapter Fifty-Six ·

Airtime Naptime

Amaryllis glared at the cards on the table.

Then, with slow and careful solemnity, I lowered my hand next to those cards. "Flush."

The corner of Amaryllis's eyes twitched. "You didn't cheat."

"I'd never," I said. "That would be unfair and mean. Only bad friends cheat."

"And you never even tried to bluff."

"I'm not good at lying," I admitted.

"How?" Amaryllis asked. She let her own hand fall next to mine, a bunch of cards with numbers on their tops and colored shapes in their middle splaying out across the table. "How?"

"I guess I got lucky?"

Amaryllis stood up suddenly, her chair squeaking back. "I'm going to go read. At least the pages in my books don't have Dirt's own luck on their side."

I held back a giggle. It wouldn't be nice to laugh at Amaryllis. She was making an effort to be a good sport about losing, too, even though this was the fifth round she'd lost. We weren't even betting anything, mostly because I insisted that gambling was wrong.

We had started playing with four of us. Amaryllis and Captain Risa explaining the rules, and Awen joining in even though she didn't seem to get it entirely.

The captain had to run off to do captaining stuff, which was fair, and I think Awen just found the game a bit boring.

Which meant that now I was all alone at the card table.

Sighing, I picked things up and shuffled the deck idly before fitting it back into its box. It was the captain's deck, so I didn't want any of the cards bent or stained or anything.

I leaned back into my seat and glanced out of the nearest porthole. We were moving—that much was obvious. Mountains surrounded the *Little*

Atlas on all sides, their sheer walls passing by at a slow crawl. The cargo ship felt like it was heavy, big, and cumbersome, despite the amount of lift it needed to stay afloat.

The *Beaver* could likely fly circles around this ship, but we weren't in the *Beaver*.

I was a little bored, which was a nice change of pace from the high-energy excitement I'd been going through nearly every day for such a long while. Still, I wanted something to do. I couldn't practice most magics in a confined place, and it might be rude to cast spells in someone else's ship besides. Training physically was right out. The passenger quarters were small and cramped and already pretty warm.

Standing up, I moved toward my little room. Maybe I could flop down in bed and take a nap? That felt very unproductive, but at least it was something to do.

I saw Amaryllis engrossed in a book in her room, then I crossed by Awen's quarters and saw her on her back, staring at the ceiling.

Maybe I wasn't the only bored one?

I walked to Awen's door and knocked. "Bored?"

Awen tilted her head up. "Yeah, a little."

I stepped in, then sat on the edge of her bed. She scooted over, so I flopped down next to her, put my feet up on the bed, then stared up at the ceiling. "I'm bored too."

"There's nothing to tinker."

"I can't make friends with the crew because they're working."

Awen bobbed her head. "Boring."

"Yup."

If I leaned my head back I could see out of the porthole in her room. It was mostly cloudy skies, but once in a rare while, a mountain's peak would float by. "Do you know anything fun about the capital?" I asked.

"You mean Goldenalden?" Awen asked. "Not really. I guess there's a lot of sylphs there. And there's some gold, I guess."

"That makes sense, with a name like that."

"Yeah, the sylphs are supposed to be very rich. They have a lot of mines all around their nation and a big army. I don't know if they do a lot of trade with Mattergrove. We're far away."

"There's a whole mountain range between the two of you, and, like . . . at least two other countries." I squinted as I tried to remember where the nations were. "Unless they go all the way around, like we sort of did."

"They could come in from the north, too, to the south of the Snow-lands," Awen said. "That's Trenten Flat's territory, but they only started to colonize that later, so it's still very wild."

"Huh," I said. "The entire bit to the north of your home is all independent, right? Like Rosenbell was."

"Mostly, yeah."

"We should visit there someday. And we should go all the way west."

"To Pyrowalk?" Awen asked. "I hear that it's a very weird place. Sometimes we'd get visitors from there."

"Oh, and the Ostri desert too. And whatever is beyond Pyrowalk. Maybe we could even find out what's south of the known world, off the bottom edge of the maps."

Awen giggled. "There's a lot of places you want to visit."

I nodded. "I want to visit all the places. And see all the cool things and make even more friends. I have a very long bucket list, you know. I didn't think I'd get to check off 'Ride a dragon' so early."

"I'd like to visit the Snowlands," Awen said. "It's cold, but they have a lot of machines, and everyone says that their airships are the best in the world."

"Then we should go there," I said. "Maybe after all this stuff in Sylphfree is done?"

"That would be nice."

"Yeah, I think so too." I yawned, jaw cracking and ears shivering in delight. I should have gotten up and moved, but instead I shifted on the bed and kept staring at the ceiling. Getting up took way too much energy.

"I'm sure we're going to"—Awen paused to yawn herself—"have plenty of adventures after this one."

"Mm-hmm," I agreed. "Maybe one day we'll have to settle down or something, but I hope not."

"Uncle Abraham never settled down."

"That's right," I agreed. Things were a little fuzzy, and I couldn't help but blink at the ceiling a bunch. Some warmth was coming in through the window. Had we flown over the clouds at last? It was nice.

Awen shuffled next to me, and I felt her head settling in by my shoulder, so I leaned to that side.

My eyes closed, and I was asleep.

"Broccoli?" Someone shook my shoulder and I blinked awake. Awen was leaning over me, blond hair tucked behind her ears. "Broccoli, I can't get out."

"Huh?" I asked before a yawn cut me off. I looked around and . . . yeah, I was between Awen and the edge of the bed. And next to me was Orange, currently rolled up into a furry ball with her face tucked in close to her middle. The sort of puffball cat shape that looked very nice to pet, but that would inevitably lead to scratches if touched. I carefully swung my legs over the edge and sat up.

"It's okay," Awen said. "I think we're nearing the city."

"We are? How long was I sleeping for?"

"I don't know. I took a nap too."

I wobbled to my feet, thankful that Cleaning magic made sleeping with my shoes on acceptable, then I wandered over to the doorway. Amaryllis was sitting at the little table we'd been playing cards at, along with Bastion, who was finishing off a plate of something that smelled nice, and Captain Galebane was there.

"Hey," I said as I stumbled closer. I flopped onto the seat next to Amaryllis. "Where are we?"

"About twenty kilometers from the capital," Captain Galebane answered. "We should be within visual range within the next ten to twenty minutes. Which means, unfortunately, that I'll need to head back up."

"That's too bad," Awen said as she joined us and sat next to Bastion. "We didn't get to talk much."

"Do you think you could show us the capital from above?" I asked.

"That should be doable, yes," the captain said. She stood up. "If you want anything to eat, Captain Bunch, Miss Bristlecone, then there should be some left in the mess. I'll be moving to the topdeck. I need to keep an eye on the crew as we come in for docking maneuvers."

"Those are pretty tricky," I said. "Can we eat on the top deck?"

"As long as you stay out of the way, you should be fine."

I stood right after the captain, then stretched until my toes and ears both wiggled in delight. "I'm going to grab a bite and see the sights!"

"I guess I'll come with you," Awen said as she stood up too.

"Oh! I didn't say hi to Bastion!" I waved to Bastion. "Hi, Bastion."

The sylph grinned. "Hello, Broccoli," he replied. "Sleep well?"

"It was a good nap. Been a while since I had one of those. What about you?"

"Well enough. I think I might have a hard time sleeping on anything that isn't an airship. I'm growing quite used to the constant rocking."

"It is nice," I agreed. "Will you join us later? I bet you know the capital really well! You, too, Amaryllis."

"I'll see it in due time," Amaryllis replied. "You enjoy yourselves."

"I'll finish up my meal first," Bastion said.

I nodded, then with a final wave goodbye, skedaddled. The mess, as it turned out, was a section at the rear of the ship's bottom deck where a small kitchen was tucked away. I think the stove used the same flue as the engine above to spew out any smoke it created. The chef, a big burly fellow—for a sylph—with a big apron and a bigger smile, was more than happy to give Awen and I a pair of bowls full of still-piping-hot stew and some wooden spoons to eat it with.

Awen and I moved up to the top deck, where sailors were busy spooling ropes, adjusting sails, and chatting amongst themselves. Mostly, it looked as if the *Little Atlas*'s crew was doing busywork while staying sharp in case they were needed.

I guessed that, on a bigger crew, that was going to happen a lot. Moments of hectic work when they were nearing or leaving port, but then long, drawn-out times when there wasn't much to do.

We moved up to the foredeck. The ship didn't have a figurehead, which was really a shame. Still, we installed ourselves by the rails there and blew across our stews while a chill wind breezed by. I had the impression that we weren't all that high off the ground, relatively speaking. It was likely the mountains around us providing all that chill.

Goldenalden appeared before us as we went around a particularly sharp mountaintop.

"Whoa!" I said as the city stretched out before us.

I'd been to some big places in my admittedly short time on Dirt. Awen's home city was pretty big, sprawling out across a broad patch of arid land. And Port Royal was quite large, the way it was split on multiple levels lending it a sense of grandness. Even Fort Sylphrot, though that city was built up rather than out.

Goldenalden was so much bigger. It spilled out over the sides of a mountain that looked as though it was shaved off at the top. Plateaus all around, built on dozens of terraces that formed walls.

That wasn't to mention the actual walls around the city.

It was obvious that whoever had designed it had added more walls as the city grew. A maze of stone walls cut all across the city, but none were as impressive as those on the exterior—huge slabs of stacked stone, with guard towers every hundred meters or so.

They didn't compare to the Grey Wall, but they were still really cool!

There wasn't just one port, but at least five of them that I could see. With airships big and small docked in place, and dozens of them dotting the skies around the city and either moving toward or away from it. And that wasn't including the military airships. Small, boxy ships, like the ones that had escorted the *Beaver* back in Granite Springs, were constantly moving around the city, like schools of metal fish in the sky.

At the very top of the city was a castle, an imposing, blocky building with towers all around it, all topped with golden roofs.

"Pretty, isn't she?" Captain Galebane asked as she walked up next to us. She looked proud, and for good reason.

"It's gorgeous," I said. "I can't wait to see it for myself!"

· Chapter Fifty-Seven ·

Final Destination

The *Little Atlas* flew into the busy port on the eastern end of Gold-enalden with short, jerky motions. I didn't notice on the flight over to the capital, but the ship didn't fly with the sweeping grace of a ship like the *Beaver Cleaver* but instead moved with careful, nearly robotic precision.

Once we were within the port, a large mechanical arm rose from below, metal fingers longer than the *Atlas* coming up on either side, where the crew tossed ropes out and hooked the ship into place. Then the arm folded itself back and pulled the *Little Atlas* into an empty berth, where another crew flew over and tied everything up.

The berth was exactly the right size for the ship to fit into. A glance above revealed a sign that read *Little Atlas*, along with a bunch of numbers next to it. So this was a space specifically designed for this one ship. Neat!

"And there we have it," Captain Galebane said as she stepped away from the helm.

I clapped politely. "That was some very nice flying."

"Ah, it's hardly a challenge here," she said. "Goldenalden is one of the premier ports in the world—plenty of tools to help a captain guide her cargo in."

I nodded, but in reality, I wasn't paying all that much attention. It was rude, true, but there were so many things to see! The sounds alone were making my ears twitch left and right. Ships coming in to dock and leaving, engines thumping away, cranes moving with hydraulic hisses to grab and unload cargo. Teamsters leading huge horses around with wagons loaded up behind them.

I flinched as a trio of teeny-tiny airships roared by above, leaving a faint gaseous trail in the air behind them.

It stank, like a highway with a traffic jam.

The mountain air swept in a moment later and washed all that away, though it brought a shiver-inducing breeze with it. I grinned. It was the nice kind of cold, dry and fresh. Awen's clacking teeth suggested that she wasn't as ready for it as I was.

"We should go get our things," I said. "Awen, you might want to grab a sweater to wear under your coat."

"That sounds like a great idea," Awen said. "Bye, Captain."

"Ah, I'll be here to show you off properly," Captain Galebane said with an easy smile. "I do hope you enjoy your time in Goldenalden. It's the greatest city in the world for a reason."

"We'll do our best," I said.

The whole crew were running about, hard at work, which meant that Awen and I had to be careful not to get in anyone's way, especially those carrying stacks of stuff so high that they couldn't see ahead of them.

We arrived at the passenger quarters to find Amaryllis stuffing her book away in a bag. "Ah, you're finally back."

"Yup! The city's really pretty!"

"I've heard of it, yes," Amaryllis said. "I look forward to judging that for myself."

"I bet you'll like it," I said. "Do, ah, you know where we're going now?" I looked at her, then at Bastion, who was tugging on his armor.

The paladin was the first to reply. "Technically, you are a group of diplomats. There are inns specifically for them and richer merchants in the Purple District. They are expensive, but their proximity to the city center and to the Gold District makes them worthwhile, at least if you intend to travel to both frequently."

"That sounds perfect," I said. "We're still a bit behind schedule, aren't we?"

Amaryllis nodded. "We are, though I don't think it matters as much anymore. Did you notice if the harpy ship is in port?"

"I didn't, but there's more than one port and a lot of ships out there."

"Then we'll need to see if we arrived first. If so, then the amount of time we have before us will determine a lot in regards to what we can do."

"You know, I don't actually know what we're supposed to be doing. Other than warning people about the war stuff," I said.

"Leave that to me," Amaryllis said. "Once we have a place to roost, we'll draw up a proper plan, one that's informed and takes into account the lay of the land, so to speak. Learning about local rumors and the like will be part of that. I don't suppose Goldenalden has a newspaper?"

"It does," Bastion said. "A few of them at that. There are political parties and groups of some import in the capital. They'll usually have their own papers. There's also the state-funded paper, which is mostly dedicated to well-researched news."

I was really looking forward to walking around and just exploring the city now. Seeing new cultures, eating new foods, meeting new friends. I was holding back the giggles. I was so excited!

I grabbed my bag and my spade, then made sure all my gear was properly cinched up. I came out of my little cabin to find Bastion looking me up and down. "I should warn you, while in the provincial towns and other cities, it's fine to carry a weapon, but it's not legal to carry an unsheathed weapon in the capital. Though that law in particular isn't enforced all that well."

"But we're strange and foreign-looking," Amaryllis said. "So any law officer might decide to make an example of us."

"You will certainly attract a lot of attention just by appearing to be different than most," Bastion said. "As long as I'm there, you should be fine."

"Ah, but . . . you're not going to be with us for very long, are you?" I asked. I couldn't help but feel a twinge in my tummy at that. I didn't want to lose a friend just yet.

Bastion nodded. "I'll be returning to the garrison tonight. I can still escort you to a safe place and fend off any trouble until then. I have . . . a lot to report. But I'm certain we'll be seeing more of each other."

I nodded. "I'm warning you now, there's going to be a whole heck of a lot of hugging when we say goodbye."

Bastion chuckled. "Certainly."

We grabbed all our stuff. Amaryllis grumbled as she stuffed her wand-knife away into her backpack. I didn't know what to do with my spade, but Awen helped by wrapping a cloth around the blade.

The advantage of Makeshift Weapons Proficiency was that it didn't really harm my ability to use it if I needed to. I could still send magic into the spade until it glowed with Cleaning magic—not that I expected to need it.

I led my friends back out of the ship and to the topdeck, where I found Captain Galebane speaking with someone who looked official, clipboard and all. I didn't want to leave without saying goodbye properly, so I waited around for her to finish up.

"We're heading off," I said as soon as she was done.

"I see that," Risa said. "It was an honor to have you aboard the *Little Atlas*, Captain Bunch. And you as well, Sir Coldfront."

"What are we, roost feathers?" Amaryllis muttered too low for the captain to hear.

"Goodbye hug?" I asked.

"Pardon?"

So I pulled her into a tight glomp and squeezed her good and proper before letting go. The captain was a bit red in the face after that. "We'll see each other again, I'm sure! And by then we'll have even more awesome stories to tell about sky captaining!"

"Ah, y-yes, I'm sure," she replied.

The bunch of us walked over to the docks. The ship's railing had been removed to make room for a gangplank where sylphs were unloading crates. We waited for a moment where it wasn't as busy and hopped over to the docks.

After that we walked to the edge of the port. My head was on a swivel, turning this way and that to see as much as I could. It was giving my poor ears whiplash.

"No harpy ships," Amaryllis muttered.

"Where do we go now?" I asked.

"I'll bring you to a reputable inn," Bastion said. "It'll be a good place to base yourselves out of while you're in Goldenalden."

"Neat!"

I crossed my arms behind my head and enjoyed the walk.

Goldenalden reminded me—out of all the cities I'd seen so far—of Fort Sylphrot in the Harpy Mountains. Unlike that city, buildings here were built tall rather than long. The roads below were mostly, it seemed, used to carry stuff, with wide paths where carts could roll by on either side.

There was only a thin sidewalk, one where older sylphs and those with big packs that prevented them from flying were moving along with easy efficiency. It seemed as if there was something of an unwritten—or maybe it was written and I just hadn't read it yet!—code that let older people and pregnant sylph ladies pass first.

I craned my neck back as we walked. "What's at the top?" I asked. I could see sylphs flitting by above us, quick shadows that passed faster than I could follow.

"Most homes have a small garden and greenery above them, as well as a small outcrop where they have their roof access. That's generally the main entrance to a home or building," Bastion said. "Mostly, it's a small staircase and a place to change out of your boots. I should add that it's considered impolite to walk into a house wearing your outdoor shoes, with some exceptions."

"Huh, all right."

"Most homes will have a greeting room on the topmost floor. If the building has multiple homes, then it's likely to be a communal area. Shops will use the space for displays." Bastion shrugged. "Once you've seen a few, you'll see what I mean."

"I look forward to it!"

"It might be tricky for nonsylphs. The air is our home, and it means that a lot of construction isn't designed for those destined to only travel in two dimensions."

"Hey now, I can jump around with the best of them."

Bastion chuckled. "Fair enough. Most places should be accessible from the ground, at least public spaces. We need to account for the older and those who are injured, not to mention the pregnant."

"So, sylphs don't lay eggs," I surmised.

Bastion turned to stare at me. "No, no, we don't."

"Good to know!"

Amaryllis trilled in happy laughter. I think she was enjoying Bastion's confused look more than anything else. That set Awen and I off, both of us joining her in a chorus of giggles.

Bastion shook his head. "The city is divided into districts. See that?" He pointed to a pole that stretched way up and over the tops of the nearest buildings. A banner hung from each arm of the T-shaped post. One had a fancy symbol on white cloth with gold gilding. The other was entirely red.

"We're in the Red District now—mostly housing, some small family-run shops that have been around for centuries. You can navigate the city by looking for one of those. They should be easy enough to find."

"Oh, that's neat," I said. "Like road signs on corners."

"The roads are numbered here, but unfortunately, due to the age of the city and the shape of the mountain it's built upon, they're not very useful for navigating," Bastion said. "Most will just name the color of the district they're in and then give directions from there."

"All right," I said. That sounded like a cute way to get around.

"Any places we should avoid?" Amaryllis asked.

"Every road and alley is well patrolled and quite safe," Bastion said. "You'll find no poverty on the streets here, or many muggers for that matter. Not in the capital. Land here is too valuable to allow for any of it to go unused."

Something told me that wasn't the full story. For there to be rich people, someone had to be poor. At least, I remembered my dad telling me as much once. Maybe the poor here were fortunate, or maybe they were just tucked away very well.

"Come on, let's get to the inn. I could use a snack! And then we can do some proper plotting!"

· Chapter Fifty-Eight ·

See Ya Later!

Welcome!" the man said with a spinning twirl that ended with a bow. "To the grandest inn in all the capital: Dewdrop Inn." Little magic whirls and sparkles took to the air behind him, flipping and twirling like teeny-tiny fireworks before they burst apart and transformed into pretty flowers.

I clapped.

"Greetings," Bastion said, obviously not as impressed by the manservant's display. "We're looking for some rooms for a few days. I was hoping that I could speak with Jared."

"Certainly, Sir Paladin," the manservant said as he rose from his bow. He took in my friends and I at a glance, then nodded, as if to himself. "I'm afraid that, while spectacular in its own right, this lower entrance is not as fabulous as the one above. I only hope its meager splendor is enough for such esteemed guests."

We were standing on the ground level of what Bastion called the Gold District. We were close to a big wall, one of the many that we'd crossed so far while navigating the city. This one had purple banners on it, so I guessed that it was the Purple District, where the castle and a bunch of other important places were.

The Gold District was filled with businesses. Every building we crossed had an understated entranceway with a plaque telling passersby what they might expect within. The topmost floors looked a lot more interesting, but I couldn't reach them without abandoning my friends, and I wouldn't do that.

"Follow me, if you please," the sylph who was guarding the bottom entrance to the Dewdrop Inn said.

We filed in after him and found a small but well-decorated waiting area. There were sofas and some potted plants, freshly painted walls, and a couple of bookcases filled with interesting books. It was spotless, and I could only imagine that they must've had a couple of people with Cleaning magic on the staff.

The far corner of the room was taken up by a spiral staircase that rose up and up, with twisty wrought-iron rails and magical lanterns casting an eerie white glow onto marble steps.

The sylph paused and bowed to us again. "Would you do me the honor of allowing me to carry your belongings to the topmost floor?"

Amaryllis gave him her bag, but Awen said she wanted to keep hers. I did give him my spade, mostly because I was worried I might bonk one of the lanterns on the way up. As it was, the room might have been downright opulent, but it felt . . . cramped?

The ceiling was tall for a sylph, but for a bun it was on the shorter side. The stairs were worse, with my ears batting against the steps above with every step. "Who's Jared?" I asked Bastion as I hopped up to be next to him.

"The owner of the inn," Bastion said. "I've stayed here before. Twice, but I suspect that's enough for him to remember me."

"Why would you stay at an inn when you're in the capital?" Amaryllis asked. "Don't the paladins have barracks?"

"We do. An entire keep in the Purple District, as well as barracks within the royal castle and estates. And it's not unheard of for a paladin to sleep in a guardhouse. Both times I was here, I was escorting someone."

"Oh, diplomacy stuff?" I asked.

"Something like that," Bastion said. "Keep it between us, but some members of the royal family like to spend time outside the castles and palaces. Less stress, I suspect, and they get to see things that they wouldn't otherwise."

I noticed Awen and Amaryllis nodded, but I didn't quite get it, not really. I had never really been stuck in any one place for that long. It was usually very much the opposite. I could still sympathize, but not from personal experience. "So they'd stay here?"

"For a night or two," Bastion said. "With a complement of guards, regardless of how safe they thought they were on their own."

"The city seems pretty safe," I said. It was definitely one of the more protected places I'd ever seen—lots of big walls, plenty of guards.

"Goldenalden is a very safe city," Bastion said. "But people who are looking for trouble tend to find it."

We reached the top floor with just a bit of huffing and puffing. It was a good thing we were all so active, or else I'd think the stairs would have been too much.

The top floor was very wide and tall, with a corner dedicated to a small garden filled with bright flowers in full bloom, and there was even a small tree, its trunk bent over to skim the roof, with a bench tucked below it.

Round tables dotted the room, with comfy chairs next to them, and at the far end was the kind of reception counter that I expected to see in an inn, though this one was a lot fancier, with a stone top and wooden sides.

"Ah, Mister Jared is right there," the manservant said with a gesture to the counter.

A sylph was behind it, sitting on a stool and examining some papers, with glasses perched on the tip of his nose. He wore an apron over a clean shirt and vest. His head rose when we approached. "Ah! Greetings and welcomes. Dewdrop Inn—there's always a seat for a new friend."

I decided that I liked Mister Jared.

"Hello, sir," Bastion said.

"Paladin Coldfront! It has been some time," the old sylph said. He bounced off his seat with a flutter of his wings. "How can I help you, Sir Paladin?"

Bastion gestured. "I have a few . . . guests for you here. Travelers from all across Dirt. They're looking for a place to stay, and I gave them my solemn word that your inn was the greatest in Sylphfree."

"Aha!" Jared cheered. "That it is! Now, what sort of accommodations are you looking for?"

"We're looking for a room with at least three beds," Amaryllis said. "I don't think we require your finest, just a place to rest for the next week."

"We can certainly accommodate," Jared said. "I have a fine suite on the third floor. Four modest rooms and a shared common area. We can include meals at your discretion as well. We have some of the finest chefs in all of Goldenalden here. Though if you want to test your palate beyond what we can provide, then I of course have some suggestions to offer as well."

"That sounds nice," I said. "Are there any neat things to see in Goldenalden? I want to play tourist!"

Jared laughed. "There's plenty! If you tell me what you enjoy, then I can direct you that way, but you must see the Orange District's parade. It's held every day at noon, rain or shine. And of course there's the museum next to the congress, which is itself a wonderful building to admire."

I oohed. "That sounds neat! What's the parade?"

Bastion was the one to answer. "The Orange District is on the far side of the Green District from here. It's where the local branches of the armed forces are stationed, at least the more bureaucratic part of the army. There's also a training camp, and every day, soldiers practice marching in formation. It draws a bit of a crowd."

"There's a somewhat mean-spirited tradition involving civilians trying to make the soldiers in formation laugh," Jared said. He looked like he was working hard not to smile. "The officers encourage it, and people tend to enjoy seeing some poor cadet being berated for failing to keep a straight face."

"That sounds mean," I said.

"Traditions are often unkind," Awen muttered.

"Shall I show you to your rooms?" Jared asked. At our nod, he flew over the counter with a buzz of his wings and quickly removed his apron to toss it behind him next to a fancy brass till. "Come along, gentleladies."

Jared walked with a skip in his step, arms gesturing grandly as he spoke about the great meals they had on offer, the wonderful wines, and the spectacularly soft beds.

I couldn't help but grin as we went back down the stairs until we reached the third floor. A corridor bisected the floor, with doors on either side of the wide passage. Jared fetched a key out from his pocket and unlocked one. "Here we are," he said with a flourish.

The suite was exactly what we needed. A wide room with some comfy sofas and a table surrounded by seats. A desk was in one corner, next to a happy potted plant, and four smaller bedrooms, with windows overlooking the street below the inn. We had a big washroom too. It would have been annoying to share it, but I think we were all used to it after the *Beaver*.

"This will do," Amaryllis said with a satisfied huff. She immediately started negotiating with Jared, whose smile never wavered as Amaryllis deployed all her trickiest tricks to lower the price. The manservant who had greeted us at the entrance brought our bags in, then left with a bow.

I spun around, then sighed. The next step wasn't going to be fun. Still, we could put it off for a little bit longer.

Once Amaryllis forked over the gold, and Jared bid us a good afternoon, we were left with just the four of us in our little quarters.

"So," I began.

Bastion nodded, very solemn and serious. "I should be returning to report and announce that I've returned. I imagine that the demand for paladins is quite high at the moment, with so many important diplomatic events occurring in such close proximity."

I pouted. "It still sucks that we won't be seeing you much," I said. "If you have time off, you have to come and visit."

He chuckled. "I will. I promise, as long as you're in Sylphfree, I'll make a point of visiting when I can afford to."

When he could afford to. That meant that he probably wouldn't have all that much time. "All right," I said. I'd take what I could get. "You were a great crewmate, and there's always going to be room for you on the *Beaver*. If you ever get tired of being a paladin, then I'm sure there's plenty of adventuring to do, and we could always use one more friend."

"Thank you, Broccoli."

"I . . . will, with some reluctance, admit that my initial impression of you was wrong," Amaryllis said. "You are as honorable as your reputation entails. I hope all your comrades in arms are as just and levelheaded."

"My initial impressions were also quite wrong," Bastion said. "For all of you, I think. You're a kinder soul than I would have imagined, with a keen mind under all your barbs. Awen's delicate nature hides the spine of a true adventurer, and I suspect she will have just as many songs as her uncle one day, and Broccoli, I think your unique morality is quite eye-opening."

Amaryllis huffed the huff of someone who didn't know how to take a compliment.

"Hugs?" I asked.

"Certainly."

I squeezed him tight-tight. I'd miss Bastion. He was stoic and hard to read, but he was a nice person, dependable and strong and willing to help others just because it was the right thing to do.

"I don't know what you'll be up to next," I said. "But make sure to make plenty of friends and keep them close."

"I'll be sure to take some of the lessons I've learned to heart," Bastion said. He sighed while glancing at the door. "I think this is goodbye for now. I would ask that you three stay safe, but I don't think you're capable of that, so I'll instead ask that you watch out for each other and try not to burn down the capital while I'm here."

"We'll do our best."

About the Author

RavensDagger is a Canadian writer who wants to make people smile. The best way to do that, he has found, is by pecking away at the keyboard and hoping for the best.

9 781039 416680